pause

PRAISE FOR *PAUSE*

First Place, Chanticleer Somerset Award for Women's Fiction

"Stamey's lovely, inspiring, often funny novel... will touch the hearts of readers.... Stamey's achievement is the realistic, down-to-earth, eminently relatable Lindsey and all she offers contemporary readers."

- Publishers Weekly Booklife Review

"Sara Stamey does for fiction what Cheryl Strayed and Elizabeth Gilbert did for memoir—*Pause* gives a voice to women who are too often invisible in contemporary books. The unforgettable Lindsey Friedland weaves together humor and passion against the backdrop of the Pacific Northwest's natural beauty, using her unique voice to deliver a must-read novel about friendship, love, and killer hot flashes."

- *USA Today* Bestselling author Mindy Klasky

"Lindsey's banter with her best friends as well as her complex family dynamics feel extremely realistic.... Lindsey herself is an appealing and capable hero, both intelligent and relatable. A solid, engaging tale about the importance of self-knowledge."

- Kirkus Reviews

"Sara Stamey's novel PAUSE—whose heroine is a feisty, determined, middle-aged woman endeavoring to restart her love life and a career in journalism—is filled with lyrical prose and pure, thought-provoking joy."

- IndieReader review, 5 stars

pause

SARA STAMEY

Book View Café

PAUSE
Copyright © 2021 Sara Stamey, LLC

Published by Book View Café
304 S. Jones Blvd., Suite #2906
Las Vegas, NV 89107
www.bookviewcafe.com

ISBN: 978-1-61138-964-7

Cover design by Dave Smeds
Woman's image by Dreamstime.com

Production team:
Copyeditor, Sherwood Smith
Book formatters, Jennifer Stevenson and Marissa Doyle

For the brave girls and women of #MeToo, for our heroic healthcare workers, and for all of us just trying to keep cool....

With thanks to:

Kathryn Trueblood for her writer's eye and true friendship.

Margi Fox, Gary McKinney, and Paul Piper for feedback.

Mindy Klasky, Nancy Jane Moore, Katharine E. Kimbriel, and Sherwood Smith for reading and excellent advice.

Sisters and gal friends who inspire me—you know who you are.

Mary Alice Kier and Anna Cottle of Cine/Lit Representation, for continuing encouragement and support.

Thor—the one up ahead of me on the trail that day—with love and ongoing amazement.

prologue

Dear Diary,

March is the cruelest month—will gray winter never end?—and no sign of the lion lying down with the lamb (or anyone else).

Shall we pause to take stock?

Female (liberated, at least from fraught marriage), age 52, height 5'5", weight 120, bone density excellent, minimal cellulite, maximal hot flashes.

Possessions: 2 Best Cats in the World; 1 degree in creative writing and journalism (what was I dreaming?); 1 dead-end job transcribing medical reports. 1 charming 1920s bungalow with 30-year mortgage and badly in need of new windows, trim, and roof. 1 aging Subaru wagon, 1 bicycle. 3 recycle bins.

Green eyes, somewhat nearsighted; long hair, braid optional (blah light-brown, but disguises the gray strands appearing); "terrific ass" (impartial testimony of ex-husband); no-longer-firm jawline; 1 and 3/4 breasts.

Months since sex: 27.

one

IT STARTS LIKE THIS:

She's twenty-three again, and that's the magic, she knows the exact year, feels it in the way her skin presses tight against braless breasts, knee and hip joints smooth, no clicking or catching as she flows down the splintery steps of that funky old cottage in the cedar grove. Her bare toes grip the rough boards, savor the moist grass for the sheer pleasure of being alive. She throws out her arms and spins across the yard, embroidered long skirt wheeling out about her legs. The sun winks on off on, striping down through the branches.

A deep chuckle. He stands straddling his bicycle, flashing a white grin as she slows, steps forward, squints against the man splitting sun rays. He shifts, summer sunlight streaming over him, and he's all golden—tanned and shirtless in ragged cutoff jeans and a strand of hippie beads, long blond hair shimmering.

Lindsey looks down and now she's naked standing there. She's all sun-gold, too, her breasts perfect round and smooth and she looks up, he's naked, beckoning, wow she's floating and she knows it's a dream then.

She's back all those years behind him on his bike and they're flying fast down the hill. His hair streams out longer and longer with the wind of their flight, twining through her own tawny locks, and she laughs. Long flaxen hair sprouting, curling, twining into psychedelic paisley swirls and birds are nesting in the profusion, a home for the honey bees, the Wonder of their Hair! But then the strands whip out tangling in the bushes, and she's yanked backwards from the bicycle as he flies on solo.

Lindsey lands on her bare feet flinching at gritty linoleum. She's walking down a long hospital hallway of gray doors and glaring white walls. She shivers, tries to wrap her hair around her nakedness but it's only long enough now to barely cover her breasts, the one withered. She's ashamed and hunches as the first door swings open.

"Washed-up." Her ex Nick's head pops out of the doorway, Jack-in-the-box on a hinged extensor, dark hair a polished cap.

Lindsey tries to run, but her feet are too heavy.

"Gotcha!" *Snap.* Another door springs open, Nick's face popping out with a painted leer.

"No!" Lindsey heaves herself past him as the corridor squeezes in on her, struggling to run as her ponderous feet hold her to a gasping shuffle. She looks down, gropes for the strands of cloaking hair but she's gone bald, flesh shrinking around the bones and all her substance sagging down around her legs.

The demonic heads snap in and out of their doorways behind her, laughing. "Think you'll do better than me?" The next door crashes open, blocking the corridor. "Get real. Look at yourself." Coiled spring unleashing, his head darts forward—that familiar crooked smile, eyes pinning her.

Lindsey sucks in a breath as her hand tightens to a fist, flinging out to punch the leering face of her so-*ex*-husband. But his head's gone rubbery, bouncing back at her. She pushes past it, but now more doors pop open before her, Nick's twisted grin on all the maniacal puppets.

"No exit, Babe. Face it, you're going nowhere but downhill." The voice, cool, amused, comes from behind her.

She whirls around, and it's the real Nick standing there, raising his palms, chuckling. He winks as he runs a hand over his dark hair, gleaming like the blue-black feathers of the raven perched on his shoulder. They cock their heads in a synchronous movement to give Lindsey a sidelong glance. The raven chortles and sidles down Nick's arm to grip onto his fist. He raises his other hand to stroke the glistening feathers.

Lindsey's rooted, mesmerized by the black mercuric mirrors of the raven's eye, Nick's eye. He turns toward her then, lifting his arms to launch the bird skyward as the graceful folds of a midnight silk magician's cloak swirl around him, and a scalpel-sharp sword materializes in his grip. He glides toward Lindsey, eyes glimmering with amusement.

"It's only an illusion, Lindsey. It won't hurt a bit." He whips the blade in a flashing ring of light, swinging it toward her neck—

"No!" Lindsey flails against the drenched sheet tangled around her legs, finally rips it off her, flings it to the floor. "Damn it!" She stomps on the crumpled sheet for good measure.

Then shivers, the sweat gone cold and clammy. Can't she divorce Nick from her dreams, too? She scrubs at her sticky face, gropes for the alarm clock, squints and blinks at the glowing display. *5:03 am.*

"Crap!" Her back hurts, bad knee throbbing. She rips the damp bottom sheet off the bed, too, and fumbles for her robe, all goosebumps in the pre-dawn.

HighJinks and Sombra twine around her ankles, mewing anxiously, tripping her as she stumbles toward the bathroom. She starts to snap at them, gropes for a lamp and switches it on, sees them staring up at her, vaguely accusing. "Oh, god," she mutters. A prayer? To whom? To what?

She drops to her knees and gathers the cats against her, hugging close. But this only alarms them and they squirm free, running for their bowls in the kitchen, mewing. "Sorry. I'm sorry." She pulls the robe tighter around herself, gropes her way into the dark kitchen and shakes out some kitty kibbles into their bowls as they skirmish for position. "No fighting, you two. You know—Peace, Love, like that?" She pulls open the back porch cupboard, feeling for the clean set of sheets, maybe she can get another hour of sleep if she doesn't really wake up, then realizes she didn't wash them after yesterday's night sweats. "Damn!"

She gives up, snaps on all the lights in the little bungalow, HighJinks and Sombra blinking in the glare as she stomps back to the bathroom and turns on the shower. Maybe she'll call in sick today, wash the sheets and go back to bed and see if she can catch up on all the lost sleep. Right.

Steam swirls around her in the shower, and she tries to let the tension dissolve into the hot streams, like all that positive-image advice says you're supposed to be able to do. But it's no good. It's always there, insects buzzing in her ears. She takes a deep breath and slides soapy fingers over her damaged breast. Feels the puckered, irradiated skin and the raised scar of the lumpectomy.

Stepping out, Lindsey tries to recapture that visceral joy of youth and wholeness from the start of the dream. Then wipes the mist from the mirror and faces the middle-aged truth—everything sagging into entropy, face going slack and gaunt despite the best efforts of high cheekbones, the ugly pucker and droop of the cancer breast.

"Get a grip," she mutters, disgusted with her own self-pity, the sad-sack expression. Four years later, she's still cancer-free. "And let's not forget husband-free, too," she can't help adding. Fourteen years of her life—prime years—gone with him.

She bangs defiantly around the kitchen. She doesn't have to tiptoe around the little house any more, paranoid she'll disturb Nick and somehow set off one of his rages. Two years since the divorce, and she still fights the reflex to duck. She realizes she's standing stiff, shoulders hunched. She takes a deep breath, sees HighJinks and Sombra backed together against the heat vent, watching her, their glassy eyes a reproachful mirror.

"Hey. Okay." She eases down beside them, giving them her imitation purr and slowly stroking—HighJinks's silky Siamese coat, Sombra's plush ebony pelt. They relax, pressing against her.

Lindsey takes her tea and granola to the table. She switches on the SAD light, wincing in the glare. It's still black out there behind the curtain, and her counselor has finally talked her into trying this light to lift the heaviness. She's tried every herbal "midlife" remedy and finally antidepressants, but those just made her feel like she was sealed in a balloon floating outside a numbed, alien body. She wishes she could be a bear and den up through the winter. But reality check means keeping her job and paying the mortgage, so she's making do. The bright light feels good, and it gives her an excuse to scribble in her journal.

Maybe she really can be a writer again. Yeah, right.

March 13

Dear Diary,
    Shall we pause to take stock?

The list makes her chuckle despite herself. Until she gets to the "1 and 3/4 breasts."

"Okay, okay." Lindsey grimaces, tries pasting on a perky smile.

Months since sex: 27.

She blows out a breath and rakes her hair back off her face, grits her teeth.

So here's how it goes:
You hunker down with the yelling, the tension and vigilance, locked in a nightmare but thinking you're going to wake up any day now. And you remember the good parts, all those years and dreams invested in this marriage, in loving him, and could you have been that wrong? It's not so bad, really. There is chemistry still there, he's a handsome man, you can't deny the charisma, and though the sex isn't tender or really making love, it's reliable. You've become adept at supplying the missing emotional foreplay, taking responsibility like a good girl for your own orgasm. At least he's there, in bed, even warms it up for your cold feet. And you shudder at the thought of being single—not to mention the horrors of Dating!—in your fifties. You'd be going in one fell swoop from the envied Married Woman to the least-desirable social unit imaginable—crone female, divorced and menopausal.
But finally it gets so bad it's either die or get free. The relief of a quiet house! You drink in the blessed silence, even the being alone. Except for the cats, of course, who snuggle with you in bed, so it's not so bad. And you think you finally did it, you showed your backbone, the hard part's over now.
No. You start to dread coming home to that empty house, to the ongoing internal soundtrack of your arguments and pleas and analysis of why it all went wrong, which by the

Nth playback is getting really old but there's no Off button.
You search for distractions. Your conversations with the cats
start to feel a little one-sided, and maybe you'd like to try an
adult, human give-and-take again. So you join a hiking club,
call your girlfriends you didn't have time for before to see if
they want to catch a movie or go to an art show. You sign up
for a book discussion group.

Time. Filling time. You're thirsty—for touch, for intimacy,
even though you recoil from questions that get too close,
shudder at the thought of some stranger's hands on you. You
wonder if you've finally just dried up, shriveled into a prune.
Then you dream about your ex and wake up horrified.

Where's the nearest convent? Will they take me?

"Shit!" Lindsey looks at the clock and jumps up, flings
her journal down, snaps off the SAD rays. *Can you OD on*
that stuff? And she's off:

Racing around the house, grabbing fruit and a power
bar, no time to pack a lunch, she can't afford to keep buying
it but she'll think about that tomorrow. Pull the curtains—
it's finally daylight and drizzling again—stuff pants and
blouse into her bike pannier, wrestle hair into a braid, forget
about makeup, and out the door. Back in to grab her
helmet. Wheel bike from garage. *Now* she's off.

The road glistens, rain just a cool misting, and she takes
a deep breath, lets it out, lets it go. She's a Pacific Northwest
person, craves that moist, cleansing air as she pulls in a
lungful and pumps fast, streaking down her winding road
along the creek. Sunlight glimmers through breaks in the
cloud cover, drizzle slacking off, and a faint rainbow
shimmers over the big cedars in the park before she zooms
in under their fringy green arms.

She remembers the dream then, that lovely first part.
Flying along on...what was his name...? Right, Newman's
bike, those carefree hippie days. He was only a fleeting
connection, and she can't even bring his face into focus, so
where's he popped up from now? Those notions of Free Love
and Peace. And that image of him as all golden sunlight, the
perfect cliché of getting back to the Garden, as if it could be
that easy. Or even desirable? She shakes her head, pedaling

faster, pushing so she can feel the burn. She realizes she's smiling.

Late to work again, but the aerobic flush of the extra lap through the park was worth it. After a hasty rinse-off and change in the employee locker room, she's hustling down the hall to Medical Records when she hears voices coming closer around the corner beyond the waiting lounge:

"...keeps letting her get away with it, it's not fair." Marlene's distinctive nasal whine.

Damn. Lindsey ducks behind the big activities calendar at the corner opposite the elevator.

"What's the deal with her, anyway?" Marlene's the data-entry clerk. She's passing by now, along with Sono, another transcriber like Lindsey. "When she hired on, Katie over at the Madrona Center was like, 'Oh, Lin Friedland! I went to high school with her, she's a hoot.' Guess they were always waiting to see what she'd pull off next, like the time some boy dared her to climb the big maple up to the third story, and she arrived in class through the window."

Lindsey bites her lip. She never had been able to turn down a dare. The climb was no problem, and the window was open. Then she'd figured, *Okay, just act casual, sit down and pull out your book and nobody will pay much attention.* Until Mr. Thornycroft was standing beside her desk, tapping his foot, everybody's faces turning expectantly. All she could think to say was, "So, I guess no extra credits?"

Headed for the hospital elevator, Sono's chuckling.

Which seems to be annoying Marlene. "So what's her problem now? Ms. Stiff Upper Lip. I mean, would it pollute her to come down for Donut Day in the break room?"

Something muffled in response as they stop at the metal doors, blocking Lindsey's escape. Sono punches the Down button and turns back toward Marlene. "...so why not cut her some slack? Anyway, Olivia's not about to give her the boot, she racks up the fastest production rate in the department." Her voice is matter-of-fact, as usual.

"I still say it's about time she got over it already."

The elevator doors open for them, then close.

Great. Lindsey blows out a breath, darts out from behind the calendar, and hot-foots it toward Medical Records. Just in time to collide in the doorway with her boss Olivia.

"Oh! Shi-shoot. I'm sorry." Lindsey kneels to pick up the cascade of chart folders she's knocked out of Olivia's arms. Thank goodness they're all stapled.

"Lindsey...."

"I know. I'm trying." She scoops the files into a neat stack, stands, and offers them to Olivia.

Who's shaking her stylishly short-cropped gray head, peering over pink half-glasses and pursing her brightly glossed lips. Then she sighs and gives Lindsey a smile. "I know that, Lin. But I have to think about department morale. Make sure you're on time the rest of the week." She starts to take the stack, then pushes it back at Lindsey. "While you're at it, why don't you run these down to Archives? I've got a meeting. Jenny's sick today, so I'm putting you on the Number Two E.R. line. After you catch that up, you can do the surgery reports. If you need any extra hours, you're welcome to stay after."

"Great. I will." Lindsey places a hand atop the thick stack to steady it. "Thanks."

Olivia's already tapping briskly down the hall, with a backwards waggle of fingers toward Lindsey.

Another long exhale, this time relief. She sticks her head into the office to tell Gayle, who's on the Number One E.R. line and typing away, that she's going down to Archives. That's where they store the backup paper charts.

Gayle, neat little dreadlocks setting off her perfect dark complexion, pulls off her headphones and makes hyper typing motions in the air. "They went nuts in E.R. last night. I've got Trauma Jock on the line, too bad we can't ship him off to Hollywood."

"Fun fun," Lindsey sympathizes. Dr. Nichols, ruler of night-shift Emergency, suffers from short-man syndrome and compensates with his red Porsche and custom *TRAUMA DOC* plates, cowboy boots, and a pain-in-the-ass reputation. Though, to be fair, he's a super surgeon with a way low complication and loss rate.

"Luck of the draw." Gayle shrugs philosophically. "You get busted again?" She tilts her heads toward Olivia's charts in Lindsey's arms.

She surprises herself by chuckling. "Yep, ran smack into Olivia and knocked them flying."

Gayle grins. "Wish I'd seen that one." She winks and swivels back to her keyboard, humming. She's the newest employee, just coming up on her six-month review, and Lindsey's never seen her anything but cheerful. Unlike Marlene and some of the others, she doesn't push for responses, just lets people have the space they need.

Lindsey heads for the hall, grappling the chart stack and a pang of envy for Gayle's mellow smile, her fresh young face. Then realizes it's not so much envy as nostalgia for her own younger self.

Hardly anyone uses the back stair, but she doesn't like elevators. Likes to think she's conserving energy, though in reality it's any excuse for a little exercise when you work at a computer all day. As she reaches bottom, she hugs the tippy stack to her chest against the ID badge, a keycard necklace, and backs through the door. It clicks locked behind her as the balky old fluorescent light on its timer flickers and crackles in the dark.

Her feet know the way to the Archives door, so she doesn't wait for the slow warmup with the light, just starts down the hall. She stumbles over something in the dark.

"Shit!" She's tripping forward. She manages to throw out an arm for balance and catch herself, but the charts go flying as she staggers back. The light flares on, and the folders shower down over a man sitting lotus-style against the cement wall.

"Ah!" Lindsey windmills back, heart jolting.

The man just sits there, calmly looking up at her as the manila folders spill over his legs and across the cement floor. "Hello," he says.

"What are you doing here?" Lindsey steps back farther, voice sharp as she gropes for her key badge and glances toward the stairway door.

He just raises his palms, then starts to gather up the files.

He's a big man from what she can tell as he sits, broad in the chest and shoulders, wearing jeans and a fleece top, wavy gray hair a bit long and shaggy, but he doesn't look threatening. No hospital ID badge.

She clears her throat. "Are you okay? You're not hurt?"

He stands then in an easy movement out of the crossed-legged position, hands her some of the folders, and crouches to gather up the rest. "I don't like elevators. Thought there was an exit down here, but there was only that emergency door down the hall that would set off an alarm. Then the stairway door was locked, and the light timed out." He glances up, eyes crinkling in what seems to be amusement. "I figured someone would come down eventually, so I might as well sit and meditate."

He rises again, holding the rest of the charts. He's tall, and she has to look up at him now. "So, Lindsey, I guess you have a key? Or else we can both sit here and practice some mantras." Another glimmer of humor in his eyes. He has a lot of laugh lines scrunched around them.

"Uh...." She glances down, sees her ID badge twisted on its cord. He must have read her name off it. "Were you visiting a patient and got lost?"

"Yes. And no." His mouth twitches. "I'm not lost, just taking a detour."

She shoots him a look, frowns, then shrugs. "I need to put these charts in Archives, then I'll take you to the exit." She reaches for the folders he's holding.

"Allow me." He tilts his head and holds onto them.

She thinks maybe he's laughing at her and she wants to get huffy after the shock in the dark, but somehow his presence is calming, like he's inviting her to laugh along with him. Though when she glances back at him, he only has a neutral, inquiring look on his face.

She spins on her heel and stalks down the hall toward Archives, thrusts her keycard into the reader, and yanks open the door, gesturing him in. Strictly against security rules, but he doesn't look like he's out to pilfer confidential patient records. "Just set them on the cart there." She adds her own stack and gestures him back into the hall. He's giving her another attentive look, and she sees now he has gray-blue eyes under shaggy brows. A square, strong-jawed face thickening around the edges with middle age.

"So. Where were you trying to get to?" She starts back down the hall.

"Harvey from the kitchen said there was a back exit, I seem to remember that from years ago. You could get to the park faster that way. But I haven't been in the hospital since the big expansion, not since my mother–"

He takes a breath, resets. "My daughter's having knee surgery, so I thought I'd take a walk in the park."

"You know Harvey?" she asks incoherently.

"I do now. Nice kid."

She shoots him another look, shakes her head, inserts the keycard into the stairway door, nods him through.

But he holds it open for her. "After you."

She gives up, lets him usher her up the stairs, surrendering to the lunacy of the day. Up one flight, she pauses at a door, this one unlocked. "Here's the door you wanted. If you go down the hall past the cafeteria, there's a back exit. Then across the parking lot to the park. There's a path—"

"I know. I grew up in this neighborhood."

"Oh." She frowns. Maybe that's it. He does look familiar somehow. She shakes her head, says briskly, "You know there's a waiting room for family. I can take you up there."

He raises his palms. "Actually, I was taking a break from that. Melani's mother's up there. She…. It doesn't work too well for us to be in the same room these days."

"Oh."

"Guess she thinks I should have asked her permission to take Melani skiing, even though it was my weekend with her." A shrug. "Kimberly's still caught up in old anger, it's really her pain body talking. She needs more time to move through it into detachment."

"Uh…."

He looks down at her, into her eyes. "You know. How everything comes to feel like a source of suffering. It'll pass."

She stares up at him, gears ratcheting. Is he a kook? That strange calmness, she's seen something like it in the way the patients in the psych ward can look right through you. Into you. Maybe he's a nut case, escaped off the ward….

But even as she thinks it, she sees he's got a gentle smile tugging his lips. She's the one spinning out.

"Thanks." He gives her a nod, pushes through the door, looks back as it's swinging closed, and the smile widens. "Be well, Lindsey." The door shuts with a soft click.

two

BACK IN MEDICAL RECORDS, Lindsey straps on her wrist-tendinitis brace and sits down to it. Pulling on the headset and plugging into Number Two E.R. line, she's relieved Gayle's got Trauma Doc and his dramatic flourishes. She goes into her patented zombie state and her fingers fly. She doesn't have to think about it any more—once she enters the patient workup info and diagnosis, the terminology's pretty well selected, and only occasionally is she jarred out of it with an unusual case or nomenclature. Her mind goes thankfully numb, just occupied enough to keep the "brain whirl" at bay, all the endlessly cycling and recycling wounds and arguments and pleas and fears receding to white noise. And when the hot flashes attack along with the nausea and vertigo they bring, she can fake it, pretend to keep typing and no one seems to notice.

Static now in the headset, then a popping as Dr. Octavio with his thick accent she's learned to decode hangs up and a new doc starts recording:

"Bennerton here. Patient Montague, Richard, male forty-five head trauma motor vehicle accident arrived via ambulance 2:45 am...."

Lindsey cringes, braces herself to keep typing. Dr. Bennerton is the backup neurosurgeon on call for emergency head and spinal injuries. She keeps praying he'll move out of town or they'll take away his surgery privileges. Everyone dreads it when they see his name on a chart, but the audit committee protects its own. She can predict the complications piling up in the next reports to come down the line after the patient's admitted from E.R. She takes a deep breath and tries to shunt the thoughts away, not summon bad luck on this faceless man, hoping the next report she types isn't about fluid pressure buildup on the brain, infection, vitals deteriorating, non-response to stimuli.

The office phone rings and she realizes she's been sitting stiff, fingers poised motionless above the keyboard, staring at the blank monitor screen.

"Lindsey."

She flinches, takes a breath, starts typing.

"Lindsey, it's for you." Gayle is leaning around from her station, pointing at the blinking red on the phone extension. "Hey you okay?"

She mouths, "Bennerton," indicating her headphones as she pulls them off, and Gayle makes a commiserating ouch face.

Lindsey picks up the phone. "Hello?" She keeps her new little cell phone off while working, per office policy.

It's her older sister Francine. "Lin, sorry to call you at work, but it's Mom. She's having another bad spell. Can you pick her up and take her to the doc?" Fran has already booked the latest appointment she could get today, but her number two grandkid's sick, and she's daycare backup for her Phyllis who's moved back home after her divorce. It's Lindsey's turn to cope with Mom. Make sure she understands the meds, make sure she doesn't try to drive. Ratcheting more gears, Lindsey figures she can make it home on her bike after work, pick up her car, and get Mom to the doc on time.

She braces to finish the Dr. Bennerton report, sends it to the printer, and shuts down for lunch break. She needs some fresh air. Then she stops short as she's passing Olivia's desk. Crap. She'd forgotten about staying late to catch up the surgery line.

"Olivia...."

They work out a deal. Lindsey can come back for a couple hours on the evening shift.

"Thanks." She ducks her head, can't meet her boss's eyes, hates having asked one more favor.

"Lin."

She looks up to see Olivia giving her a motherly look. "It's okay, Lin."

Her eyes are burning, damn she's so tired of losing it.

Every time she lets a little crack open, feels anything, it turns to tears. *"You know. How everything feels like a source of suffering."* The stranger in the basement stairwell, calmly seeing through her careful mask.

She blinks, gives Olivia a quick nod, bites her lip and makes it to the stairs before the tears spill.

Lindsey bursts through the back exit, desperate for open air and movement, figures she just has time for the shorter trail-loop through the park. She'll grab a sandwich at the cafeteria afterwards and eat it while she works. That's another splinter festering, she can feel the resentments in Marlene and some of the others, she doesn't join them for lunch to sit and gossip and do the female bonding thing. They think she thinks she's above it.

She sucks in a cool, drizzly lungful and lengthens her stride past the patient dropoff circle, past an idling medi-shuttle and parked cars. Well, maybe they're partly right, she hates all that hen-pecking at the latest intrigues and outrages, but mostly it's just survival. She can't let them pry her open. And she won't make it through her days, cooped up in that windowless office, without this break to move in the free air, in the watery winter daylight.

"A cancer in our community!"

Lindsey flinches at the shout, back for a second in her nightmare of looming faces and scalpel. She shakes her head as more voices chime in:

"Save the park!"

"No more land grabs!"

Placards and people in rain slickers are milling around at the access turnoff to the hospital. Someone's shouting through a bullhorn, "It's corporate greed! Don't let them sucker you with their spin about saving lives with a new emergency access."

Protestors are blocking Lindsey's dash across the arterial and the gate to the park entrance.

"Here's one now!" A clot of them converge on her. Shoot, she's forgotten to take off her ID badge.

An earnest, bearded young man pushes a green flyer at her. "United Medical owns the hospital, you know. They've posted the highest profits of any other hospitals in the state. Let them pay for a new access exit from the freeway."

A silver-haired woman waves her sign in Lindsey's face. "Save the park! The nesting hawks and owls! Don't let them put a road through it!"

Lindsey carefully pushes the sign away from her face. "I'm voting against it. No way am I letting them gut the park."

"More power to you, Ma'am!" A dark-haired young woman presses closer with a petition to sign.

As Lindsey grits her teeth at the "Ma'am" and tries to explain that she's already signed it, the bullhorn roars again: "Down with corporate greed! Up with real community health!" What look like students from the local environmental studies college–all dreadlocks, beards, and neo-hippie garb—dart out into traffic, pushing the green flyers at cars they've forced to slow. A few drivers roll down their windows and take the papers, but most just scowl and honk their horns.

"Slow down and look at the park! It belongs to you," the bullhorn continues its irritating rant.

"Will you sign, Ma'am?" The young woman is still nudging her with the petition clipboard, and Lindsey recognizes her then with a jolt.

She turns as the man with the bullhorn lowers it. Sleek graying dark hair, wiry build, deliberately oblivious to the rain in a thin wool shirt, the arrogant thrust of the chin. Nick.

He sees her then, too, and his trademark crooked smile tugs his lips to the side, the smile that charms until you know what's behind it. Lindsey feels that too-familiar, sickening empty blow to the gut. She falls back from the pretty young woman, his new girlfriend, at least not the earlier one he was having the affair with.

She jerks around, pushes away blindly through the ruckus, all the voices and car horns just a roaring in her ears as she darts through traffic. A horn blares right behind her. She leaps forward and narrowly misses getting hit. "Damn it!" She's losing it again and right in front of him, great this is just great.

In the park, fringy arms of the cedars bend down for her, drooping wet fronds brushing her face. She runs down the muddy trail, deeper into green shadows.

"You're not like most women, thank goodness." Nick emerged from the tree-shadowed trail on that years-ago backpacking trip, following Lindsey onto a flat boulder beside the river.

She shrugged her heavy pack off onto the boulder, stretching in the sunshine and rushing river song. "What do you mean?" she ventured. She'd taken it as a compliment when Nick had first said that same thing, but after five years with him, she was starting to wonder. She perched on the flood-smoothed granite jutting into the pool below the rapids, dipping a hand into the current.

Nick crouched down beside her, brow furrowing. "Come on, Lin. You know what I mean. Don't try to tell me you're not into it, leaving most guys in the dust."

"Then why do you single out women?"

An exasperated sigh. "Hey, it was your dad started it, not me— introducing you to all his pals as his 'boy' who'd whup their sons at fishing and splitting firewood." He chuckled. "Anyway, how many guys do you see fussing on the trail about breaking a fingernail?"

Lindsey examined her ragged nails, three days worth of camping dirt imbedded beneath them. "Definitely not an issue here. I could use a bath, though." She started stripping in the warmth of noon sunlight streaming down between high rock walls of the ravine.

Unlacing his boots, he suddenly sat upright and grabbed her wrist. "Listen." He leaned toward his pack to grab his binoculars.

"What?" She strained to hear anything over the rush of the upstream rapids, finally caught the trill of a dipper and spotted it bobbing on a rock across the river, but glanced at Nick and saw him sighting upwards. Then she heard the shrill hawk call and reached for her own binoculars.

"Where?" She couldn't spot anything.

"Listen. Watch the breeze on those vine maples hanging over the lip of the cliff." He jerked his chin upwards. "Tell me if it's a sharp-shinned or a Cooper's. It went behind the cliff, but it's riding the upward thermal so it'll come around in a sec. See if it's a new species for your life list."

Lindsey tried to summon the image of that page from her birding guide. She knew now to watch with hawks for the barred tail, longer than on falcons, the distinctive wingbeat, and note the chest and head patterns for a positive ID. She squinted against the sunlight, then saw the quick form rising in a spiral above the river. Putting her binoculars to her eyes, she swept, found it, focused. Caught a quick breath at the beauty of the little hawk, its fierce eye and curved beak, felt a visceral connection to its flight up into the sun.

"See the white patch on its tailtip? Is it wide and rounded, or just a thin stripe? That'll clinch the difference." Nick's voice jarred her out of her spell.

Lindsey blew out a breath. "I'm not.... Oh, now I see it. Just a stripe, it's a sharp-shinned. Is it a male or female?"

"Pretty sure it's a male. They're smaller, of course, but hard to tell size from a distance. That's why you look for the other identifiers."

Nick lowered his binoculars as the hawk soared out of sight again. He grasped Lindsey's shoulder and squeezed. "Good job." He nodded. "And you spotted that pygmy owl before I did yesterday. You're really learning to *see* in the forest."

Putting her binoculars back in their case, Lindsey paused to meet his approving look. She shook her head. "Nick, I did spend four years as a river-rafting guide." And most of her life hiking since she was a little kid. "It's not like I didn't see anything before you taught me about bird-watching."

"Birding." He gnawed his lip. "Lin, don't be so uptight. I just meant you notice a lot more now."

She turned to watch the river's flow, feel its eddies and surges like her own blood singing to her. She felt a pang of missing those footloose-free whitewater years before Nick, and before the torn shoulder in the rafting accident. But the shoulder had healed well enough for all her other sports, and the guiding was never meant to be a long-term job anyway.

She took a deep breath. "Nick, I appreciate learning the birding lore, the scientific names." She had to admit she'd been lazy that way. "But there's another way I wish you'd...."

She glanced up to see that stiffness coming over him, the rigidity of resistance, and she gave up trying to explain the way she took in things differently from him, had to feel the energy of a place not so much with her logic. How abstractions sometimes interfered with becoming part of the whole picture. But she didn't want to spoil the day with another argument, see him slam the shutters against her "irrationality."

She shook it off, putting on a smile. "That pool is calling my name." She pulled off her shorts, tossed her underwear on top of the pile.

Nick was sitting back watching. He grinned, white teeth flashing between dark beard stubble.

"What?" Lindsey stretched in the luxury of warm sun on skin.

He chuckled. "Just admiring the wildlife. You are one hot forty-year-old, Babe." He reached over to stroke the curve of a still-firm breast.

"And about to cool down. Last one in...." She reached a cupped hand into the river swirl and flipped water at him. Jumping up, she ran down the boulder and dove into the clear, deep pool.

The cold was a total-body jolt, but she relished it as she glided underwater through liquid jade. Rippling lights and shadows, and the quick silver dart of a fish. Breaking into the air, she gasped and shook her head, drops flying. She stroked back to the flat boulder, heaved herself up. Throwing out her arms, she flung more drops to be jewelled by the sun. "Whooo! Now I know I'm alive!" The surge of the river pulsed through her, skin tingling.

Nick had stripped now, strong wiry body sun-browned, and she reached out to touch the familiar patch of dark, curly hair over his chest, trace the line down his ridged belly. His penis was stirring in its thatch.

He took a stride and pulled her close, his sweaty heat delicious on her river-chilled skin. He rubbed, hardening against her. Licking her neck, he worked his way up to her ear, nipped the lobe. "Lin the water witch," he breathed. "I'm gonna fuck your brains out." He gripped her harder, plucking her off her feet and plopping her down on their piled clothes. He licked her breasts, tugging one stiffened nipple with his teeth, and then he was thrusting hard into her as she gasped at the suddenness but then opened for him. That heat and power in him always turned some hidden key to lay her bare. He was the river in spring flood, sweeping her along in the spray and churning whitewater as they rushed on wild through the rapids.

"Linny! Watch out!"

"It's all right, Mom. There's half a block of clear road."

Lindsey's grateful to be nudged out of the Nick memory as her mother Opal clutches the armrest on the passenger side of the Subaru, as if pulling out of the clinic parking lot is a death-defying road race.

"Who's clearing the road? Should we stop?"

"Easy, Mom. We're fine." She has to raise her voice for Opal now. Her mother's gotten so frail and tremulous, how did it happen? Was it gradual, and Lindsey didn't notice until suddenly Mom's this birdlike gray-haired old lady whose bones might snap if you give her a real hug? She's afraid to be alone, and Dad at eighty-five is still barreling along oblivious to anyone else's needs. What is it this time? Off on a fishing trip, and they can't let Opal drive.

"No wonder I was feeling such pain, Doctor says it's my arthritis. He upped my ibuprofen by 500 milligrams." Opal's smiling, pleased with the attention.

Lindsey bites her lip, trying not to be exasperated with the way her mother, a former nurse, still worships "Doctor" and lives for these visits when she can trot out her lists of minutely calibrated symptoms, confer about dosages.

"I told Doctor he needs to get a decent office nurse. These new gals, and they even have men now, they're just incompetent. They don't go through the kind of training we had. Why, during the war we were practically running the ward *and* studying for exams, and we'd never leave a patient sitting there without...."

Lindsey nods and makes the proper agreeable noises. She's heard these stories so many times she could recite them verbatim, Opal's voice receding to a background drone as she navigates town traffic and heads onto the county roads, dark clouds lowering into an early twilight.

She comes out of autopilot with a start as Opal grips the

door frame and cries out, "You're going too fast! It's hard to spot the driveway."

"Mom, it's okay." *I've only made this drive hundreds of times.* "I'm going the speed limit." She slows for the turn.

Down the long oak-lined drive through the hay field and into the big empty house where yapping Bingo awaits. Lindsey gets Opal settled in with the terrier and dinner and her new meds. She prays Arlen hasn't given her another gun after Fran and Joanie confiscated the pistol she was keeping in her bedside drawer, ready to fend off burglars and rapists she was sure lurked behind every tree. She'd always tried to scare Lindsey into ladylike safe behavior with tales of pirate slavers and sexual predators.

"So when's Dad coming back from his fishing trip?"

"Two more days. I'm paying Skip to come out and sleep here while Arlen's gone."

Lindsey bites her lip again and wonders when her youngest nephew is going to get a steady job, cut back on the beer. Maybe she better call and remind him to give Opal a buzz before he heads over, so he doesn't get met at the door with a shot of mace to the face.

She blows out a breath. "You're so isolated out here in the county, Mom, and Dad's gone all the time. Why don't you think about one of those assisted-living condos in town? We could visit more often. You'd make new friends."

"You know Arlen would never give up his shop and the garden."

"Then leave him here! All he does is yell at you all the time, anyway." *And push you around.*

"Don't you start that again!" Opal pulls her crocheted afghan tighter around her shoulders. "That's just Arlen. I don't want to be alone. He's not so bad—he doesn't drink, and he's a good provider."

Lindsey closes her eyes, a hot flash igniting at the base of her spine, flames roaring up into her face as sweat breaks out. Blackness, red sparks sweeping over her.

She was six years old, pain flaring over her bare back-side and legs after Dad broke the heavy stick beating on her for daring to correct him when he screamed at her about leaving the hose running and she wasn't even the one who did it. She was trying not to cry as her mom dabbed salve on the bruises.

"Mom, please! Please take us away! I hate him! Why is he so mean?"

"Shush, now, they're only spankings. He doesn't mean those things he says, he just gets upset when the bosses give him a hard time. And don't you go bad-mouthing your dad to people. He works hard, he doesn't drink. He's a good provider."

Lindsey, swaying now eyes-closed in her parents' overheated, echoing empty home, swallows and takes a deep breath. Is it too late to talk to her mom about her life, her choices? How does Opal hold onto her pieces of identity—the former nurse in charge of the hospital cardiac unit, shouted down and mocked viciously by her husband, disassembled bit by bit over the years, until she's given all her strength away?

Lindsey gives Opal a careful hug, eyes still prickling. How did Linny learn at six to seal off the tears, and now at fifty-two any little thing just sets her off like that faucet she can't shut? She rips off her sweater and fans herself with her T-shirt as another wave of the nauseating hot flash blazes through her along with a surge of helpless love for her mother. She remembers Mom young and vital and pretty, always singing.

Lindsey can't tell Opal how grateful she is to her: It was the final straw with Nick, running to barricade herself behind the locked bathroom door as he stormed through the house breaking furniture and she huddled with her face in her hands. Looking up, she saw herself in the mirror becoming her mother.

She lets herself cry in the car, then it's a cold water splash and a fresh mask face for evening shift in Medical Records. She's cranking along on the surgery line when the report on the knee surgery comes down–sixteen-year-old Melani Zender.

Lindsey blinks, pulls her fingers off the keyboard. She shakes her head.

"Be well, Lindsey." The big man smiling gently as the hospital's stairwell door clicked shut behind him.

She finds herself standing, pulling off the headset,

stepping over to the stack of active charts and pulling out the only "Z."

Melani Zender. Parents at different addresses. Father: Newman Zender.

She's back in the absurd dream–was it only that morning?–back on Newman's bike zooming along, their long hair tangling together in the trees. She bursts out laughing.

"Lindsey?" Carol's head pops around the partition from her station. And that only cements the dream images of those nasty Nick puppet-heads springing out at her. She can't stop laughing, seeing the bafflement on Carol's face. She stares like she's thinking Lindsey's finally lost her mind.

"That's right." She waves the chart, as if that explains everything, and manages, "It's the official diagnosis."

three

"IT'S A SOULMATE CONNECTION, gifting you with that dream about him." Crystal, wrapped in fringy scarves and tribal necklaces, broad beautiful face serene, delivers her truth. She channels her information from a ten-thousand-year-old deity, so it tends to reduce complications of ambiguity in her life.

Lindsey's been doing some spiritual seeking herself since the cancer diagnosis, but isn't quite ready to accept Crystal as guru. She refrains from a skeptical rebuttal as Crystal forks up some veggie salad and smiles, bathed in an appropriate halo of light. The sun's broken through the cloud cover to shimmer off the marina ripples and in through the window of the Bayside Café.

Megan, across the table, does roll her eyes, short hair gleaming with new reddish streaks. "Lindsey, you dodo-brain! It's no big mystery." She cuts off a piece of rare steak and pops it into her mouth, talks around it as she chews. "I told you Newman moved back to town a few years ago. And how he ended up getting divorced a year ago. Remember? You were so wrapped up in the Nick stuff, I guess you weren't listening."

Megan's an old friend of Newman's from high school days, has kept in loose touch as he moved at large through the world, from living on an East Indian ashram, to selling Nepalese handicrafts at fairs from his hippie van, to now consulting in third-world countries, helping villagers set up self-sustaining cottage industries.

Lindsey pushes her empty chowder bowl away just in time for their server's tattooed hands to whisk it onto his tray and slosh more water into her glass. "Thanks." She shrugs at Megan. "Well, at least I got a good laugh out of it. Here I am in the hospital basement, thinking he's some wacko out of the psych ward and can I get the door unlocked fast enough to flee." She shakes her head, chuckling. "I think he knew all along who I was." Was he laughing at her? It didn't feel like it at the time.

Crystal, with the authentic warmth that shines through whichever New Age trend she's on, reaches over to squeeze Lindsey's hand. "It's good to hear you laugh, Lin. Accept these gifts from the universe."

"Tell you what, my dear." Megan fixes her with a practical eye. "What you ought to take is the opportunity to give him a call." She flips open her cell phone and taps at it, whips out a business card, and writes down a phone number on the back. "He's one hot prospect for the right gal. Financially secure, and he's into all those outdoors things you go for." She gives a little shrug, unusual for briskly efficient Megan. "So, okay, those guys I tried to set you up with were geeks, at least it pried you out of the house. But Newman's different." Her voice sounds wistful. "He...he's a really *good* man."

Lindsey's touched by their caring, but she's jittering away from this conversation. She pushes her palms out, fending off. "Look, that's not where I'm going." She's damaged goods, but not about to be an object of charity. She cringes at the memory of his eyes, that clarity seeing way too much. She's not ready for that. And what could she offer a man? Anyway, he recognized her and didn't say anything.

"One of these days, Lin, you're going to look in the mirror and see how beautiful you are. Haven't you been using that ylang-ylang essence I gave you? It'll open up your heart chakra, help you balance your male-female energies." Crystal is giving her the Earth Mother gaze.

Lindsey wishes she could find something that made sense to believe in, but maybe that's the trouble–she both wants and is skeptical of easy answers.

Megan snorts. "What she needs is a close encounter with a big, hard—"

"Megan." Lindsey waves her down, glancing over at the next table, where two men in suits have fallen silent, eavesdropping.

"Linny, I know you! What's it been, over two years?

You've got your juices so backed up by now, your teeth must be floating. Do you wonders to have a good, screaming—"

"Megan! Cut!" Lindsey slices crosscuts through the air with her hands. "You keep this up, I'll be forced to use my blackmail material." She's come armed this time. Reaching into her purse, she pulls out a yellowed letter from Megan, dating from their twenties when Lindsey was in the Peace Corps in Honduras. She'd found it when she was going through some old boxes, tossing out reminders of Nick. Opening the folded paper, she reads from mid-page, "...and was he hot!! Honestly, we were so revved, and I'd never done it on a pool table before, but his frigging boot laces were in knots and we couldn't get the damned things off him. So I grabbed the kitchen knife, and—"

"Lindsey Friedland!" Megan, face reddening, grabs at the letter as Lindsey pulls it out of reach.

She sits back, pouting. "*You* better watch it, Lin! Don't forget I've still got the photo negatives from that bicycle trip on Orcas Island. You know, the ones with you wearing nothing but sea kelp? Not to mention the topless hiking shots...." She makes another lunge and this time rips the letter from Lindsey's fingers.

"Careful! That's got historical value."

"My God, I can't believe you saved this." Megan scans the page, laughs, flips it over. She reads on, sobering, fingers gripping tighter.

"No, not that part." Lindsey tries to take the letter back.

"No, no. Wait." Megan finishes the page and drops the letter into her lap. She looks up at Lindsey, her eyes brimming. "Hey, gal friend," she says softly. "You *were* my angel, you got me through that shit with Brent and the...." She bites her lip and shakes her head, mutters, "To think I might have married that jerk just because I got knocked up."

"Hey, I didn't mean to rake that up."

Megan reaches over and squeezes her hand.

Crystal is looking baffled, turning her face from one to the other. "What's going on?"

Megan smiles, squeezes Lindsey's hand again, and releases it. She turns to Crystal. "Lin got me through some kind of heavy-duty stuff back when we were roommates, finishing up college. Then she was off to the Peace Corps. That was before her river-rafting gig. Talk about Amazon woman! She was my hero."

"Wow." Crystal blinks, turns to give Lindsey a surprised look.

Lindsey's shaking her head. "Megan's never been known for exaggerating."

"No way!" Megan slaps her palm on the table. "You saved my silly butt back then, my dear, and now I'm returning the favor. I think Newman's got just what you need, give you a little jumpstart back into your sassy old self." She reaches over to stick the business card into Lindsey's purse. "So you've got his cell number now. No excuses!"

Dusting her hands, she briskly pulls out her daytimer. "Okay, Crystal, it's your turn to choose the spot next month. But have a heart. Not that place with everything made from goat milk curds...."

April 23

Dear Diary,

Red and purple tulips up in the garden! April showers bring phallic spring flowers.

HighJinks brought in a black-capped chickadee—catch and release—for the morning's entertainment. I managed to trap it in the livingroom curtain, the poor thing quivering so I thought its heart would burst. Put it in a paper sack and warmed it under the lamp, then held it in my hands on the back porch. I swear it looked into my eyes before it flew off.

Hunters and hunted. Where do I fit?

Lindsey pauses, tapping her pen on her teeth. She's phasing out the SAD light, bundles up to sit on the porch for breakfast and catch the morning sun when it's not raining.

Speaking of running like a scared rabbit.... Let's list the fiascos. "Hot prospects" friends have sent my way:

MEGAN: BRUCE
Technically not a "date," so she's off the hook. Felt like I

was the worm on it, wriggling away. Okay, he was funny at her family's traditional July 4th barbecue, hanging with Megan and Joe and me, but those clouds of his men's cologne enough to choke you. So then he showed up at the house! Didn't invite him in, figured I'd take him on the yard tour down to the creek in back, show him my native-plant restoration project, then I'd send him on his way.

"You're so tense," he said. "Let me give you a shoulder rub." Therapeutic massage? Is this a sure-fire date tip they learn in the locker room??

I politely declined, edging toward the driveway and an appointment, "Darn," I just remembered.

Then, cross my heart, he lunged at me, grabbed my shoulders, started digging in. By then I was tense all right. Jumped five feet.

So there I was, leaping away across the lawn like a scared rabbit with Mr. Cologne in hot pursuit.

Is this what it's come to?

CRYSTAL: RAVEN SKYWALKER

Past-life regression facilitator and repurposed plastics sculptor C. invited to her annual Capricorn-Aquarius Birthday Party. Tall with little silver ponytail (nice) but mostly bald (shiny scalps not my thing but trying to be open-minded, it's luck of the genes for the poor guys.) Arrived on a Harley in serious black leather.

When Leon introduced us, I trotted out something lame like, "How are you?"

"For the primal how, you might ask my mother. For the rest, I always say, 'When you play with God, it's for keeps.'" All the while fixing me with a meaningful look.

"Oh. Well. But…. Is that true?" I fumbled. "Seems like God might have a heart. You know, give us a second shot."

He laughed and cocked his head to give me another look. So then it appeared I was his designated partner for the evening. I got used to the Koan-flavored quips, even though I didn't have a clue what he was saying half the time. I figured out that if I just answered something mysteriously illogical, he'd find a hidden meaning in it and nod sagely.

So then Crystal was taking us all on her garden tour—she'd made some new wire sculptures and bird houses—and Raven S. took this as his cue to guide me along, taking my *arm, rubbing his hand between my shoulders. I eased away a couple times, figuring he'd get the message.*

No. (Is this where Skywalker goes to the Dark Side?) He actually started jabbing me in the ribs!

"What are you doing?" I stared at him.

"You're so uptight!" And then he shook my arm, gave me a bit of a shove. "Let your body move with it, instead of resisting. It helps you let go of your past-life traumas. I could help you with that, some deep-release work along the spine, and the groin area."

I think I managed not to shudder. "No, thanks, I'm feeling perfectly adjusted. Now, if you'll excuse me...." I tried to move past him without stepping on Crystal's violets.

"That's only denial talking." Then he shoved me again!

"Stop it!" Now I was getting pissed off.

"I was just being playful. Loosen up." He was drilling me with his eyes again. "You know I'm an expert at reading body language, and—"

"Good. Then read this." I actually flipped him the bird! And then I was hightailing it out of there.

"Lindsey, what—?" Crystal, calling after me. "Where's she going?"

The last thing I heard was Raven answering her, "Your friend's holding a lot of latent hostility...."

MEGAN AGAIN: GERALD

From the terrorists to the timid!

Met "Gerry" at the student flute recital Megan tricked me into attending so I could help cheer on her Cathy. "Just happened" to see single-dad Gerry there, who "just happened" to really like hiking. "Isn't that amazing? Lindsey does, too!"

He was decent-looking in a Clark-Kent sort of way, clean-cut and with a knife-edge nose and jawline, though almost nonexistent lips. But very polite!

We went on a couple of low-key outings, rambles on local trails. Talked books, gardening, and his son's baseball league. At least he knew how to be quiet on the trails, and someone to share driving with is always a bonus. No chemistry whatsoever between us, so a relief to just relax and be casual friends.

On the third hike, we were sitting on a log with our water bottles, taking a break. Maybe we were talking about the latest logging outrage near the North Cascades forest preserve. Apropos of nothing, he cleared his throat and turned to me.

Another prolonged throat clearing, then he asked, "May I kiss you?"

CHARLOTTE: DENNY

For an ice-breaker, he announced, "Yeah, what I'm really looking for is a woman in her thirties who wants to make babies."

And way way back, in the days when men seemed to fall off the trees like ripe apples at Lindsey's feet, there was Newman.

By some arrangement of Megan's—roommate with Lindsey in that funky cottage in the cedar grove while they both returned to Hometown U. to finish their bachelor's degrees—her old pal was coming by on his bike after returning from a couple years in the East Indian ashram. Only Megan never mentioned it to Lindsey. And she never made it home from her hot date the night before.

Lindsey was out in the yard reading and sunning topless when she heard the "ting" of a bicycle bell.

"Shit." She rolled over, fumbling for her shirt.

A deep chuckle. She squinted against the sunlight. A dark silhouette split the rays, then shifted, walking the bike closer.

"Hi. I'm Newman." He dropped the bike, stepped over to her blanket.

She blinked up at this sleepy summertime vision. Sunlight caught in his long blond hair and beard, gilded his deeply tanned skin. He was tall, shirtless in ragged cutoff jeans, a single strand of blue glass beads around his neck dangling some kind of medallion. He was grinning.

Lindsey got herself together and stood up, tugging her tank top down over her shorts. "I'm Lindsey. Can.... I help you?" The rehearsed line from her part-time waitress job popped out.

He tilted his head like he was thinking it over, then

reached out a hand and took hers, but he didn't shake it. He turned it over and gazed at the lines on her palm.

She retrieved her hand, brushed her palm over her hip. "Uh...are you lost?"

"I don't think so." Another slow smile. "You must be Megan's roommate. Is she ready? We're going for a bike ride."

Lindsey shook her head. "She didn't mention it. She... she's not home."

"Hmm." He took that in calmly. "Well, Lindsey, how about it? I was thinking over to Mosquito Lake, take a swim."

It was easy in those days, all the time in the world and life meant for exploring. Mosquito Lake was a leisurely ride. More a muddy pond, really, lined with rushes, shallow and warm in the summer sun.

Newman flattened a sort of nest in the tall grass, and they dangled bare feet in the water, watching the red-winged blackbirds flit around as he told her about his travels, and his studies with the "Teacher" at the ashram. Then Lindsey finally put it together: he was the one Megan had said was studying to be...what was it? A Buddhist monk?

"Here's a good way to practice, you can learn to tune out bodily distractions. We'll just lie here in the mud. Just feel it and let it pass over you, let the bugs crawl on you and be part of it."

Okay, she was game. So they stripped and lay there in the mud and Lindsey almost thought she could do it, ignore the grit on her skin and the flies landing, and she tried to be serene and let time be only the moment. Like Ram Dass advised: *Be. Here. Now.* But then something wiggly was going on under her thighs, some creature burrowing. She gritted her teeth and kept her eyes closed, desperately willing it away, but there it was, some bug or crawdad crawling higher between her thighs and what if it bit?

She cheated and brushed under her leg, pushing the bug away. Then squinted to see Newman sitting up, caked with mud. He gently touched her hip, lifting a squirming worm off her. He smiled.

She shook her head. "I don't think it's working."

He just kept smiling, shifting to lower himself onto her. He settled his weight carefully over her, pressing her deeper into the mud. She felt strangely disembodied, while completely aware of his chest against her breasts, the gritty slippery feel of the mud oozing along their joined skin, his penis settling soft between her legs. Some part of her mind was asking all the usual questions like what the hell was he doing? but it was all so oddly peaceful and nonthreatening. He didn't move or grind against her, just lay still over her, not crushing her at all, and a new kind of light and warmth seemed to radiate through them both. Serene.

And Lindsey thought maybe she was getting it. It was about transcending physical desire, making a spiritual connection, all the things the hippie songs and poems talked about only she'd never understood really even though she'd smoked her share of pot and sampled the psychedelics. But now she couldn't help feeling a hot twinge in her loins, wanting to pulse against him. He really was gorgeous and his hard bod on hers felt good, and how could he just lie there so still and not give way to it? Maybe that was what they learned, studying to become monks.

Lindsey felt her face flushing and suddenly she could feel the flies and bugs squirming again, and was that something else stirring, hard, between her thighs?

He sighed. She was too confused.

"I think that's enough for me!" She pushed against him.

"Okay." He smiled and lifted quickly off her, then plunged out past the cattails into deeper water, waving her in for a swim.

The next day Megan told her he'd left for India again. Lindsey chalked it up to Transcendence 101.

four

MAY 1. MAYDAY. MAYDAY.

Dear Diary,

I'm tired of being tragic.

Hot Flash Queen of America reporting in: Yesterday I timed them—like perverse labor pains—2.6 per hour averaged, a new record. By the end of the day, I was exhausted with the surges and the sheer effort of ripping my clothes off and then putting them back on. The blazing heat and drenched clothes are bad enough, but it's the nausea and vertigo that really whack me. Lucky Lindsey, you win the rare triple whammy!

So I was going through the checkout line at Food Land (ha! no more Nick telling me where to shop) and there in the impulse-buy rack was this battery-powered Chinese plastic purse-size fan. On special at a buck! I slipped one in with my groceries, hoping no one was noticing.

Then of course the little cutie with the curly hair and soul-patch goatee picked it up, cocked his head, and gave me a puzzled look. "These are selling pretty hot lately, but it isn't even summer yet."

The gal in line behind me started chuckling, gave me a nudge. "Oh, honey, you got the reverse curse, too? Men just don't know how lucky they are!"

Then down the line a blue-haired granny type piped up, "Don't worry, you'll be glad to put all that behind you. Think of the money you'll be saving on those glad rags." In her cart I saw she had a packet of adult diapers.

By this time the whole line was chortling, and the poor checker had gone beet red, whipping the rest of my stuff through the scanner as fast as he could.

So naturally all this triggered another flash, roaring up my back prickling and blazing. Broke out into a sweat, face ready to burst, but I'd be damned if I was going to cap off the performance by tearing off my sweatshirt right there to the applause of the crowd.

And the beat goes on....

"Hrrm. Lindsey? Ted Horner here. Hrrm. Yeah, well I thought I'd just say hi. How you doing?"

Out of the blue, it's a phone call from an old friend—no, really just an acquaintance—from high school days. Or maybe not so out of the blue. The hometown web seems to be wired, signals going out and in. Seems Ted ran into Cheri, living in Seattle now but up for a visit, and she'd been talking to Don, who mentioned he'd seen Nick with his new girlfriend.

Ted keeps clearing his throat. "You know, when I saw you last winter out with Megan and Joe at the Grizzly Bear, I don't know why I didn't ask you to dance."

Lindsey doesn't remind him that was when Megan asked about his wife who wasn't in evidence.

"Well, since Zhia and I split, I figure I'll get out more. Hrrm. I've got two tickets to the Theater Guild this Friday...."

All that sticks in Lindsey's memories of him is a vague image of shaggy brown hair and a motorcycle. He was on the football team. Now he tells her he owns a commercial fishing boat in Alaska, where he captains it during the summer salmon season.

What the hell, he's being straight with her, so she says yes.

The play's a farce—a bedroom bedlam of closed and opening doors, lovers and would-be lovers hiding in bathroom and closet while jealous wives stalk and disguises get swapped. Lots of pratfalls and exaggerated facial contortions. She and Ted are sitting front row, where they can literally see the actors spraying spit. And Lindsey can't stop laughing.

She always used to embarrass her big sister when she'd

tag along to the weekend movie matinees. Fran would threaten to gag her. And now Lindsey's doing it again, breaking out even during the beats when no one else in the theater is getting tickled, her helpless laughter echoing over the pause. It's almost like she gets possessed—like those Voodoo dancers when the gods take them over and they eat coals—and the line between pleasure and pain gets blurred, her gut spasming, and she breaks into a sweat it's so absurd. Joni Mitchell had it right on so many things: it's the same release, laughing and crying.

By this time the woman sitting next to her is looking over pointedly, but Ted doesn't seem to mind. In between her laugh attacks, he whispers questions about the plot or makes comments like, "Oh, it's really the boyfriend in the Italian tenor's costume." Which makes Lindsey laugh even more helplessly, when she realizes he's serious.

She's limp by the end, and he ushers her outside, apologizes because he forgot to open the car door for her. He explains again about his other car—the Mercedes— that's in the shop so they had to take his SUV. And even though the evening's mild, they now have to wait while the huge vehicle warms up, so he can demonstrate the features of the leather seats. She feels something weird under her butt, really pretty unsettling, then she laughs some more when she realizes it's a heater and not some new insane menopause symptom.

Which thought in itself triggers another massive hot flash prickling down her back, blazing out through her skin. She manages to resist the urge to rip off her jacket and run the car window all the way down for the short drive back to her place.

It's only polite to ask him in for a glass of wine. HighJinks strops himself on Ted's legs while Sombra, still suspicious of men after Nick's raging around the house, sits atop the scratching post fixing them both in the high beams.

"Nice little place you got here," Ted says. He's average height, but stocky, and somehow seems to crowd her small living room as he paces over to check out the windows. "Nice, looks like the original wood trim. Good investment, houses in this neighborhood. Hrrm. I've got a rental like this, fixed it up and I've had the same tenant for twenty years, she could have bought the place twice over by now.

But I never sell. That's my rule. Just live in them for a while, fix them up, use the collateral to buy a new place. I'm good as gold now, any bank will loan me a hundred grand no questions asked if I just walk in. I planned it all out that way, it's working out good."

"Oh," Lindsey manages. "And you like the lifestyle, fishing? I guess you'd get a lot of time to travel during the winter."

"Well, I stay busy trading online. I like to buy cars, too, drive them while I detail them out, then sell and I come out okay. I like Mercedes."

"Oh." Now she's the one hrrmming. "And you go to plays a lot? I haven't been to the Guild for ages, didn't realize they were so ambitious with the productions. That was really pretty tightly choreographed tonight—"

"Well, it's something to do, get out of the house. I watch cooking shows, too. I got this incredible new high-def TV, gets direct satellite downloads. The picture is so sharp you can really see the moisture in the people's eyes, see inside their mouths. You've got to come over and see it. You won't believe how real it is."

All Lindsey can manage is "Hrrm," as he goes on to explain his longterm investment strategies and retail philosophy in buying only quality. He shows her the label inside his jacket: "One hundred percent camel hair. That's why it's so warm."

Which Lindsey pounces on as his exit cue. "Well, I have an early morning tomorrow." Gets jacket on him, and he's out the door Stage Left. Sagging back against the closed door, she lets out a long breath. Outside, a stretched-out silence. Then, finally, his SUV starts up, growls down the road, and fades. Curtain.

From: HotDawg Horner
Subject: Good Time, etc.

Hey, Lindsey,
    Great to connect with you last night and spend the evening together. I'm planning to get rush tickets tonight for the jazz band concert at the Starlight—if you get tix on the

day of the show it's a big discount and you sit up on the
balcony where the sound quality is great. I bring my Fujinon
binocs for closeups. If you're free, I'll pick you up, got the
Mercedes out of the shop. Dinner first? My treat.

Got a confession: I am smitten....

Luv, Ted

"Megan, my god, what am I going to do?" Lindsey clutches her new phone—she's finally accepted the inevitable and purchased a simple cell phone so she wouldn't be completely left behind "progress." She glances down the hall and over to the patient waiting lounge, trying to keep it to a whisper in case anyone from Medical Records comes by. She's finally managed to catch Megan between meetings. Megan's always juggling meetings, when she's not juggling kids and husband and nieces and nephews, and Lindsey can't grasp how she clearly thrives on hyperdrive. She takes a deep breath. "I don't know whether to laugh or cry."

"Well for heaven's sake don't get all wrought up over it. Just tell Ted you'd like to be friends but you're not ready for anything else."

"I already did that. He doesn't seem to get it, keeps emailing and calling."

"Well then I guess you have to explain it. Different interests, the chemistry's just not there, blah blah. Ted's a decent guy, just maybe not the sharpest tack in the box. He needs things spelled out." Of course Megan remembers him, she probably has the entire Fairview census databank downloaded in her social matrix.

"I feel awful. I really wasn't leading him on, just thought it would be fun to get out. Reconnect with some of the old crowd."

"Don't think so much! Just a sec...." Megan rattles off something about extra chairs to someone, then gets back to Lindsey. "Look, men are wired different. They don't get so complicated about this stuff, sometimes they just keep swinging at the balls, figuring it'll up their odds of scoring. Maybe 'smitten' doesn't mean the same thing to him as it does you."

"Oh." Lindsey never was able to figure out the dating

scene, even when she was young. Maybe the Pacific Northwest hippie worldview soaked into her since childhood, and she can't get over believing that if everyone were just open and sincere, everything would be clear. "Why am I so clueless?"

"Lindsey." Megan's voice has softened. "You are a total sweetheart, and I love you to pieces. Just lighten up, have some fun with this stuff." She clears her throat. "How's your mom doing?"

Bingo, she's zeroed in. And that's what Lindsey loves about Megan, she really does manage to care about all the multitude of people in her "clan." It puts Lindsey to shame, but she can only handle letting a few in that close.

"Lindsey? You there?"

She clears her throat. "It's getting bad again. We've got to come up with a plan. But Fran's got her hands full managing the furniture store and mothering all her kids and their kids, half the time she's got one or more of them living back home with her. And Joanie—now Eric and his girlfriend got back on the drugs, they have to go through treatment again, and Joanie's got custody of the baby. Plus *her* full-time job. So it seems like I'm the only one with time to think about where all this is going...."

She sighs. "Dad fights us any time we try to get them to reorganize. Mom, too. It's like they hate their lives and each other, but would rather die than change anything." She takes a deep breath.

"Time we had lunch, kiddo." Megan is laser focused now. "How about Friday? I'll pick you up at the hospital entrance, 12:30, we'll zip over to Murphy's for a bite."

Lindsey's eyes are prickling again. "Thanks, Megan."

"Keep smiling, sweetie."

Lindsey furtively wipes her eyes on her sleeve before turning toward the hall, heading back to Medical Records. And comes up face to face with Marlene, Jenny, and Sono. Damn. She sniffs, hopes her eyes aren't red.

"Break time!" Jenny shakes out her fingers, rotates her wrists. "They've got Crispy Cremes in the cafeteria today!" She flashes a mouthful of braces.

"Oh." Lindsey blinks. "You mean those donuts? I've never had one."

Sono shakes her head, chin-length glossy black hair

bobbing. "Never had a Crispy Creme? Are you serious?" She pushes her thick glasses up and focuses on Lindsey.

Lindsey takes a breath. "I guess it's time. Do you mind if I come along?"

Marlene blinks in surprise.

Sono pushes her glasses up again, then cracks a grin. "Let's go before those greedy docs snap them all up."

"Oh, no!" Jenny—thirtyish, plump, and single—has one of those high, breathless little-girly voices, and Lindsey is never sure if her matching persona is for real. "We better hurry then, those creepos!" She grabs Marlene's arm and tugs her down the hall, breaking the awkward freeze.

Lindsey and Sono fall in behind, regroup at the elevator doors. Lindsey balks then, glancing over at the stairwell door—it's only one flight down for heaven's sake—but she bites her lip and goes along.

"Watch out if you go for one of your walks today, Lindsey, those protestors are out there again." Jenny tugs her sweater down over her skirt. "I could hardly get through them this morning."

"Yeah, I got more of those flyers about the park stuffed under my windshield wipers," Marlene grumbles in her nasal tone. "If they're so damn environmental, maybe they should stop wasting all that paper. Think they're going to convince me some frogs and birds are more important than saving human lives?"

Lindsey takes a breath as the elevator door opens. "You're right, I think they're just antagonizing everyone by now. It doesn't have to be black and white."

Marlene frowns, then shrugs. "Well, I can tell you I just get the urge to strangle that jerk in charge. The puffed-up asshole with the bullhorn."

A choking sound from Sono. Lindsey bursts out laughing.

Jenny stops where she's hurried ahead to the cafeteria doorway, turns wide-eyed and puzzled.

Marlene's looking a question from Sono to Lindsey.

Lindsey waves a hand, drags in a breath. "My ex."

"What?"

"The guy with the bullhorn. My ex."

Marlene's jaw drops. "Oh." She looks chagrined. "Oh. I didn't mean...."

"No, you're right on. He is a jerk."

Sono ushers them all onward. "I can smell those artery-clogging fats calling."

"Now don't start on that, Sono!" Jenny giggles and hustles toward the line, skirt swaying over her wide hips.

"I'm in recovery from a deprived childhood of rice cookies and sushi." Sono winks at Lindsey.

They pick up trays and hot drinks, corral the Crispy Cremes that just look like regular glazed donuts to Lindsey. After all the hoopla, she was expecting something like custard-filled at least. But anyway they've broken the ice, maybe she can do this after all. Fit in like a normal person.

"Can you believe those new forms?" Sono starts in, talking around a mouthful. "Act like we don't have anything better to do. Like, oh yeah, just add on an hour's worth of paperwork, and of course work twice as fast to catch up the backed-up transcription lines."

Jennie wipes her hands on her paper napkin, shakes them out, and holds them up. "They're starting to tingle at night, all the typing." She rubs her wrists. "Lindsey, does that wrist brace help?"

"Well, bad keyboard position is the real killer, but especially at night if you get one of the braces with the rigid support and strap it tight enough, it does help. I'll show you how to strap it."

"Oh, thank you! That's sweet." Jennie smiles.

"...say they're working on new standards for the audit committee," Marlene's telling Sono, the two having veered off onto a new topic. "But all it amounts to is shuffling around the HDCA codes." She sniffs, air laboring through clogged-sounding nasal passages. "If they were serious, they'd look at the complication rates for Dr. Bennerton—"

"Sshhh!" Sono leans forward to grab Marlene's shoulder, looking alarmed. "She's sitting over there by the window."

"What?" Marlene looks startled.

"Keep it down," Sono whispers, rolling her eyes toward the window, with a tiny jerk of the head. "It's Mrs. Montague. She comes every day."

"Who...?" Then dismay dawns on Marlene's face. "Oh, no."

Lindsey bites her lip, darts a look over toward the

window tables. By herself, a middle-aged woman in a blue parka she hasn't unzipped sits hunched, staring into a coffee cup. Montague. Her husband is the one Lindsey transcribed that emergency report about, the head injury over a month ago that Dr. Bennerton botched. The one they moved to the longterm care wing. The one on IVs and intubation. The one with no evidence of brainwave activity.

Nausea, sour and hot in her mouth. She wants to jump up, shout it out, tell Mrs. Montague what they've done to her husband, but she's choking on the words. So many words swallowed. Burning sparks, molten lava roiling from her gut up her throat.

Lindsey drags in a breath, pushes her half-eaten donut away, stands in an awkward scraping of chair legs over linoleum. Her face is burning, boiling, she's a pressure cooker ready to burst.

"Lindsey, what—?"

"Hot flash. Gotta get some fresh air." To get to the outside door, she has to edge past Mrs. Montague, who doesn't look up from her coffee cup.

Bile rises on the crest of more surging heat. Lindsey pushes out the glass doors and into the blessed coolness of gray drizzle in the garden off the waiting area. She sinks onto a damp bench, taking in deep breaths as the nausea subsides, fixing her gaze on the drops beading the tulip buds. She wants to fall to her knees and embrace them, but she just sits there, letting them fill her vision. They're beautiful, perfect, a delicate pink veined with peach, swelling egg shapes of plant flesh on their vibrant green stems rising toward the sky and kissed by silver rain.

five

IT WAS THE "EGG incident," as Lindsey labeled the memory, that started her seriously wondering about Nick's mental health. Over the years with him, it had come to seem normal to tiptoe around his anger-triggers, the same way as a child she'd learned to watch for the signs of a Dad explosion, keep herself braced for getting grabbed by the neck or whacked with his wooden paddle. With Nick, too, it was better not to question too much, not push for connection he wasn't willing to offer. Finally, that day—when she found herself literally walking on eggshells—she had to face what was happening.

It was a Sunday morning, and Lindsey had planned a surprise. When they'd first started living together, they'd enjoyed making pumpkin waffles, eating them in bed and licking any maple syrup drips off each other. So this weekend she'd made sure they were stocked up on all the ingredients, had pulled the waffle iron out of the back of the cabinet the day before to dust it off.

"Come on, I need some help in the kitchen!" She dragged him protesting away from his newspapers, and the head of steam he was building over "the bullshit EPA trying to fuck us over again with lower standards." She had all the ingredients laid out, ready, the waffle iron plugged in and heating up.

"I got a new bottle of real maple syrup." She waggled it at him, raising an eyebrow.

He hesitated, then grinned. "All right. I guess I get to help with the...cleanup?"

She laughed, relieved. "If you treat the cook right, maybe."

He snorted and pulled a knife from the wooden block, started slicing a lemon for their tea. "No way, I'm the head chef around here. Whose recipe is it, anyway?"

She shrugged. "You got a point."

"Okay, I'll whip the egg whites and you can heat up the syrup, mash the pumpkin."

"Done. I bought canned, didn't want you smelling the pumpkin cooking and ruin the surprise."

He paused, holding the knife. A little frown. "It's better with fresh."

"This is organic, I've used it in pies before."

He sighed and turned to the egg carton lying on the counter, flipping the lid open with the tip of the long knife. Lindsey hoped the eggs had reached room temperature by now.

"Where did you get these?"

"What?" Lindsey, pulling the can opener out of a drawer, peered around Nick and realized it was the styrofoam carton he was staring at. "Oh. I didn't have time to go to the co-op, so I had to pick some up at Food Land. I was surprised they actually have a little organic section now."

"But it's styrofoam packaging. Lin, you know how bad that is for the ecosystem...."

"Nick, I know. It was just this once. And I think we're doing our part—I mean, I rode my bike over there, don't I get points for that?"

He still had the frown lines creasing his forehead. "I just don't get it, Lin. It's not that hard to establish new shopping habits, the co-op even does most of the research to find 'green' producers. For one thing, we can recycle our old cardboard cartons and buy the bulk eggs there."

"I've been doing that." She spread her hands. "Nick, if you want to do the shopping, that's fine with me."

"Oh, that's just great!" He swung around, the knife still gripped in his hand, and she had to take a quick step back to avoid it.

"Nick, be careful." He tended not to be aware of the usual body-space considerations. Like the way he'd let a branch snap back at her on the trails, so she'd learned to give him plenty of room.

He rolled his eyes. "I'm just asking you to get with the program, Lin! Don't you think I have enough stress with the new job? I'm paying the bills, so I figured you'd be happy to carry the household end."

She opened her mouth, then shut it and made herself take a deep breath. "Nick, it's not like I'm a housewife with nothing else to do. I've got a job, too, even if it is only part time. I had to take what I could get after you applied for the transfer here."

"Wait a minute. You were the one who wanted to move back to Fairview so you could be closer to your family. So I took the transfer, even though I inherited a real mess up here."

Lindsey blinked. All she could do was stare in disbelief. It had been "the bureaucratic bullshit" and "jerk administrators" at Nick's previous posting at the environmental watchdog agency that had driven his blood pressure through the ceiling, triggered his insomnia. She'd given up her job and the beach cottage she'd loved, so they could get a fresh start.

This was his second transfer. Lindsey was beginning to wonder if "impossible working conditions" were really the problem.

She took another deep breath. "Nick, you're working hard, and it's for important causes. I just want some credit for all I do, too. It's not like I'm sitting around. I've put in most of the labor getting this house in shape, and I take care of almost all the upkeep. I mow the lawn, weed the garden, put out the recycle bins even when it's your turn, plus doing the housework. I've been trying to help you, I know you're stressed over the job, but can't we just lighten up today, let this go? Maybe go for a bike ride, have some fun?"

He turned abruptly back to the counter and thrust the knife clattering into the sink, scowling down at the egg carton.

"Nick, please." She took a step closer to touch his arm.

He jerked like she'd stung him, then swung sharply around, and his elbow rammed hard into her sternum, between her breasts.

Lindsey fell back, jolted. "Nick! Watch it. That hurt." She rubbed the tender spot.

"Come on, I barely brushed you. Don't blindside me when I'm trying to cook."

"What? You weren't—"

"Damn it! Don't tell me what I'm doing!" His face had gone red, that look he'd get like it was ready to explode. "Fuck this shit!" He grabbed the egg carton and hurled it across the room. It hit the wall by the door and burst open in a spattering yellow mess. He strode toward the door.

"Nick, wait. I'm sorry, I didn't mean to...." Lindsey tried to catch his arm, slow him down so she could explain what she'd meant. They could talk it out.

He whirled around, ripped her hand free, shoved her away from him. She slipped in the mess, stumbled back over crunching eggshells, and then her feet slid out from under her and she landed on her butt in the slimy goop. She sat stunned as he grabbed his keys and slammed out the door. The car revved, loud, and roared off down the road.

She sat, ears ringing. What had she said? All she could hear was the echo of her own voice, saying, "I'm sorry." *I'm sorry sorry sorry.*

The next time it was HighJinks. When he was still a kitten, Nick grabbed him and threw him against the wall when he was mewing too much. After that one, he walked off into a near-freezing winter night wearing only a thin sweatshirt and jeans, and didn't return until the early morning hours, in time to shower and head to work. Refusing to discuss it.

Lindsey started doing research on syndromes, started keeping a calendar of the sleepless phases, the rage attacks, the flurries of pacing and spouting off, the weeks when he'd drag in from work, skip dinner, and go lie on the couch staring at the ceiling. She was convinced he was suffering from a serious medical condition, and she wanted to help him, but she couldn't seem to find a pattern.

His family didn't seem that surprised when she called with her worries. Nick had repeatedly refused to see a doctor or therapist, so his parents offered to pay for Lindsey to consult a psychologist about him.

Katherine McDonald, PhD. Clinical Psychology.

Lindsey checked the polished brass sign on the office door, one of a half dozen, then pushed through to sit on a scratchy upholstered chair, gripping her calendar and diary. The other people in the waiting room, an older man and a young couple, carefully avoided eye contact.

"Mrs. Friedland?" One of the inner doors had swung open. A big-boned woman in slacks and print blouse, graying blond hair pulled into a loose bun, stood in the opening.

Lindsey hastily stood, flushing, dropping her calendar. The psychologist waited calmly while she retrieved it.

"Hello." Lindsey stepped closer, sticking out her hand to shake, then wondered if that was the right move here.

Dr. McDonald flashed a quick smile and gave Lindsey's hand a squeeze, then ushered her into the room, indicating a pale-green velour couch. She picked up a folder from a wooden desk and then sat facing Lindsey in a leather chair.

"So, Mrs. Friedland...may I call you Lindsey?"

She nodded.

"Call me Kate, if that feels comfortable to you." She glanced at the folder that had the paperwork Lindsey had sent in clipped to it. "I understand you have concerns about your marriage?"

"Yes. Well, I mean, it's about Nick. My husband." She cleared her throat. "I'm afraid he might have some kind of psychological problem, something wrong with his brain chemistry. Or it could even be some other medical condition, but he won't see a doctor. I'm worried he's going to have a breakdown."

"I see." Dr. McDonald leafed through the papers. "It indicates here that his family shares your concerns?"

"Well, I talked to them about it, and they thought I should talk to you...I mean, you were recommended to them. To me. That is...." She took a breath. "I was wondering about some sort of intervention. Is that possible? I mean, is he hurting himself, banging his head against the walls, not sleeping? Is there a way to get a diagnosis? I've been reading up on manic depression, started keeping a calendar to see if there's a pattern to it...." She lifted the calendar and her diary.

The counselor glanced at them, pursed her lips, and made a note on the papers. She looked up into Lindsey's eyes. "Let's back up a bit. Why don't you tell me how this started, when you first noticed something wrong? And what's going on now?"

Lindsey told her about Nick's two work transfers, how he'd get so angry about the environmental abuses that he couldn't wind down after work. Then it was his coworkers getting him steamed up. Then Lindsey herself, like everything she did was wrong. But when she tried to talk with him, discuss things calmly, it just seemed to add to his agitation, and he'd think she was criticizing him. His blood pressure was high, and she was afraid with the stress and sleep deprivation he was going to have a breakdown.

Lindsey realized she was gripping her diary so hard her fingers hurt, her shoulders tight and tense. She made herself take a deep breath and set the diary and calendar aside.

"And what about you, Lindsey? How do you feel with all this stress?"

"Me?" She blinked. "I...don't know." She closed her eyes for a second, then opened them. "Upset. Worried."

"Of course you are." A pause. "Why don't you tell me about the most recent episode of his rage. Can you remember what led up to it?"

To her mortification, Lindsey felt tears prickling.

"It's all right. Take your time." Dr. McDonald—Kate—leaned over to place a box of tissues beside Lindsey.

"All I did was ask him if he could put out the recycle bins because I'd strained my back that week."

Lindsey hesitated, and then it all came out in a rush. "He thought I was complaining because he hadn't been doing it, but I tried to explain that wasn't it at all. He said then why did I ask him with this tone of voice that was so insulting, like I was just setting him up and being a martyr, and he was sick of being manipulated. I tried to explain that wasn't it, truly it wasn't, but then he said I was just trying to have the last word, like I always did—but I don't, really—and he wasn't going to talk about it any more. So he went off to work at his computer, and he was muttering and getting upset about the failure of the government to fine the polluters, so it wasn't worth pushing it. The bins were full, and it's an early morning pickup, so I just figured I'd lift them carefully into the wheelbarrow and take them out to the road. It wasn't that big a deal. Then I did strain my back again, but I didn't want to say anything. I guess he saw me doing my stretches and then he just exploded. Started screaming at me...."

Lindsey had her eyes closed, but the tears were leaking out anyway, and her throat was seizing up, the way it did when she tried to talk with Nick and she knew it was hopeless. He would just turn anything she said around on her and he couldn't seem to understand what she really had meant, and by that time she couldn't even think straight, let alone get any coherent words out.

"Take some deep breaths, Lindsey." Dr. McDonald's voice was slow and soothing. "When you're ready, tell me what happened next."

Lindsey couldn't meet her eyes. "He was screaming, said I was trying to make him feel guilty, all I had to do was ask him straight out, I was driving him crazy and didn't I realize he had important work to do?" Her voice was shaking. "Then he started hitting his head with his fists. I tried to get him to stop, and then Sombra—she's one of our cats—got in his way and he started to kick her aside. He'd thrown both of them before, and I couldn't let him do that again, so I grabbed her and ran into the bedroom and shut the door. But he came in after me and he was really crazy, yelling that I was trying to make him look bad, I was pretending he'd hurt Sombra."

Lindsey rubbed at her eyes. "He just started raving then, I don't even know what he was saying, but I wasn't going to let him get near Sombra. So he grabbed this photo print off the wall. He'd given it to me, it was framed, the river where we'd gone backpacking on our honeymoon. He smashed it against the dresser and took off."

Silence for a while. Then Dr. McDonald asked quietly, "What happened when he returned?"

"Well, that time he stayed with a friend for a couple of days. When he came back, he just pretended it didn't happen. He seemed more upbeat, so I didn't want to push it. When I tried to talk about it, he said he was just blowing off a little steam, everybody did that, and I was making a mountain out of a molehill."

Lindsey rubbed her eyes. "Maybe I am. I can't tell any more, maybe it's because I'm so jumpy. He says it's just me, like I'm in constant PMS and acting bitchy, the whole perimenopause thing, and it's driving him crazy the way I'm imagining things. Maybe I *am* crazy, thinking he's going to hurt me when he swings around with knives in the kitchen and I'm standing right beside him. I swear he comes really close, I have to jump back, but he says it never happened. Only I know it did. Does."

She took a deep, shaky breath. "I really think he doesn't remember the scary things he does, like the time he went into a rage on the freeway and almost killed us swerving around, and he wouldn't stop or let me out. And it seems like he'll look at the empty spot on the wall where the photo was and not even notice it's gone."

Lindsey blew out a long breath. "That's why I think there's something physically wrong. His brain chemistry must be out of whack." She wiped her eyes.

Dr. McDonald was contemplating the view out the window. She cleared her throat, shifted her gaze to Lindsey's. "Of course, I can't diagnose him at a distance. I wouldn't rule out a medical condition, but I'd strongly urge counseling for him. Meanwhile, it's more important to talk about you."

She stood up and walked over to a bookshelf, pulled out a paperback, and came back to hand it to Lindsey. "I think you should read this."

Lindsey blinked, then focused: *The Traumatic Relationship Trap: Abuse Victims and PTSD.*

"What?" She stared at the red and purple bookcover. Post-traumatic stress? Wasn't that for Vietnam Vets? Confused, she looked up at the counselor.

"It's a common pattern, Lindsey. Too common. You need to learn to protect yourself, then we can talk about healing. Before you leave today, we should discuss an emergency safety plan for you."

Lindsey pushed the book aside and launched to her feet. "You're saying this is all about *me* being a victim?" She shook her head. "I'm not the victim type!" She straightened her shoulders. "This is crazy. My family calls me the Amazon Woman. I used to be a river rafting guide, I'm not afraid of camping around bears, I've travelled solo in Central America, gone diving with sharks. I'm not some cringing little crybaby!" But the damn tears were prickling again.

Dr. McDonald sat calmly watching. "Please sit down, Lindsey." She waited until Lindsey did. "Clearly you are a strong woman, or your health would have broken under this longterm stress and confusion, like a state of siege where your body is always on high alert."

But Lindsey was already losing faith in her strength she'd always taken for granted. Was it the prolonged "siege" that had led to her cancer?

"Lindsey." Dr. McDonald was leaning forward for emphasis. "I strongly urge you to take this seriously. You could be in danger, and you need to know when to get out if the episodes escalate. Take the book home and read about 'power over' versus 'power within.' It's a huge problem in our culture."

"I'm not a victim."

"There's no shame in recognizing it. That's one thing you can learn now—how to refuse to be shamed. How to stop having that sick feeling in your gut when you've tried so hard to communicate with him, and he makes you wonder if it's all your fault because you just didn't explain it carefully enough. When he 'accidentally' shoves you or rams into you, and you find yourself saying, 'I'm sorry.'"

Lindsey opened her mouth, then closed it.

"Do you want to make a safety plan? We can start there." Dr. McDonald paused. "It's your decision. Your power."

She sat still, waiting. Lindsey looked down at her clenched hands, swallowed, and nodded.

six

Dear Diary,

That book my counselor–Kate–gave me was a page turner all right. All those years when I thought I was maybe going crazy, and worrying so much about Nick's health, it turned out that I was the wife in a movie "The Shining II" and Nick was following its classic script of abusers. Wow. I've been taking a look at the book again lately, a refresher to remind myself how to stay out of traps like "gaslighting," when Nick got me doubting my own perceptions.

Still reclaiming my "power within." And since the cancer, thinking more about the spiritual side of life. So far, not scoring too high on finding faith that seems so important for most people's happiness. Off-the-shelf Christianity I was raised in not my thing–most organized religions have inspired way too many atrocities in the name of "truth."

So, my floundering forays in the last couple of years:

TRANSCENDENTAL MEDITATON: Still a hippie at heart, I really resonate with the idea of "Be. Here. Now." If only I could get that anxious brain whirl to dissipate into the white light of no-thought, maybe I would feel that universal Oneness and peace. So I tried a meditation class and flunked out. Managed to sit in almost-lotus position and ignore my whining knees, but the harder I tried to banish thoughts, the wilder they attacked! I tried so hard to not-try that I was sweating, and then of course that triggered cascading hot flashes. I may have groaned aloud. Anyway, the instructor took me aside and said I was "disturbing the force field" (should I call in Luke Skywalker?) and maybe I should just practice at home. Alone. The Force is definitely not strong with this one....

GODDESS ENERGY: Crystal invited me to join her women's circle to raise group Goddess Energy and ground ourselves with organic essential oils. Found out I was allergic to the strong flower scents. And opening up my chakras just made me paranoid. Also nauseated. Crystal says I'm over-protecting myself against past-life trauma. Oh, good. This-life trauma not enough?

WICCA: Didn't realize it's officially a religion, but "do as you will, as long as you hurt no one" seems like a decent guideline. Have gone to a couple of seasonal celebrations— like dancing around a Maypole, chanting, singing, feeling good will and connection. I like honoring the turning of the seasons, tuning into nature, but the mashup of ancient and new deities to honor is kind of confusing. When one of the women started talking about casting spells, I got queasy. Again.

SHAMANIC DRUMMING: Went to a drumming circle at the local college, led by an anthropologist/shamanic practitioner who explained that these ancient practices are similar worldwide, not necessarily culture-specific. What I liked was the honoring of spirit in all natural beings, not just humans. The drumming was somehow powerful and peaceful all at once, resonating through me, or maybe it just drowned out the brain whirl. I was ready to join, but then a protest group got it shut down for cultural appropriation. I guess I see their point–so many things already stolen from the natives, who can blame them for circling their wagons?

Next???

It's June, time to celebrate summer, so what if this is the Pacific Northwest and it's still raining half the time. Lindsey decides to host the next lunch gathering in her back yard, gals garden party. It's a sunny weekend! And she'd managed to mow the out-of-control lawn the day before, drag out her rusty garden tools and make some inroads in the rampant weeds.

"Lindsey, you are so blessed to have this place right in town! It's like the Garden of Eden!" Crystal throws out her arms and spins across the lawn past the sprawling red rhododendrons and the old lilac tree, her embroidered long skirt wheeling out around her pale legs and bare feet.

Lindsey recalls that vivid dream, months ago now—twirling young and barefoot across the grass in her hippie skirt—and she feels a rush of gratitude to Crystal. She sets down the picnic basket and kicks off her flipflops to feel the earth beneath her feet. She grabs Crystal's hands and twirls them both across the moist grass.

"Whoa, girls!" Megan's chuckling, waggling her bottle of Chardonnay. "You haven't even fueled up yet!"

HighJinks, overstimulated by the visitors, yowls and darts to the back porch to jump onto a rounded beach cobble Lindsey uses as a doorstop. He slides onto his side, embracing it, kicking his legs to get it spinning.

Crystal claps her hands. "Did you teach him that?"

"Try teaching a Siamese." Lindsey snorts. "It's his latest obsession, humping that rock."

"Way too much sexual frustration bottled up in this household!" Megan gives Lindsey a significant look, waving the wine bottle. "Mister Mojo there is ready to roll, anyway."

"And I am so ready for summer." Lindsey pulls off her fleece zip and ties it around the waist of her jeans, savoring the breeze on her bare arms. She's been wearing tank tops all spring so she can cool off when the flashes hit her, has figured out how to pad the left cup on her bras so the lumpectomy breast doesn't look so unbalanced with the other one. And now that it's officially summer, she and the underdressed coeds aren't the only ones wearing skimpy tops.

"Yep. Figured it was time to show a little leg." Megan strikes a pose, extending a rhinestone-encrusted sandal to show off shiny pink toenails, then going into a modelling turn to display what look like brand-new purple capri pants. "So where do we set up camp, Kemosabe?"

"It's still pretty mucky down by the creek, let's eat up here." Lindsey shakes out a heavy blanket, spreading it over the grass beside the border of native groundcovers she'd planted under the rhododendron hedge, fringy foliage of bleeding-heart with its pendant blooms setting off the glossy leaves of wild ginger.

"Wait, I have to visit the appleblossom devas before we eat. I want to see who else is popping up back here." Crystal meanders deeper into the yard toward the old orchard and the creek ravine, stopping to poke here and there at wildflowers struggling up through the weeds Lindsey has let take over since the divorce.

"Let's pop *this* sucker." Megan plops down onto the blanket and whips out a wine opener, cranking into the Chardonnay cork and yanking it out. Lindsey hands her glasses from the basket, and she pours. "Better corral Crystal before the fairies take her away." She hands Lindsey a glass, then stands and takes hers and Crystal's. "So how's it going with your mom?"

Lindsey raises crossed fingers. "We got the new meds ironed out, I think, so we're in a holding pattern."

"Good." Megan tilts her head, auburn tints catching the sunlight. "You look better, too, Lin. But you could still take ten pounds from me, you skinny minnie." She reaches over to click glasses with Lindsey. "Though I have to say, you look hot in that tank top."

"I'm hot all right. Still up at night with those damn hot flashes. Crystal gave me a couple of Reiki treatments—that's her latest thing—but it didn't help any more than the herbs." She blows out a breath. "I'm about to say to hell with the cancer risk and try hormone replacement for a while. It's the nausea along with them. Sometimes I just hit the wall with it."

"Well, maybe some hormones wouldn't hurt for a bit, just to get you through the worst of it." She heads after Crystal toward the apple tree. "My family, we're good peasant stock. All I noticed was I stopped bleeding, never had those flashes."

"I could kill you."

They duck under the gnarled apple boughs, white petals drifting down. Crystal's poking around in the tangled foliage by the fence that separates Lindsey's yard from the neighbors' backyard barbecue area. Luckily it's a six-foot fence, since the Jorgensons are earnest Born-Agains and

Lindsey still indulges in nude sunbathing.

"So how long *has* it been since you had sex?" Megan's voice booms across the lawn.

"Ssshh!" Lindsey waves her down, tilting her head toward the fence. She can hear the Jorgensons on the other side now, sounds like they've got the Bible-study group out there again.

"Oh, shit!" Megan giggles. "Tell 'em you invited Mary Magdalene over," she stage-whispers. Raised Catholic, Megan has never let notions of sin cramp her style. "Crystal, come and get your wine!"

Crystal drifts over to claim her glass.

Megan raises hers. "To Lin getting her brains fucked out."

"Megan...." Lindsey rolls her eyes.

"Goddess! You're kidding!" Crystal bursts out. "Lin, don't tell me you have a new guy?"

"No. Megan's hallucinating."

Megan laughs. "Just you wait, my dear. You better get serious, or *I'm* going to call Newman, sic him on you. Do you both good, his ex did such a number on his head I think he might go turn into a monk again."

Lindsey can feel her face burning, not a hot flash this time. She's been thinking about that phone number Megan gave her. "Give me a break!" Lindsey turns away, irritated now, tired of advice and the focus on healing that seems to have taken over ever since the cancer. She just wants to *live* her life.

And then she's more irritated, with herself, when she realizes she's hunching protectively around her breasts, crossing her arms. Every time Lindsey lets herself think about connecting, maybe making love again, she has to remember. Nick had flinched away from the lumpectomy scar, didn't want to touch it. So how would a new man see her now, this aging body? The misshapen breast?

"Sweetie." Megan's voice has gone soft. "Don't do that to yourself. Nobody who deserves you is going to mind a little missing piece." She touches Lindsey's shoulder, the faint scar from the years-ago repair she rarely thinks about. "Who the hell at this age doesn't have scars? Like this one never slows you down. Shows you're winning the fight, if you ask me."

Lindsey bites her lip, gives Megan a wry smile. "Yeah, here I go with the pity party." She moves toward the fence, where Crystal is poking around again, picking forget-me-nots.

A voice is reciting on the other side of the cedar boards, "And lo, when Delilah saw that Samson had told her all his mind, she sent and called the lord of the Philistines...."

"Lin!" Crystal's kneeling beside the bird bath Lindsey and Nick had made years ago, a concrete basin formed over the impression of a huge rhubarb leaf. "I never saw this before. It's wonderful!"

"Nick and I made it."

Crystal leans forward to rub moss off the deeply incised veins, runs a finger up the deep folds of the leafy basin. "You two did have a strong creative synergy, when he could stay centered in his true self."

Lindsey pauses. "You're right." She kneels beside Crystal, reaches out to pull weeds away from the basin.

"...and she bade him sleep upon her knees while...." The low voice rumbles on from the Jorgensons' yard. "Then she began to torment him, and his strength left him."

"It's pure Goddess energy for your garden!" Crystal turns on her knees, raising her voice to call over to Megan. "Come and look at this! It's the perfect fertile female shape, the way the leaf is opening, beckoning the male penetration."

"Crystal...." Lindsey tries to hush her.

"I mean, just look at these labial folds. Did you realize what you were creating here?"

The voices beyond the fence have fallen silent.

Crystal spreads her arms, raising her face to the sun in smiling rapture. "Goddess, Lindsey, it's a celebration of sacred sexuality! Completely vulvular!"

seven

LINDSEY ROLLS DOWN THE window and takes some deep breaths as she turns off the country road into her parents' drive—a long stretch through a field of tall ripening grasses and darting goldfinches. At the end of it, the artificial pond and waterfall, green watered lawns, trimmed flowerbeds, and what she calls the Friedland Folly–the ostentatious house her parents built for their retirement.

The two-story, three-bedroom oak and tiled "dream house" has become an oversized mausoleum for mother Opal to rattle around in. Coerced into moving from the house in town she loved, now she's isolated out in the county with her failing strength and vision, unable to drive and depending on visits from her daughters. Meanwhile, Lindsey's father Arlen roars around in his huge diesel pickup truck, wheeling and dealing with his cronies, or gone on fishing and hunting trips.

Lindsey suspects he made a deal with the devil to stay so energetic at eighty-five. When she was younger, she'd blithely assumed she could just choose what she'd inherit: her father's toughness and adventurous vigor; her mother's songs and gentle spirit. Now as the days come down to her (more Joni Mitchell playing on her inner soundtrack), she has to face the flip side of these traits: Dad's restless self-absorption and hair-trigger anger; Mom's singing voice turned to a fussy whine of suffering.

Lindsey suddenly puts on the brakes. Still partway down the dirt drive, she shuts off the motor, closes her eyes, and takes another deep breath. She gets out and walks into the hayfield. Moving slowly, holding out her arms to feel the scratchy stems, she lets the fringy tops slide through her fingers. Childhood habit kicks in, and she breaks off a stem, strips out the tender inner shoot, tastes the sweet greenness. Chewing on the bobbing stem, she returns to the Subaru, pulls out the audiobook reader she's bought Mom, and heads to the house.

"Linny!" Opal blinks through her thick lenses, then beams. She struggles to rise from the oversized lounger where she's propped up with back and neck cushions, heating pad, afghan, and napping shapes of striped cat and spotted terrier.

"Don't get up, Mom." Lindsey sets down the box and hurries over to perch on the arm of the lounger, leaning over to give her a kiss on the cheek. She fluffs the thinning gray strands her mother still has permed into a pouf that now reveals a lot of scalp. "How's it going?"

"Oh, I decided to add another half pill at night of the Remeron. I just couldn't get to sleep worrying about Eric and the baby."

"Mom, did you talk to Dr. Nichols about that?"

Opal loves to tinker with her meds, which sets off Lindsey's alarm bells. Last time, she overdosed herself by upping her antidepressant.

"These young doctors, they just don't understand how I suffer!" Opal looks indignant, and Lindsey makes a mental note to call Dr. Nichols. She's the new GP, really sharp and specializing in geriatric patients. The family doesn't want Opal changing docs again.

"Mom, remember what your counselor said. It's best if you just pray for the grandkids, try not to worry so much about them." The latest on Joanie's oldest is he's lost his job after falling back into the heroin habit, and his now-ex-girlfriend's in jail for stealing to support hers. How Joanie is coping now that she has custody of their baby, who has developmental problems, Lindsey has no idea.

"Here, Mom." She resets, puts on a smile. "I brought you something, I want you to try it out." She steps over to the box and opens the flaps, sets aside the audio books she's checked out of the library, then pulls out the compact player.

She wants to plug it in and demonstrate with the earphones while she's caught Mom in position, let her see this could work, since she refused to try the magnifying reading lamp with the large-type books she can't read any more: *"It's too bulky, it won't fit by the lounger. I've got my little table there with my pills and everything."*

"Okay." Linsey turns back to Opal, ready to plug it in.

But by this time her mother's already struggling upright, plucking at the afghan with helpless little movements, fumbling with the button that releases the extended leg rest. "I've got to get up and get lunch ready. Your dad will be in from the shop in a minute."

"Wait, it won't take long...."

Too late. The window of opportunity creaks shut as Opal pulls herself to the edge of the lounger, grimacing and rubbing her back. Spike the cat and Bingo the terrier protest the disruption. Opal grunts and bobs forward in a false start at launching herself to her feet. Lindsey drops the player on the cushions and takes her mother's thin shoulders, gently eases her up onto her feet.

She sways for a second, knit pants and matching top with appliqued roses hanging loose on her shrinking frame. She finds her balance and shuffles toward the kitchen on the other side of the breakfast counter.

Lindsey goes ahead and plugs in the audio player, sets it temporarily on her mother's side table, where there's plenty of room once she eases aside the water jug and tray holding all the prescription bottles. She inserts a book CD, slips on the headphones, and fast-forwards to the first chapter of an Agatha Christie novel.

"Okay." She follows Opal around the counter to the sink, where she's holding a kettle under the faucet, hands shaking. "I can do that, Mom." She takes the kettle, fills it, starts to set it on a burner on the stove.

"Wait!" Opal plucks up a tea towel, clutches Lindsey's arm, and wipes a couple of drops off the bottom of the kettle before she'll allow it to be set on the burner.

Lindsey refrains from rolling her eyes, the old teenage response, and lets Opal direct the lunch preparations, lets her explain for the hundredth time the right way to set out the plates, how to use the can opener and which container to put the fluorescent orange preserved peaches in, the exact thickness the American cheese must be sliced "or Arlen will growl."

"Who's the goddamn idiot blocking the driveway?"

Having announced his presence, Lindsey's dad slams the door. Still a handsome man with his deeply tanned face and most of his formerly-black, wavy hair, he stomps over in work boots and coveralls to give her a rough hug. "Where the hell you been? Figured you must've moved off to Oregon again." From Arlen, this is a big display of affection.

"What about you? The last couple times I was out here, I figured *you'd* moved to Canada." Lindsey plays along, doing the good ol' gal back at him. "You score any fish?"

"Big waste of time. Humpies weren't running yet, goddamn river all screwed up." He turns to Opal. "Where the hell's my sandwich? I told you I've got to get to town this afternoon."

Opal's hand tremor is noticeably worse as she hastily picks up the spatula, checks the white-bread cheese sandwich toasting in the buttered pan. She utters a little exclamation, flips the sandwich, reaches to turn down the heat. Black charring streaks the bread.

Lindsey finds herself moving quickly over to hide the sight from her dad, figures they can scrape off the bit of burned bread. But Arlen's already spotted it.

"Goddamn son of a bitch! Jesus Christ, you're worthless! All you do is sit there popping pills all day, can't you manage one little thing for me?" He strides over, jostling Lindsey, and grabs the pan off the stove. He jerks around with it, face flushing, thrusts it clattering and hissing into the wet sink, as Lindsey pulls her mother aside, feels her trembling.

Something snaps inside Lindsey, her spine straightening in protest of that hunched-in posture of her mother's. She guides Opal back to the lounger, tells her to just sit a minute, then she strides back over to her fuming father, who's ripping into the fridge and throwing out packets of bread and cheese, slamming condiments onto the counter, swearing in a nonstop rant.

"Stop it!" Lindsey plants herself in front of him as he turns.

He stops short in surprise, then glares at her. "Get the hell out of my way."

"Not unless you stop swearing." Lindsey has no idea where this is coming from, or going.

He scowls, takes a step closer, fists clenching as he uses

his height to force her to look up.

"Don't." Lindsey fights her own urge to back off, cringe.

Arlen still glowers, but he's shifted somehow, not trying to loom over her now. They stare at each other for a minute, punctuated by some heavy breathing. Then he shakes his head, turns away, stomps down the hall into the bathroom. Bingo, yapping, runs after him.

On the lounger, Opal is crumpled over, a trembling hand patting Spike's striped fur. Tears are sliding from under her glasses, catching in the soft wrinkles of her cheeks.

"Mom." Lindsey sits down and holds her, rocking. She blows out a long breath as she realizes it's the way Opal used to comfort her when she was little.

The back door slams, and a minute later Arlen's truck rumbles into life, starts to roar off down the drive. Lindsey remembers her Subaru then, blocking the way, and braces herself for a crash. Instead, a blaring horn. She just sits there, patting her mother's back.

It takes a while, but finally the blasting horn stops and the truck reverses back up the drive. Arlen comes to the glass patio door, opens it, stands there staring at Lindsey and Opal.

"You gonna move your goddamn—" He breaks off, shakes his head. "You wanna move your car?"

June 12

Dear Diary,

God—Goddess—the Great Pumpkin—if there's anybody out there, give me patience. How much longer can we keep the juggling act going? Always one more egg to keep up in the air—now it's Mom's macular degeneration, and Dad just doesn't get it that he's not going to have his perfect grilled cheese sandwiches on demand any more. One of these days the whole shebang's going to come down cracking and splattering all over their custom tiled floor.

(Eeek, shades of Nick!)

Fingers crossed: At least Mom's accepting the new housekeeper to clean once a week—now that she can't see the stray dust streaks or check that the upstairs carpet is vacuumed in precision parallel rows—and Dad hasn't driven this gal off yet with his temper tantrums. But the way Dad's running through their retirement funds like no tomorrow— now it's a new boat!—if Mom needs to go into a care facility, how long could they pay for it?

Sisters and I have lost count of the crises with Mom and Dad, like the time she admitted he yanked her down the steps because he was in a hurry, and she fell and broke her shoulder. She always refuses to report him, lied about the black eye that other time. Back when I was off in the Peace Corps, Fran had actually talked Mom into leaving him, had rented a trailer to move her stuff. Opal backed down when Arlen threatened to burn down the house. I've talked to a lawyer, my doc, and Mom's doc, and we can't force her to move, can't report Dad unless one of us actually witnesses the physical abuse. Fran and Joanie are clearly burned out after all the rescue attempts, and dealing with the crises with their own kids. Should I give up trying to save her? Have I even managed to save myself?

After the Mom and Dad visit, Lindsey's ears are buzzing louder, tension clamping down on her jaw and neck. The hot flashes are accelerating with warmer weather, and she's down to tank tops with no more clothing layers to rip off. She's not quite ready for public nudity. Though that might come next, maybe a nice stint in a padded cell would be just the ticket. She and her mom can move in together, if Opal's latest medication doesn't keep the depression and anxiety in check—

STOP.

Lindsey holds up the imaginary Stop sign to her "whirling brain," one of the tricks she learned from Kate in counseling. She takes some deep breaths, waits for the fiery prickles to subside, dabs sweat from her face and upper back. Even though it's a gray drizzly day, low clouds brooding over the hills, she's searching for the pocket fan she managed to misplace.

She visualizes Coolness, and an image of Fern Lake pops into her mind. Its perfect round bowl cupped in a cedar and huckleberry and alder-rimmed ravine, fed by rocky little snowmelt streams off the mountain. Voice of the forest calling, and she hasn't listened lately. But it's her day off.

When Lindsey gets to the trailhead and shoulders her knapsack with water and lunch, she realizes why she's been resisting a visit to her favorite lake. She steps into the shadows under the ancient moss- and fern-covered maple that bows a curved limb over the trail to make a gateway, then she takes a deep breath of cedar bark and rich black soil. She waits, a reflexive pause.

But the old magic doesn't kick in. The voice of the wilderness, the resonance alive in her blood and bones—she'd always arrogantly taken it for granted as her birthright here in her native forest—doesn't happen for her now. All she can hear is the buzzing in her ears. And the panicky, angry, whiny, relentless voices in her head telling her she's lost it forever. It was fading in the years with Nick and now it's too late, she dulled her senses to bear the pain, thinking she could revive herself later, but maybe it's a one-way street. And now she's too old anyway. Who does she think she is—some twenty-year-old hippie? Grow up and face the facts, the world isn't about joy and your pathetic dreams and complaints so face it from here on out you just slog through on duty and memories—

STOP.

She tries the halt-traffic drill again, but it's no good, the voices of brain whirl are a constant for her now, only silenced by loud enough distractions. The wilderness song is too quiet to overcome her overwired nerves.

She presses her hands against her ears, but it only makes the buzzing louder, more insistent. She closes her eyes, a wave of dark dizziness washing through her.

Night. Car lights flaring toward them on the black highway, flashing to blind her and then fading behind. Lindsey winced, hands pressed over her ears futilely trying to block Nick's tirade.

"Christ! What do you want? You trying to drive me crazy? Telling me I'm a liar now? It was your brilliant idea to bring the fucking kitten along!"

She hunched in silent misery on the passenger seat. Way past the point of trying to reason with him. Anything she said now would just stoke his rage.

"And don't go into your goddamn martyr routine on me!"

Little HighJinks, trembling on her lap, mewed in shrill distress, and Lindsey lowered her hands to stroke him.

"You happy now? We've never left the cabin early before! It's my vacation you're screwing up. But what do you care?"

Lindsey shudders, blinks up at the towering maples and cedars, the vibrant palette of greens, remembering how she used to melt into their serene embrace, the whisper of breezes. Not today.

"Shit! Keep the goddamn cat off me, can't you at least do that?" Nick had been ranting nonstop for the last hour. Even in the dim dashboard glow she could see arteries standing out on his neck, his hands clutching the wheel, blood pressure going sky-high again.

She scooped HighJinks back onto her lap, the kitten distraught and crying, struggling to climb up Nick's shoulder and escape out the sliver of open window. Lindsey wanted to dive out into the night with him. Nick had been screaming at her ever since she finally couldn't take more of his complaints and accusations, and suggested they cut short their vacation at the mountain cabin.

She'd been so pleased the week before, when he seemed upbeat about the trip, and he thoughtfully suggested they bring HighJinks along, since the kitten was too young to leave at a kennel. And now Nick was blaming her for ruining his "plans" to go backpacking, which she'd never heard him mention.

"Easy, now." She rocked the crying kitten, trying to soothe him.

"Damn it! Shut him up!" Nick swatted backhanded at HighJinks.

"Stop it!" Lindsey finally snapped. *"Let us out!"*

Nick jerked his face toward her. An awful smile twisted his lips, and he gave the wheel a tug, squealing into a swerve that threw Lindsey against the doorframe.

"Nick, please!"

Kneeling beside the trail, Lindsey digs her fingers into the damp moss, as if it can anchor her. "Please, just.... Please," she murmurs.

She pushes herself upright again, almost decides to turn back, but her body craves the release of movement. She brushes past a sword fern, cool drops sprinkling her bare legs, and strides fast up the first few switchbacks. She pushes herself to the point of gasping, feeling as if through a veil the flex of muscle in her calves, her heart settling into a deep pounding rhythm, fingertips tingling with the blood flow, lungs expanding to take in the cleansing moist air. Maybe she still needs to be numb, just keep going through the motions and someday the veil will lift.

The buzzing in her ears drives her on.

Lindsey's ears were ringing, HighJinks yowling desperately to escape as he clawed his way out of her grip, sharp pain in her arms almost a welcome diversion from Nick's shouts echoing in the car, but then the kitten scrambled toward him again and Nick grabbed him, threw him hard against the back window.

Lindsey screamed, "Stop it! Stop the car!" She unbuckled her seatbelt, started to crawl into the back to find the wailing kitten.

"Fuck you, bitch!" Nick tugged the wheel again, and the car was slamming crazily back and forth, throwing her against the back seat, then against the door. She hit her head hard on the window, stars flaring. Headlights loomed, sweeping out of the dark, a horn blaring as Nick swerved again. "You want out?" he taunted her, and swerved again.

"Nick, please! Just stop and let us out." She'd found HighJinks now, the kitten a frantic ball of terror, scratching her as she folded him into her sweatshirt and hunched around him in a fetal curl on the back seat. "Please," she begged.

Lindsey shudders, pushing faster up the trail to the overlook of massive granite opening a glimpse of the river valley and clouds lifting for a moment to reveal jagged snowcapped mountains.

Feeling at least the burn in her legs and lungs, sweating and panting, she crests the rise and drops into the lake ravine. Rain-beaded lacy huckleberry bushes shower her face, the trail turning mucky past a bog of skunk cabbage and rotting logs. In the subdued gray light, the mosses coating every rock and tree trunk somehow glow a brighter green than they would on a sunny day. Breaking through the deep foliage, she stands on a finger of rock extending into Fern Lake, its perfectly round, deep green bowl reflecting the calm gray clouds, the glossy dark green cedars and brighter spring green of alder leaves.

The lake waters are perfectly calm and flat under the overhanging alder boughs. No one else here on a drizzly day. No sound but the distant chortling call of a raven. Water striders glide beneath her on their sticklike insect legs as she steps out onto the gnarled root mass forming a suspended nest over the lake.

Lindsey scrubs at her face, takes a deep breath, and concentrates on quieting the ringing in her ears. She sets her knapsack aside, pulls off her boots and socks, settles into the meshed, mossy roots that make a perfect cupped perch for her butt. She dangles her feet in the water for a moment, taking a quick breath at the cold, then pulls them in to sit crosslegged. She gazes out over the lake.

The buzzing fades, and she almost hears a gentle voice: *Let it go. You're okay now.*

A trout jumps, ripples spreading in circles. Nosing along the far shore, maybe a couple hundred feet from her, a pair of mallard ducks spread another set of ripples, iridescent green of the male's head catching the light in a flash of brilliance.

Lindsey looks up, sees the clouds are breaking apart, gray wisps thinning, letting in the sun.

A breeze shivers the surface of the lake, glittering bits of sun flashing in a sweeping arc across the water. Shimmering reflections of light off the lake pulse along the silvery alder limbs overhead, strobing over Lindsey's face. She holds out her bare arms to see the waves of electric energy alive on her skin. And suddenly there's no separation—she *is* that branch reaching down to touch the water in pulsing reflections of light and shadow, its crooked mirrored arm stretching across the rippled surface toward her.

The limb grows, flowing across the water and up her chest, into her, piercing the brittle shell of her skin. It twines deeper, down into her heart, and rips her open. Lindsey can feel the pain now—ruthless, ecstatic. She's alive. She gasps in a breath like the first breath of being born into the suffering and joy of the world. She's alive. *Alive.*

She flings off her clothes, dives into the cold shock of the lake, gasps again and strokes fast across it, breaking the smooth skin of the surface with her own ripples. Concentric rings pulse outward, and she's the center.

eight

Dear Diary,

All right, okay—I called Newman Zender. And what did he say? "Lindsey, you're feeling better now?" Like we'd just talked the day before, and he was expecting me. (Megan swears she didn't make the threatened call to him.)

He chuckled when I told him I didn't recognize him in the hospital basement, thought at first he might have been an escapee from the Psych Ward. (Did I really tell him that?? He seemed to get a kick out of it.)

Then he asked if I wanted to come over to his place on the lake today. "Don't we have an unfinished conversation to...not finish?" (Did he mean from this winter, or from almost three decades ago? Egads.)

So what popped out of my mouth? "Is that a Zen question?"

He laughed again. "No, Zender. A Zender question."

Lindsey's heart is beating fast on the drive over to Emerald Lake (which used to be Toad Lake back in her high school skinny-dipping days, but a few years ago the trendy developers decided the old name wasn't dignified). She wipes her damp palms down the thighs of her jeans, tells herself she's acting like a ridiculous teenager. Then, just to remind her how really ridiculous that is, a massive hot flash roars through her, and she has to pull over to the side of the road, yank off her fleece zip and fan herself with it.

It's another typical June day in the Northwest—anywhere else the height of summer, the longest day of the year, and here it's cloudy and sixty-five degrees. At least the cool air calms her prickly heat. She tilts the rear-view mirror and blots her damp face, starts to twist the mirror back into position, then halts.

She's startled by the face looking back at her: green eyes wide, their color amped by the flush in her cheeks; long hair fluffed with its natural waves coming out in the dampness. It could almost be her twenty-three-year-old face looking out of a shadowy time-tunnel.

"Right. Just means I'm ready for bifocals." She snorts as she briskly puts the mirror straight. Maybe Newman will be seeing her in soft focus, too.

Her heart is fluttering too fast, feeling like it's up in her throat as she pulls off the gravel lake road into a grassy drive. It leads past a wooden dock and a shed surrounded by willows leaning over the banked shore, toward an old farmhouse set among lichened fruit trees. She parks, gets out, and listens to the silence for a moment. Not seeing anyone in the yard, she opens the back door of the Subaru and bends over to retrieve the pickle jar with a rhododendron bouquet from her garden.

"Ah!" She startles as she straightens and turns.

Newman's standing there, holding pruning loppers, a wide white smile on his tanned face.

Lindsey blinks, tilting off balance and caught in one more disorienting trip back through that time-tunnel.

"Sorry." He drops the loppers and reaches out a big hand to take her arm and steady her. "Guess I better stop spooking you."

She shakes her head, thrusts the flowers toward him. "From my garden."

"Thanks." He glances down at them, then back at her face, and that glimmer of humor is still in his eyes. "Good to see you again, Lindsey. Again," he says.

Lindsey can feel the heat rising in her face, imagining the picture her snug jeans must have presented as she leaned over into the backseat. Oh well, at least according to Nick, that portion of her anatomy offers viewing pleasure. So, "Likewise, Newman. Again."

When he laughs she can tell he's doing it with

enjoyment, and she takes the moment to enjoy her own view. He's aging well, Newman, wavy hair gone gray but still plenty of it, square-jawed face and blunt nose like a lion, thick eyebrows lowering over clear blue eyes. It isn't fair that men get to look stronger, more defined, with the age lines setting in, while every media message hammers home to women that they're turning into dried-up rejects. But to hell with that, she's not going there today. Looking up at Newman, she lets herself appreciate his height and solid masculine presence. He's gotten thicker with the years, but not paunchy like so many men their age. He looks way too good, in fact, barefoot in cutoff jeans, a worn flannel shirt hanging open over a faded blue tee.

Then he sobers, and their glances catch. A palpable jolt of recognition crackles through Lindsey. Raw attraction, and they both clearly feel it. She hastily looks down, her face flushing again.

"Let me show you the garden. I finally got my beehives moved over here from the old house." He seems unruffled, ushering her toward a path around the side of the house. He sets the bouquet on the porch and leads the way to the back, where raised vegetable beds are sprouting lush greens. Beneath more arthritic fruit trees, bees dart and buzz around the white boxes of stacked hives. A steep hill backs the property, dense with fir, alder, and cedars climbing toward the ridge.

"This is a beautiful spot." Lindsey turns to take in the gnarled clematis vine engulfing a tilting trellis on the back porch of the house. "I can't believe the developers haven't hacked away at the ridge yet."

"They'd like to." He moves over to the raised beds and picks some strawberries, hands her a few, and pops one into his mouth. "It's a standoff right now. Some environmental groups have managed to get a moratorium on more building until they study impacts on the lake. That one outfit—Green Life—they do a good job."

"They do," Lindsey admits, then has to add, "Nick, my ex, he's a wildlife biologist with them." She looks toward the lake, again appreciating the quiet Sunday morning. "Thank goodness they never allowed motorboats here, it's so small. How on earth did you luck onto a place like this? Was it in your family?" She pops a strawberry into her mouth, savoring the sweetness.

"I'm just renting from a friend. Since the divorce. My daughter Melani loves it here, too, I'm hoping I can talk Ron into selling. We're working on a deal." He leads the way back around the house, through the overgrown grass and past a stand of big purple poppies busy with bees. "I've got business contacts in China, and Ron wants to get an import trade going, something like my own handicrafts wholesale line. So maybe we can work something out."

"I hope you can." Lindsey finishes the last strawberry. "Is your daughter here?"

"It's her weekend with her mother. Then I get her back for a couple days this week, before I fly off to Bali."

"Bali? On vacation?"

"I wish." He leans over to pick up the jar with the rhodie blossoms, ushers her ahead up the wooden porch steps. "Though I might get to do some snorkeling while I'm there." He opens the screen door and stands back to let her through. "There's a group I consult with there, helping them set up community cottage industries."

"Oh, that's right, Megan told me that's what you were doing now. I guess you get to travel a lot?"

"More than I want to right now." He puts the flowers on a scuffed, round oak table with a pedestal base, set on a faded rag rug over the hardwood floor. "Maybe Kimberly was right, might have been one reason for the divorce." He shrugs. "I'm trying to shift things around so I can spend more time with Melani. Before I know it, she'll be graduating." He turns to look at Lindsey. "You never had kids?"

She shakes her head. "Never seemed like the right time. I was traveling a lot, too, when I was younger. Did a Peace Corps stint in Honduras, then was working as a river-rafting guide. Then, when Nick and I got married, it wasn't—" She raises her palms, lowers them. "Long story."

He nods. "Well. Why don't you sit a minute?" He tilts his head toward a couch with an afghan. "I'll make us some herbal tea. You have to taste my honey." He heads through a doorway into the kitchen, runs some water.

Lindsey wanders across the pleasantly shabby Craftsman-style front room, admiring the thick wood trim and tiled fireplace with its flanking built-in bookshelves.

She wishes her own little bungalow had one just like it. Browsing the shelves, she sees several titles about India, some paperback novels, a pile of maps, foreign-language dictionaries, and a shelf of poetry. She pulls out *Rumi: Poems of Spiritual Love*, and takes it over to the couch.

The book falls open to a marked page:

> *Birds write freedom in the air.*
> *Who teaches them?*
> *They fall, and falling,*
> *they grow wings.*

Lindsey's sitting transfixed, staring at the words, when Newman comes back with two mugs. He sits and leans over to see what she's reading. "My favorite poet."

Lindsey takes a breath. "This is beautiful." She amends, "More than beautiful."

"You've never read Rumi?"

She shakes her head, touches the verses. "I'll have to get a copy of this."

"Borrow mine for now." He hands her a steaming mug, clicks his against it in a toast. "To summer solstice." He takes a sip, then chuckles. "I guess hot tea is better than a cold beer today."

"Thank you." Lindsey sets the book aside and sips. The gingery tea is thick with sweet honey, perfect for the cool day.

"You want to sit on the porch where we can look out at the lake?" Newman rises, and over by the bookshelves a musical cell phone starts chiming.

"Shoot, I forgot Melani was going to call. Do you mind? It'll be quick, then I'll turn the damned thing off."

"No problem."

Lindsey heads out to the front porch, can hear him answer, "Hi, sweetheart, how's that math homework going?" Then he's gone into a back room. She settles onto a padded bench swing on the front porch with its overhanging roof and square columns, enjoying the tea and the wispy mists rising from the lake. It's another of the county's overgrown ponds, nestled among steep encircling trees and ringed by aging summer cottages and docks. A couple of kayaks pass beyond the willows, stirring a brief commotion among the ducks browsing the shore grasses.

"Okay." Newman comes out and sits beside her on the swing.

"Everything all right?"

"Fine. She just got a little behind. We're all still feeling the divorce fallout. And then her knee surgery this spring, all the physical therapy and missing her riding competitions. Sometimes she needs a pep talk from Dad to stick with the program and the makeup assignments."

They sit quietly sipping the tea for a few moments. Lindsey is surprisingly relaxed, gazing out over the lake as Newman tucks one knee under him and pushes with the other foot to rock them gently. She looks over to see him watching her.

He smiles. "This is peaceful. I don't get to slow down much these days."

"Don't you meditate?"

He leans back, looking up. "Not as much as I'd like to. Somehow I've turned into one of those multi-taskers. Like juggling a dozen raw eggs, waiting for one big splatter."

Lindsey blinks. "I was just thinking that exact thing myself, dealing with my parents on top of everything else. It doesn't seem like life used to be so hectic for everybody."

"Guess I didn't realize how lucky I was to have those years in the ashram. Simplicity. Devotion to one path." A little shrug. "I tell myself now the challenge is to hold onto that peace. Practice detachment when things get intense...." He sips his tea. "And of course when you need to meditate the most, that's when you tend to be 'too busy.' Let it slip."

"But you seem so calm. That's what I remembered most about you, what I...." Lindsey gives her own shrug. "I guess I envied that, even way back when."

"Well, it is a practice. You can learn it. I'll teach you a mantra, if you like."

"I'd like that. I tried a meditation class, but they kicked me out because my energy was too distracting. Too much whirling brain, I guess."

"Whoa, that teacher needs a talking to. But I get what you're saying—the monkey-mind syndrome."

"You?" She glances over at him. "I guess this is silly, but I figured you were somehow past that. I mean, when Megan said you were a Buddhist monk, I thought...." She's flustered now. "Well, you know, that day we went for the bike ride to the pond all those years ago, and we were lying there in the mud, and I was trying to meditate. I didn't know what...." She's digging herself deeper, floundering. "Well, maybe you don't remember." She waves a hand. "I figured it was all about transcending base desires or something." She's staring down into her mug.

He chuckles.

She looks up quickly, embarrassed. Why did she burst out with all that nonsense? He probably doesn't even remember that day.

"I remember well enough." He touches her hand briefly. "Especially the part about *not* transcending desire."

She can't help laughing at his wry expression. "Oh."

"And another thing Megan got totally wrong—I was never a Buddhist. I was studying with a Hindu spiritual teacher in the ashram. I did take a vow of celibacy for a few years...."

"Really?" Lindsey turns toward him again. "How did you do it? I mean, isn't it sort of like starving yourself? It's been two and a half years since I split up with Nick, and sometimes it seems like forever since—" She snaps her mouth shut, biting her lip.

But he's just nodding, considering. "It wasn't easy, especially when I was in my twenties. But it was about spiritual discipline, the path I was on at the time. I guess all that practice ended up helping, with my marriage. It wasn't...." He looks down at his hands cupping the mug. He starts to take another sip, sees it's empty, and sets it on the porch boards. "I didn't want to be a monk in my marriage, but it sort of ended up that way with Kimberly and me."

"Oh."

He turns to look at her. "Sounds like we're both still healing from some pretty deep heart wounds, Lindsey. What happened in your marriage?"

Lindsey hesitates, starts to give him the politely edited version, then finds herself confiding the nightmare and the slow waking back to life. And how hard it still is to let herself feel sometimes. *Be* in the moment. Newman listens quietly, gazing out at the lake, nodding as he rocks them on the swing.

"I got so tied up in knots, I started wondering if I was going crazy when Nick would tell me he never did those violent things. That I was making them up. I mean, if Nick was mentally ill, I wanted to be a loyal wife and help him. But then it got so bad, I was putting myself in danger by staying." She takes a deep breath. "Living in fear, till it soaked into my whole life. And then I started to hate him. That was the worst part. I'd never felt that way before." Lindsey shudders, thinking she *is* crazy to dump all this on him. But he has this aura of taking things in and not judging

She shrugs then, tries to laugh it off. "So. Here I am, another statistic, right down to the two cats. Every cliché I never figured I'd be."

He straightens abruptly to face her. "Don't say that! Don't put yourself in that kind of box." His voice is emphatic, gaze snapping onto hers, and again Lindsey feels a jolt. This time it's a bit daunting, a glimpse of some powerful energy held beneath the calm surface.

He blows out a breath and leans back into the swing, gaze returning to the lake. "It's a trap, Lindsey. Those definitions and expectations we get drilled with from when we're kids. I should have known better, but I let it happen in my marriage, too. Trying to fit what you're 'supposed' to be. What other people define you as. Then we become our own worst enemies because we're starving our souls. Living on illusions."

Silence hangs over them as Lindsey thinks about it. "You're right. Of course," she says slowly. "But that's all kind of...abstract, isn't it? I always considered myself a pretty free spirit, but where I get stuck is in the practical details." She blows out a breath. "I mean, things just roll along, and where do you say, 'I'm getting off'?"

He glances sideways at her. "I guess we both did that in a big way. But I don't want to let things go that far off center again. I won't." For a second he looks surprisingly grim, then he shakes his head. "Hey, let's lighten up." He rocks quickly forward and stands. "What do you say we take a sauna? I built one into the old boathouse, put a little wood stove in there. It's great for opening the pores, purifying, then I take a dive into the lake. You up for it?"

She blinks at the sudden shift, but responds with her old reactions to a chilly gray day. "Sounds perfect." *Right,* her menopausal self inserts, *the perfect way to trigger a world-record hot flash.* Then she realizes that even in her fleece jacket she's felt blessedly calm and cool since she arrived at the lake.

"All right. Sit tight, and I'll go fire up the stove. It heats up quick." He strides off across the grass toward the dock.

Then Lindsey remembers she didn't bring her swimsuit.

Her heart is beating fast again as she follows Newman over the damp grass toward the boathouse. She feels lightheaded, not quite sure where her feet are landing as she walks.

He's got a couple of towels over his arm, and that somehow comforts her. She'll just leave her underwear on. Her sports bra is close enough to a swimsuit top.

"Ron was letting things kind of fall down around the previous renters, so I'm chipping away at repairs when I have time." Newman stops to lift a hanging blackberry vine aside so Lindsey can duck past the corner of the plank boathouse. "I boarded off half of the boathouse and lined it with cedar, put in a little stove. When I can, I get up early to meditate, then come down for a sauna and a swim. Starts the day out clean."

He pauses on the mossy wood deck by the boathouse doorway. Native willows and wild roses overhang a ramp that leads down to an old dock, grass sprouting from its gray boards.

"After you." He gestures toward the doorway.

Inside it's a cramped space, blocked off by the new inner wall and door that looks like a hobbit-hole entrance with its curved top and round brass-rimmed porthole from a boat. A dim jumble of faded life vests, fraying line, and tools take up part of the floor beneath the one small window that filters shadowy daylight through cobwebs.

Newman hands her a towel and pulls off his tee, matter-of-factly shucks his shorts to stand naked as Lindsey bites her lip and averts her gaze. He opens the inner door and starts to go in, then stops.

"Better get some water so we don't get too dried out." He picks up a wooden bucket with a rope handle and heads out onto the dock, where he squats to scoop water from the lake.

The way he moves at ease in his nakedness reassures Lindsey. It's the way she always felt uninhibited and free of clothes in the wilderness, out camping, where the civilized trappings didn't matter. And on backpacking trips with Nick and the neo-hippie "green" crowd, nudity was simply a given. A way to reset, everyone meeting at ground zero.

Lindsey's not quite sure that applies to the current situation, and it was certainly easier not to be self-conscious when she was younger. But she's sick of overthinking everything. She hastily strips off her jeans, fleece, and underwear, hoping to get into the dark sauna where she can hide her disfigured breast. Then she can't resist sneaking a peek out the doorway toward the dock.

Newman's heading back with the full bucket, moving with an easy swing up the ramp. Again she's surprised by what a big man he is—she hadn't remembered that from all those years ago—broad across the shoulders, with a thickness and heft to his torso, smoothly packed and very different from Nick's wiry musculature. She feels an odd sliding dislocation—simultaneously transported back in time to Mosquito Lake with her younger self and a leaner, tanned Newman, his long blond hair and beard lit up with sunlight, while standing rooted here with this gray-haired, handsome naked man striding toward her, smiling.

She takes a quick breath, fumbling with her loose hair to cover her breasts. Too late, she moves toward the dimness of the sauna as he comes in beside her with the sloshing bucket.

She takes a hasty step back in the cramped space, hair swinging aside to reveal the misshapen lumpectomy breast.

Newman stops short, gaze fixing on it, then darting to her eyes. He slowly lowers the bucket, face stricken.

Lindsey, mortified, hunches and turns away, bringing the folded towel up over her breasts.

"No, please." His voice is gentle, a hand on her shoulder halting her, turning her back toward him. She can't look up as he eases her clenched hands open, lowers the shielding towel. He touches her damaged breast very carefully. His fingers are surprisingly warm, a soft heat penetrating her chilled skin, spreading deeper.

She blinks, looks up into his face.

He meets her gaze. "I'm sorry, Lindsey. It's just...my

mother. She died of breast cancer. Are you okay now?"

She nods, eyes stinging but held in his gaze. And that's it. All her fears of how disgusting she'd appear to him are just smoke, vanished. There's some kind of glow enfolding them both, palpable.

It seems like they stand that way for a long time, but it may be only a few seconds. He smiles then and nods, tilts his head toward the sauna door, gestures her in. "Careful, don't touch the metal on the porthole."

He bends down for the bucket and follows her into the tiny space where dry heat and the fragrance of cedar close around her. Newman shuts the door as Lindsey climbs up onto a short bench built into the wall opposite the wood stove, puts her towel down, and sits on it. He sits on the other end, placing the bucket between them on the floor. He glances up at her. She can barely make out his face in the dimness, but thinks he's smiling still as he reaches into the bucket, scoops out a handful, and flicks cool drops over her.

Startled at the shock of cold through the enclosing heat, she laughs. She leans over to scoop up her own handful and fling it at him, stray drops hissing over the hot stove.

"Ahhh. That feels good." He leans back against the wall, facing her on the bench, raising one leg to cock his knee. His foot rests against hers on the bench.

The contact is warm, comfortable. Lindsey feels tenseness in her body she didn't even know was there begin to uncoil, release, as she sinks back against the wall, sinks into the heat and quiet. Only the popping of wood in the stove. Dancing flickers of firelight through the vent grating. A sigh rises from deep inside her.

Silence reigns, then, and Lindsey's glad he's not the type to have to fill it up with talk. She can listen to her heartbeat slow down, feel her pores opening as her skin turns slick with sweat. She closes her eyes. She's here. Now.

Finally she rakes back her damp hair and takes a deep breath. "I'm about cooked through. You ready for a swim?"

He sits up, rubbing his eyes. "Either that, or I'm off to dreamland." He stands and leads the way out, so Lindsey doesn't have to feel awkward again in the daylight. "Watch the ramp for splinters." He pauses on the dock.

Lindsey reaches the bottom of the ramp, skin a tingling interface between internal stoked heat and the cool air. She takes a deep breath, savoring the unruffled gray surface of the lake shimmering like quicksilver. A crazy exhilaration she barely recognizes fills her suddenly, and her legs are launching her past Newman's startled face as she runs down the dock and plunges into the lake.

The shock of cold to her overheated body is almost orgasmically intense. She strokes underwater through murky green dimness, past waving weed fronds, then bursts back up into the air. "Eee-yah!" She grins, sucks in some air, and strokes fast across the surface.

A splash behind her as Newman follows. She circles around, past him, and he matches strokes with her for a bit before he turns back. She dives under again, savoring the cool caress over her body, reveling in weightlessness. Finally, the cold penetrating into her deeper layers, she heads back to the dock.

Newman is sitting watching her. As she reaches the dock, he stands, and before she can brace her arms to heave herself out of the water, he's lifted under her armpits to pluck her up beside him as if she weighed feathers.

She's face to face with him, close and dripping. "Thanks."

He tilts his head. "You're welcome."

They both laugh, for no reason.

She shakes her head. "I keep getting these time displacements. Here we are, back in our birthday suits."

"Lindsey, maybe we're just fated to get naked together." Still chuckling, he spreads his palms. "You ready for more heat?"

"Definitely." She slaps water off, goosebumps shivering her skin.

Back in the fragrant dimness of the sauna, she sighs and loosens to the welcome heat, leaning back against the wall. "This is perfect."

Newman puts another stick of wood in the stove, then climbs up to face her on the bench. He pulls his feet up, again touching hers. They sit in silence as they soak up the warmth, but this time the contact of his foot against hers is electric, alive. She can almost hear a hum swelling, growing between them.

She opens her eyes to see he's watching her in the flickering firelight. She meets his gaze, and suddenly her heart is pounding again.

He sits up, reaches to touch her hand where it's resting palm up on the bench. Slowly he draws a fingertip along the lines of her palm, and she shivers. One more flashback to their younger days, the long-haired stranger dropping his bike and stepping over to her blanket to take her hand and study her life lines.

Newman takes a deep breath, raises his hand to run his palm down her shoulder and arm, tracing a tingling connection everywhere he touches. Lindsey can see in the flickering light his penis swelling, rising toward her, and something inside her wrenches, then springs open, heat flooding her. He lifts and shifts her effortlessly so they're sitting closer, facing each other with her legs over his.

He touches her face, gently, leans closer to brush his lips over hers. She catches a quick breath, pulls him closer, and then they're kissing madly, deeply, as waves of velvet-black shadow and red-tinged firelight wash through them.

He eases back from the contact. They're both breathing hard, and he looks almost startled.

He takes another deep breath, touches her breasts as the nipples rise hard to his palms. He leans forward to kiss the damaged breast, licks his tongue down over the puckered scarring, takes the nipple into his mouth. It responds to his touch, alive, and suddenly Lindsey is weeping, a crazy mix of grief and joy.

He straightens, touches her face and smooths the trail of tears over her cheeks. "We can stop now, Lindsey, if you want. Just touching you like this is enough for me." A glimmer of humor then. "Though I guess you know what my body wants." As if to second this, his penis throbs between them, brushing against her.

Lindsey's flooded with an uprush of arousal so intense it makes her feel faint. She moves closer against him, feeling his hard penis now against her moistness. She rocks, and he slides against her. He groans, reaches to her hips and starts to lift her, then halts.

"Phew." He shakes his head. "I don't know how to do this."

"What?" She blinks. "Believe me, you do."

He chuckles, but he's still out of breath, and that crazy charge is zinging between them. "Lindsey, it's been over twenty years with one woman, and in the last years sex wasn't really happening. So what kind of conversation are we supposed to have first, these days?" He looks chagrined, glances down. "I mean, besides that one we're having."

Lindsey has to laugh, the wild bubbling joy bursting up as her voice shakes. "You're asking the wrong gal, Newman. It's been two and a half years since I so much as kissed a man. But I did get tested after Nick's affair, so looks like clear sailing to me."

"But…birth control?"

"That's the least of my worries these days."

"Oh." He looks taken aback, then laughs, too. "Looks like we're making ourselves a new way here. That's good." He sobers, gaze holding hers, and again she glimpses that powerful charge held beneath his surface.

"It's good." Her voice is still shaky, but the words ring true.

He pulls her close then, kisses her to banish words and bring back the deep, pulsing tidal heat. Everywhere they touch, her skin is electric, lit up. When he lifts her by the hips and slides her up and then slowly down onto him, there's no more separation. Only something new, two currents merging in an endless wave rolling toward shore but never breaking.

nine

Dear Diary,
   Bliss.

Lindsey floats in her ecstatic daze for the next few days, despite a sharp twinge of disappointment when Newman calls to cancel their plan for another sauna and a meditation lesson. He can't get free to see her again before he flies off to Bali for a couple of weeks.

"There's a crisis with one of my textile sources in India, got to get that straightened out before I go. And I need to spend some time with Melani, she has to come first." A pause over the phone waves. "Lindsey, just hearing your voice is stirring me up. I'll be holding the thought of you until I get back." Somewhere in his rush out of town he manages to leave on her porch the Rumi book she'd forgotten to take with her, wrapped in a beautiful pale-paisley silk shawl.

Lindsey hugs to herself that solstice turning with him, feels her cells still humming with the visceral imprint of their lovemaking. With the way they simply flowed on into the early morning hours, opening their hearts to each other about their lives, the pains and setbacks, the dreams old and new. And the way he encouraged her to "turn down the volume" on self-doubt and dive back into her writing.

When Megan calls to chat, Lindsey doesn't mention Newman. She doesn't want to share this yet, let it out into the daylight. If it weren't for the fringed shawl to wrap herself in at night, and the book of poems, she'd wonder if it were all a dream. Wouldn't believe that she could feel this way. Only now can she let herself realize how fearful she'd been that her heart had died to cold ashes, that she'd never feel the fire again. She has to admit it's a major relief to discover that all her parts still work!

> *Birds write freedom in the air.*
> *Who teaches them?*
> *They fall, and falling,*
> *they grow wings.*

Lindsey reads the poem again, tracing the worn page with her fingertips. She doesn't know if she can learn that kind of trust. But here she is, mid-air.

She manages to show up at work, get through the shifts, and again she's relieved by the routine of it all, requiring just enough focus to siphon some of the effervescent bubbling energy and hold her feet on the ground for the daylight hours. At night she's untethered, soaring in the widening gyres so high and swinging so far out from center she wonders if she'll ever find her way back to her old self. Then realizes she doesn't care to.

She's head over heels.

Lindsey reminds herself this is totally insane, she really doesn't *know* Newman, and she can't be doing this. It's too reckless. She's not strong enough yet. But every time she tells herself that, she's back there beside him, feeling the warmth of his fingertips soaking in through her breast to her wounded prisoner heart and freeing it.

"Earth to Lindsey!"

She startles, realizes she's been staring at the computer monitor gone into screensaver mode, fingers poised above the keyboard.

"Whoo-Hoo!" It's Gayle, popping her dreadlocked head around the edge of the partition like another of those grinning puppet-heads Lindsey can't quite exorcize from the weird dream months before. She waggles her fingers, lifts her pierced eyebrow with the little silver barbell through it.

"I've been trying to get you to answer for like five minutes! What's up with you? Anybody'd think you were major crushing...."

She trails off, staring, as Lindsey feels her face burning.

"Holy shit! You *are*! No wonder you've had that crazy grin on your face even when you had to transcribe all those catch-up charts of old Doc Beasley's." Gayle's head disappears momentarily, then she comes whizzing around the partition, wheeled chair and all, halting against Lindsey's like bumper cars. She giggles, looking around conspiratorially, then whispers, "Okay, spill! Who is he?"

Lindsey bites her lip, not ready to be outed this way. And though she likes Gayle, they've hardly been confidants. "It's nothing. Just an old friend I got together with." She manages a shrug, not convincing even herself. "It's way too early to be making a big deal out of it."

"Yeah, right." Gayle digs an elbow into Lindsey's ribs. "You've got that glow, gal. Like you just got your socks knocked off in the bed department, huh?"

Lindsey's shaking her head, face really hot now with another flash coming on. She rips off her cotton zip and fans herself. "Give me a break, Gayle. Aren't raging hormones enough?"

Gayle, probably half her age, purses her lips, giving an assessing once-over to Lindsey in her tank top. "Hey, you are one hot-looking older babe, and I don't mean those flashes. Anyway, my mom calls them Power Flashes. So c'mon, dish! I want to know what I have to look forward to."

Lindsey just keeps shaking her head. "I'd take the curse back any day over these hot flashes." She nudges Gayle's chair back from her keyboard. "And if we don't want the wrath descending, we better back to work."

"You're not getting off that easy. I'll worm it out of you later." She starts to push her chair back around the partition, then pauses. "Oh, speak of the devil, I almost forgot!" She smacks her forehead with the heel of her hand. "That's what I was trying to tell you—Olivia's stuck in that meeting, but she wants you to switch over to the E.R. line. They need the reports from last night."

Lindsey groans. "Trauma Jock?"

"No, I think it was Aufhauser's night on." With a thumb's-up, Gayle gives a push of her feet and rolls backwards into her own cubicle.

Lindsey switches dictation channels and cranks out the reports on a minor accident, with some contusions and a broken arm, a six-year-old admitted for observation of possible appendicitis, a homeless man with the D.T.'s. Aufhauser is easy to transcribe, speaks clearly and cuts to the chase.

Then there's a pop and static, and a new voice comes on the line. "Bennerton here."

There's a sinking in her gut as the backup neurosurgeon rattles off the patient ID, date and time of motor vehicle accident. All she can see is the face of Mrs. Montague in the hospital cafeteria as she sits not drinking her coffee, eyes blanked-out windows. On coma watch.

Lindsey takes a deep breath, backs up the recording to catch the patient name. Bennerton's reciting so fast, she can't nail it and has to try a third time. Finally she gets it: Kevin Spieler, age 20, motorcycle accident, head trauma.

Cold dread settles in the pit of her stomach. She's not sure of the last name. Doesn't want to be sure.

Her fingers keep typing on auto-pilot. Patient a student, leaving restaurant server job at one a.m., lost control of motorcycle and impacted head-on into a cement abutment. The familiar phrases float up from her robotically clicking fingertips: *Cranial fracture...fluid pressure buildup...emergency neurosurgery...EEG activity irregular...family consent—*

"Uhn." Lindsey's hands jerk upwards, off the keyboard, pushing her back, away. But it's finally penetrated beyond denial. Nausea rising in her throat, she stands, takes a deep breath, moves shakily to the stack of new admitting forms to verify the name.

Kevin Spieler. And under parents: *Robert and Marcia Spieler, 1228 Gardenia Lane.*

Rob and Marci, best friends of Lindsey's sister Joanie. She closes her eyes, seeing the crowd at last summer's 50th birthday barbecue for Dan. Kevin always a fixture in these extended-family affairs, his lanky height and curly mop of dark hair as he galloped Fran's grandkids around on his back, laughing.

Somehow she's back at her keyboard, finishing the surgery report with grim determination. Maybe they've called in another consultant, and they need the report. She finishes it, sends it to the printer, hurries over to pull it out and attach it to the admittance sheet. Her body efficiently going through the motions, she looks up the Intensive Care location and starts out the door, numbly noting that Olivia isn't back yet.

She halts, turns back to tell Gayle she's running the report up herself. "They need it Stat," she lies. Usually the records clerk waits for a pile of transcribed reports, takes them around to add to the charts at the nursing desks.

Gayle looks up, the start of another grin fading as she sees Lindsey. "Are you okay?" She pulls off her headset.

Lindsey fans herself with the paper, faking another hot flash. "Yeah. But I think I'll take a break after I deliver this."

"Maybe you better lie down in the break room. You look kind of green."

"Maybe I will." Lindsey hurries off to the stairwell, grips the rail and takes some deep breaths. Then launches toward the third floor, hurrying and hoping it's not too late to hurry.

She passes the long windows of the ICU rooms, beds surrounded by tangles of wires, fluid lines, portable monitors all clustered around sheeted shapes barely recognizable as people beneath all the attachments and bandages. At the nursing desk, she hands over the report to a nurse she doesn't recognize.

"How's he doing?" she asks as he pulls out the metal chart cover, inserts the emergency surgery report into an already thick collection of color-coded lab and EEG reports.

The nurse looks up, tall guy folded into a short chair, squinting behind wire-rimmed glasses. "Too soon to tell, looks like. Why?"

Lindsey manages a shrug. "It's just—such a young kid. Seems like a shame." She takes a breath. "If there are any other consultants coming in on it, and you need any other reports transcribed Stat, just let us know in Medical Records."

He frowns, checks the chart again, gives her a sideways look. "Well, sure. But I don't see any request here. Just a couple of progress notes from Bennerton this morning. Did someone call you?" He's giving Lindsey an odd look. This is not standard procedure.

"Oh, no." Lindsey waves it off, turning, tosses back,

"Just letting you know, we can prioritize if you need the reports."

"Oh. Well, okay." A buzzer goes off, light blinking outside one of the windowed rooms, and he drops the chart on the desk, hurries past Lindsey.

She sucks in a quick breath, her glance darting over the busy, pale-green suited figures attending the rooms. Her ears are ringing. She seems to be watching from far away as her hands reach out, flip open the chart to the progress notes. She scans, flips to the EEG readouts. The ice in her gut swells heavier.

"Can I help you?"

Lindsey startles, drops the chart, and turns.

It's another nurse, a young woman with curly red hair, giving her a questioning look, glancing at Lindsey's ID badge.

"No, no, I just brought up the emergency report from Medical Records, wanted to make sure it was slotted in the right spot."

"Oh. Okay, thanks. That's Spieler? Doctor wants it now."

"Oh. Here." She watches the nurse bustle over to the second room down, move in past the monitors and hand the chart to a tall, balding man in a rumpled shirt and tie. It must be Dr. Bennerton. Lindsey's never seen him before, only knows his dreaded voice over the lines.

She hurries past the glimpse of a long figure in the bed, one leg swaddled and raised in traction, head wrapped in bandages, face covered with an oxygen mask, lines and tubes plugged in everywhere. She heads for the stairwell again, down to the family waiting area on the second floor. Halfway there, she suddenly reverses, ducks into a handicap toilet room and locks the door. She grips the edge of the sink and stares at herself in the mirror. Her eyes look wild, face pale and damp. She's surprised the ICU nurses didn't call Security. She pulls in a deep, shaky breath, splashes water over her face and blots it, takes one of the little paper cups and gulps down more water.

Think, Lindsey.

She stares into her cloudy green eyes. *Whistleblower?* Is she ready to risk it—again? Take the wrath for speaking up? Like voicing those earlier forbidden words: *"Your son's psychologically unbalanced. Rageaholic. He needs to be in treatment.*" Nick's parents chose "loyalty" to their offspring and turned on her, after Nick convinced them that *she* was delusional, lying about his rage attacks. With a surgical knife-stroke, they cut off the "daughter we never had before."

So how does she find the words now? *"Marci, Rob, your son's surgeon is incompetent."* Then brace for the backlash? She signed a confidentiality oath when she hired on here. Does she swallow more words, more damned secrets? Is she still afraid to find her voice?

It's her own eyes she's got to face in the mirror. To hell with privileged information and the hypocrisy of the medical bureaucracy. She takes another deep breath and hurries down the hall.

Marci and Rob and Kevin's younger sister Patty are there, hunched over in chairs in the waiting room. Their faces snap up as the door opens, hope flickering across them for a second, then surprise.

"Lindsey?" Marci shakes her head, face gone blank.

Rob stands, starts to step toward her, then stalls, looking down at his hands.

"I just found out," Lindsey explains uselessly. "I'm so sorry."

Marci frowns, then gets it. "Oh. Lindsey. I forgot you work here." She stands, makes an aborted movement.

Lindsey comes over and gives her a hug, reaches to touch Rob's arm. Patty is still hunched in her chair, crying.

"Lindsey, it's so...I can't...." Marci sinks back into her chair as Rob paces across the narrow room, stops facing away from them. "It's so awful! He wasn't drinking or anything, he was just coming home from work. They don't know what happened, why he went into that wall. He cracked his skull, they had to do surgery, and we don't know...."

"I know." Lindsey squeezes her hands, gives her a minute. "Have they told you anything yet?"

Rob clears his throat, makes surreptitious motions wiping his eyes, drops heavily into a chair. "We talked to the doctor this morning. The neurosurgeon. He says it's too early to tell if...if there's brain damage. We have to wait."

Lindsey pulls over another chair to face them, and sits. "Was that Dr. Bennerton? There isn't anyone else working with him?"

"Bennerton...." Rob seems to go inside himself for a moment, gathers himself, focuses on Lindsey. "Bennerton, that's right. He's the neurosurgeon. He said he'd let us know as soon as...as the signs stabilize." He looked down at his hands again. "He's in Intensive Care," he added.

"I know. I was just up there," Lindsey says.

Marci turns quickly from stroking Patty's back. "Did you see anything? They won't let us see him yet. Well, just for a minute from outside the windows after they got him settled in there from surgery. Did they tell you anything?"

"No, but—"

"Mom, is Kevin going to die?" Patty has finally raised her head, her face blotched and red. "Lindsey, is he going to die?"

"Honey, the doctors are doing the best they can. They're not going to let him die." Marci hugs her daughter. "Why don't you go down to the bathroom and rinse your face? If you could bring me back a cup of water, that would be really nice."

Patty bites her lip, gives Lindsey an imploring look, hurries out.

Marci stiffens, looks Lindsey in the eye. "What?"

She takes one more deep breath, searching for the way to say what she needs to. "Marci. Rob. I want you to listen to me. I could get into trouble for telling you this, but it's important."

Rob straightens in his chair. "Okay."

"You need to get another neurosurgeon to take over. Right away. Call Dr. Peters, he's good. Or his partner, Steinberg. Just get Bennerton off the case."

Marci gasps. "What? What are you talking about?"

Rob leans forward to grip Lindsey's wrist so hard it hurts. "What are you saying?"

"I type up the reports all the time. I see the complication rates." The roaring in Lindsey's ears is so loud now, she can hardly hear. This is a nightmare, maybe she shouldn't be doing this, maybe it's too late already and there's no point.

Maybe she's taking away their hope, that faith relationship you're supposed to have with your doctor. Maybe everything will be okay with Bennerton in charge, and she shouldn't meddle. But it's too late.

"Lindsey." Rob's grip tightens, and she flinches, but he doesn't seem to notice. "Tell me."

"Bennerton's been audited more than once, but they never kick him out. His patients don't do well. Lots of complications. Way too many. You need to get someone else working on Kevin."

Rob leans closer, staring right into Lindsey's eyes. "You're sure of this?"

She nods. "Everyone in the hospital knows, but no one stops him."

Rob jerks to his feet. "Well, by God I will! He's off the case right now. What's this other doc? Peters? I'll call him." He starts toward the door.

"Rob, wait." Marci half rises, sinks back into her chair. "I don't think...." She shakes her head. "This is crazy." She shakes her head again, slowly. "I volunteer with Dr. Bennerton's wife, at the Womencare Shelter. Renee. They're terrific people, they're involved in all these community-service projects."

Lindsey spreads her hands. "I don't know him. All I know is there's no way I'd let him take a scalpel to anyone I care about."

"But he's a doctor! He's respected. He comes in on all these emergency cases. The hospital wouldn't let him keep working if he was messing up that way."

Lindsey rubs her eyes, takes a deep breath, tries to find another way to explain. "It's the system, Marci. The insurance companies and the doctors are all afraid of malpractice cases maybe. I don't know. But the docs protect their own. We process the audit reports, it's all on paper, Bennerton's complication rates are way higher than they should be. But they just keep letting him operate."

Marci's still shaking her head, staring unfocused, like she can't get it to make sense.

Rob steps over to touch her shoulder, then looks Lindsey in the eye. "You're sure of this?" he repeats.

She nods.

"Well, I don't believe it!" Marci stiffens and pulls away

from Rob's hand. "It doesn't make sense! We're all supposed to pull together. I'm not going to alienate Dr. Bennerton, get him thinking we're the enemy. We need him focusing on getting Kevin better."

"Great! You want to make all nicey-nice with your fucking high society pals while our son's life could be on the line?" Rob glares.

Marci glances at Lindsey, back at Rob, twisting and twining her fingers together. "I just don't think we should fly off all...crazy."

This is worse than Lindsey could have imagined. She stands. "I'm sorry, this is horrible. But I had to tell you. I couldn't just let it go." Eyes burning, she starts toward the door.

"Lindsey." Rob stops her, gives her a hug. "Thanks."

Ducking her head, Lindsey hurries out, down the hall to the stairwell, managing to avoid seeing Patty. She clatters down the steps and out through the nearly-empty cafeteria, heading instinctively for the garden. She remembers those beautiful tulips glistening their fleshy egg shapes in the rain. But today, as she sinks onto the bench in the dappled sun beneath a vine maple, she sees the tulip petals have already dropped, bare stalks all they offer to the sky.

ten

JUNE 30

Dear Diary,

From ecstasy to grief. Feet back on the ground with a thud. Kevin in a coma, EEGs deteriorating, we're still hoping but it doesn't look good. Doc Steinberg finally agreed to come on as a "consultant." Rob's talking to a lawyer about getting the hospital audit records. Bennerton let Steinberg do a second surgery with the fluids still building on poor Kevin's brain, along with a nasty staph infection. It was probably too late by the time Steinberg came on.

Should I just have let it alone? This is tearing everyone apart, Marci and Rob fighting when they should be pulling together, Joanie furious at me for butting in—"Who do you think you are, God?"—and there's a sort of no-contact zone around me at work, like I'm carrying something infectious. I can feel the whispers....

Grief and longing. No word from Newman. And I feel guilty for even thinking about him with all this going on. Anyway, it's way too much weight to be putting on that one day of magical connection, but I want so badly the comfort of feeling his arms around me or just hearing his voice saying I didn't imagine it. Why did he leave me the silk shawl and the Rumi book?

Broke down and left a message on his cell phone, asking when he'll be back, telling him I was feeling like Rumi's "Guest House" full of rampaging visitors/emotions. It's another poem from his book:

> *Being human is being a guest house.*
> *Every day a new emotion....*

Welcome them in the door!
Even a mob of sorrows with axes,
They may be making space
for a new delight....

How could Rob and Marci be expected to be grateful for this mob of sorrows? Am I supposed to be grateful for Nick and the cancer? Right now, I don't feel like I'm making any steps forward at all, just circling around to the same place. Heartsick.

Or is it a widening gyre? Are these the new wings, bringing me around on a rising spiral? Now that my heart's laid open, I don't get to choose joy over sorrow, have to feel it all.

Did I forget what it means to be alive?
Kevin hasn't had much time for that.

"Lindsey?"

Her fingers jerk on the keyboard, and she blinks, hopes they were actually transcribing the voice droning away in her headphones. She's been in robot mode again. She lifts her foot off the pedal, silencing the dictation, and looks up to see Olivia standing beside her.

Lindsey pulls off the headset.

Olivia's studying her, lips pursed. She pushes her pink half-glasses up on her nose and tilts her head toward a cart by the door, piled with chart folders. "Lindsey, would you run those down to Archives?"

"Oh. Sure." Puzzled, Lindsey saves the half-finished admitting exam file and sets the headphones on her desk.

Olivia's already back at her desk, flipping through a stack of reports, her glossy red nails flashing over the papers. Lindsey passes the cubicle where Sono's stolidly typing, not looking up. Marlene does glance up from her diagnostic coding, giving Lindsey a look of self-righteous indignation. Lindsey hasn't received any invitations to join the staff for breaks this week. And the ever-sunny Gayle is off on vacation.

Lindsey pauses at Olivia's desk. "Just stack them? Or do you want them filed?" She's confused as to why Olivia's sending her down to Archives. Especially right now. The second time she went up to ICU to look in on Kevin, she could see the blond nurse—the one who'd caught her going through Dr. Bennerton's progress notes in the chart— whispering to another nurse and gesturing toward Lindsey. Now she's just waiting for it all to catch up to her.

Olivia sets the papers aside, pulls off her glasses, looks up at Lindsey. "Just stack them for now. If Natalie has time on evening shift, she can file them." She gives her a wry smile. "Then go ahead and take a break, dear."

Shrugging inwardly, Lindsey rolls the cart into the elevator, punches Basement. The light refuses to light up. Hot, then cold flash over her for no reason as she stares at the obstinate button. The elevator doors open again at First Floor, where she entered, and someone gets on behind her. She tries Basement one more time, but it won't engage.

The person behind her clears his throat. It's a nursing assistant, waggling his ID card on its cord. "You have to use your card, for the basement."

"Oh. Right. I usually take the stairs." Lindsey inserts her card into the reader, then hesitates before punching the button again, paranoia taking over. Maybe they've blocked her access to secure areas, and this is Olivia's way of telling her. Then the button lights up, and the elevator drops smoothly.

This time Lindsey waits a few seconds for the fluorescent light to kick in before she rolls the cart past the stairway door where she tripped over Newman in the dark. Her footsteps echo off concrete down the empty hall.

She can hear his voice: *"Be well, Lindsey."*

Somehow she gets through the Friday afternoon. Before she leaves, Olivia casually drops a sealed envelope beside her keyboard. Lindsey blinks, glances around to see that no one else has noticed, sees Olivia's back heading out the door. She slips the envelope into her shoulder bag, waits to open it as she's retrieving her bike from the rack outside.

Lindsey, I just wanted to let you know that Administration will be asking to talk with you Monday morning.

Olivia had typed it but hadn't signed it.

Lindsey closes her eyes and blows out a long breath. So. She violated her confidentiality agreement, she knew what she was doing. She could be in deep doo-doo.

But somehow, despite a sick feeling in her gut, like she's just stepped off another cliff, she doesn't care. Maybe they can't save Kevin, maybe it's too late for Mr. Montague, but maybe the next accident victim won't end up under Bennerton's scalpel.

"Hey, Lindsey!"

She looks up, realizes she's been wheeling her bike on auto-pilot toward the parking exit. A young man in shorts and Birkenstocks lifts his hand toward Lindsey as he waves a protest placard at the employees leaving in their cars. The students are still keeping up a presence as the drawn-out negotiations continue over the proposed new hospital park access route.

Lindsey takes a breath and smiles. "Joshua. How's it going?" She's gotten acquainted with a few of the students over the past months. He's the one who was handing out Birth Announcements a month earlier, with photos of the engagingly homely barred-owl chicks spotted in the area of the park proposed for road construction.

Joshua grins and pushes back his billed cap. "Thank God I survived finals. Got an internship this summer with Northwest Stream Stewards."

"Hey, that's great. You know they helped me with my native-plant project. I'm downstream from here."

"Awesome!" He gives her a thumb's-up. "Any time you want to take a turn here, we've got plenty of flyers to pass out." It's an ongoing joke he's been playing off Lindsey as he's seen her leaving work over the past weeks.

This time she pauses. "You know, I might just do that. See you around, Joshua."

The encounter cheers her briefly, as does the bike ride. She takes a second loop through the park and dismounts to walk her bike along a narrow trail threading a grove of old cedars and big-leafed maples.

As she pauses to breathe in the moistness and the quiet of this oasis in the midst of town, she feels a light touch on her bare arm. A green bit of maple leaf is stuck to the skin. She peels it off and notices a couple more pieces drifting down past her face. She squints upward.

Above her on a big, mossy limb of an old maple, two fledgling owls—all downy fluff, gangly talons, and comical feather tufts emerging around their faces—clutch the branch and lean out to watch the drifting leaf bits. Shoulder to shoulder, they sway side to side to the rhythm of the leaves' swooping glides. When those reach the ground, one of the pair sidles along the branch to an intersection of another leafy bough, where it plucks a new piece with its beak. It returns to its nestmate and leans out to release the green bit. Again they sway, leaning together like Tweedle Dee and Dum, rapt in contemplation of the dance of the leaf through the air.

Lindsey, craning upward, feels a grin stretching her face. She's filled with the sheer wonder of this world she's lucky enough to inhabit along with these experimental young owls.

She turns her bike back along the trail, then stops short. Red surveyor's tapes dangle from wooden stakes following a path beneath the big maple, right through the cedar grove toward the hospital. It hits her in a sudden kick to the heart: This is the proposed route for the new access road.

Dear Diary:
    Damn!

Lindsey tries to get a grip on the shock and anger surging through her as she paces her bungalow, unable to grasp the monumental cluelessness of the road plan. And she's got the weekend ahead of her to wonder about this upcoming "talk" with Administration. Plus there's no message light on her phone. Should she try Newman's number again? Her pride won't let her.

Nightfall, and she's back to pacing the cramped measure of her walls, trailed by HighJinks and Sombra anxiously mewing—furry mirrors of her agitation. Another hot flash assails her, and she grabs a spiral-bound notebook to fan herself. Then she opens it to a blank page, picks up a pen, and sits down to write out her confusions.

It's a mystery, our connection to special places. I can't explain why the one bend of my favorite trail quickens my heartbeat as it brings me down a dip where I veer off the path, over a windfall cedar, to crouch beside a tiny pool fed by a spring seeping from under gnarled alder roots. The smooth surface makes a reflecting glass for the doubled branches reaching skyward, reaching rootlike deep beneath the surface. I'm stilled, peering into what someone else might call a puddle, the way I'd label homely some beloved face only one person finds beautiful.

She's writing not just to herself now, but trying to reach wider. Why not make it an essay? She'd once dreamed of being a writer, before Nick convinced her it was a waste of time. *"Maybe you just don't have what it takes."*

She takes a deep breath and flushes his voice where it belongs—down the toilet.

How do we feel when our personal nature-refuge is suddenly wiped off the map, crushed under bulldozer treads and scraped flat of trees, moss, birds? Reduced to mud? We're slapped right down into the mucky stages of grief— shock, anger, denial—just as inevitably as facing the traumatic death of a loved one. So maybe a turn toward the rituals of grief might find us a path toward environmental recovery.

Lindsey writes about the young owls and the senseless proposed road that could easily be located elsewhere. She writes about her uprush of blind anger and then righteousness, the gut feeling of wrongness that must be rectified. She wonders how the Native Americans could ever be expected to recover from their shock over the ways of the settlers ravaging their land. How the words of Chief Seattle still ring compassion down the decades. *"We are all children of the Great Spirit, we all belong to Mother Earth. Our planet is in great trouble, and if we keep carrying old grudges and do not work together, we will all die."* Maybe there's a place for healing—for regeneration?—in that primal mud this "civilization" is laying bare as its blank slate.

I flinch when I pass a clearcut or a ravaged hillside slated for more urban sprawl. Don't want to look at it. Seal myself off and go in search of a new "natural" refuge. But it's the wounded places that need our love.

Suddenly Lindsey realizes that's part of Nick's sickness. He can offer only anger against the environmental short-sightedness and greed, can feel only his personal pain at each loss. Ultimately, it's all centered on himself. And she wants to be bigger than that. Is there a way?

All of this finds its muddled way into the essay. She writes and rewrites all weekend, wondering if she's finally gone around the bend, and what difference can these words make, anyway? Whether anyone ever reads them or not? But it's somehow become an act of love, and faith.

She titles it "The Stages of Environmental Grieving," prints up a clean copy, and addresses it to an anthology soliciting women writers on the environment. Then, what the hell, sticks a second copy into an envelope for the *Weekly Whiplash*, the local alternative newspaper.

Sunday night she lays the two stamped packets by her bike pannier. She shrugs and stretches her tight shoulders, shakes out her hands she should have given a rest from typing. Who knows? Maybe soon, after this meeting with hospital Administration, she'll have a real long break from typing. These days, she looks for things to be grateful for: She's managed to get through the weekend.

eleven

THAT NIGHT LINDSEY REALIZES she was counting her chickens before they hatched—she *hasn't* quite made it through the weekend, and the brain whirl won't let her sleep. She lies in bed, throwing off the sheets and thin blanket for the hot flashes, pulling them back up when she starts to shiver. She surrenders to the insane rhythm of it, turning and shifting in efforts to find a cool spot on the sheets, finally driving the cats off their curled hotspots flanking her knees.

She checks the alarm clock. *2:03 am.*

Desperate, she tries the chakra-opening meditation Crystal told her about. Then a progressive-relaxation positive-imaging exercise.

2:57 am.

Another hot flash attacks, and it feels like her skin is crisping under a heated iron. She throws off the sheet one more time, grabs the towel off the nightstand to blot her face and back, then lies back down and gives way to the grief and longing she's been trying to tamp down all weekend. She's mourning for Kevin, freaking out about her job and paying the bills, worrying about coping with her mom's frailty. And wanting Newman's touch. She remembers the "Guest House" poem and just gives in, flings open her doors before they get torn off their hinges by these unruly visitors.

Maybe the heart-chakra thing worked, after all, because suddenly she feels an expansion in her chest. A shift. She's back at Fern Lake, sitting on the intertwined roots, dipping her feet into the cool water as backlit leaves whisper overhead. She slides into the water, floating eyes closed, and she feels another touch to her heart. Inside her closed eyelids, she opens other eyes and sees it's Newman. They're floating together now, and he's smiling, touching her wounded breast with his fingertips.

She blinks, startled, and the images start to dissolve into static. *"What—?"*

"Sshhh...." He takes her hand.

A deep ocean blue lulls her in its waves. *Peace.* She sighs and sinks deeper, sinks into sleep.

July 1

Dear Diary,

Such a lovely dream! Or was I actually meditating? That peaceful ocean blue, the color of Newman's eyes....

But today is Monday. Time to get my feet on solid ground, so I don't turn into one of those eccentric crones with twenty cats, house a labyrinth of piled-up old newspapers and magazines. The one they find a week later trapped under a collapsed pile with her desperate cats feeding on her body. Which reminds me, when am I going to do some housecleaning around here??

Time for the shock treatment: I'm off to the hospital for that meeting with Administration....

The Director of the Board and the personnel manager keep Lindsey waiting for twenty minutes while she dies a slow death under the scrutiny of the secretary and what seems to be the entire staff of the hospital just happening to pass by the reception area on urgent errands. She wipes damp palms down the nice slacks she wore for the occasion. Right on schedule, a hot flash ignites just as the inner office door swings open and the manager beckons her in.

Her skin's burning, prickling under her summer-weight blazer. She was determined to keep it on, present a professional image, but her face feels like it's going to explode with the heat. Sighing, she pulls off the jacket. She manages to resist fanning herself with it.

"Are you alright?" Ms. Landon, the manager, frowns

slightly, waiting in her office doorway. She's wearing a blue blazer and skirt, tinted blond hair sculpted and sprayed into rigidity.

Lindsey just looks at her.

She lowers her gaze, ushers Lindsey past and follows her into the office, where a paunchy man in a rumpled white shirt, thinning dark strands combed over his bald spot, is drumming his fingers on the armrest of one of the chairs in front of the manager's desk. Another man, in a suit, stands looking out the window over the parking lot toward the park.

The first man stands when Lindsey comes in, straightening his tie and taking a step toward her. A big, shambling fellow, he smiles jovially and extends a hand, takes hers in a damp grip. "Roger Stone. I'm on the Board. And this is Allen Dunshire." He indicates the other man.

He's a slight, shortish man, dapper in an immaculate gray suit, sandy hair crisply curled tight to his head. He gives Lindsey's hand a brief, brisk shake and hands her a business card. "Nice to meet you." He doesn't meet her eyes.

Lindsey looks down, sees the long name-conglomerate of a legal firm. The heaviness in her gut settles deeper.

"Sit down, Lindsey." Big smiling Roger indicates the chairs facing the desk with its nameplate, *Alicia Landon.*

Alicia shoots Roger a narrow-eyed look—some kind of turf war going on?—and moves around to assert her position behind the desk, sitting in her leather chair. She picks up a folder, makes a show of opening it and laying it flat on the desk.

A pause, as the three of them settle into the curve of chairs, Lindsey flanked by the two men, the contained erectness of the attorney on her left, expansive bulk of the director on her right. *"See no evil, speak no evil, hear no evil"* pops absurdly into Lindsey's mind, along with the matching monkey poses, and for a moment she thinks she's said it aloud. If she bursts out laughing, maybe they'll just cart her off to the Psych wing and they can save going through the motions here.

"Well, Lindsey," Alicia starts, clears her throat, and continues, "I see by your employee reviews you've been an asset to the hospital. Aside from a bit of a tardiness issue, you're rated excellent, with a top production rate in transcription. So, in light of that—"

"Okay, Alicia, let's not beat around the bush." Roger leans forward with his affable smile, spreads big pink hands topped by black hairs. "I'm sure Lindsey would appreciate it if we just cut to the chase." He turns to raise an eyebrow at Lindsey, who nods mutely, waiting to see what their game plan is. On her left, the attorney makes a small movement, quickly checked.

Roger runs a hand over his head, smoothing the dark strands. "The Spielers are family friends, I understand?"

Lindsey bites her lip, then nods again.

Roger's smile morphs into an expression of sincerity, sympathy. "The accident—a terrible tragedy. Believe me, everyone at the hospital is pulling for that young man. He's getting the best care available." He glances at Alicia, who is sitting rigid behind her desk, then turns back to Lindsey. "I'm a churchgoer, myself, but sometimes I have to admit it's hard to see God's plan in these things. So I can understand how upsetting it must have been to have to type up that accident report on your friend."

Lindsey's gripping the armrests of the chair, another hot flash blazing through her, and she can hardly hear over the roaring in her ears. She wants to jump to her feet, tell the man to shut up, but she's the one in the monkey lineup with the gag over her mouth.

No, she realizes then, that's the old program. She's here because she *did* find her voice. And now more words are boiling up in her, angry ones—the effrontery of this oily jerk, trying to push her buttons about Kevin! She opens her mouth, ready to spew her hot contempt, but then realizes she has a choice here. She can wait to see what they'll reveal.

"...but here's the thing," he's continuing, and she lost something there but it doesn't matter. "That's where you should have stepped back, talked to your supervisor, ah...."

"Olivia," Alicia supplies tersely. "Lindsey, you do remember signing the confidentiality agreement? It's here in your file."

Again the attorney makes a movement, but checks it.

"Now, Alicia, of course Lindsey remembers. She's a very bright woman."

Lindsey, despite her distaste, meets his eyes. She recoils from their hard shrewdness. How much do they know? She left a message for Rob over the weekend, but he never called back to tell her what actions his attorney has taken, if they're pursuing a malpractice case.

"Believe me, Lindsey," Roger's going on, "we've agonized over this, Alicia and I and all the Board members. It's a hard one. I'm sure, like us, you'd like to move on."

Alicia pulls out another paper, pushes it over the desk toward Lindsey. "We're giving you layoff status, Lindsey, effective immediately. It won't look bad on your record. You should have no trouble getting another position, with your skills."

When Lindsey doesn't move to take the paper, Roger leans forward and takes it, lays it in her lap. "We agreed— the Board talked it over with Allen here—not to pursue legal action against you. Go ahead, read it, it's straightforward. You'll see we're being generous, giving you through this pay period's salary to tide you over."

On her left, Allen Dunshire clears his throat, finally speaks. "There are two main clauses. The hospital agrees not to pursue legal action for violation of your agreement in revealing confidential information about audit reports, and you agree not to be part of any legal action against the hospital." He's still not looking at Lindsey.

She tries to read the paper, but her focus is blurred by a red mist of rage at their manipulation. She resists a startling urge to jump up and throttle smug Roger Stone, playing on the suffering of real people as if they're only counters in some chess game. Her face is burning, throat swelling with the choked-down rage—where has all her anger gone, these past years? Into more cancer?

She drops the paper unread, looks up at Roger again, and asks, "What planet are you from, anyway?"

He stares at her, nonplussed, as the lawyer makes a little choked-off sound that might have been laughter. Lindsey darts a look at him to see his lips twitch, but then he's holding a blank, neutral expression.

Roger stands, shaking his head, and hands her a pen. "Take your time, Lindsey," he says, back into his script. "Sign it, and you can put this mistake behind you." He wanders over to the other side of the desk to confer in a muted voice with Alicia.

Lindsey glances again at the agreement, folds it, and

puts it in her purse. She stands. "I'll take it home, and get back to you."

Roger swings around toward her, starts to protest, but the lawyer cuts him off, telling Lindsey, "That's fine. Call me if you have any questions."

"Thank you." Lindsey meets Allen's gaze.

He nods quickly, then looks away, and she thinks, *How odd. He's the lawyer, and he's the one feeling ashamed.*

She picks up her jacket, turns to go.

Roger straightens on the other side of the desk, starts to say something, moves toward her. Allen holds up a hand, and Lindsey's out the door.

"Excuse me, Ms. Friedland?"

She blinks at the man blocking her way past the receptionist. He's an earnest-looking young Latino she doesn't recognize, wearing a white uniform shirt and a Security badge.

"I'll just take your ID badge and escort you to Medical Records to retrieve your things, Ma'am."

"Ma'am?" She stares at him. "Oh, God! *Ma'am!*" And that does it. Lindsey's hysterical laughter trails them like a banner down the hall to Medical Records.

She celebrates her liberation from the ranks of the gainfully employed by pushing the protesting Subaru past its comfort speed zone on the way to the Fern Lake trailhead. Might as well take advantage of weekday solitude, and she can't bear to spend another day pacing the bungalow walls. She pushes herself past her own comfort zone, making the lake in record time, legs and lungs burning. The aerobic flush and a brisk, cold swim finally push her Reset button on the brain-whirl, and she can go slow on the way down, notice a big pileated woodpecker tearing into a pockmarked snag, feel the dappled lights sliding over her face, breathe in the cool moisture of the mossy creek ravines. On the overlook cliff above the rocky river canyon, she catches sight of a great blue heron, gliding past her on motionless extended wings, riding the air down the winding path of the waters.

That evening, she leaves another message for Rob,

hating to intrude but needing to know where she stands before she signs the termination agreement. Maybe she should talk to an attorney, too.

The summer light finally fades after 10 pm, and she tries to settle on the couch with Sombra and HighJinks and the Rumi book, reading about spirit and wings, seeing the heron spread its wings to glide effortlessly down the winding course of the river and past sight. She closes her eyes, feels that deep blue serenity of last night's...dream? Feeling that heart—soul?—connection. Then she's over the edge again, vibrating with the urgency of wanting Newman. She sends out an incoherent prayer a la Joni Mitchell, wondering who's there to hear as she asks for a man who's "somewhat sincere." She gets up and does her yoga stretches. Makes a cup of chamomile tea.

Finally, at midnight, she crawls into bed, goes through the deep-breathing chakra-opening relaxation drill, and manages to drop off into sleep. She dreams of flying, feeling her chest expanding with the rhythm of her wingbeats, a smooth undulation carrying her into cobalt-blue skies.

The phone rings, jarring her out of her wingspread glide down the heron's river course.

"Uhn!" She gropes for solidity, pushes the sheets down, blinks at the lighted clock: *1:08 am.* The phone rings again, goes into answer mode, and she can hear her own voice, *"This is Lindsey. Please leave a message."*

Then Newman's voice, blurred by static, "Lindsey, it's probably some godawful hour, but this is the first I could get to a phone and I wanted to—"

Lindsey, fumbling in the dark for the phone, finally clicks it on. "Hroa." All that comes out is a heron croak. She clears her throat. "Hello."

A chuckle, sounding far away. Well, yeah. "Lindsey, I'm sorry, I woke you up."

"No. Yes." She clears her throat again, takes the phone back to bed with her and gets under the covers. "I mean, I was dreaming. I was flying."

"That's good." A crackle of static breaks up the connection for a few seconds. "...my cell phone, or maybe it got stolen. Then the village elders invited me on a retreat with them, we went up to the mountain temple I helped them build back in.... Man, how long ago was that?" He laughs.

"Then a monsoon hit, it's early in the season for that, every-thing got flooded out, I finally got back to town but I don't know how long this connection's gonna hold...." More static.

"Newman?" Lindsey grips the phone, wants to shout into it. "Newman, are you still there?"

"*There?*" her own voice echoes.

"...but anyway," Newman comes back on the line. There's some kind of strange delay effect going on, so she's not sure what she missed. "It's been a wild ride!" He sounds exhilarated. "I wanted to tell you about the bird sanctuary. It's a white heron rookery, on the river. They're beautiful. Like angels, when they fly." A pause. "Lindsey, did I lose you?"

"Herons?" she croaks. She clears her throat one more time. "Newman, that's—"

But with the delay he's started talking already. "...be quick, before I lose you. I—" He stops, waits, then, "What?"

"Newman, I just saw a great blue heron up at the river. I was dreaming about flying with it."

More static. Then, "You're okay, then? I got some worried vibes about you."

"You got my message?"

"...phone message? Can't retrieve them here yet, but—"

"No never mind!" She's flooded with embarrassment over the neediness of that message she left. "Just delete it."

He chuckles. "Now I'll have to listen to it."

"No, please don't—"

"...kidding." He continues hastily, "Listen, Lindsey, this may not hold. Are you okay?"

"Well, it's been kind of awful...but I'm okay. It's Kevin. A family friend, a terrible accident, he's in a coma.... It's complicated, but I told his parents some confidential info about his surgeon's incompetence. They fired me."

"What? Fired?" More static. "No wonder I felt your—"

Static.

"Newman? Newman?" Lindsey's straining to hear, gripping the phone, but the connection's gone.

Not quite. As she gives up and crawls back into bed, she can hear something like a whisper. She closes her eyes and lies quietly, and then she feels it—lips gently brushing her forehead. She sighs and flows like the river emptying into blue ocean.

twelve

"HELLO, MS. FRIEDLAND? LINDSEY Friedland?"

"Yes. This is Lindsey." She doesn't recognize the caller.

"Great, glad I caught you." The voice on the phone is male, a bit breathless. "This is Damon Perrera from *The Weekly Whiplash.*"

"Oh. Hello."

"I'm the editor, I just got your essay. It's terrific, we want to run it."

"Oh." Lindsey stares at the phone, gathering her thoughts, and he beats her to a response.

"No problem, then? We're pushing a deadline for this Friday's issue, but we got a big hole with another article not arriving in time, and this is perfect timing what with the community forum Tuesday about the hospital road proposal."

"Well." She blinks. "Okay, go ahead and run it."

"We can only offer you a hundred bucks, but we don't take any rights, you're free to submit it elsewhere." The voice is enthusiastic. "It's a strong piece, I'd like to talk about some more articles for us if you're up for it."

Lindsey smiles. "Yes! I mean...great."

"Awesome," he says, and she visualizes him as one of the environmental-studies students at the hospital protests, though surely he must be a little older than that. "Well, hey, we'll go ahead with it, but just to dot all the i's, could you stop by the office front desk and sign our little permission form? And you can give us your info to send the check. Soon as we put this baby to bed, I'll call you and brainstorm some more article ideas. We've got lots to cover!"

"All right, I'll stop by. On Railroad Avenue, right?"

"You got it. Hey, great talking, Lindsey! See you soon."
Click.

Lindsey's still standing, holding the phone, as it starts beeping. She slowly hangs it up. Her words made a connection!

Gears start turning. Is this a sign? She can actually make money as a writer? She has to chuckle as she calculates all the hours that went into the essay. At this rate she's making, what? Less than ten dollars an hour for actual writing time, of course that's self-employment at a higher tax rate, with no job benefits, and how to factor in all the time pondering and finding inspiration to write? Though the editor did remind her of the option to sell the piece elsewhere as well....

Then Lindsey closes her eyes and blows out a breath. What about the termination agreement with the hospital? Once the essay comes out—if anyone in Administration reads the radical *Whiplash*—will this affect their "generosity" in not pursuing legal action? Should she sign and get it sealed before Friday?

She takes a deep breath, taps in Rob and Marci's number again.

It rings five times, then goes into their message, with a long, stacked-up beep behind it, and she almost hangs up, then starts, "Rob, it's Lindsey. I'm really sorry to bother you guys again, but—"

"Lindsey." A clunk, something crashing, then Rob comes back on the line, "Damn. Just a sec." A scuffling, clattering, a chair dragging, then, "Okay. Yeah, Lindsey, I never got back to you. It's...." His voice raises, "No, Patty, just take it outside to your mom, okay, Hon?" He comes back to Lindsey. "Listen, Lin, I don't have much time, I've got a meeting with the lawyer today, but I want to talk to you. Marci's real...upset. Well, of course we all are, but she...well, she doesn't think I should talk to you. Or the lawyer. It's...." His voice is rough, choked-off.

"Rob, I'm so sorry." Lindsey takes a deep breath. "Anything new on Kevin?"

He clears his throat. "No. The new doc, Steinberg, he's great, but it's just...that infection, and the earlier pressure buildup seems like it caused permanent damage, they aren't reading much brain function...." Another throat-clearing.

"You haven't heard anything up at the hospital, have you?"

Now it's Lindsey clearing her throat. "Well, I got fired Monday."

"What?" A pause. Then, "Those goddamn bastards! This is it! I'm gonna nail their butts so bad—"

"Wait, Rob." Lindsey gives him a second. "They have grounds. I just wanted to ask you if—"

"Shit. Marci's heading back inside, I don't want another big scene here. Listen, Lindsey, you need to talk with my lawyer. Meet me in front of his office before my appointment. Can you be there this afternoon at a quarter to three? It's on Cornwall, across from the old Newberry building."

"Okay. I'll be there."

Marci's voice in the background, "Who's that?"

"No thank you," Rob's voice shifts, "and take us off your list." *Clunk.*

Rob's pacing back and forth on the sidewalk in front of the attorneys' building, smoking again after he'd quit when Kevin was maybe five.... His face looks ten years older in this past couple of weeks. This secret meeting with Lindsey, and lying to Marci.... It's bad.

Maybe Lindsey should have just kept her mouth shut. It's looking grim for Kevin, as Rob fills her in:

"The staph infection is really taking him down, Lindsey. Doc Steinberg is doing the best possible, but Kevin's EEGs are getting worse, no response." Rob scrubs at his face. "Christ, even if he pulls through, will he just be a vegetable? This is gonna kill Marci." He stops, struggling for control.

"Hey." Lindsey moves to give him a hug.

But Rob backs off, shaking his head, wiping his eyes. "Let's go up." Stone-faced now, he ushers her into the building, into the elevator.

Lindsey's trying to keep her own face under control. Maybe her sister Joanie was right, she shouldn't have interfered. Maybe it would have been better to just let Dr. Bennerton stay on, finish Kevin off faster. Oh, God. If anybody's out there, don't make him linger in a coma, stringing the family out forever.

"Lindsey, how do you do?" The attorney Doug Trundall

stands to shake hands with her as they're ushered into his office with a view of Mt. Baker in the distance.

Rob cuts through the niceties. "Clock's ticking, Doug. When are we gonna get hold of those audit reports?"

"It's not that easy, Rob." He sits, runs a hand through his graying hair. "The hospital is lawyering up, of course, and they'll be putting up plenty of roadblocks before we can—"

"Roadblocks!" Rob loses it then. He's practically foaming at the mouth, funneling the grief and anger into a crusade to take down Bennerton and the hospital. "I want them to suffer!"

Doug, quietly reasonable, tries to keep him from flying off the handle, but Rob barrels on:

"Lindsey should sue the hospital, too. The way they fired her!"

"Rob, they're part of a large parent corporation. They have all the big-time attorneys and money and time at their disposal," Doug points out. "That would be a very tough battle."

He does take a look at the hospital's "generous" termination agreement they're offering Lindsey, and tells her flat out that she'd be crazy to sign it. The hospital's on shaky PR ground right now with the park access controversy, and the last thing they want is more bad press about Kevin and firing Lindsey. He advises her to ask for four months' pay in return for signing the "no involvement in legal action" and confidentiality clauses.

And that gets Rob all fired up again, mad at Doug for "stabbing Kevin in the back." He insists that Lindsey should be a witness in the malpractice case against Bennerton.

Doug keeps explaining that it's highly unlikely they'll need to go to court. The hospital and Bennerton's insurance company will be eager to settle out of court, and they don't need Lindsey to testify anyway, since the hospital eventually will have to hand over the audit committee reports. They just need to hang in there and give it time, see how Kevin's going to do....

"Wait and see how Kevin's going to do!" Rob's spitting mad by that time, face going purple. "Jesus Christ! You want to go up there to ICU, Doug? Look at how my son's doing? Watch him shriveling up day by day? He's gone!

There's nobody home! And I want those bastards to pay!"

He turns on Lindsey then. "Damn it, you started this! You going to chicken out now? Take your four months' pay and walk away? Well, fuck you, too!" He slams out.

Doug and Lindsey stare at each other.

"Look," she finally manages, "I'll testify if you think it will help get Bennerton stopped. Forget the termination agreement."

He shakes his head. "Lindsey, don't go there. Rob's just blowing off steam, it's his way to grieve. I've seen it a lot. He's not really mad at you, in fact he's said more than once how they owe you for speaking up. Just give it time. A little space."

He fiddles with his papers. "You know, preparing a case like this isn't just about the facts, it's about how you orchestrate the presentation. Especially if it goes to trial. It's like a theatrical play in a lot of ways...."

He adjusts his wire-rims, gives her an assessing look. "I'll repeat, I don't think this is likely to go to trial. Right now, Ron's ready to go any distance for what he thinks is justice, and he's right—you don't even want to know about all the abuses the medical system gets away with. I've been chipping away at efforts toward reform for a long time. Most clients just don't have the staying power, or they don't really want the spotlight focused on them, they just want their lives back into some kind of stability. The ones that can hack it, or have the time to put into it, sure, a big splash of a lawsuit can make a difference."

"Like that Ryan family? The little boy poisoned at the fast-food joint?"

"Right. That mother's a tiger, she sank her teeth in and wouldn't let go. But that costs a family, financially and emotionally. A lot." He shakes his head. "And on top of the original trauma, that's just too much for most."

Lindsey knows that Rob wants to set up an action fund with any settlement they get, to use toward reform of physician's self-policing practices with the audit system. Is he only dreaming?

Doug pulls off his glasses and rubs them on his shirt, squinting across the desk at Lindsey and looking tired. "I'm not sure why I'm telling you this."

"I appreciate it. It helps me understand what's at stake."

"You'd be a good witness, if it does come to trial. Which wouldn't be for a couple years. Even if you sign a non-involvement clause, it would be highly unlikely the hospital would bother to pursue it."

She nods. "I'll do whatever would help."

"Good. If you ask the hospital for new terms, I know another attorney who could look at the agreement. I'd advise it, and she won't charge much."

"Thanks, Doug. I appreciate this, and I know Rob does, too."

"I just wish I never had to see another case like Kevin's...." He spreads his hands, a good man up against the Goliath.

July 4

Dear Diary,

It's bad.

How long will Kevin linger? Have we all given up hope too soon? Looks like the handwriting's on the wall, but it's only been a couple weeks. Maybe it's not too late to hope for a miraculous turn-around. All this legal stuff—are we just writing Kevin off like he's already some inanimate object to be bartered over?

Lindsey closes her eyes, sees his smooth, freckled young face, brown eyes eager even as he ducked his head shyly when she asked to read the science fiction story he'd written. That was last summer, the barbecue at Joanie and Don's. Kevin sat watching her while she read, hands thrust anxiously between his knees, and they were both so relieved when she really liked the story that they burst out laughing.

Damn it all! He's such a good kid! Maybe Marci's right, this legal battle's pulling Rob away from the real fight—Kevin lying there trying to keep body and soul together.

So, do I hope Rob drops the malpractice lawsuit, after all? What about Bennerton's next victim? Am I a coward, not walking my talk? When I look at myself in the mirror, I have to admit I was relieved to take the easy out that Doug Trundall offered. I don't want to be the whistleblower again, like I was with Nick. Don't want to be the scapegoat, see them turn on me with that rage and scorn and shaming, the way Nick and his family twisted everything to make it all my fault—even his affair—for "emotionally abandoning him."

Was it my fault? Did I not try hard enough?

Happy Independence Day.

Lindsey has decided to skip Megan's family Fourth of July barbecue this year. She needs some quiet amid the swirling chaos, save her energy for her own family's do set for the coming weekend. Arlen's in one of his manic whirls, laying in all the supplies for charring his trademark venison shish kebabs around the firepit at Friedland's Folly, calling everyone to inform them they're coming and what they're supposed to bring for side dishes.

Lindsey girds her loins for the usual sister skirmishes, Dad rants, Mom martyrdoms, drunken nephews, and over-stimulated grandkids. Added to the mix this year will be the specter of Kevin's coma. She doesn't know if Joanie will be speaking to her or not.

She sighs and calls Megan to beg off.

"Okay, Lin, we'll miss you, but everyone will under-stand. You've got your plate full with all this awful stuff up at the hospital. You hanging in there?"

"Yeah, I'm okay, a lot of changes but aside from Kevin, it's not bad. Let's go for a walk around Stimson Pond one of these days. Catch up." Is she ready yet to tell Megan about Newman? What exactly is it that she can say, anyway?

"Okay, do my butt good to get it moving. And, listen, just so you don't feel too deprived missing out on my mom's kielbasa and potato salad, Bruce has been asking about you. He's gonna be there today in all his cologned glory, hot to trot."

Lindsey laughs, hangs up relieved.

So she hunkers in with the cats to survive the neigh-borhood onslaught of fireworks and illegal M-80s from the tribal stands. Last year HighJinks and Sombra burrowed under the couch cushions and refused to come out when she got home from the barbecue.

So this Fourth, she closes the windows and gathers them onto her lap to watch a Disney DVD about a boy adopting an orphaned leopard. They shudder at the louder explosions outside, but stay with her, heads following the action onscreen.

The next morning, she calls Allen Dunshire, the hospital's attorney. She leaves a message with his assistant, and Dunshire surprises her by calling back within the hour.

"Hello, Lindsey. You have a question about the termination agreement?" His voice is neutral.

"Well, not really a question." She takes a breath, plunges in. "I'll agree to the terms, if the hospital agrees to give me four months' severance pay."

Silence. Then, "I...see." Another beat. "And you'd like me to present this counter-offer to the hospital?"

"If that's within your job description."

"That's what they retain me for. I make a good buffer zone." A hint of humor in his voice now?

"Well.... Then you'll let me know?"

"I will." Another pause. "You're a talented writer, Lindsey. Have a good weekend."

"Oh. Thanks." She hangs up, staring unfocused out the window. He must have read *The Weekly Whiplash* essay about the park access. She'd forgotten it was coming out today. Oh, boy. Was that amusement in his voice? Is this some lawyerish setup?

Es la vida. The useful everyday phrase from her sojourn in Honduras rises from the murk. *That's life.*

HighJinks, who's been insistently nudging her legs while she was busy with the phone call, reminds her of priorities by biting her ankle.

"Ouch! All right, all right." She crouches to stroke his back, behind his silky gray ears, under his chin. "Where's your mouse?"

He's instantly alert, eyeing her. She looks in the usual hiding places—under the couch, in the corner of the bathroom counter overhang, the bottom shelf of her nightstand, finally finds it in his food dish. That means he's pointing out a serious attention deficit.

"Okay, I get the message. Lighten up, Lindsey." She brings the frayed mini stuffed mouse back to the living room, lobs it across the oak flooring so it gets a good slide going. "Get the mouse!"

HighJinks launches himself over the area rug, gets a

push with his back legs, and goes into a controlled skid over the slippery wood flooring. He banks off the bookshelves in a turn, snaps up the little mouse by its tail, and trots back over to Lindsey, dropping it at her feet.

"Good boy!"

He turns his tail to her, cattishly pretending to ignore her praise.

The phone rings again, and her heart gives a lurch as she picks up, hoping it's Newman. "Hello?"

"Hey, Lin, congratulations." It's Nick.

Lindsey closes her eyes, gripping the phone, gears spinning. First survival instinct: hang up. She never did get around to signing up for that caller ID her lawyer recommended during the divorce when Nick was harassing her, threatening her and her friends, accusing her, cursing her.... But somehow her fingers are frozen, like her voice, and she just stands there.

"Lin, you there?" His voice so casual, like they'd just talked that morning. "Lin?"

"Oh." She clears her throat. "Yes." Not sure what's she answering.

"Well, I read your essay. It's terrific. Just wanted to say...." He trails off, sounding oddly indecisive.

"You mean *The Whiplash*? I just realized it was coming out today, I need to get a copy."

"You haven't seen it yet?" He laughs. "You are one of a kind, I have to give you that. Everyone here's talking about it. I knew you had it in you!"

Right. Like when he'd talked her out of writing stories because she didn't have "what it takes."

He's still talking. "You could do some environmental pieces for the agency, branch out. So get your butt in gear and pick up a copy."

"I'm on my way." Exit line. Take it. "Bye—"

"Wait." Another pause, then, "Word is, you got fired from the hospital. Those assholes! Something about a friend they messed up on? What's going on, Lin?"

She can't trust him. There's always some catch. She has to remember not to give him any information he can use to pull her into his manipulations. "Nick, it was nice of you to call, but I don't want to talk about it. You...take care." She starts to hang up again.

"Wait, Lin! Don't—" His voice sharpens, then he lets out a gusting breath, lowers the volume. "Just, if you're in a bind, don't be afraid to ask. I could front you some money."

She stares, startled. "Oh. That's—" She's started to thank him, but remembers that's another dangerous hook. He wants her gratitude. Always wanted her dependence.

She steadies her voice. "I appreciate the gesture, Nick, but that won't be necessary. I have to go now. Goodbye." She carefully hangs up.

Her ears are ringing, and her gut feels empty, sick. A hot flash gears up, flames licking through her, sweat breaking out on her face and back. "Shit. Shit." Just his voice is enough to trigger the old panic. "Damn it!"

She rips off her shirt, takes some deep breaths. This is ridiculous, he was trying to be civil—maybe—and she should just be calm and detached and cool. But she's not there. Yet.

She throws on her bike shorts and sports bra, grabs her helmet, and she's out the door. Once she's on her bike, pedaling fast down the creek road, she can remember the essay, let herself feel the excitement again and banish Nick's voice claiming a piece of it. She'll do her favorite loop around the harbor and then pick up some copies of *The Whiplash* on her way back.

She takes her usual route to avoid traffic, over the creek bridge and along a gravel trail that brings her out behind the tech college parking lot. From there, she zips onto Marine Drive so she can drop down steep Salish Street to the harbor loop.

The turnoff onto Salish is still blocked off by a construction detour barrier, she's been dodging it all week while they fixed potholes. Lindsey gives a quick glance for lurking cop cars, then darts around the barrier onto the cracked sidewalk, bounces over the curb and skirts the patch jobs that look like they should be okay by now, anyway. At the bottom of the drop, she slows just enough to check for rare cars, sees only another mountain bike coming from the trailhead parking lot by the reclaimed industrial beach. She lets her rear wheel go into a controlled slide to carry her around the turn, dropping a foot on the inside in case she needs a pivot, but she's got the momentum and it carries her on.

She's cranking along past warehouses and along a spur rail line when the other bicyclist overtakes her, surprising her as he pumps past. He's panting, covered with mud, really pushing it.

Lindsey blinks, then tightens her grip on the handlebars and pushes harder, too, thinking she could use the aerobic burn, see if she can pace this guy.

She rounds the curve past some parked boxcars and over the tracks, then sees up ahead there's another road barrier at the stop sign giving onto the main industrial harbor drive. A couple cars also block the way, except for a narrow slot through, and some people are standing around. A cry goes up as the cyclist ahead of her shoots through.

Lindsey frowns, glances behind her to see two more mountain bikers strung out behind her. They've both got numbers pinned to their skintight jerseys.

"Oh, boy." Lindsey barely has time to register the mud-spattered number pinned to the biker ahead of her, too, as she sweeps toward the open slot and arms waving her through.

"Go, go, go!" People are chanting as she zooms past, still cranking along in the wake of the first cyclist.

Now she sees the banners draped along the route, the parked cars, the people cheering. She's blundered into the second-to-last-leg of the annual Snow-to-Sea relay race.

Looking for a place to pull over, she shoots another glance behind her and sees the other racers aren't catching up, she's in the clear, so suddenly she's just riding the adrenaline rush. *What the hell!* She grins at the spectators lining the route and waving her on, cranks harder and is about to overtake the first biker as she nears another barrier and people with flags waving her through the slot and a turn toward the handoff to the kayakers for the final leg of the race.

A cop car is parked there, lights flashing to add to the festive color.

People are cheering. "Yeah! Go for it! Go, girl!"

Lindsey sails through, grinning, raising her hand to flash a Peace sign. Then reverses it: V for Victory.

thirteen

"SURRENDER THE CHOW, OR walk the plank!" Arlen greets Lindsey as she reaches the deck toting her mini-cooler with beer and potato salad for the family do. He's brandishing a croquet mallet like Thor's hammer, sporting the horned Viking helmet he bought after a dig-up-the-ancient-family-roots phase a few years back.

"Dad, I don't think Vikings did plank-walking." Pirates, Vikings, Arlen's probably channeling both today.

"Well, get your butt out here for an obstacle-croquet match. Loser goes in the pond, whether we've got a plank or not." He grins, then roars scarily and waves the mallet, chasing five-year-old great-grandson Chad, who tears off across the yard.

Lindsey blows out a breath of conditional relief. Dad's in a jovial mood, at least for now. She sets down the cooler and checks out the two long picnic tables arranged on the deck, tablecloths secured with clothespins.

Fran, flopped on a lounger in the thin strip of shade next to the house, tilts her head toward Arlen and holds up both fair-skinned hands with crossed fingers. "So far, so good." She looks tired, not surprising with her job managing a local furniture store, plus her Phyllis divorced now and moved back in with the kids.

Lindsey nods. "How's Mom holding up?"

"The usual. Fussing around with the condiments and place settings, won't sit down and rest. I gave up, sent Phyl in there while I watch the kids." She waves a hand toward the yard where her oldest, Ross, and the clan's assorted grandkids and great-grandkids are setting up croquet hoops in the most difficult-to-reach spots like behind shrubs or next to Arlen's twenty-foot pole flying high the American flag. It was Lindsey who first came up with the obstacle-croquet concept when they were kids and spread the game out into the woods behind their old house in town, so every year she's designated to explain the "rules." Which leaves plenty of room for creativity in interpretation.

A rumbling roar and gust of exhaust fumes as towheads Jesse and Connor barrel around the house and down the driveway on Arlen's four-wheeler, heading for the newly mown hayfield. Bingo races after them, yapping.

Fran shudders. "God, I was hoping that contraption was out of commission. Death on wheels. Christie said no, but of course Arlen fired it up anyway."

"Linny, Linny!" It's Bitsy in one of her trademark frilly dresses, tugging on Lindsey's shorts. "Gramps says you have to help put those wire things up."

"Okay, just a sec. I'll be right out." She pushes through the screen door as Fran claims a "kiss for Grandma" before releasing Bitsy back to the game.

In the kitchen, petite, curvy Phyl is looking especially pretty in one of Opal's gingham aprons. She's managed to persuade her "Gran" to sit down, at the counter, where she can supervise the slicing and layout of the shish kebab fixings, make sure the proper platters are being used. Joanie's daughter Sharon winks at her Aunt Lindsey as she lines up the dishes on the counter for Opal's inspection.

"Anything I can do?"

"Nope, we're about set, just waiting for the fire to die down to coals. You better get out there for that game," Sharon tilts her head toward the door, "or we're gonna have Grampa in here stomping around again. I made him put down the skewer he was using for a sword."

"Good job. Potato salad's out there in my cooler." Lindsey gives Opal a kiss on the cheek, then heads out to join the fray. She skirts the fire pit made from a tractor wheel rim, lawn chairs circled around it and metal shish kebab skewers clustered upright at ready position like so many bristling bayonets. At least Arlen's not charging around with one of those poised to put out somebody's eye.

Joanie, in sun hat and dark glasses, is sitting in the circle with Don, Sharon's husband Kyle, Fran's husband Lonnie and their youngest Skip, Ross's wife Christie, and

Eric's baby napping on a blanket beneath an umbrella. Lots of empty chairs. Then Lindsey remembers that Eric's back in drug rehab. And, of course, this year there's no Marci, Rob, Patty, or Kevin.

Lindsey waves as she passes. Joanie pointedly ignores her, and Lindsey prays they can avoid another blowup about her "meddling" over Kevin. Maybe it's easier for Marci and Joanie to blame her instead of Dr. Bennerton, especially for this revenge campaign Rob's on, and maybe they're right. She hasn't told anyone about being fired. Why add to Opal's worry quotient? She already has a lot of family members on her prayer list.

Christie waves at her, and the men raise their beers.

"Lonnie, I want a rematch after the way you cheated last year," Lindsey tosses out.

He pats his paunch. "Yeah, I've been in training. Maybe the second round. I need some more painkiller first, before I'm ready to play with Arlen." He waggles his beer bottle, then takes a long pull.

"Taking your goddamn sweet time, you yard-bird!" Arlen roars across the lawn at Lindsey. "Take those hoops over to the other end and plant 'em. We already got the post in, down by the pond."

Last year they had to dive for the wooden balls lost in the "water feature." That was after Don had lobbed one high with a golf-chipping swing (since banned) and narrowly missed braining Phyl on the sidelines. Maybe that was why she was safely indoors today on Opal duty.

Lindsey rounds up the kids. "Okay, remember, we hit one at a time, right? And you duck and cover your heads if the ball goes up into the air?"

The kids nod, then grab her hands and drag her toward the pond to finish setting up the course. Which involves lots of shrieking laughter and waving of mallets. Oh well, so far the only injury has been the year Fran hit her own foot trying to knock Arlen's ball into the woods.

This year the closest call is Bitsy getting too excited and losing her grasp on the mallet, sending it instead of the yellow-striped ball flying toward little Daryl and his blue stripes. Skip drops his beer bottle and jumps in to pluck Daryl out of the way, but Bitsy's so upset that Lindsey decides to deliberately miss the last goalpost and let Bitsy knock her ball into the woods. By some miracle, nobody's gone into the pond. Yet.

The brass ship's bell on the deck rings out. It's Opal, summoning them to assemble the shish kebabs. So far, so good.

Lindsey steps back to gauge the level of tension—these noisy family gatherings always a fine balance between exuberant chaos and vigilance for the signs of irritable exhaustion, which in her dad lead to outbursts of rage. It occurs to her, not for the first time, that the family reflex of monitoring Arlen's emotional state is right on a par with watching the kids for signs of overstimulation and crankiness. It's just that his tantrums wreak more destruct-ion.

Today they might sail through the shoals unscathed. As if by unspoken agreement, nobody's talking about Kevin. No political arguments yet, and even Lonnie, longtime employee of the local pulp mill, hasn't baited Lindsey about being a "tree hugger." Arlen has traded his Viking helmet for his baseball cap with the Navy veteran's insignia, and the guys are mellowed out with beer. The kids are just tired enough from the game to let Phyl shepherd them through the messy art project of putting together their shish kebab choices without skewering each other. Fran's beside Opal, stepping in right in time to take a heavy fruit platter just as her shaking hands are about to drop it and provide Arlen the perfect excuse to launch into one of his tirades. Everyone pulls up a chair around the fire, breathing out a sort of group sigh as the skewers ray out, propped on the metal rim, and the bacon-wrapped venison sizzles over the coals.

Lindsey, hanging back on the deck, pops a rare beer and dribbles a grateful libation over the edge onto the grass, a ritual she picked up in Central America. She takes a swallow and moves along the decimated table, assembling her own concoction of venison, fruits, and mini potatoes.

Over in the circle, even Joanie has loosened up, and Lindsey can hear her launching into one of her funny stories:

"Lordy love, I think I'm too old for this!" She gestures toward Eric's baby Kendra, now sleeping peacefully on her blanket in the shade. "I mean lugging around a big old baby on one hip and that huge diaper bag hanging on the other arm, and my back keeps reminding me it's fifty...." What she doesn't need to explain is that Kendra is over a year old now, but what with being a preemie, and who knows what drugs Tammy was on before or during the pregnancy, Kendra hasn't learned how to crawl yet. Joanie has to take her to physical therapy, and ends up carrying her a lot.

"...at work the other day. I mean, I was just telling myself I've got this under control. You know, I am Woman, I am strong...."

Lindsey hangs back on the deck, doesn't want to break up Joanie's flow, remind her of her grief and anger over Kevin, just as she's got everybody chuckling.

"So mid-afternoon the phone rings, it's the daycare center, looks like Kendra's got an ear infection and I need to get her to the doc. So I call the clinic, get the latest appointment I can but I still have to leave early, and you know what a crab the boss is. So I pull in to daycare to pick her up, then I realize I left the frigging diaper bag in Don's car because we had to make a last-minute switch that morning. I'd been thinking, well, it's only a ten-minute drive home, so I'll just give her a juice bottle and we'll be fine.

"Anyway, Kendra's screaming a blue streak, they practically lob her into my arms and slam the door, so I cuddle her right up and then realize she's got applesauce smeared all down her front and now I do, too. Well, okay, I can handle that. So I strap her into her baby seat and give her the bottle. I know we're supposed to be weaning her onto a sippy cup, but I just can't deal with it sometimes. She can't seem to get the hang of how to hold onto it, and she loves her bottle...."

"Hear, hear!" Ross raises his own bottle in recognition.

"Yeah, when are you guys gonna graduate to sippy cups?" Joanie shoots at him.

"Whatever works," Don interjects.

"Well, that's what I was saying to myself. I'm super-Grandma, just whisk her into the doc's, get some ear medicine, we'll be home in no time." Joanie shakes her head. "But noooo.... You don't *even* want to hear about the ordeal at the pharmacy. I'll get to that later. Anyway, I pull into the clinic lot, we're pushing it, but they better not cancel the appointment for only being five minutes late. Good! Kendra finished off the bottle. But she's still crying.

Then I realize she didn't drink it, she managed to spill it all down her front and she's sopping wet. And sticky purple. And her diaper's full. Oh, Lord."

By this time, everyone's laughing. Clearly Joanie's going for the comic release.

"So of course no diaper bag, no change of clothes, and she's screaming now, rubbing her ear, I've got to get her in there. The only thing in the car is Don's ratty old sweatshirt—"

"Hey, that's my favorite soccer team shirt!"

"Right, well now it's Kendra's dress. I strip her down and put that thing on her and I drag into the doc's office like some street druggie all smeared with goo and the baby in rags and would they by any chance have a diaper so I could change her? They're looking at me like, Social Services took the baby away from the mother and gave her to *you*?"

Hooting laughter from the circle. Joanie's shaking her head, and Lindsey stands frozen in awe that her little sister can be this strong. Just emerging from the self-absorption of her own double-whammy with the cancer and the divorce, she's grasping all that the family has been enduring.

Joanie's shoulders are shaking now, and Lindsey realizes she's not laughing. Don stands up, takes her shoulders and gets her to stand, guides her toward the deck steps. They come face to face with Lindsey.

She sets down her skewer, moves toward Joanie and starts to raise her arms, wanting to hug her.

Joanie stops short, scrubs angrily at her eyes, glares at Lindsey. "Not you. Don't *you* come looking for—" She breaks free of Don and stalks off into the house.

Don stands with his hands half-extended, staring. He finally shakes his head. "Hey, Lin...."

She blows out a breath. "It's okay."

"Goddamn!" Arlen breaks in helpfully. "What the hell's wrong with her?" Then, "Son of a bitch, her goddamn shish kebab's burning! Don, yours, too. Wake up, birdbrain!"

"Got it!" Lonnie struggles up from his chair, lunging over to grab the two skewers with the flaming bacon fat, but he trips and knocks into Fran's chair, tips his beer bottle spilling over her feet. The burning skewers, jostled, fall into the coals, taking along Opal's.

"Jesus fucking Christ!" Arlen roars and jumps up,

grabbing skewers and pulling them aside. "What the hell are you goddamn idiots—"

"Stop swearing!" Fran's dabbing at her sandals with her napkin.

Arlen thrusts the skewers onto the edge of the fire pit, steps over to grab her arm. "Don't you tell me what to do, you know-it-all little shit! Think you're the queen around here, the way you boss everybody around."

"I boss? *I* boss?" Fran scowls up at him. "Here's Mr. Lord of the Universe telling me—"

"Oh, don't!" An anguished cry from Opal. "I can't bear it!" Then she slaps her hands over her mouth and hunches over, rocking herself.

Arlen whirls and glares at her. "Oh, go piss on yourself, you old bag! Now it's one of *your* pitiful-me routines?"

"That's enough. We're out of here." Phyl stands up, face grim. "Come on, kids, you know the rule." The nieces and nephews have decided they won't subject *their* kids to the verbal abuse, so if Arlen starts in, they'll just pick up and leave these gatherings.

The kids start to protest, and Bitsy bursts out crying. "I want my shish kebab!"

"We'll stop at McDonald's, honey. You can get a toy." Phyl rounds them up in record time, brushing past Arlen, who's still ranting at Opal. He kicks a couple of the half-cooked skewers that have fallen over the edge of the metal rim. Fran commandeers Lonnie and Ross, and they're all moving, collecting their stuff.

Lindsey's still rooted on the deck, hot flash blazing through her on a surge of anger. She gives herself a shake and hurries down the deck steps to Opal, who's hunched over, hands covering her ears as Arlen vents, yelling down at her.

"Stop it, Dad!" Lindsey moves between them. "Can't you hear yourself?" She pulls Opal to her feet and guides her shuffling steps toward the house.

"You fucking whiners can all go straight to hell!" Arlen stomps off past the flagpole, kicking a croquet mallet aside as he heads for his shop. Black smoke rises from the charring skewers still propped over the coals.

Skip comes weaving drunkenly around the edge of the deck, pulling a hose. "Yeee-ha! Happy Fourth of July!" He grins and lets loose the spray over the charring mess, steam and smoke billowing in the breeze past the snapping red-white-and-blue.

fourteen

Dear Diary,
*   SOS! Take me away from this insane family! Reformat my genetic code! Now would be a good time for an alien spaceship abduction....*
*   Flashback: I'm four or five and hunkered in the sort of musty greenery-cave the shrubs made in the back yard, my arm around Ginger our golden lab, sending out pleas to the fairies to come and get me. I'm convinced they've abandoned me with this crazy human family, and I'm ready to go back to my real home. Not so much has changed since then....*

"Crap." Lindsey pushes her journal aside, shaking her head. "This was supposed to be funny, HighJinks."

Prince-of-the-household, enthroned on her lap over-seeing the writing process, yowls his opinion, then jumps up and sits on the page to make a more definitive statement.

"Critics," Lindsey mutters.

Sombra winds her usual circuitous path into the spare bedroom Lindsey has turned into her writing/library/"stuff" room. She makes a furry turn around Lindsey's ankles, then jumps onto her lap, kneading and giving a soft cry.

"Okay, lunchtime."

Both cats streak off toward the kitchen, Lindsey following. The phone rings.

"Lindsey. Hi." It's Newman.

"Oh." She grips the phone as lightheadedness ripples

through her. "Newman?"

All she can hear is static on the line now.

"Newman?"

"—and I'm.... Oh." Something clunking, clattering, then, "Oops! Lindsey, you there? I think I'm in the clear now."

Lindsey's anything but. Just the sound of his voice is sending her into the spins.

"Lindsey? Did I lose you?"

She clears her throat. "Newman, where are you? Still in Bali?" How long has it been since that other phone call? A week?

"No, just got out of SeaTac, I'm heading north. Man, every time I leave the country it's a jolt to get back on the freeway here, see all these cars with only one person instead of packed to the max."

She takes a steadying breath. "I felt the same way after Honduras."

"Listen, Lindsey." His voice sounds oddly rushed. "I'm kind of up against it, what with the trip running over with the monsoon and all. I've got to get some orders together, they're overdue already, everybody wants a piece of me, including Kimberly, she's out for blood again. I need to pick up Melani this afternoon, but...." A gusting breath, and Lindsey can feel the reset. "Could I stop by to see you first? Before it all hits?"

A smile spreads over her face. "Of course. I mean, I'm here."

"Lindsey, I...." There's some kind of static again. But it's not coming over the phone line, it's more a feeling. "Lindsey, when I finally got a replacement cell phone, I wasn't going to listen to your message, since you asked me not to. But... I gave in to temptation. I want to—"

More of that odd static, then a jolt of eagerness knifing straight through it that sets Lindsey's heart racing. But there's something else that blocks it, some kind of push/pull going on in his voice. "Lindsey, when you said you felt like Rumi's 'Guest House,' all those emotions running wild, you're not the only one. But I don't know if I can—" He cuts out again.

"Newman?"

"...timing. Damn! I'm losing reception. Listen, I'll be there in about an hour. Okay?"

"Oh. Yes." She's feeling lightheaded again, off balance.

"Okay." His voice settles, gentles. "See you soon."

Lindsey stands holding the receiver until the disconnect message starts nagging. She hangs up slowly, shaking her head. Her heart is pounding, and she can taste him, his kisses, the feel of his hands on her.... But what was that in his voice? What's going on? Why did she leave that ridiculous message, so needy?

"Damn!" A hot flash ignites, blossoming out from her core like a prickling rash. She rips off her shirt, then her sports bra. Lifts her hair off the back of her neck and heads to the bathroom for a cool washcloth. She blots her back and chest, her face, then stands braced over the sink, eyes closed and taking deep breaths, until the heat subsides. Her ears are ringing. Maybe that's where the static is coming from.

She looks at her watch. Heading for the bedroom, she halts, looks at the mess of scattered tea mugs, books, and magazines in the living room, rugs crying out for the vacuum, dust bunnies breeding with a deplorable lack of restraint under the couch. Not to mention that sink full of dishes in the kitchen. She starts forward, stalls, turns toward the kitchen, looks down at her bare breasts. Right. First: What to wear?

She opens the built-in closet in her bedroom, built for a simpler age—or midgets—and surveys the hangers jammed in. That soft olive-green silk blouse she treated herself to for her birthday, the one that sets off her eyes so nicely? Too fancy for an at-home day. A sundress? Skirt? She doesn't want to look like she's primped for a date.

She slams the cupboard closed and pulls open one of the drawers beneath it. Her favorite worn-smooth jeans she just managed to put a toe through when she was yanking them on, so now they're stylishly ripped in the knee? Just throw on a T-shirt like she'd ordinarily wear slopping around the house? But she doesn't want to look like she couldn't be bothered to make an effort. And, hey, why not wear something a little form-fitting? Show off her bod a bit?

Lindsey glances at her watch again. "Shit!" She opens the closet and yanks out a skimpy sundress she wears as a swimsuit coverup, pulls it on, makes a turn in front of the clouded old mirror mounted on the back of the door. Nice, but she really needs to wear a bra with it. She pulls open the underwear drawer, realizes most of her bras are outside drying on the backyard clothesline, gives up on the idea of the sundress and lets it drop around her feet. She pulls out an exercise tank with built-in shelf bra. Tugs it on and then remembers she has to fill out this one on the lumpectomy side, imagines Newman sexily sliding off her top only to have a piece of foam padding fall out. Not good.

She rips off the tank, rummages for one of the bras she's sewn pads into, but there's only older ones at the bottom of the drawer. "Damn."

She throws on a T-shirt at random, grabs a pair of running shorts from the other drawer, wads up the discarded selections and crams them into the bottom of the closet, slamming the doors once more. She heads for the back door to see if anything's dry on the line, but by this time she's worked up a sweat again, so she makes another dash into the bathroom to blot her face and chest. A glance in the mirror confirms the worst: hair straggling out of a loose braid, and to top off the hot flashes, this week her face has decided to break out in what looks like teenage acne. Thank you, berserk hormones.

Another glance at the watch. "Shit. Shit." More deep breaths.

Lindsey makes herself slow down, wash her face and brush her hair out. It doesn't look so bad after all, nice waves from the braid. Then she dabs on some spot concealer and a touch of eye shadow. She can't stand goopy makeup, and after all she doesn't want to scare the poor man, for heaven's sake.

Back on track for the backyard clothesline, cats picking up on her agitation and trailing her, darting around her ankles and tripping her. HighJinks nips at her bare toes.

"Please! Not today!" She resolutely ignores the dirty dishes and checks the old-fashioned line threaded between wheels on the garage and the porch. The bras are still damp, but one of them is almost dry. She grabs it off the line, hooks it around her waist and pulls it on under the tee.

Time check: "Damn." He'll be here any minute. What on earth is she wearing, anyway? She squints at some upside-down printing on the mud-brown shirt, something about the "Clamfest Fun Run" years ago, at least she can find a better shirt than this. So she dashes back through the kitchen, but the cats are really anxious by this time, mewing, and Sombra darts forward just in time to get accidentally kicked. She cries out and shoots away for the living room.

"Sombra, I'm sorry! I'm acting like a hormonally-deranged teenager." Is this love? Or "this is your brain on menopause"? She slows down, heads quietly into the living room to crouch next to the alarmed cat, who's backed against the armchair. "I didn't mean to hurt you, sweetie."

Lindsey takes slow, deep breaths, stroking gently down Sombra's back, finally lifting her against her chest.

Sombra starts to purr, then heaves and upchucks a messy fur ball and slimy grass down the front of Lindsey's shirt. Outside, a car pulls into the drive.

Great. Lindsey sets down the cat, darts back into the bedroom to yank open a drawer and blindly grab another T-shirt. She rips off the slimy one and drops it at her feet, pulls on a turquoise one with a dolphin and something she hopes is innocuous printed across the front.

A knock on the door.

Lindsey's ears are ringing again, jolts of eagerness and trepidation alternating through her. She takes one last deep breath and opens the door. The static roar in her ears peaks, then falls away.

Newman stands on the porch, hair rumpled, looking jet-lagged in a faded blue T-shirt with ripped-off sleeves, but all tanned and somehow glowing in the sunlight. He looks terrific.

"Lindsey. You look terrific."

He starts forward, hands raising, then stalls, pulling back. Lindsey is caught between that forward and backward movement, her own outstretched hand left hanging. She drops it. He's looking at her, something clouded in his eyes, conflicted.

Then, "Damn," he says, and takes a stride forward, wraps his arms around her, pulls her in close, her head against his chest. She can feel his heart thudding. His lips brush the top of her head.

Time melts into warm honey. He rocks, arms tightening around her as her own encircle his waist and they're moving together in a slow rooted dance. The heat pools where they're pressed together, rises up and outward, and he's hard, rubbing in a side-to-side rocking against her pelvis. She's flowing, she's the honey, he is, the warmth and taste of it as he's kissing her so deeply she's faint, losing her footing.

She pulls back to catch a breath, steady herself against his chest, and he strokes her hair, his hand oddly trembling.

"Lindsey, I'm dying to make love with you. But I don't know if it's fair. I don't know if I can be there for you, be the lover you need—"

She raises her fingers to his lips. "I want *you*. Now. It's okay."

He picks her up then, wraps her legs around his hips, carries her through the open doorway into the bedroom and lays her on top of the bed. He lowers himself slowly over her, hips still pulsing against hers, and now the honey's dissolving into those rolling blue waves from her dream. They surge, cresting and ebbing and cresting again, ocean deep power flowing through them. They are nothing in that immensity, just part of the tides and the salty currents.

Newman sighs, kisses her once more, then pulls back to reach down, loosen her clothes, finding entrances, palm sliding over her skin. Her hands are gliding, too, burrowing, and she's finding him, his broad warm chest and then lower to free his penis to her touch as he groans.

Footsteps outside, slapping up the porch steps.

Lindsey startles, realizes they left the front door open.

The footsteps clatter onto the wooden porch, and there's a rustle of papers. A pause then. A cough, a sharp rattle and clunk of the metal mailbox mounted against the outside wall, and then footsteps hastily retreating. Lindsey cranes her head to look out the open bedroom window toward the porch, looks back into Newman's eyes. They burst out laughing.

"Hoo, boy." Lindsey struggles upright, shaking her head to clear it. She staggers out into the living room to shut the front door. When she returns to the bedroom, Newman is pulling the gauzy curtains to soften the light to a pale suffusion of green.

He turns, smiles into her eyes, reaches out to tug at her shirt. He pauses and tilts his head to read from it: "Divers do it deeper?"

Lindsey looks down at what she now remembers was a souvenir from a long-ago Caribbean trip. She raises her palms. They both laugh.

Newman sobers, holding her gaze. He eases the shirt off her, reaches around to unhook her bra, runs his palms slowly over her breasts. "You are beautiful." He kneels to tug her shorts down, leans in to press his face against her belly, breathing her in, kissing her.

Somehow she gets his clothes off him and they're back on the bed, back in those salty waves, and diving is nothing to this immersion. They're sliding and rolling dolphin-slippery over and around each other, he's inside her, and she's gone, she's completely here, she's the ocean taking him in, he's taking her deeper, and when she can't contain any more she cries out and dissolves.

She's drifting away, but he's still there. Inside her, pushing down to another layer through the soft darkness, carrying her along. He's unfolding her, unwrapping her core, unwinding long ribbons of undulating touch and she doesn't know if she can do this, open so far into annihilation and yet be filling simultaneously with so much. But her body knows better, and it leads now—down so far, it's up. Streams of light are swirling around them, shimmering and twining and floating them up and down in a new kind of pulsing rhythm as they're weightless and flying into the heart of this flesh mandala.

They reach the center of unbearable intensity, and he cries out, shattering the glowing web. She echoes him, reverberating. They sink back into themselves, rocking slowly down into two joined bodies on the bed.

"Oh, my...." Newman touches her face, draws his fingers down over her contours as if to restore her to herself. He's still pulsing gently against her, within her, as they lie there cradled in their joining. His lips softly brush hers, and he breathes into her, takes in her breaths, kisses her lightly, their lips barely touching as they share this breathing. Suddenly, lancing between them, a bittersweet longing—strange, with their bodies still entwined.

Newman rolls onto his back and pulls Lindsey to lie with her head on his shoulder, his arms around her. "Mmmm...."

He slides into deeper breathing, into sleep, as she lies there floating just above it, basking in this peace. An uprush of delight fills her, fountaining over them. She settles into him, smiling.

Newman's heartbeat, beneath Lindsey's ear, has settled into a slow, even rhythm. He begins to snore quietly, and she smiles, wondering when he last slept. He twitches then, arms tightening around her, and he wakes up with a funny little snort, to blink into her eyes.

He smiles. "I can't remember when I've felt this... completely relaxed."

She touches his chest, over his heart. "Feels like this is how it should be." Another uprush of emotion fills her, and her vision blurs.

"Lindsey." His voice is gentle, his hand stroking her hair. "This is...." His hands lift like wings, then settle again. "I am so drawn to you. Seems like we hardly have a choice but to make love if we so much as look at each other. But... I'm mixed up. I don't know if I'm ready for this."

A cold stab in her gut. This is what was in his voice on the phone. "Oh." She starts to pull away, brushing her fingers over her damp eyes.

"No, stay here. Please." He urges her back down to rest on his shoulder. "Lindsey, I'm not a talker, seems like words don't always communicate the best way for me. But I want to tell you about being in Bali this time. Maybe it was sharing with you, being with you, before I left, but...."

He takes a deep breath, blows it out. "Being there, with the monsoon hitting and hunkering down with the villagers, and going out to see the temple we'd built years ago. It was exciting again. Being alive. I guess I didn't realize how those last years of my marriage had sort of shut me down, and then the divorce was so bad. Still is, dealing with Kimberly.... But I reconnected in Bali. I remembered how life used to be an adventure. How the work I was doing then meant something, building the temples, passing on my teacher's wisdom, and I was living fully in the moment." He shakes his head. "This isn't coming out right."

She nods into his shoulder. "Keep going."

"I was thinking about you. A lot. Wanting to feel you again, make love to you, open you up like a gift to both of us and find out all about you." He sighs. "And I just don't know...It was taking me away from that being back in the moment, that coming back to myself." A little shrugging movement. "Maybe finding healing."

"But...." Lindsey doesn't know what he's trying to say. "You think this is bad? I'm hurting you?" She touches his chest again, hesitantly this time.

"No. No, that's not it." His arms tighten around her for a moment, then loosen. "It's just...when I heard your message, talking about the 'Guest House' poem, and I heard all that in your voice, too—so much turmoil like I've been going through over the divorce, and way before. I felt overwhelmed, Lindsey. Like this is too much, too fast."

Lindsey pulls away from him, sitting up to take a deep breath, stabbed by the ice again. "But—how can this be bad, Newman? What we just.... Don't tell me you didn't feel that! It's so...right. That's how it's supposed to be between lovers." She can't start doubting her perceptions again, the way she did with Nick, letting him drive her to questioning her own sanity.

He reaches for her hand, squeezes it. "I'm not denying that connection, Lindsey. It's what I'm going to do *about* it."

She shakes her head. "So what about that Rumi poetry you gave me? What he says about the true lover being a lunatic.... How can we really *be* in this life unless we surrender to the mystery, maybe the chaos? Stop trying to control it? I've been tight for so long, guarding myself against being hurt, the way being with Nick was hurting me. But I can't live that way anymore. I think I'd rather be dead than go back to that."

"Don't, Lindsey. Don't go back to that." He tugs on her hand, so she meets his gaze, intent on her. "Don't close your heart. Just maybe...guard it a little." He sighs and looks up at the ceiling. "You know, with Rumi, he's talking about spiritual love."

She nods. "Like the way John Donne wrote those love sonnets to God. But there's a reason for the sexual metaphors. It's the same in the end, isn't that the point? It's *loving* that matters."

Silence for a moment. Then he swallows. "I don't know. I never had this...chemistry in my marriage. I got hurt by those years. Sleeping beside a beautiful woman who'd taunt me, then deny me, so I sort of shut off sexually."

"Newman! What a fool she was, doing that to you. Throwing away such delight for both of you. You're a *wonderful* lover."

"Thank you." He kisses Lindsey's palm. "You are beyond wonderful."

"But how could you go on like that?"

"The marriage actually got easier once she finally shut me out of her bedroom. We were living in opposite ends of the house, but I thought we could stay a family, for Melani. By that time, I'd pretty much accepted that I just wasn't a man who *could* be a proper lover to a woman, and I got used to living like I was a single parent, not needing that other kind of intimacy. I figured since I have such deep connections in spirit with my teacher and my own... students, I guess I'd call them, maybe that's enough? And now I have to be honest and tell you I'm confused. I don't know if all this passion with you is what I want to get swept up in. At least right now. I don't know if I can afford to."

Lindsey sits back, staring at him. The cold has spread into a sick heaviness inside her. After what they just shared, he can say this? Didn't that connection *mean* something? She looks at him, and suddenly he is the stranger her rational self has been warning her about.

"Lindsey, please." He's looking her in the eyes again. "It's not that I don't feel tempted to dive right in. Just now, that was...." He shakes his head, lifts and spreads his hands. "But my life now is so complicated, I'm juggling like mad to hold it all together after the divorce." He takes another deep breath. "Kimberly really went after me when I finally had to get out, she got these hardcore lawyers and maybe I gave in too much, but I needed it to be over with. Anyway, the settlement, buying her out of the business, pretty much wiped out my credit line for my wholesale trade. I'm scrambling to get back on decent footing, making these extra consulting trips to get some cash flow, had to sell some of my land where I'd been hoping someday I could build another temple, a place where people here could come to meditate...."

He sighs. "And Melani needs a lot right now, she's in a rough stretch, still doing P.T. and counseling. She and Kimberly fight all the time, and I need to be there for her, need to be calm...." He closes his eyes, lets out a breath.

"Newman." Lindsey puts out a hand to touch his. "I didn't realize how hard it's been for you, too. You seem so serene most of the time."

He opens his eyes to meet hers, and his lips quirk into a wry smile. "Sometimes I'm on autopilot. I mean, maybe I'm better than most at letting things flow over me—it's my training, learning not to be attached. I call on my teacher when I get all tangled up, and he's there with me in spirit. So when I ask him for guidance with all this, now, of course he says to listen to my heart. And it says I need to put Melani first, take care of her, keep it together for her until things settle down."

Lindsey tilts her head, considering what's behind the words. He did try to warn her, and she plunged ahead anyway. She gives him her own wry smile. "Newman, I'm not asking you to throw your life aside, for heaven's sake. Of course you have to take care of Melani first."

His face lights up. "Lindsey, someday you have to meet her! She is incredible. Just looking at her sometimes, I feel so full, I'm ready to burst."

Lindsey eyes are prickling again. She'll never know that feeling.

He blows out a breath. "Then other times I think I'll never survive having a teenager." He reaches to stroke Lindsey's arm, tug her gently down to rest on his shoulder. "After I gave in and listened to your message—I can't believe I was that weak, that's another thing I...."

He starts over, "Lindsey, I realized things were moving so fast between us, I was building all kinds of scenarios in my mind, putting us both in those boxes we're just crawling out of. We're still healing, we need to find out who we are now without a bunch of expectations getting put on us. I decided I had to tell you I couldn't do this. I decided I was going to be celibate again until my life settled down."

He tilts his head to look at her face, and raises his eyebrows. "Well, that resolution lasted a whole day."

He chuckles. "The minute I saw you, felt you, that was out the door." Then he sobers. "Lindsey, what I was trying to say when I got here is I don't know if I can give you what you want. You deserve a man who's really *there* for you. I can't give you that right now. Maybe it's not in me."

"I don't believe that. I can feel your heart, Newman."

"Then can you be with me, when we get time to be together, and not expect the standard package? Some pre-set definition of what lovers are *supposed* to be? Can we just *be* with it?"

Lindsey thinks about it and has to admit, chagrined, that in the whirl of infatuation she's been plugging Newman and herself into the old scenarios, painting pictures of him as her new life partner. If she's honest with herself, she also has to admit she's been indulging in every fairy-tale cliché right down to the tinkle of wedding bells. (Maybe that's the ringing in her ears?) And after Nick, the last thing she needs is another husband. She certainly has enough on her own plate to deal with these days.

One more chill at the thought of always being on her own—cold comfort being a liberated woman all alone—but maybe that's the point. She can't be the lover she wants to be if she isn't strong, first, in herself.

She shrugs, lifting her palms. "Somewhere along the line, somebody told me, 'Expectations are what kill you daily.' But it's not so easy to live without *some* kind of plans." She leans down to inhale the delicious scent of his skin that's teasing at her attention. "Like maybe what I want to do with you next time I get your clothes off...." Her lips wander down over the curly hair on his chest, then lower across his belly.

He chuckles and catches her hand, pulls it to his lips and kisses her palm. Then admits, "Parts of me are saying, 'Enough with all this philosophy, pal—we're ready for some good old attachment, right now.'"

Lindsey pulls her hand free, sliding her tongue down over his belly to find his erect penis. "And this part would be Livingston, I presume?" She licks its salty length, and it pulses to her touch. "Mmmm."

"Oh, boy. That does it." He grips her shoulders, pulls her up over his chest and presses her pelvis tight against him, kissing her, sliding his palms down over her buttocks and thighs. The electric pulsation crackles between them, Lindsey's breath catching in her throat.

Newman rolls her over onto her back, starts to lower himself onto her, then pauses. "I have to warn you, Lindsey. I'm...maybe I'm dangerous these days, if you're not careful.

You may be opening up Pandora's box."

Lindsey laughs, feeling suddenly wild, reckless, the taste and touch of his skin on hers driving her crazy, and she just wants him, needs him, inside her again. "Newman," she manages, "the only thing dangerous here was the mailman spying on us."

He doesn't laugh, just kisses her again, fiercely, and they're off and flying once more.

Finally they lie there, catching their breaths. "Phew. So much for being all sane and mature past fifty," she manages.

"If I have a heart attack, I'll die happy," he responds.

They laugh, shaking together. Lindsey cranes back to see his face, and he's looking a bit shell-shocked, the same way she's feeling.

The phone rings.

"Damn. What time it is, anyway?" Newman's making untangling motions among their sprawled limbs.

"Just ignore it," Lindsey mumbles.

"It's my cell phone. Must be Melani, I'm probably late." He heaves himself upright, drops to his knees among their pile of discarded clothes. He gropes, finally coming up with his phone as it stops ringing. "Damn. It's her, I *am* late."

He rises to lean over the bed, runs a hand down Lindsey's side, gives her one last, deep kiss. He sits on the edge of the bed. "I hate to do this, but I've got to go. I promised Melani I'd pick her up and take her to a horse show this evening. She can't compete again yet, with the knee, but she wants to cheer on her friends." He leans over to gather up his clothes.

Lindsey groans.

"Welcome to my life." He turns to meet her eyes. "I won't be able to see you again until next week. You sure you want to do this?"

She answers honestly, "Do I have a choice?"

"Always."

"Then, yes." Like Scarlett O'Hara, she'll think about it tomorrow.

"Okay." He smiles, jumps up. "I better rinse off and head

out." He motions her down as she starts to sit up. "Stay there. Take a nap so I can have one vicariously."

He starts toward the doorway, then halts, lifting one foot to peer down as he's balancing with his arms full of his clothes. "Uh, what did I just step in?"

Lindsey raises herself up to see the discarded brown T-shirt. "Oh! Sombra's upchucked fur ball." She snorts, fall back onto the bed. "Welcome to *my* world."

He chuckles, and Lindsey subsides sleepily into the tangled sheets, drifting as she hears the shower spatter. It sounds like rain after a drought. She's almost asleep when Newman comes back into the bedroom, starts toward the bed, then turns to pull the paisley silk shawl off the chair and drape it gently over her. He leans down to kiss her forehead. He's here. He's gone.

fifteen

Dear Diary,

Back in the saddle! I'd forgotten how it feels to be walking bowlegged the morning after...that womb-deep, sweet aching when your lover has well and truly plumbed your depths.

sigh I do wish he could have stayed to sleep with me—two days later, and I'm missing him already—but maybe that's just life/love at this age. So many commitments tugging at us all, we can't just plunge into immersion in a love affair the way we did when we were young. This is feeling out new territory. And if I'm honest with myself, I have to admit there's a safety net in knowing he's got all those ties on his time, that we can't over-indulge the impulse to just swim in being together. I keep my own space as my quiet retreat. After Nick and the way he sucked me dry on a daily basis with his demands for emotional caretaking, his possessiveness, his out-of-control venting, a little detachment may be just the ticket.

Of course I write all this very maturely in the daylight hours. Then at night I drown in the longing, that aching to be filled with Newman's touch, thirsting for his voice. Wanting to wake up beside him.

He did call to see if I was okay with the "hit and run," so he sees it, too. I will be brave. Strong. Independent. (Rewind and repeat....)

Lindsey puts a bold face on it and marches herself off to the hospital's community forum on the park access proposal. More delayed July fireworks!

The players:

Hospital Director and Board. Meeting hosted by none other than her friend and yours, Mr. Sincerity Roger Stone. Disarmingly "just folks" in a golfing shirt and friendly grin.

Allen Dunshire, the hospital attorney, in his crisply trimmed hair and suit, discreetly posted to the side. As Lindsey slips anonymously into the back of the packed conference hall, he lifts his head to catch her eye. Was that a raised eyebrow?

City traffic planner, harassed-looking forty-something woman in a rumpled linen jacket.

Citizens of all ages, shapes, and colors, packing the folding chairs, restlessly prowling the coffee urns and decimated donut boxes (Crispy Cremes?) at the back of the hall.

The Environmental Coalition staked out in the front rows, passing fact sheets along the aisles, strategically seeded throughout the seats to trigger "spontaneous" ripples of protest, catcalls, boos to the hospital infomercials. (Technique #5 in Nick's agency guide to public demonstration dynamics.)

And speak of the devil: Ex-husband Nick Papetti, minus bullhorn but front row center. Smug and too-handsome, graying dark hair sleeked back, a little longer now. His pretty young brunette girlfriend in Sierra Sports fleece, earnest and nodding, passes instructions down the line.

Silent observer, ex-wife ex-hospital employee midlife-crisis expert Lindsey Friedland hunches in the back row, listening to the bland assurances from the hospital entourage. Then they open for questions.

Weekly Whiplash editor Damon Perrera stands in the audience to introduce himself. (Hel-lo! Fortyish with long black hair in a braid, luscious coffee-with-cream skin, and flashing dark eyes.... Hmmm. Every straight woman with blood still circulating turns to take in the eye candy.) A glimmer of humor in those Latin-lover eyes? as he earnestly? lobs a question at the city traffic planner:

"With all due respect, our readers would like to know, just to clear up any appearance of irregularity in the due process here, why there has been no publicly-posted environmental-impact assessment before this meeting...?"

And the fireworks ignite!

First to his feet among the chairs, one of the watchdog agency field workers, bellowing, "That's what we've been asking for, for months! Cut the bullshit and give us some straight answers!"

A blue-haired raging granny pushes forward with a "Save the Nesting Owls!" placard, managing to whack one of the hospital ushers in the noggin with it.

Head of the neighborhood coalition stands with a clipboard, pointing her pen, futilely raising her voice against a swelling growl.

The traffic planner taps her microphone. "We're pursuing the best balance to serve the taxpayers...."

She's drowned out by an angry roar whipped up on cue by the flashpoint hecklers.

Roger Stone stands, still all "aw-shucks, folks." He starts, "Just let us explain how this process works" into his mike, a bead of sweat rolling down his face.

There's a familiar, crooked little smile on Nick's face as he stands and tilts his head toward the back. Into the hall comes streaming a line of schoolkids in Campfire Girl and Boy Scout uniforms with crayon drawings of frogs, hawks, cedar trees, and baby owls, raising a banner: SAVE OUR PARK!

Everyone is on their feet then, applauding, cheering.

Worth the price of admission: Damon Perrera whips up a camera just in time to snap the look of dismay on Roger Stone's face as he sinks back onto his chair.

Lindsey joins Megan at the Grizzly Bear that Friday night, where the funky country-rock band Joe has recently put together is playing. He and his cronies—all old rock'n rollers who've shaken their performance personae out of mothballs—are getting down on the stage, gray or balding, maybe a bit paunchy and jowly, but pouring it out in sweat and foot-stomping rhythms.

"Hey, if this is his midlife crisis, I'm grooving on it!" Megan shouts over the throbbing bass and drums. "Better than an affair or a red Corvette any day!" She beams, dangly earrings bobbing as she raises her beer mug. She's morphed into her younger Lindsey's-roommate self, strutting her stuff tonight in a swirly ruffled cowgirl skirt and boots, a lowcut blouse displaying her Rubenesque cleavage.

"Yazzuh!" Crystal's ponytailed life-partner Micah leans over to click his mug against Megan's and Lindsey's, beer sloshing.

Crystal laughs and clicks her Pure Springwater spilling its own libation over the table. "Come on, let's dance!" She leads the way, hippie skirt trailing as she tugs Micah's hand. He, in turn, grabs Megan, who snags Lindsey for a conga line onto the dance floor.

They snake through the crowd—a mixed bunch from gray hairs on down to the summer college contingent—and pick up some more attachments to the line, swaying and kicking out in unison. Laughing, they break apart into partners and singles all doing their thing to the beat. Joe, the front man on electric guitar and vocals, launches into a cover of "Love the One You're With" just as Lindsey feels a tap on her shoulder from behind.

It's HotDawg Horner, grinning. Lindsey hasn't seen him since their "date night" at the Theater Guild. He shouts over the music, "Lindsey! You're looking fine! Wanna dance?"

Lindsey raises her palms in a "here we are," and gestures him into the fray. She's feeling frisky, even wore a short skirt to show off her tanned legs, which Ted is checking out as they dance. Megan spins closer, and it's a threeway as she gives Ted a high-five and he gestures toward Joe, gives him a thumb's-up over the crowd.

"Whoo-Whee!" Ted goes into a comical barnyard strut, winking over at Lindsey.

She laughs and spins just to enjoy the dizzy silliness.

Joe revs into a repeat chorus about loving the one you're with, as the band builds to a crescendo and the dancers are raising their hands to clap overhead and sing along, even the young kids who weren't born yet when these songs first rocked Lindsey's generation.

She shrugs inwardly with a little pang, wishing Newman had been able to break free of his "dad night" to come down. The days of loving whoever's handy are water under the bridge of all those old hippie notions, but, hey, "dance with the one you're with" she can go for. She laughs as Ted moves in to take her hand and give her a swing spin and a dip into the final chords.

"All right!" The crowd is cheering Joe and the band.

"Peace!" Joe beams and flashes the peace sign. He takes a drink from his water bottle, wipes his face on the sleeve of his plaid shirt hanging open over a black tee, confers with the drummer, then turns back to the dancers. "Okay, we're gonna mellow out for a few—"

Roars of protest from the dancers. "Come on! Keep it up!"

Joe laughs, and the bass guitar guy, whom Lindsey doesn't know, cracks, "Despite Tina Turner, sometimes it's *good* to go 'nice and easy.'"

Joe adds, "No heart attacks tonight, folks." He strums a chord. "Since we're ambling down memory lane, this one's for the heart of my heart. And is Megan looking hot tonight!"

Everyone laughs as Megan beams and does a spin, skirt flaring.

The band starts in on "Our House," and Megan goes still, giving Joe a look that brings tears to Lindsey's eyes. Megan blows Joe a kiss, then they all head back to the table. Ted, staying close to Lindsey, puts a hand on her back and pulls out her chair.

"Thanks." She looks up, then past him to the tall man standing by the bar, watching. She blinks. It's Newman.

He smiles and heads over to the table.

"Newman! You made it!" Megan jumps up, gives him an exuberant hug. "Thought you were tied up?"

He gives her a squeeze. "I got away for a bit. I have to pick up Melani in an hour, but I wanted to catch Joe for at least a couple songs."

Megan beams and gestures toward the stage, where Joe is singing the love song for Megan. She blows him another kiss, then tugs Newman down onto a chair beside her.

She starts introducing him to Crystal and Micah, who lean forward, cupping their ears over the ruckus, then to Lindsey across the table from them. She shouts, "And you remember Lindsey, of course."

A hiccup in the flow, as the music carries on. Lindsey hasn't shared with Megan whatever it is going on between Newman and her, has no handy label for it.

Newman raises his brows, eyes glinting with amusement as he tilts his head toward Lindsey. "Oh, yes. I remember."

Lindsey gnaws her lip, biting down on an insane surge of lust for him. "How are you, Newman?" she manages, playing along.

"Fine." He gives her a slow smile.

"Hi. I'm Ted Horner. Guess somehow we never met," Ted bellows over the music. "But I think Megan said you went to Northshore High?" He sticks his hand across the table, and Newman shakes it.

Ted settles back into his chair beside Lindsey, managing to edge closer, laying his arm possessively across the back of her chair. She gives him a surprised look. She glances back at Newman, who is still looking amused. Then Megan leans over to say something to him and he shakes his head, points to the band as the music is revving back into some loud country-rock and the dancers are streaming onto the floor again. Megan leans closer to his ear, talking, and Newman nods, answers something Lindsey doesn't catch.

Ted raises the arm behind Lindsey, presses fingers against her shoulder, asks if she wants to dance.

She raises her palms, points to her ears, pretends she can't hear him and gestures toward the cutesy "Bucks and Does" sign hanging under an antique rifle, making her escape as Newman's still busy catching up with Megan. In the Doe room, she takes a deep breath and pats cool water over her face, looks in the mirror. She's flushed, hair curling in damp tendrils around her face, eyes vivid green. She takes another deep breath, resists the impulse to fly back to the table and sweep Newman into her arms. Her ears are buzzing again.

She manages to walk sanely, making it halfway back to the table when Crystal, dancing with Micah, catches her arm and leans in to shout in her ear, "That's the Newman that Megan's been talking about?" She points back toward the table. "Somehow I pictured him taller. That other guy, the one who just came in"—she points toward Newman, she's managed in the ruckus to confuse him and Ted—"he was watching you dance, Lindsey. There's some kind of vibe there. *He's* the one you should go for!" She beams and flows back into the dance, arms weaving the air.

Lindsey, shaking her head, starts back toward the table. She takes another deep breath, taps Newman on the shoulder, and leans down. "Do you want to dance?"

He turns in his chair to look up at her, smiling. He hesitates, then says, "I'm not much of a dancer. I'd rather sit and watch you."

Lindsey's standing there awkwardly, appreciating the traditional male predicament, how they risk it being the ones who ask.

Ted stands up quickly, comes around and takes Lindsey's arm. "Let's dance!" He tugs her toward the crowd, and Lindsey glances back at Newman.

He's looking amused again, damn him.

What the hell. She throws herself into the driving rhythm and gets down with all the dancers, Ted grinning and stomping along. The band segues immediately into another rough and ready rock song, and by the time the drums crash into a climax, she's sweating and Ted looks ready for the coronary care unit. He shouts something over the din, and she laughs, blots her forehead on her arm.

Back at the table, Newman leans over to refill her glass from the beer pitcher. "That looked like thirsty work." He winks. "No 'nice and easy' for you?"

"Man, that's for sure!" Ted says, pushing his glass forward.

Newman tops it off for him, then turns back to Lindsey. "I remember you used to ride your bike a lot. You still like to ride *it* hard, too?" He gives it an innuendo no one else seems to catch over the pulsing music, but Lindsey nearly bursts out laughing.

"Definitely," she says, holding his gaze and licking the rim of her beer mug. "Sometimes I wake up saddle sore."

Newman chokes on a sip of beer and hastily sets his mug down.

Megan's looking back and forth from Lindsey to Newman, a puzzled frown creasing her brow.

"Well, I've got to run, or I'll have one testy sixteen-year-old on my hands." He stands.

"Hey, great to meet you, Newman." Ted offers his hand to shake, managing to edge closer to Lindsey in the process.

Newman raises a hand to everyone, starts to turn, then leans down toward Lindsey. "Say, Lindsey, I saw a bike club flyer up front about a...ride you might be interested in." He gestures, and Lindsey follows him toward the door.

He grabs her hand and tugs her outside onto the sidewalk.

Lindsey's chuckling. "Did you see the look on Megan's face? She's wondering why you're suddenly such a cycling aficionado."

He shakes his head. "Hope this doesn't make us public property, but I couldn't resist. You know, Megan's been after me to ask you out."

Lindsey rolls her eyes. "She's been all over me to call *you.*"

He tugs her closer. "Saddle sore?"

She laughs. "A little. But ready to climb back on...."

"Good." He pulls her into his arms and kisses her.

Damn, his lips feel good. She's pressing in close, and his hand's on her butt pulling her even tighter, those hot waves pulsing between them as she feels him harden against her.

"Oh, boy." He pulls back with a rueful laugh. "Now you've got me going! And I'm late to pick up Melani again." But he doesn't go, he draws her in for one more slow, delicious kiss, and Lindsey is ready to melt right down into her high-stepper dance shoes.

Finally he pulls back. "I *will* get back to you soon. To... un-finish this." He's off.

Lindsey, reeling, staggers back toward the doorway.

"Holy shit!" Standing there, her eyes round with astonishment, it's Megan.

Saturday night, and Lindsey's working on transcendence.

It shouldn't matter that it's the weekend—she's on her own work schedule now—and she's home alone. Well, with a book on her lap and a cat pressed close on each side. She's longing for Newman and those crazy kisses in the street.

Her ears are buzzing, the sound of static crescendoing. She closes her eyes and she can feel him, that solid male heft of him pulling her close, merging into her, but this is no deep blue ocean peace, more a raging gale and choppy waves flinging foam. She's tossed up and plunged down into the troughs. Then his arms are catching her, pulling her in as his lips open her up and he's thrusting inside her—

The phone rings.

"Phew." Blinking, shaking her head to clear it, Lindsey leans forward on the couch to grope for the phone. HighJinks and Sombra, affronted, leap down.

"Hello?"

"Lindsey." It's Newman, his voice an oddly agitated sort of whisper.

"Newman." She tries to catch her breath. "I was...just thinking about you."

"And you're sending out tsunami waves." A short laugh, his voice husky. "Lindsey, I keep feeling you, even long distance."

Lindsey doesn't know what to think about these...co-incidences? Astral connections? Newman seems so matter-of-fact about the spiritual dimension, like it's just another aspect of reality, and Lindsey can't decide if she's drawn to learn more, or wary about that very attraction.

Newman's clearing his throat. "I'm not used to this kind of energy, Lindsey." He's still speaking just above a whisper. "I can't wait to be inside you again."

Lindsey blinks, puts aside her confusion. "Why don't you come over?"

A gust of breath. "I've got Melani again tonight. I always take extra days with her when I've been gone on trips. We've been having fun today, took her and her friends out for dinner, and now they're inside watching a DVD movie. Then I have to take them home, try to get her settled down to bed before midnight so I can take her to visit my Dad tomorrow. I'm out on the dock right now."

With that, Lindsey gets a visceral flashback to that solstice day with him, standing close, naked and dripping wet. And inside the sauna, heat of the fire and more penetrating her to the core. "Mmm."

"Mmm is right." Another breathless little laugh. "I'm hard just thinking about you, Lindsey. And when I picture you in that sexy little skirt you had on last night.... Man, you better watch it. I wanted to rip it off you right there."

"I wanted you to. Right there in the street."

"Is this what they call phone sex?" he asks. Then,

lowering his voice again, "Oh, man, I better keep it down, sound carries like hell over the water. I just—" A break, then he comes back hastily, "Damn, that's Melani out in the yard looking for me. They must be done with the movie. And here I am with a big old hard-on. Gotta calm down." He blows out a breath. "Listen, Lindsey, I was hoping to take you for a hike later in the week, but can I come by tomorrow? I have to drive down to Seattle for business after I drop Melani off, but I could squeeze in.... I mean—"

Lindsey chuckles. "I'd like to squeeze you in, Newman. Squeeze you in real tight."

"Don't do that to me!" He laughs, too. "All right, down boy. About noon, then?"

"Okay."

"Okay, gotta go. Sweet dreams, Lindsey."

TO: Lindsey Friedland
FROM: HotDawg Horner
SUBJECT: Good Times take two, etc.

Lindsey, what a blast dancing with you to Joe and the boys cooking up some groovin' tunes! Let's do it again soon.

Don't worry, Megan just told me you and Newman have something going. I wouldn't have guessed.

Hey, he better treat you right! If I was your man, I'd make you feel like a queen. You deserve it.

Luv (just friends unless you tell me different),
Ted

"Lindsey, you sly dog! What's the idea keeping secrets from me?" It's Megan on the phone.

"Oh." Lindsey, caught with an armful of laundry and grabbing the phone thinking it's Newman on his way over, spins gears. "I didn't...."

"Looked to me like you definitely *did!*" Megan laughs. "What's with this coy routine at the Grizzly Bear? Here I was clueless, figured oh well, all my matchmaking talents really fell flat on this one. Then he's practically taking you down in the street! Whoo-whee!"

"Megan...." Lindsey rolls her eyes, drops the damp laundry into a basket, and sits on the back step with the phone.

"So how long has this been going on?" She chuckles. "Isn't that a song? Dish me the dirt, girl!"

"Megan," Lindsey repeats with a sigh, "I don't *know* what's going on. That's why I didn't tell you. It just happened."

"When? Friday night? You're kidding!"

"No, no. Right before he left on his trip to Bali. So we haven't had much time together." She takes a deep breath, lets it out. "It's kind of confusing."

"Oh, really."

"Yeah, really." Lindsey laughs, despite the flutters in her gut as she glances at her watch. Almost noon. "Listen, Megan, Newman's dropping by any time now, so I can't really talk. How about we get together for lunch?"

"It'll have to be next week—I've got a conference I'm heading off to on Wednesday. But listen, Lin," her voice settling into serious mode, "what's up with the secrecy routine? When I was hinting around to Newman, before, about asking you out, he told me he wasn't ready to date. And some bilgewater about not wanting to upset Melani, no room for anyone else in his life right now, yah-da-yah. Is this some kind of head game he's playing?"

Lindsey blows out a breath. "It's not like that. We're both a little confused maybe, like how *do* you go about all this at our age? And he got really hurt in his marriage—"

"Yeah, like you didn't."

"Well, that's a good reason to take it slow, feel out what we want out of this."

"Hmm. Didn't look too slow in the sex department there." Megan won't cut her an inch of slack.

"Well, okay, it's insane. I mean, the chemistry is wild."

"That was moderately obvious."

"But we talked about it. We want to...stay out of the box with this. Just let it be what it's going to be. Stay in the moment."

"Lin, are you having an acid flashback on me? That sounds like some old hippie mantra."

Lindsey sighs. "This isn't coming out right."

"Listen, girlfriend." Megan is serious now. "I love both of you to pieces, and I know Newman's a good guy, maybe he's just mixed up right now. But don't you dare let him treat you like booty call, you hear me? You stand up for yourself! If he wants you, then he treats you with respect around your friends. And his. Right?"

"Megan...."

"Right? No more being a man-pleaser for a guy who doesn't treat you right. Remember, Lin?"

She stiffens, gripping the phone. "Megan, I hear you. I know you're trying to protect me." She takes yet another deep breath. "But I'm *okay* now." She wants to believe it, despite her own nibbling doubts. "I'm exploring again. So let's leave it at that for now. Let's talk when you get back to town."

"Well." She sounds a bit huffy. "Don't let me inter*fere.*" Then she laughs. "Okay, you called me out on that one, sweetie. I just...hey, I love you. Don't get hurt on me again, okay?"

Lin's throat tightens. "Okay. Talk soon." She swallows. "And Megan? Thanks for being there."

"Can't miss me. So go for it, you little hottie!"

Lindsey sets down the phone and sits staring out at the yard, poppy pods swaying on their stalks in a warm breeze. Sombra darts out from under the rhodies, comes over to her for a pet. HighJinks, who's been flopped out basking on the sunny driveway, streaks over to pounce on Sombra, who boxes his ears and huffs off. HighJinks sublimates by jumping the beach rock again, humping it wildly.

Lindsey groans. "Not now...."

Is Megan right? Is Newman's talk about staying free of expectations and rigid roles just so much hot air? Is she getting "gaslighted" again? Does he want to keep her *in* a box, as "booty call?" The ugly phrase stirring her doubts. But at the same time, she sees what Newman was talking about, everyone already jumping in to define them as what a couple should be.

The phone rings again.

"Megan?" More last-minute advice?

"No, it's Newman."

"Oh, hi. I was just talking with Megan."

"Oh. Right. Listen, Lindsey," his voice sounding rushed,

"I'm sorry, but it's just not going to work out today."

"Oh."

Static, then, "Damn, the phone's cutting out under these freeway overpasses, so I better be quick. My meeting in Seattle got moved up, Namgul has to fly back to India tonight. Then I've got to stay a couple days and do some inventory work in my warehouse down there, get another shipment ready. It's—" He cuts out into static again.

"Newman?"

"—back probably Wednesday. Can I call you when I get a window?"

A *window*? The static is back, and it's not just the cell phone connection.

"Well. Okay. Let's set a day for that hike."

"I'll have to call you. I'm not sure how long—" He cuts out again. "Lindsey," he's back, "can we hold that thought from last night? I—" More static. "—when it can be—" He's cutting in and out.

"Newman, I can't hear you." She raises her voice into the phone, like that's going to help.

"—on top of this crazy traffic. I'll—"

"Damn it! Can't you call me back from a real phone?"

Nothing but static now. "Shit!" Lindsey throws her phone across the yard.

sixteen

LINDSEY LEANS INTO THE turn off Bayview Boulevard, gliding down the easy curves toward the south harbor enclave that was a separate township in the late 1800s. She grew up in this once-seedy neighborhood when the old brick buildings were mostly boarded up and the gingerbread Victorian homes derelict "haunted houses" the kids would sneak into for a good scare. Now, with the influx of California retirees and Seattle dot.com millionaires, it's been restored and tarted up with trendy boutiques and condos overlooking the bay. And what cannot be prettified out of existence behind its greenbelt—the sewage treatment plant.

She grins into the salty mudflat breeze. A Subaru wagon swings wide to pass her bike, shadowed driver turning his head to give her a once-over. Her grin widens.

Lindsey's getting over her surprise at how often this is happening lately. She's actually been the object of catcalls from guys cruising in packs, and it's funny when they look back to see her face and realize she's not some young babe. Maybe it's her change in attitude, or maybe the fact that she's letting herself cool off the summer heat in her skimpy tank tops and short-shorts again. Hey, as long as her tight butt's holding the line, why not enjoy it? There's some kind of shift that has the cutie checkers at the co-op flirting with her, people on sidewalks smiling as she passes, and it's not just men, it's women, too. Can they feel the vibe? Lindsey's in love with life again.

"Well, duh!" she can hear Megan saying. "You're *smiling* these days."

She celebrates the feel-good rush of the bike ride, swooping down toward the rack in front of the bookstore coffee shop, swinging one leg over to ride the last momentum sidesaddle and step off with a flourish onto the curb.

"Nice move!" A tenor voice from behind her.

She turns to see it's the Subaru driver, standing beside his open door, flashing a white smile in a handsome dark face, long black hair pulled into a ponytail. He also happens to be Damon Perrera, here to finally meet her and brainstorm article ideas.

Well, here comes the "Oh, Ma'am" moment. Lindsey pulls off her helmet and shades, waits for the age-recognition reset when he sees her face.

He blinks, then smiles wider, holding her gaze.

Lindsey, her bluff called, glances away from those gleaming dark eyes. *Phew.* She clears her throat. Before this can get too convoluted, she steps toward him, holding out her hand. "Damon? I'm Lindsey."

"Oh." He does look surprised then. "Wow." He laughs and steps closer, takes her hand and gives it a firm squeeze. "Hey, great to meet you!" He gestures toward her bike. "You're making me feel lazy, should've walked my talk and ridden my bike today."

Lindsey shrugs and leans her bike against the rack. "Okay, you can work off the guilt by buying me a latte."

"Done."

She pulls her cable lock from her pannier, as out pops, "You're too easy." Then she flushes at this boldness and hastily turns away to secure the bike.

"Not usually."

She glances quickly back at him. He's flashing those white teeth again.

She straightens, spreading her palms. "I better confess, I'm a big fake. I get all these environmentally-conscious credits, when I really just love to ride my bike."

"I can see that." A glance up and down her, and he doesn't bother to conceal it.

Up close, he's even more gorgeous than she'd realized at the hospital meeting. As if that coffee-and-cream skin and those long-lashed Latin eyes aren't enough, there's the high cheekbones, assertive nose offset by a strong chin, and he's bursting with a palpable vitality. Is he this... *on* with every woman he meets? Puddles of melted-down ladies everywhere he passes?

Just then, perfect timing, a hot flash ignites. Prickling heat flares up Lindsey's spine, sweat breaking out on her face and back. She turns away again, grabbing her bike pannier and clutching it against her chest, pulling out a kerchief to blot her damp face. "Guess I worked up a sweat. Maybe iced tea instead of that latte," she lamely manages.

"That's good. Have you noticed—the more fit you are, the easier you break a sweat?" He gestures toward the coffee shop. "After you."

As Lindsey bites her lip and strides past him through the doorway, he's glancing down again, checking her out. And Lindsey, hopeless, is enjoying it.

Damon acts the perfect gentleman, escorting her to a window table in the cozy cellar coffeeshop with its antique brick walls, relaying her iced tea request to the server and insisting she order a dessert "for energy on the way home," but all the while those dark eyes glimmering with mischief. She pictures a doting mother throwing up her hands in protest while indulging his every whim. He compliments her again on the "Stages of Environmental Grieving" essay, then gets her laughing with his wicked take on the hospital road access meeting, a little preview of his forthcoming editorial for the *Whiplash*. His gaze meanders again over her tank top and bare arms.

Watch it, girl. Lindsey pulls out her jersey and slips it on. But what the hell, how often is she flirted up by such a handsome hunk of maleness? So what if she's sublimating, she's not going to sit around waiting for that return phone call from Newman that hasn't materialized. All she's felt coming from his direction is that sensation of static.

"So, if you're up for it," Damon pulls a notebook and papers out of the battered courier bag he'd set on the floor, "I've got some ideas for more articles. Plus, here's a printout of some good markets, what you might call the literary-enviro readers, they go for the personal-experience, dig-deeper angle you've got going."

Lindsey blinks at the shift into business mode. She clears her throat. "These places don't mind if I publish first with you?"

"No problem." He waves a long-fingered hand. "Little outfit like us, they figure minimal distribution and it's no competition. They'll just take second North American

Rights, and you can negotiate anything else—like that anthology you mentioned. If they accept your essay, they'll want to pin down all kinds of possible subsidiary and reprint rights. But that's great, more exposure for you if it flies."

"Guess I better do some homework on all this."

"No sweat." He grins. "Just run any contracts past me, I can sniff out the land mines in the dark."

"Thank you." She won't look a gift horse. "So it's not like you're aiding the competition?"

Again a dismissive wave. "Like I said, we're still pretty small potatoes, though I've got ideas for expansion, taking it a step at a time. And, to a certain extent, it's 'you scratch my back, I'll scratch yours' among editors. I wouldn't give just anybody this list." He taps it.

"Well...I'm flattered," Lindsey confesses, giving him a quizzical look. "You're willing to do this on the basis of the one essay?"

"I've got a feeling about you, Lindsey." He shrugs. "I think we're gonna do some good work together."

"You hit me at the right time, anyway. I just got...laid off from my job at the hospital."

"No shit? You worked there?" His eyes spark, this time all firebrand editor spotting an angle.

She laughs. "Yeah, I've got some dirt I can dish. But—" She holds out a palm as he leans closer—"Not until I get the papers on my termination settlement." According to Allen Dunshire, the hospital has accepted her terms, and the paperwork "is in the mail."

"I can hardly wait." His eyes crinkle. "Whenever you're ready.... Meantime, I've got a project I'd like to run past you. It's...." Surprisingly, he hesitates, a blip in his assured manner as he looks down. He blows out a breath, looks up. "You could say I've got a personal stake in it. It's a little complicated, but I'm not really the best person to write this one. I can give you a lot of inside info, and I think you've got the right touch for it. I'm thinking a series, and there's a good potential to get it circulated widely into regional publications. Kind of a hot topic in environmental circles." The last comes out in a rush, as if rehearsed.

Lindsey's intrigued. "Okay, let's hear it."

"I'd like to do some in-depth pieces on the Kwamish

fishing and whaling rights controversy. Drill down, get past the finger-pointing."

Lindsey blows out a breath. "You like setting off fireworks?"

"Hoping not to." He lifts his palms. "So where do you stand on it?"

She pauses, getting her thoughts together. "I don't have a stand per se. I mean, given how all the natives got royally screwed with the treaties and reservations, how can you blame them for claiming what rights they have left? And wanting to preserve, or maybe reclaim what traditions haven't been lost." She takes a breath. "But, man, killing whales? Endangered, and so intelligent? There must be something else that would be meaningful for the tribe. I mean...." She shook her head. "Maybe I'm the wrong person to say this, but just because something is a tradition, does that make it the right thing to do?"

He's watching her intently, and she wonders if she just lost her new assignment. Then he slowly smiles. "Thanks, Lindsey. That's what I thought you'd say, after I read your essay. There doesn't have to be bad guys and good guys— gals here. And I think there's a lot of learning that could happen."

"Well, I'd love to get involved. You mentioned you have some research done?"

"Yeah, well, I'm part of it." He gestures, open-palmed, toward himself.

She lifts inquiring eyebrows.

"The Kwamish. My tribe," he says.

"Oh." She blinks, takes another good look at him. The long black hair and strong cheekbones. "Perrera?"

Another lift of the palms. "Half-blood. My mom was tribal, my dad's second-generation Mexican immigrant."

"Mom was?" she asks quietly.

He glances at her, then away. There's been another shift, into some other side of him, and she likes him for that glimpse. "Lindsey, I don't know what it is about you...."

Oh, boy, she thinks. Is this the classic line?

He gives a little shake of the head, still looking out the window. "I don't usually talk about my mom. She...died when I was eight."

"Oh." She hesitates. "I'm sorry." Maybe there *is*

something about her that seems to draw people to confide in her. She'd always guarded her privacy against what seemed like the too-quick intimacy of these revelations, but now she's starting to feel maybe it's a good thing.

Damon is looking down at his hands. "Long story.... Later, my dad remarried a gringa. I've got the cutest blondie half-sisters with these killer tans built in." He looks up at her again, the humor back in his eyes.

Lindsey chuckles. "They must have to fight off the guys with sticks."

He snorts. "About it. Anyway, to most everyone, I'm just Perrera and Latino and that's it. I haven't kept up my... tribal obligations, I guess you'd say, too well. That's part of the complication with this story. That, and tribal politics. In-fighting."

He purses his lips, pushes some papers across the table toward her. "Tell you what, maybe the best thing is if you read these article excerpts and my notes, then we can talk about it, do some brainstorming. How about we go for a hike? I'm dying to get out of town, up to the mountains."

"Terrific." Lindsey takes the papers, tamps them into a stack. "I'll read this tonight."

"All right! How about we do Goat Mountain on Friday, beat the weekend crowds? I'll pick you up at eight in my trusty Subaru war-pony." His eyes are glimmering with mischief again.

"Good, that's one of my favorite hikes." Then Lindsey hesitates. "Wait." Damn, what about that hike with Newman? Since he hasn't called? "I need to check my...calendar first."

The lifted eyebrow again. "That means a boyfriend?"

Lindsey blows out a breath, tells him, "I'm not sure."

He shrugs. "Well, give me a call, and one way or another we'll firm it up." Another sly innuendo? That irresistible smile spreads over his face again, starting slow and sweet, then widening. Does he have any idea how old she is? She can't quite figure out a socially-graceful way to insert that topic into the conversation at this point. Maybe ask the server if they have an AARP discount? She gives up as Damon jots his home number on a business card and slides it toward her.

"Okay, I'll call you," she says.

July 21

Dear Diary,

Hot flash news flash: They're tapering off! (Despite recurrence under smoldering glance of Damon Perrera.) Remedies tried to date:

HYPNOSIS/GUIDED IMAGERY: *I did get "very sleepy." Attempted to descend mossy cool steps and float out on mountain lake to lower core body temperature. Very pleasant until I ignited into a floating pyre. Picturesque.*

PROGRESSIVE RELAXATION: *Tighten and release muscles from head to toes. Try to continue while pulling off clothes and fanning self.*

DEEP BREATHING: *Good for the lungs, at least.*

WILD YAM CREME: *"Natural" building blocks for lagging hormone production. Still lagging? Try leftover goo on Thanksgiving leftovers?*

NATUROPATHIC SUPPLEMENTS: *Black Cohosh, Dong Quai, Super Bs, Cramp Bark, Valerian Root. Excellent for reducing bank balance.*

GODDESS ENERGY, *TAKE TWO: Crystal summons healing spirits with rattles. Use half-empty supplement bottles?*

PAST-LIFE REGRESSION: *Crystal's friend Mary swears by Raven Skywalker. Took her back to former life as a witch during the "burning days." She screamed through burning at the stake, and after that the flashes went away. How desperate am I?*

ACUPUNCTURE *and low-dose estrogen creme: Halleleuia!*

My doc agreed that a low-dose estrogen creme was a

sensible trial, and of course we'll keep an eye on the risk of cancer recurrence. But given all my lost sleep, the nausea, etc., etc., we have to consider my overall health. Thank you! Down from peak two or three flashes per hour to one or two a day, usually not rip-off-the-clothes variety. (Saving that activity—wishful thinking?—for Newman.)

Questions: Does using needles make me an addict? Should I stick needles in a Newman voodoo doll? He finally called to say he couldn't get away for a hike this week, after all, and he was on "Dad duty" for the weekend. How long am I supposed to be on hold?

So I called Damon to agree to that Friday hike! Hoo, boy....

It's Thursday, and Lindsey's trying to focus on a short news piece she's writing as a last-minute thing for the *Whiplash,* about speculators buying up prime county farmland for housing subdivisions, fueling population sprawl gone crazy. Damon asked her to write the piece when she called to arrange the hike. Which is tomorrow. Which is giving her queasy butterflies in her belly.

Maybe it's the way his voice dropped into a sort of caress over the phone line as he said, "Good night, Lindsey."

Maybe it's the way Newman's didn't, when he finally called to again postpone getting together.

Maybe she's going to scream.

Or she could take a page from Nick's book and run around banging her head on the walls and breaking furniture. Is this life in the trenches, in what one of her friends calls the post-dating era?

Plus, her mother's been calling all morning, fussing over arrangements for Joanie's birthday lunch. Now, just as Lindsey's finally getting her article's lead line together, the phone rings again. Lindsey curses and grabs it, about ready to fling the damn thing through the window. "What?!"

"Lindsey? Are you okay?" It's Newman.

She blows out a breath. "What do you think?"

"You're angry at me?"

"Newman, I'm tired of getting jerked around. We're on. We're off. So, yeah, I guess I'm angry."

"Well, that about makes it unanimous," he says. "I think I've managed to piss off everybody in my life right now. You want to let me have it? Take a number?"

"No, I don't want to take a bloody—"

"Kidding." He sighs. "I'm sorry, Lindsey. All I can say is I'm getting pulled so many directions right now, sometimes I lose track of what I *want* to do, in all the supposed-to-dos. My life isn't always this way. It won't always be." A pause. "Anyway, I got it together—at least for the moment. Cleared some time tomorrow, so we can do that hike after all. If you still want to."

Now Lindsey does want to scream. A burst of anger, longing, frustration detonates inside. She has to grab her desk, grip it tight until she can catch her breath.

"Lindsey?"

"Damn it!" comes out through gritted teeth.

"Is...that a no?" Is he laughing? Then she'll really be pissed off.

She takes a deep breath, fights the urge to blow off Damon and say yes, she's dying to see Newman, eager for time in the wilds with him away from his goddamn cell phone, longing for his touch, so more than ready to swim with him into those deep blue ocean waves, or the mud, or both. *Damn it.*

She takes another deep breath. "Newman, I can't go tomorrow. I've already made other plans."

Silence, static over the phone line. Finally, "Oh." Then, quickly, "Well, I just thought maybe we could finally connect. I don't know when I can get another free day. Not until next week, I guess." Another pause. "It's not something you can shift?"

Again Lindsey fights the temptation to give in, seize the day with him. But something holds firm in her—pride? pique? drawing those boundaries and "holding to her integrity" the way counselor Kate urges when Lindsey checks in with her? She can't be on call for any man this way.

"I'm sorry, Newman. I was looking forward to it, but when you said you couldn't get free, I agreed to go with...a new work associate."

"You got another job already? Wow. What is it?"

"Well, not really a job, but some writing assignments for *The Weekly Whiplash.* I'm going hiking with the editor, so we can talk about some big environmental pieces he wants me to write."

"Hey, Lindsey, that's great." His voice is quiet. "Do you want to try for next week?" He blows out a breath. "Damn, I guess this is what I was talking about the other day, how I couldn't always be there for you. Only I didn't realize how... physically frustrating this could be. Maybe I kept it all so compartmentalized, in my marriage. I figured, okay, I need to be celibate to keep the family together, and it was settled. Then these past weeks I was getting so distracted, thinking about you, maybe I went back to that old habit and walled you off. I guess that's not fair. I'm feeling out my way with all this...."

That odd sensation of static peaks then, and falls away. Suddenly Lindsey can feel him loud and clear, a surge of desire sweeping over and into her. Despite herself, she sighs.

"Oh, boy," Newman breathes into the phone. "Lindsey, is it awful to want to rip your clothes off right now and just dive into you?"

"Damn it, Newman, don't do this to me."

"Sorry. I'm doing it to myself. I'm on my way to an appointment, and just thinking about you is getting me all hot and bothered."

"Newman...."

"Okay. I'm trying. Can we set a day next week for that hike? And if Melani goes out with her friends this weekend and I get some time, could I call? Would you be open to something last-minute?"

She wants to fly through the phone line and jump him right then. She takes another deep breath, trying to settle her voice. *"Carpe diem?"*

He chuckles. "I'd like to seize more than the day. Respectfully, of course."

She can't help laughing. "I give up on being sane."

"Good." Another chuckle. "Listen, there's something else I think might help. You asked me about meditation before. Do you want me to teach you a mantra to practice?"

She blinks. "I'd like that. Do we...set an appointment in astral time for that?"

"I'll check my calendar." Then hastily, "No, you check yours. Any days for a hike that *won't* work for you next week? I promise I'll call this weekend, and we can set a day."

"I'm setting my own schedule these days, working on my writing projects."

"Good. Okay, I gotta go now. Enjoy your hike, Lindsey."

Right.

seventeen

THE WORLD HAS GONE still, poised on the fulcrum of Now. Lindsey takes a deep breath of fir needle resin and listens to the forest hush.

She's halted at a switchback on the Goat Mountain trail, confronted by the flaring skirts of two giant cedars flanking the trail, making a gateway to the filtered light beyond—a soft green frieze of lacy bleeding-heart, red huckleberry, and backlit vine-maple leaves. She steps through, outstretched fingertips brushing the rough bark on either side. Before her on the steep slope rises another big cedar, this one a hollowed-out husk surviving an old lightning burn. It's a favorite spot, an intricate sculpture in brown and charred black, scooped and hollowed into a windowed tube and resting impossibly balanced on narrow spikes of intact trunk. Lindsey holds her breath, feeling the slightest breeze might crumble the fragile balance, send the whole thing crashing at her feet. And yet it's clearly stood this way for decades.

Overhead, a raven chortles.

There's an answering raven call behind her, full-throated.

Lindsey turns to see Damon stepping through the twin-cedar gateway, face turned up as the hidden raven overhead calls back to him. He smiles and flattens a palm over one of the flaring trunks.

"Wow." He steps closer behind Lindsey, staring at the hollow burned cedar. "I'd forgotten about that."

They stand quietly taking it in.

Damon lifts the camera hanging around his neck. "How about a shot of you standing beside it?"

She shakes her head. "Better without me."

"It needs you at its feet, gives proportion."

"Oh. All right." Lindsey moves carefully to avoid crushing the delicate wildflowers. "How about if I crouch down? Less intrusive."

"Perfect." He snaps a couple shots, taking his time, and when Lindsey thinks he's done and she's relaxed to gaze up at the play of filtered light over cedar bark, he snaps one more. "Nice. If you'll sign a release, I can use it in one of our hiking features."

She bites her lip, starts to protest about not being photogenic, then shrugs.

"Look. It's beautiful." He gestures her closer, tilts the camera—an expensive-looking digital with a big lens—so she can see the monitor screen. The soft lighting glows over the sinuous lines of the burned sculpturing, casts a warm hue on Lindsey's uptilted face. He's caught a very flattering angle on her.

She blinks in surprise. "You're an artist."

He brushes her bare shoulder lightly with his fingers. "No. You're a natural."

She shivers—from his touch, or just cooling off after the sweaty push up the steep switchbacks? Adjusting her knapsack straps, she moves quickly on up the trail. "Looks like more light breaking through up ahead. We're almost to the meadow."

A snowmelt stream gurgles down the slope and across the trail, silencing whatever response Damon might have made behind her. Lindsey can feel the heat in her cheeks, the unspoken vibe between them. He's been quiet on the trail, after their animated brainstorming session in the car about article ideas, but she can feel his gaze on her back, can't help noting his appreciative glances at her bare legs and arms when they take a water break.

Damon has surprised her in the forest, the way he's carried a sort of stillness that meshes with the forest hush. They have a good matching pace and rhythm for hiking, something Lindsey doesn't find in many companions. She's grateful he doesn't feel the need to talk much, can just tilt his head toward something he's noticed, or catch a movement of hers toward a bird or wildflower. They've got a groove going with the trail.

And yet, part of her isn't fully here, is somewhere else wrestling with the enigma of Newman in her life. She has to remember what she's learned the hard way: Be watchful for the signs of manipulation. Don't let herself fall into another Nick scenario of push-pull. Can she ever trust herself to know when a heart connection is true? Trust that core goodness she feels in Newman, past this static of confusion? Do they each need to go off and lick their old wounds a little longer?

Why did he have to pick last night to call? Stir up that wild pitch of arousal one more time, for one more wait-and-see? Just in time to divert her pleasure in Damon's company, insert his Zender static into this vibe that's building today, whether it's flowering into a creative work partnership, a new friendship, the *frisson* of sexual flirtation or more—and why the hell shouldn't she enjoy Damon's appreciation of her female self? Newman's certainly made his ambivalence clear.

Clearly ambivalent. Now there's a Zender koan. She can't help chuckling—better than twisting herself into a pretzel over it all.

She blinks as she steps out of forest shadow into full blazing sunlight, a meadow opening at her feet rampant with crimson fireweed, lavender lupine, and delicate yellow glacier lilies nodding at the edge of a melting snow patch. A stream meanders from under the snow, braiding over the lush, soggy grass—a rainbow carpet shimmering under the incandescent alpine-blue sky.

"Ah!" The intensity of light pierces her heart, breaks it open to gratefulness. Tears sting her eyes.

"Hey." A soft voice behind her. "You okay?"

She didn't hear Damon stepping closer on the moist dirt of the trail. She ducks her head, brushes at her eyes, and nods.

He squeezes her shoulder briefly. "Sometimes it's hard to take, this beauty, eh?" His voice has taken on the slow native cadences, so different from his pace in town. "Almost to the overlook. We can have our lunch there. Take your time."

He moves around her, up the trail, not pushing her to respond. Again she's taken by surprise by him. She takes a deep breath, breathing in the shimmering light and color, the pure cleansing air. She smiles, sending out an incoherent *Thank you*—to what or whom she isn't sure. Her feet are light on the path as she moves on, higher, deeper, into overarching blue.

Damon's waiting on the granite knob of the Goat Mountain overlook, shirtless and sprawled out on his back, eyes closed, smiling. Lindsey is smiling, too, as she rounds the last switchback and crosses a lingering snowbank in the alpine meadow. Somehow she's been released into the joy of the day. She steps forward into a nearly three-sixty panorama of jagged snowy peaks cutting a razor-sharp border into the ultraviolet sky.

"Wow." She drops her knapsack and stretches.

Vibrant light pulsates over the glaciers and mountain lake almost close enough to touch across the steep valley, a glimpse of the river glittering far below. The intensity of light throbs in her eyes. Shimmers over Damon's brown skin, a startling contrast of warm, vulnerable flesh against the starkness of black rock, white snow, blue sky.

He opens his eyes, blinks, and sits up. "Man, this is where it's at." His white teeth flash as he opens his arms to the view.

Which, for Lindsey, includes his beautiful presence. His long black braid falls over one shoulder, bare torso nearly hairless and smoothly muscular. "Let me take a shot of you, here," she says.

He looks surprised, then shrugs and hands her the camera sitting beside him. Lindsey moves the knapsacks out of the way, backs up and crouches, sighting into the viewfinder. She angles around, backs up some more, and finds the best spot to catch him sitting crosslegged on the weathered dark rock, its upward thrust launching him into mountains and sky. "Got it! This is the one you should put in that hiking column."

She sits beside him as he purses his lips, scans the shot, and laughs. "No way! I look like the fucking shaman on the mountaintop."

"I want a copy, at least."

"Okay, but you have to promise not to show it around."

"Why?" She tilts her head and studies him. "Don't go all fake modest on me. You'd make a terrific scenic trailside attraction." She waves a hand as he laughs. "But it's more, right there in that picture. Like you're rooted here. Why do you want to hide that?"

He shakes his head. "Lindsey, you just put it right out there, don't you?"

She bites her lip. "It's just lately. I mean—" She laughs at herself then. "I don't know, it's not the way I used to be. But now it...doesn't seem worth it to dance around things anymore."

He turns to face her, wincing a bit in the glare of sunlight off stone, and reaches to pull off her shades. He looks into her eyes. "You have the most amazing eyes, Lindsey. The color of growing things."

He touches her face, leans in to brush his lips over hers. She starts to stiffen, pull back, but then it feels right to see what this is. He returns with a slow, lingering exploration, drawing her out, drawing her in, and it's suddenly very clear what those earlier sparks were promising. He has a gift of sensual touch, not rushing or pushing, just savoring, and Lindsey joins him in a warm uprush of delight. Along with the deep stirring of arousal.

Finally she pulls away, lightheaded. "Oh." She lies back on the warm rock, closing her eyes to feel sunlight pouring over her, penetrating.

"Mmm," he breathes, and lies down on the rock next to her, taking her hand and slowly running his thumb over her open palm. "I knew that was going to be good."

She chuckles, still lying eyes closed. "I guess I knew it, too. But, Damon, I have to warn you. I'm sort of...a loose cannon these days. Since my divorce." She squeezes his hand and releases it.

He blows out a slow breath, pulls his arms up to cradle his head. "Yeah. And the boyfriend?" His voice sounds unruffled.

She shakes her head, still with her eyes closed. "Don't know if I'd call him that, it's still really new. And pretty confusing. If he wants to pursue it or not." Somehow it feels perfectly comfortable to be talking this way with Damon.

"I figured it was something like that. But there's something else going on here. We had to at least get a taste of it.

And man, oh man, it would be really sweet with us, Lindsey."

At that, she sits up, looks over at him. He's lying there smiling up at her, for a second pure Raven Trickster, and she has to laugh. She puts her face in her hands and shakes it. "Too crazy."

"Kind of like life, eh?" Then he sits up, reaches over for his knapsack. "Hey, let's eat!" He winks at her. "Just keep it in mind. You never know."

She turns to her own knapsack and digs out her lunch bag. "I've got some plums from my tree."

"I've got smoked salmon and crackers. What else are you hiding in there?" He reaches over to grab her sack and peer inside, lifting an eyebrow. "Chocolate! I knew it!"

They laugh and lay out their offerings to share.

Lindsey's worked up a ferocious appetite, and manages to demolish several crackers loaded with tender smoked salmon, along with her own contribution of pita bread and cheese, fruit, and chocolate.

Damon's lying back on his elbows, watching her. "I like a woman with an appetite." The flirtatious innuendo is back.

"Mmm. I can't resist this salmon." She finishes the last crumb of it. "Should have brought along a little red wine, perfect mountain gourmet eating."

"Don't tempt me. I don't drink anymore."

She gives him an inquiring look.

He lies back on his braided hands, gazing out toward the mountains.

"Hey, I don't mean to pry—"

"It's—"

Their words collide, then he snorts and starts over. "Lindsey, it wasn't some line when I said there's something about you. Makes me want to tell you stories. I mean real ones."

"I'd like to hear," she says quietly, licking her fingers and then settling back with her head pillowed on her knapsack.

"Mom and Dad—they were drinking pals, really liked to party. When I was little, it was pretty wild. Mom was so beautiful...." Silence for a moment. "I still miss her. Even though sometimes it wasn't so great. She...alienated people in the tribe. Well, that's complicated. But, anyway, Dad was driving them back early one morning from one of their binges, hit another car. Killed an old man and lady. And Mom."

"Oh, no." Lindsey sits up, looks at him. "That's really rough."

He doesn't meet her eyes, but goes on, "Dad did some jail time, then disappeared for a while. I was raised mostly by my *abuelita*. That's—"

"*Sí. Entiendo.*"

As he glances over at her, she shrugs. "Peace Corps in Honduras."

He nods, continues, "Well, that was until I was fourteen, I guess. Then Dad showed up again, married Danielle, wanted me back with him. But before that, during the summers I lived with my Nana on the rez. Nana and Abuelita, they're both fantastic. Both tough as nails in their own ways. Beautiful." He sits up then, turns to look at Lindsey. "Man, that's it! You've got to meet Nana, you two would just hit it off. You need to spend some time with the tribe if you're going to write these pieces about the fishing rights. You could stay with her. She'd love it."

"That sounds perfect. Thanks."

"No—thank *you*."

"Why?" She raises her eyebrows.

"I don't know...." He looks at his hands. Opens and closes them. Then glances back at her face. "Yeah, I do know. You remind me of her."

Lindsey laughs. "Now that's an interesting development."

He shakes his head, serious. "I mean it. It's like you're a messenger, reminding me it's time I went home. You're beautiful in the same way Nana is."

"I...don't know what to say. That's quite a compliment."

"Lindsey, you must hear it all the time."

She shakes her head. "Oh, I never had any illusions about being that pretty. And now, at this age...."

"Hey, you're talking to the gray hair here!" He laughs, tilts his head to display a few silver threads along his dark temples. "That's why my Abuelita—and Nana—keep on me. I was pretty wild when I was young, along with the drinking, pretty much a radical, too. Always off half-cocked on whatever cause sounded good and angry. So now I'm all respectable—even civic-minded, *caramba!*—they're all over me to settle down, make them some grandkids. Especially on the Perrera side. *Es la vida*, you lived among Latinos, you know all about *machismo*. Still a bachelor at forty-two, they'd all be calling me *mariposa*, if it weren't for...."

"Yes?"

"Okay, I admit I've gone through my share of pretty women."

"Never would have guessed."

He chuckles. "I finally realized it's empty just having those...flings." He blows out a breath. "Anyway, most of the women I've met lately, they either have kids already or their biological clocks are ticking away, and they just want a man to plug into the picture as Daddy. I don't know if I want that. Kids. And like I said, I haven't exactly had a great record with long term relationships...."

He glances aside at Lindsey. "You know, I've just been assuming you don't have kids."

She nods. "My marriage wasn't.... Well, it didn't happen."

"But you want them? I'm not knocking it, you know. I'm just talking about my own confusion here."

"Damon, how old do you think I am?" Time to get that straight.

"Well, we're in the same ballpark, right?" He shrugs. "It's one thing I liked right off about you. I'm tired of younger women. You've got depth. And, hey, you're in way better shape than most people in their twenties."

Lindsey blows out a breath. "Damon, you're forty-two? Well, I'm fifty-two."

He goes still, staring. "No way."

"Way." She raises her palms. "Maybe that's why I remind you of your Nana."

"No." He grasps her wrist, gives it a little shake. "That *is* no way. But hey, this is really interesting. I like it." He studies her. "You are one damn sexy woman, Lindsey." He grins. "This is coming from an expert."

She laughs. "You just want to explore new territory."

He shrugs. "Why not? We'd be good together, Lindsey. I can feel it."

She spreads her hands. "Damon, obviously I find you attractive. I like you. But I'd rather be friends, colleagues, not get all messy with some kind of affair that might sour things. And I need to find out what it's about with my friend Newman."

"Newman? The maybe-boyfriend?" He shrugs. "Hey, I'm cool with sharing."

She laughs. "You are impossible!"

"No, just flexible." He picks up her hand, runs his thumb over her palm again. "Let me show you. You'll like it." He gives her hand a little tug toward him.

She shakes her head, suddenly uneasy, hunching away from him.

"Hey. Sorry." He backs off, holds up his palms. "Truce? I like to tease a little too much."

Lindsey takes a deep breath. "It's not you. Sometimes I still...." She pokes a finger into the lichen along a crack in the granite beneath her. "Sometimes I get flashbacks to the times with Nick, when he'd push me around...." She adds hastily, "Not that you were being like him at all."

"Nick? That's your ex?"

She nods. "You might know him, he works for Green Life. Nick Papetti."

"Papetti? That jerk?" Damon sits up straight.

"I guess you know him."

"Hey, Lindsey, you don't need to say anything else. I'm sorry." He reaches over to gently squeeze her shoulder.

She shrugs. "A lot of people like him."

"Not me. I mean, he gets things done, but I don't like the way he insists on confrontation. Sets it up. He's a real manipulator." He runs a hand over his head, smoothing back his hair. "Yeah, sometimes pushing is what you need to get things moving. But not always. I like what you were saying about finding common ground, in your essay. It's where the new environmental activism is moving. Looking for the win-win instead of war. So that's where I think we want to head with these pieces about the Kwamish. There's already enough head-butting going on."

She turns to him, eager. "I was hoping that was your take on it. You know, after I read your notes, I called a friend of mine in Seattle. Ayako does communications-facilitation consulting. She's done some work with regional tribes, and there's an interesting model she uses for getting fruitful discussions going. Sort of sidestepping the usual authoritarian models where conflicts get triggered. She calls it 'circularity.'"

"That's it!" His face lights up. "Linear doesn't work too well with us Indians. You got to circle around. Circle up." He traces one with his finger on the rock. "I've got a feeling about this—there's a lot that's ready to come out into the light. Not just for this region, or even this country. Maybe shed some light on some wrong turns we went down a hundred years ago. More."

Then he raises his palms. "Yeah, pretty grandiose, Perrera. Never had too big a problem with that false modesty stuff you were talking about. But really, Lindsey, if you're into this, it could unfold into some in-depth essays, maybe even turn into a book. We could do a collaboration. Who knows?"

Lindsey blinks, startled. "You know, why not? Ayako was talking about the experiences she's had with different groups, how this model of communication really gets to the heart of issues, generates all kinds of ideas. Somehow frees people up to talk about the nuts and bolts. Ways the imbalance of power, from family on up to government, can be shifted." She presses her hand flat on the warm granite, over the place where he'd traced the invisible circle. "You could say it hits home with me, in more ways than one."

He nods. "We're on the same wavelength. Let's go for it!" He purses his lips. "I think I can get my *Whiplash* investors to front a little cash on this. Some of them like to…seed liberal notions, see what comes up. Best if you go first, spend some time on the rez without me. I've got too much history there. It'd just be inflammatory."

She frowns. "You think they'll take me into their confidence without an inside connection?"

"That's why you're going to stay with Nana!" He beams.

"Hmm." She tilts her head, studies him. "This is about a lot more for you than writing those pieces, isn't it?"

He takes a deep breath. Looks out at the mountains again. Lindsey lets the hush settle around them.

Finally Damon nods. "Yeah," he says quietly.

eighteen

Dear Diary,

Caramba! Who am I? What am I? Where am I going? If it's off to the loony bin, it's one hell of a ride. Launching off into clear blue skies (Take Two?), like Damon in that photo I snapped. Which just arrived by courier this morning, "as promised," along with the shot he took of me at the foot of the sculpted cedar trunk.

He enlarged that one of me as an 8x10 and double matted it in lichen-green and gold, with an invitation to his photography show opening at the Blue Horse Gallery, and a note asking if he can include the photo in the show! Didn't even know he was showing his work seriously. And it's scary—he really did make me look beautiful in this photo. Is that me?

He included just a standard 4x6 of the one I took of him, but I'll have to demand an enlargement! No artistry needed to make him look beautiful.

Does not compute. No way this gorgeous, dynamic, artistic man can be pursuing plain old Lindsey Friedland. Maybe I'm just the Older Woman, the only category he hasn't yet conquered. And I said No, so it's a challenge. (One reason I'm so hot and bothered over elusive Newman?) Watch it, Lindsey. Am I so fickle? Heading into the "love the one you're with" zone?

Pros and Cons:

NEWMAN
Sexy. Wow, and how!!

Tall, Gray, and Handsome—but not showy. Good!
Funny and smart. Excellent!
Complex, rich life experience. Essential.
Citizen of the world. Inspiring.
Spiritual depth. Resonating.
Devoted father. Reassuring.
Post recent nasty divorce. Caution!
Talks to his Teacher via spirit. Confusing.
Self-assured to point of arrogance. Off-putting.
Open to compromise? Doubtful.
Wounded heart. Not ready for love?
Inconsiderate about calling. Not good.
Commitment-phobe push/pull. Frustrating!
Times has said I am beautiful: 1

DAMON
Sexy. Also (Pow)Wow!!
Fantasy-material gorgeous. Spoiled?
Funny and smart. Also excellent!
Complex life experience. Seamy past?
Civic-minded activist. Also inspiring.
Spiritual depth? Searching?
Family connections unsettled.
Self-assured, with chinks. Human.
Open to compromise. Good.
Jaded heart? Too ready for "love"?
Considerate. Good.
Expert flirt. Too smooth?
Longtime bachelor. The habit is set?
Times has said I am beautiful (on short acquaintance): 5

"Lin, you are beautiful."

Nick had always been good at saying it. And that day—
what was it? Four years ago?—Lindsey believed he meant it.
Especially since he'd just grabbed her off her bike the
minute they'd pulled into the drive, dragged her all laughing
and sweaty onto the living room rug, couldn't wait to get her
completely undressed before he tugged off her shorts and
took her by storm.

Then he was kicking away his own shorts still caught

around one ankle, settling in beside her to stroke tendrils of loose hair from her damp face.

"Phew." Lindsey smiled into his eyes, then sat up to tug her sticky tank top over her head. "How hot is hot?"

She saw it in his eyes then, as he winced away from the puckered lumpectomy breast. Since the surgery, he'd bought her a couple of lacy camisoles, seemed to like having sex with her partially clothed.

She closed her eyes and took a deep breath, lay down beside him again and stroked his face. "Nick, I know it takes getting used to. But I could use some help not feeling...self-conscious about it."

"Lin, I mean it. You are the most beautiful woman, ever. It hasn't changed that."

"But you don't want to see it. Touch it."

"I'm afraid I'll hurt you. It makes *me* hurt, for you."

"It's healed up fine. Could you at least touch the other breast, the way you used to? I'd really like that." She took his hand, guided it toward her intact breast.

He pulled away, sat up shaking his head. "Lin, you can't...script it like that. Just give me some time, okay?"

"All right." She sat up, turning away from him, pulling the sports top back on so she could hide the puckered breast. It really wasn't looking so bad now, the burns from the radiation therapy had faded and the skin looked normal, sensation returning. Nick had raised the possibility of reconstruction, but with a lumpectomy and radiation she wasn't the best candidate for that. The procedure hadn't been extensive enough for reconstruction to be covered on their insurance—which was good news because the tumor hadn't been that big. And Lindsey, for what complex of reasons she wasn't even sure, didn't want to go the implant route anyway. She'd hoped Nick wouldn't be so bothered by it.

It wasn't like it was that extreme—not like those photos she'd seen of post-mastectomy women proudly displaying their scarred one-breasted Amazon torsos. Celebrating being alive. Facing down the death threat and those fears of being seen as ugly. Lindsey wasn't that strong.

She ducked her face, feeling the tears coming again, and she didn't want Nick to see them. It would only make him more upset. But she couldn't help it, she wanted him to take her in his arms and comfort her, care about how *she* was feeling about her body now, not just his feelings. But that was pathetic. She was wallowing. She should be grateful she was cancer-free, almost a year later. Recovering. And Nick obviously hadn't lost his desire for her. It was just a little different now.

"Lin, where'd you get that killer tan?" Megan activates the door locks on her SUV and heads over to Lindsey, who's waiting at the park trailhead for an aerobic walk.

"Right here at home. Well, I did get up to the mountains. Just one of the bennies of being laid off."

"Right. I could use some of that, look at these pale legs. Can't believe I'm sneaking off on Sunday. Thank God Joe decided to take the gang to the fair. So lead on, Amazon woman! I mean—"

"It's okay. I'm over it." Lindsey smiles, realizing that now she can reclaim her "Amazon" family nickname without the wince.

But Megan isn't smiling. She hesitates, then blurts out, "*Are* you okay, Lin? You're coming up on the five-year mark real soon, right?"

Lindsey blinks, taken aback. "I'm due for my mammo next month, then I'll officially be in remission. You kept track of the date?"

"Gal friend." Megan puts her hands on her hips. "I've got a vested interest in you sticking around." She blows out a breath. "You don't know how scared I was for a while there. I couldn't stand losing you."

Lindsey peers closer into Megan's face. "I didn't realize."

She swipes at her eyes. "You've had enough on your plate without worrying about keeping me sane."

"*I* keep *you* sane?" She starts down the trail.

Megan laughs then, hustling to catch up. "Guess it all depends on how you define your terms." They head into the shadow of the cedar grove where the surveyor ribbons are still dangling. The road-access issue is still dangling, too, but looking less and less likely to pass environmental review.

"But, seriously, gal friend." Megan gives her a sideways

look. "I didn't want to push you, what with all the shit hitting over Nick and the divorce and all. I was praying a lot for you, even if you don't go that route. But I never asked. Weren't you afraid? I mean, of dying?"

Lindsey thinks about it, as the filtered light flickers over them. "You know, it's funny. But...well, of course I thought about it, the whole cancer scare. And once you land in the middle of the medical system, they really work on you to be sort of paranoid with all these percentages and rates and risk groups and all." She shrugs. "I just can't buy into the Christian dogma, but I do believe there's...a force for good, so I'm not really afraid of dying. Not that I want to!" She bites her lip. "Well, for a while there with how bad it was with Nick, I did kind of feel maybe I'd be better off dead than slogging through the nightmare day after day. I'd wake up and think, 'Please let it all be just a bad dream.' Then I'd remember it was real."

"Oh, honey!" Megan stops short on the trail, forcing Lindsey to stop and face her. "You'd tell me, wouldn't you, if you felt suicidal? We should have gotten you help sooner!" She grips Lindsey's wrists. "You still see your counselor when you need to, right?"

"Every once in a while. But...." Lindsey sighs. "Now that I'm off the hospital insurance plan, I had to get cheaper coverage, and it doesn't pay for Kate visits."

"Oh! Damn." Megan frowns. "Look, Lindsey, you know Joe and I would help you get through this—"

"No, no, I'm okay, I just have to watch expenses."

"Promise me you'll ask, especially if it's your health. Call it a loan if you want. We just need to keep you on track."

"Thanks, but really I'm okay now." Lindsey eases free of Megan's grip. "I just didn't realize how far down I'd gone before. But now it's like I pulled the Get out of Jail Free card. Everything looks so good out here!"

"Oh, Lin," Megan repeats. "Nobody knew how bad it was with Nick."

Lindsey starts walking again, urging Megan back into motion. "I guess that's part of it—hide the truth from every-body, even yourself. The Friedland family motto. Maybe we should all get it tattooed on our foreheads."

She ups the pace, swinging her arms. "You know, when I finally got into counseling, had to face it about Nick and the abuse, and then they diagnosed me with that Post-Traumatic Stress Disorder, it was so weird. I mean, I thought that was just for combat vets or something. But it's really a physical thing, once your nerves get so shot with the chronic stress. Being braced all the time for the next no-warning explosion or ducking out of the way of his 'accidental' swinging-around-with-knives in the kitchen or grabbing the cats out of range when he's looking for something to throw. Lucky I have good reflexes! But after a while, my body got tapped out—the whole 'fight or flight' response gets shorted out. It's like you're paralyzed, in this dark place."

"Oh, honey."

"Hey, I can talk about it now without getting over-whelmed." She puffs out a breath. "So, anyway, I guess that's the long answer to a short question. I was just trying to get through day to day, so I didn't have much energy for thinking about mortality. Or immortality."

She shrugs. "Lately, I have been thinking more about… the spiritual end of things."

"Good. Doesn't matter what religion, it's all God." Megan's panting now, pumping her arms to keep up the pace on the trail. "So…what about Newman? Dish me the dirt, gal. How's the romance going?" She smirks over at Lindsey. "Holy shit, that's it! I swear you look a year younger every time I see you lately. It's being in love! Or lust, whatever. Can you bottle it? I'll order a case."

Lindsey blows out a breath as they pass under the baby-owl maple. "Not much to report. He can't make up his mind whether or not he's up for it, I guess."

Megan snorts. "From what I could see the other night, getting up for it isn't the problem."

Lindsey shakes her head. "No problem there." She shrugs, pushes up the pace a bit. "Maybe it's *too* intense. It's freaking him out."

"Well, don't let him string you along for *too* long. Newman is a real sweetheart, but maybe he's just not ready, after the divorce. I had a couple run-ins with that ex of his at our kids' school, and I don't like to throw the 'B' word around, but if the shoe fits.…" Megan pauses to catch her breath. "Phew. You know, Newman's always been like every-body's mellow big Dad, maybe he just can't get himself wrapped around being a lover. So if he can't make up his mind, there's plenty of fish in the sea."

She purses her lips. "Wait, I know! I should introduce you to Jeff. He's an engineering consultant on that new project at work. Nice guy, travels, too, and I think he said he's a kayaker. Looks pretty buff." She winks.

"Megan, I thought you were laying off the match-making."

"Well, Newman's never around, so why not branch out a little?"

Lindsey feels her face heating and covers by countering, "There's always a catch. So what is it this time, out-of-control earwax and nose hairs? Drives one of those jacked-up pickup trucks on balloon tires, with Playboy mud guards? Calls his mother twice a day?"

Megan snorts. "Come on, Lin, you've gotta give these guys a chance. He's funny, an interesting guy. There's just the one thing...."

Lindsey rolls her eyes. "Here it comes."

"Well, it's not that big a deal, I mean everybody seems to do it these days."

"Do what? Spit chewing tobacco? Snort heroin?"

"Lin." Megan flips a hand, puffing. "The online dating thing."

"Oh, God. Remember the architect? So what is it with this guy—he trolls those sites for young, willing Russian brides or something?"

Megan bites her lip. "No, Thai."

"What?"

"We got talking, and he told me he can't seem to meet the right gal here, so he put up a page on *ThaiLove.com*."

"Megan, you've got to be kidding!" Lindsey stops short, forces Megan to meet her gaze. "He's one of those guys who wants a meek little wifey slave? Young, of course, preferably a virgin?"

Megan looks at Lindsey's face and bursts out laughing. "All right, all right. Maybe it *is* weird. He did tell me he was 80% okay with the 'contractual aspect.'"

Lindsey shakes her head. "Just spare me any more hot prospects, okay?" She starts walking again. "I've got enough on my plate already."

"But seriously, how do you think you're going to meet

this Mr. Perfect you're holding out for? Maybe you're being unrealistic. You've got to get *out* there, Lin, you know gorgeous men don't just fall off the trees."

Lindsey feels her face warming again, hopes the exercise explains it.

"Whoa! Is that a hot flash, or what?" Megan's caught it, naturally. "Come on, gal friend. What's up?"

She blows out a breath. "I'm kind of getting the come-on from another guy."

"Hmm." Megan shoots her another look, eyebrows raised. "And you're liking it?"

"Well...yes and no. It's complicated."

"Isn't it always?"

"I'm working with him on writing projects. Damon Perrera. He's the—"

"Oh, my God! The *Weekly Whiplash* editor? You've got to be kidding!" Megan comes to a standstill again, staring.

"You know him, too?" Lindsey manages weakly.

"Well, yeah, I've met him at some of the community forums. Lindsey, are you serious? Mr. Romance-novel-cover-art?"

Lindsey rolls her eyes. "Not to mention ten years younger than me." She flips a dismissive hand. "Hey, it's probably just flirtation. He's not exactly shy."

"I gather he's got a track record."

"He admitted it himself. That was after he kissed me."

"Oh, my God!" Megan repeats, eyes widening. "This is.... Are you...?"

"Just a kiss." Lindsey urges her back into action down the trail, heading toward the hilly section. "Though, mind you, a very good one."

"Lindsey, you sly dog!" Megan laughs. "I bet he's one hell of a kisser. So, what now?"

"I told him no, thank you very much, I'm waiting to see what's up with Newman."

"But?" Megan's still chuckling, shaking her head.

"Well, he doesn't seem discouraged." Lindsey shrugs, then admits, "It's not exactly hard on the ego to be pursued a bit."

"Maybe hard elsewhere?" She winks. "Lordy love! Reminds me of the old days in that funky cabin, roomie."

"Come on, I never kept up with you. I swear you had

them lined up at the door, taking a number."

"Just don't tell Joe!"

"I think maybe he's figured it out. But the way he was looking at you the other night at the Grizzly Bear, you have nothing to worry about."

"Newman might. He better get his buns in gear or he might miss out. He may be Mr. Transcendental, but it never hurts to let a guy know he's got competition."

"Megan, don't you dare tell him!"

"How much is my silence worth?" She raises her eyebrows.

Lindsey just shakes her head, relieved they've reached the foot of the hill. She revs up, forcing Megan to save her breath for the climb. By the time they've reached the top, Megan's gasping and Lindsey's getting a nice flush. "Ready for another round?" she asks, just to get even.

Megan groans, dabbing her face with a kerchief. "Give me a break!"

"Okay, next time." Lindsey blows out a breath, sobering. "Anyway, I'm heading up to the hospital. Thought I'd visit Kevin."

"Oh." Megan winces. "Any news?"

"No. He's still in a coma, in the long-term care facility." She shakes her head. "Not looking good. But they're thinking it might reach him if people come and read to him."

"Oh, Lin." Megan reaches over to squeeze her hand. "They still working on getting that doc kicked out?"

Lindsey nods, feeling a little guilty she hasn't talked to Rob for a couple weeks about the malpractice suit.

She says goodbye to Megan, heads up the road to the facility behind the hospital. Bracing herself, she signs in on the visitor sheet, heads toward Room 212. The too-familiar smells of antiseptic and bedpans permeate the air, reminding her how she doesn't miss the hospital job. She'd just been numb for so long. Maybe she needed to be during those years.

It hardly looks like Kevin lying there on the bed. There's his body, hooked up to the life-support lines and blinking monitors, breathing without oxygen now, but otherwise there's no sense of life here. No wild mop of dark hair, just stubble growing in around the angry-looking scars. Face slack as an old man's or infant's. Despite the work of the physical therapists moving and stretching his limbs, he seems to be sinking in on himself, curling into fetal position. Preparing for the next passage.

Lindsey takes a deep breath, banishes those thoughts so she won't send that dark cloud toward him. "Hello, Kevin." She steps around to the chair beside the bed, touches his hand that's tightened into a fist but is still warm. "It's Lindsey. It's another sunny day. The poppies are really gorgeous in my garden—purple and pink and orange."

The caregivers say it's good to talk to him and read something he likes. There's still a chance he's perceiving the contact, even though the CAT scans aren't showing much activity. People have come out of these states.

Lindsey blinks quickly, pulls open the bedside cabinet and takes out the dog-eared paperback she's been reading from, in there with some dirt bike magazines. *Lord of the Rings: The Two Towers*. Marci had found it in his bedroom.

Lindsey notes the bookmark has shifted forward from where she left off reading last time. She feels a momentary pang at missing those sections, then smiles. It's good to revisit Treebeard and the hobbits after so many years. She reads a passage of the Ent's amusing pontification, then comes a ballad about summer and green woodlands, and a golden land where "hearts may rest."

Lindsey sits silently holding the book. She doesn't have the heart to read more right now. Carefully inserting the marker, she leans over to replace the book in the cabinet.

"What are you doing?" The voice from the doorway is sharp.

Lindsey jerks upright and steps back, looking across Kevin's still form to see her sister Joanie, her lips pressed tightly together, hands gripping the bar of a baby stroller.

Lindsey takes a deep breath. "I was reading to Kevin." She glances at him, sees nothing shifted since her arrival, but tells him, "Kevin, Joanie's here, with Kendra." She steps around the bed to lean over the stroller and tickle Kendra's pudgy belly. "Hey, cutie."

Joanie's face softens. "You want to hold her?"

Lindsey nods and unbuckles the restraints, grips

Kendra under the arms to hoist her up. "Ooof! She's growing!" She thinks of her as a baby, though at sixteen months she's really a toddler. Except she's just learning to crawl now, with the physical therapy Joanie's been getting her.

"Yeah, she's making progress. Set her down. If you hold her hands, she can stand now. I think she'll get walking soon."

"That's great, Kendra! Who's a good girl?" Lindsey holds her out from her chest.

Kendra beams and claps her hands.

"That's right, Kendra's a good girl!" Lindsey kneels to set her on the ground, where she wobbles but grips tight to Lindsey's fingers, moving her feet as if ready to launch. She laughs, her eyes still slightly crossed, and they haven't gotten to the bottom of what's caused that—the drugs her mother Denise was on, or Kendra being a preemie—but she's such a happy baby, she seems to bubble with delight.

Lindsey looks up at Joanie, who's moved over to sit bedside Kevin, gazing at him. "You want me to take Kendra for a ride while you read to him?"

Joanie shakes her head. "I think she likes listening. Maybe good for her, too."

"Okay, kiddo, back in the stroller you go!" Lindsey lifts her in, fastens the straps, and steers her over beside the chair.

"Well." Joanie clears her throat. "Maybe you better head out. Marci's gonna meet me here."

Lindsey stiffens, starts for the door, then turns back. "You're both still mad at me?"

Joanie shrugs, not looking at her.

"What would you have done, Joanie?" Lindsey's sick of the silent treatment.

She whips her head up then, glaring. "Well, maybe I would have thought it through first! All it's done is put a big split between Marci and Rob. You ask me, he's gone off the deep end, obsessed with this lawsuit. Nothing there for Marci or Patty. And for what?" She gestures choppily toward Kevin shrouded in his web of tubes and wires.

"I'm sorry. But...."

"But what? Easy for you! You get to feel all virtuous about outing that doc, but everybody else has to deal with the fallout."

"Hey. I did lose my job over it."

"What?" Joanie stares at her. "What are you talking about?"

Shit. She hasn't told the family yet, asked Rob not to tell.

"You're kidding! Now you're playing the silent martyr? Just like Mom?" Joanie's itching to be mad about anything these days.

Lindsey's about to snap back at her, then glances at Kevin's empty face. Damn. Here they are arguing over him, like he's already dead, just a slab of meat?

She takes another deep breath. "Let's go outside. I don't want to do this here." She tilts her head toward Kevin, and Joanie presses her hands against her mouth, blinking.

Joanie rises quickly, grabs the stroller and pushes Kendra hastily into the hall. Lindsey follows her to a lounge area with bright orange faux-leather settees that make her wince. She sits slowly, rubs her face, and blows out a breath.

"You got fired over this?" Joanie sits a ways away, nudging the stroller back and forth as Kendra nods sleepily.

Lindsey nods.

"Whoa." She shakes her head. "How are you paying the bills? I mean, Nick the Prick didn't exactly leave you with much in the piggybank, right?"

"I didn't want anything from him. The hospital gave me a severance package, I'm okay for a few months. I'm doing some freelance writing." She shrugs. "Probably pie in the sky, thinking I could support myself on that, but what the hell."

"Well, it's what you always had a gift for, Lin. Go for it."

Lindsey looks her in the eye, surprised. "Thanks." She clears her throat. "I wasn't trying to be a martyr, you know, just figured Mom had enough to worry about right now, the way she frets. She's really worried about you and Eric and Kendra."

"Yeah." Joanie blows out a breath, leans over to hide her face and adjust Kendra's pacifier. "Sometimes I think I've just hit the wall with all this, Lin."

"I know." Lindsey moves over beside Joanie and gives her a hug. "I am so proud of you."

"Oh, God, I'm such a mess! If it weren't for Don and Sharon, I think I just couldn't go on. I mean, I'm too old to be raising another baby."

Lindsey rubs her back. "It won't be forever. You'll work it out. Maybe Eric will get it this time, after rehab."

Joanie pulls back, digging in her pocket for a tissue and blowing her nose. She nods. "Yeah. I just take it a day at a time." She smiles then. "And Kendra really is an angel."

"Well, you know me—not exactly a baby person, and I'm smitten." Lindsey leans over to stroke Kendra's pudgy smooth arm, gets a sleepy smile from her. She sits back, takes a breath. "I wish Marci would talk with me. I just saw so many lives get hurt by that Dr. Bennerton. I had to tell them, see if there was a chance to turn it around for Kevin. Maybe there's still a chance for him."

Joanie gnaws her lip. "I don't think so. I can hardly stand to come here and look at him. It's like there's nobody home."

Lindsey nods reluctantly.

"I can't even imagine how it would feel to lose one of my kids! It's like it's killing Marci by degrees. And now what's happening between her and Rob. He's crazy with all this anger. And they used to be such a perfect family—I could at least look at them and think, yeah, it's possible. I don't know.... I mean, why them? It's not fair!"

Lindsey closes her eyes. "I know. Maybe we're all taking our anger out in different ways. But if Rob's out to get revenge on Bennerton, at least that's going to do some bigger good. His lawyer's a really decent guy, he wants to stop the corruption, the way the docs cover for each other. And if Marci needs to be angry at me, that's okay, too."

"She's still in her pain body. It'll pass." Newman's voice echoing from that day in the hospital stairwell.

Lindsey blows out a breath. "I've been kind of beating myself up over this, too. Maybe I shouldn't have interfered? Then I wonder how we'd all feel if it *had* made that difference and he was recovering. I mean...." She throws out her hands. "I don't know what I mean."

"Yeah, I get it." Joanie takes her hand, squeezes it. "Let's give it some more time, okay? Maybe it's not the best idea yet to run into Marci here."

Lindsey nods, gives her another quick hug, and heads

for the garden exit. She turns in the doorway, says, "Be well, Joanie."

Lindsey walks home through the park, passing under the big mossy maple where the fledgling owls played their leaf game. As the dappled light plays over her upturned face now, she sends out a prayer for Kevin. For all of them, really.

Back home, HighJinks and Sombra take advantage of her mood, finagling an extra portion of kibbles for lunch. She's giving Sombra a cuddle when there's a knock on the front door.

"Lindsey?" It's Agnes from two doors down, peering through her thick trifocals.

"Agnes! How are you?" Lindsey has to speak loudly for her.

"Oh, not too bad, not too bad." She holds out an envelope, her hand trembling. "This came in our mail yesterday, dear. Didn't see it until this morning. Got mixed in with our bills." She coughs. "Shame, Gordy was all excited, thinking we'd got a real letter."

Lindsey takes the envelope, glances at the return address, a green tree and *Evergreen Publications.* Her heart lurches. A rejection letter, already, from the anthology where she'd sent the essay.

She takes a deep breath, pushes aside the pang. She knows the odds. You just have to keep sending things out there. "Thanks, Agnes. Do you have time for a cup of tea?"

"No, no, got to move the sprinkler. You ought to give that apple tree a deep drink, too, dear."

She smiles. "I will." As Agnes weaves slowly down the walkway, she promises herself she'll send them a card so they can get some real mail. She sits on the front porch step, HighJinks coming out to mew and beg petting. She shrugs and rips open the envelope.

Dear Ms. Friedland,

We received your essay just as we were closing our selection process for Women and the Wild....

Lindsey sighs. Oh, well. She starts to set it aside, then reads on:

We're delighted to inform you that "The Stages of

Environmental Grieving" fills out our spectrum with just the right touch. We'd like to include it in the anthology....

Lindsey grips the paper. A grin spreads over her face, and she jumps up, tossing the page and letting out a whoop. HighJinks, offended at being dislodged, complains shrilly. Lindsey picks him up and dances over the lawn. "Hey, we're in business, big guy!"

HighJinks, unimpressed, wriggles free and huffs off under the hedge.

Lindsey laughs and picks up the letter, reads the terms. A thousand dollars! Plus some complicated percentages of possible royalties. Her eyes widen. "Wow."

She goes inside, takes a random turn around the living room, laughs again, spots the phone. She picks it up, taps out Damon's number.

"Hey, Lindsey. Good to hear your voice," he says. "Did you get the package?"

"I did. Thanks." Lindsey laughs again. "I didn't realize what an artist you are! You managed to make me look pretty good in that photo. And I love the one of you—I want an enlargement of that, too."

He snorts. "I only sent it because I promised. But, hey, are you gonna make the opening?"

"Of course. I had no idea, Damon. How many pies do you have your fingers in, anyway?"

A rich chuckle. "Probably a few too many.... So what's up? You sound jazzed."

"I am. Guess what? I just got my essay accepted to the women's anthology."

"Fantastic! Lindsey, that's terrific! What did I tell you?"

"Hello?" A tap on the half-open door. "Lindsey?"

"Oh!" Lindsey turns to see Newman in the doorway, peering in at her.

"What?" Damon is asking on the phone.

"Oh, sorry, I'll wait." Newman backs off to the porch as he sees she's on the phone.

Lindsey braces herself, as a surge of excitement washes through her. She fights the impulse to throw down the phone and race out to leap into Newman's arms.

"Lindsey, you there? Did we get cut off?"

You could say so. She takes a deep breath. "Damon, sorry, I've got a visitor at the door."

"Oh." A pause. "Mr. Maybe?"

Lindsey bites her lip. "Yes."

Another pause. "Well, okay. Let's talk tomorrow about the articles. I've got meetings in the morning, so how about after two?"

"All right. Damon, thanks again for the photos. And the hike."

"My pleasure.... Tomorrow, then."

Lindsey hangs up, takes a moment to settle herself, acknowledge the connection with Damon. She takes another deep breath and walks over to the doorway. Newman's sitting on the step, scratching HighJinks behind the ears, her fickle Siamese purring in closed-eyed ecstasy.

"He's shameless." Lindsey plops down beside Newman.

He tilts his head back toward the living room. "Who, your friend?"

She rolls her eyes. "I'm talking about HighJinks."

He chuckles. "Am I interrupting? I just dropped Melani at her riding lesson, doc said her knee's strong enough to start up again. I thought I'd see if you were home."

"I'm glad you did."

He smiles then, and she smiles back, and everything else—all the static and confusion—falls away into irrelevance. He touches her chin, brings her face up toward his, leans down to give her a kiss. It's a light touch, lifting away and leaving her wanting more. She sighs. He takes her shoulders, pulls her toward him, kisses her again, this time deeply, and that wildfire ignites at the base of her spine, flares up through her and reduces her brain to a hopeless molten puddle.

He pulls back, groaning. "Oh, boy, that does it. Lindsey, I'd really like to...*talk* with you, but every time I get near you, I...." He shakes his head, spreads his hands.

"You're not alone."

He sits back, takes her hands. "In about two minutes I'm going to pick you up, carry you into the bedroom, and do some really...thorough things to you." He adds quickly, "With your permission?"

Lindsey's toes curl with anticipation. "I guess I could stand that."

"But," he raises a hand, "first I want to ask you something." He runs a thumb over her palm, and for a second she's displaced onto the mountaintop with Damon again, only this connection with Newman is like the high-voltage just got switched on. He smiles into her eyes, nods. "Okay." He raises her hand to his lips, kisses her palm. "I've been running on overdrive lately, Lindsey. But I figured out a way we could have some time together. Will you come on a trip with me next week? I know it's short notice, but I've got to check in with my handicrafts sources in Guatemala, and it would be great if you could come with me. We can take some time just to...be. What do you say?"

She stares at him, gears spinning, then smiles. "I'd like that." She squeezes his hand, then shakes her head. "But I can't afford the plane fare right now." She shrugs.

"Lindsey." He squeezes her hand back. "Don't be silly. I'm asking you, I'll cover your expenses. I've got all these frequent flyer credits, anyway, so you don't have to feel... awkward about it."

She blows out a breath, fixes her gaze on the orange poppies glowing over the grass. "Let me think about this."

"Don't think." He takes her hand again, jiggles it. "Look, if it'll make you feel better, you can go as my assistant buyer." He laughs as she gives him a dubious look. "Seriously! I could use the help keeping track of inventory, I'm not exactly the most organized person in the world. And remind me what I agree to with those *caballeros*. You can take notes, keep us all honest."

She shakes her head again. "You're tempting me."

"Good! Then it's settled?"

She lifts her palms. "All right."

"Yes!" He jumps to his feet, takes her wrists and tugs her up off the step. "Okay, on to Plan B." He grabs her, tosses her over his shoulder, and starts up the steps as Lindsey dangles, kicking her feet.

"Oh, Lindsey, here's another one!" It's Agnes coming back, rounding Newman's car and waving another letter as Lindsey raises her face through her curtain of dangling hair.

"Oh, my." Agnes stops short. "Well, you're busy, my dear. I'll just...."

Lindsey chokes.

Newman swings around with her, says, "Hello."

Lindsey, upside down and helpless, gestures. "Agnes, this is Newman. Newman, Agnes."

"Nice to meet you, Agnes." Laughter bubbles in his voice, as he grips Lindsey's legs to steady her over his shoulder.

"Well, yes, here's your letter, dear." She steps forward to hand the envelope to Lindsey, still hanging there like an idiot. "You two have fun now." She totters off down the walkway.

Newman carries Lindsey in through the doorway. "Smart neighbor you've got. Excellent advice." He turns to shut the door and emphatically lock it. "No more postal visitors!" He carries her into the bedroom, heaves her laughing onto the bed, where she bounces and kicks the air. He grabs her ankles, eases her feet down onto the coverlet. "Coming in for a landing...."

He slides down over her, presses his solid warmth against her, and finds her mouth.

"Mmmmm." Lindsey pulls back for a breath. "Landing, or launching?"

He laughs, slips his palms beneath her shirt, over her breasts and around to her back, pulls her hips up tighter against his own.

All systems go. They're off and flying.

nineteen

AUGUST 1

Dear Diary,

(Now officially my travel journal.) We're flying! En route to Guatemala City on the red-eye from Miami, only flight we could get on short notice, which seems to be Newman's modus operandus. It's the middle of the night, but I'm too buzzed to sleep. Must be ten years since I've been back to Central America.

Sshhh. Everybody's asleep, there's just that visceral hum, lifting and dropping through the air currents. Newman's leaned back, dozing, long legs stretched out in the aisle. Told him I needed to jot down some travel article ideas, but I'm really memorizing the angle of his jaw, and I can admit here how I get this ridiculous pang of tenderness for the little extra age roll softening the edges. How vulnerable we are in sleep and aging, in these crazy bodies we wear.

There are also the lighter lines raying out from his eyes, that are usually crinkled with animation. I like the way he laughs. And now I can lean over, inhale a good whiff of his salty, sweaty essence. Mmmm.

XOXOX! I luv N. Is this a flashback to 8th grade math class, giggling with Carla and getting caught passing our silly notes about the crush of the week?

What I'd really like to check out is another portion of Newman's anatomy. How about if I flip my blanket over his lap and—

MS. FRIEDLAND, YOU ARE A VERY NAUGHTY GIRL! THIS BEHAVIOR WILL BE SUBJECT TO AN IN-DEPTH INVESTIGATION, AS SOON AS WE'RE BACK ON TERRA

FIRMA....
   Firming it up?
   WATCH OUT, LINDSEY!

The Jeep growls around twists and turns on the rutted dirt road, brick-red dust billowing in clouds behind them. Lindsey leans back, slitting her eyes to let the strobe of light-shade-light through overhanging pandanus palm and pine boughs play over her face. She turns her face to watch Newman's big hands on the wheel, raises her gaze to see him flash a grin at her.

She stretches, luxuriating in the dry heat like a massage for aching joints. They're weaving along the folded green skirts of one of the humped-back mountains pushed up close in the highlands like rumpled cloth—up and down, in and out, following the contours of the land.

Newman slows and pulls wide around a soot-grimed man in ragged pants plodding the edge of the road toward them, a huge load of charred branches on his back balanced by a tumpline over his forehead. A yellow-nape parrot zig-zags past. They round one more curve, and before them opens up a narrow green valley cupped by volcanic mountains, cradling the deep turquoise-blue waters of Lago Atitlan.

On the slopes above the lake, a cluster of pale colonial buildings in miniature glitters under the sun, the spire of a church stabbing above the rest.

Newman tilts his head toward it. "Solola. We'll stay there tonight." He reaches for her hand, squeezes it.

She returns the pressure, then pulls free to peel one of the melting-sweet miniature bananas off the cluster they'd bought earlier from a campesino standing beside the road with a wooden crate of fruits. She licks the banana suggestively as Newman laughs, then she takes a bite and leans over to push the rest into his mouth.

He licks his lips. "Here we go!" And accelerates over the crest, down a long swooping plunge through light and shadow and flashing lifting wings toward the lake.

"*Si, Señor, aca. El cuarto matrimonio, para el hombre grande.*" The short, graying proprietress gestures Newman through the doorway toward the double bed, then shoots a sly glance toward Lindsey.

There'd been an awkward moment when they'd checked in downstairs, and Lindsey had referred to Newman as *mi marido*—"my husband." It was common practice for unmarried couples travelling in conservative Latin America. Luckily married women retained their own last names here, just added on the appellations of their husbands, so the passports were no problem.

But Newman had stopped short, turning to give Lindsey a wary look.

The proprietress had glanced from him to Lindsey's bare ring finger and then raised skeptical eyes to her flushed face.

Belatedly, Newman had stepped forward. "*Si, un cuarto matrimonio.*"

But Lindsey's still feeling that moment of chill now, as she crosses the threshold into their room.

"*Bueno. Gracias.*" Newman accepts the big old-fashioned key from the proprietress. The woman, clearly more Spanish than native, smooths her polyester flowered dress, gives him a smile that flashes a gold front tooth, and retreats.

"*Perfecto.*" Lindsey steps into the high-ceilinged room and across the tiny black and white mosaic tiles, over to the open French windows where gauzy curtains flutter toward her. There's a balcony overlooking the plaza with its fountain and the whitewashed church beyond. The iron grillwork is maybe or maybe not safe to step out onto, but it's certainly picturesque with that seedy charm of old Latin America.

Newman drops his bag and steps over to the *matrimonio*-size bed, dropping onto it and bouncing to test the sag factor.

Lindsey, veteran of countless antique *hospedaje* mattresses, raises an inquiring eyebrow.

"Not bad." Newman pats the threadbare embroidered coverlet. "Shall we give it the acid test? *Señora?*"

"Hey, that was for—"

"Come here." He smiles. "I was just slow on the uptake. Hope you're not the Scarlet Woman now."

Lindsey shrugs. "I think our landlady's on to us. It'll give her some gossip material."

As she steps over, Newman tugs her onto his lap. "Then I guess it better be racy." He pulls her against him as the heat mingles their sweaty, dusty, fruity scents. He licks her neck, nibbles his way to her mouth. His lips are warm, delicious, inviting her deeper into red-gold darkness closing around her.

"Mmmm." She eases back. "Maybe we should rinse off first? Since we scored the luxury room with its own shower." No doubt cold water, but you can't expect the moon.

Which summons back the señora's sly smile downstairs as she looked from Lindsey to Newman. "*Hay un cuarto perfecto para la luna de miel.*" *The perfect room for a "honeymoon."* And despite herself, Lindsey feels a secret thrill at the word.

"The shower can wait," Newman's saying. "I want you just like you are, all salty and sweaty." He falls back onto the bed, which sags only moderately, pulling Lindsey along on top of him and tugging her blouse loose from her cotton skirt. Slipping a hand beneath it, he cups her breast. "Ah. *Que lindo.*"

"*Mejor sin vestido.*" And suiting action to the words, Lindsey sits up, straddling him, feeling his hardness stirring as she unbuttons his shirt and pulls it open. She leans over to inhale his spicy scent. Then pulls off her blouse, drops it over the side of the bed, loosens her hair from its clip and leans over to trail the dangling strands across his bare chest.

"*Deliciosa.*" He closes his eyes, smiling, and pulls her down onto him, bare skin on skin sliding, heated, light fading beyond the window to a dusty coppery haze, his mouth opening to hers.

The foot-passenger ferry slows, motor gurgling and coughing, to allow for the passage of two native dugouts paddled by fishermen. Lindsey leans over the rusty gunwale to trail a hand in cold ripples of deep blue mirroring the clear skies of high altitude. Across the lake, the sharp cones of volcanic peaks rake the air.

The motor revs again, and they swing in toward the steep, lush green shoreline and a distant wooden pier below a scatter of low buildings. Newman shifts on the bench, pulling out his cell phone to click through his message list one more time, then stuffs it into his pocket.

"Still no word from Melani?"

He looks over, blows out a breath, and shakes his head.

"She's probably fine, Newman. You know kids that age, they get swept up in stuff with their friends, and you said she was going to music camp. Why don't you call Kimberly?"

"Left her a message, but she never called back. Should have known better."

"Another chance to punish you?"

He darts a questioning look, and she shrugs. "It's what Nick would do. You leave an opening, and...well, you know."

He nods, reaches over to squeeze her hand. He still looks bothered.

She squeezes back. "She *would* let you know if anything was wrong with Melani, wouldn't she?"

He shrugs, then nods again. "You're right." He looks out over the lake. "It's just...well, Melani knows I always call her when I'm travelling. We've always been so tight."

"Hey, she's sixteen. Not exactly the most considerate age."

He raises his palms. "Right, look at me. My teacher would be reminding me about attachment."

"But you're a dad. You're *supposed* to worry."

He chuckles, glancing at the pier they're approaching. It's a ramshackle affair on wobbly-looking wooden posts, with a tiny, colorful figure waving toward them from the end. "*Entonces, Señora Friedland*," Newman changes the subject, "remind me again how many tablecloths and tunics we've already ordered? You're earning your wages on this trip."

Lindsey decides to save her questions for another day. The Eastern philosophy of non-attachment has never made sense to her—how can you love someone and *not* be attached?—and it seems like Newman hasn't exactly mastered it, either. Thank goodness. She pulls her notebook from the woven shoulder bag the manager of the last *cooperativa* insisted on giving her when she admired it—a rich purple with figured borders and wide strap of Mayan-motif animals including jaguars, plumed quetzals, parrots, and tapirs. Consulting her inventory, she points out the totals.

"*Gracias.*" He tilts his head, giving her an appreciative glance. "You're really scoring points here, not to mention adding to my prestige, having such a classy assistant along on this trip. And your Spanish is way better than mine. It's a big help."

"*De nada.*"

"This group we're visiting today is special. Pretty much what's left of one of the high-mountain villages the soldiers wiped out. What's the polite term? Ethnic cleansing?"

Lindsey shakes her head. "It's hard to grasp it when you're here, right in the middle of all this." She gestures toward the lake, the mountains, the rich greenery bursting with life. And not far away, those hideous army camps with their grotesque *mascotas* painted on the gates, all fangs and claws dripping blood. "What I heard was they'd kidnap the young village men to brainwash, turn them into soldiers. Send them back to kill their own people."

He touches her hand. "The shadow side finding one more outlet? Seems like the more we refuse to look it in the face, the nastier ways it finds to burst out."

Lindsey tilts her head to meet his gaze. "That's taking the long view."

"The only one that lets me bear it sometimes." He puffs out a breath. "Maybe it's time we turned the world over to women to run." Then he adds wryly, "Though I can testify some of them know all about abusing power, too."

"At least it might be a chance to do something different."

He squeezes her hand and releases it.

"So what about this family we're going to see?"

"Well, really an extended family. They're amazing. Headed up by great-grandparents, part of the old village *cofradia.*"

"That's the ritual hierarchy?"

"Right. Basically they ran things in the villages. These folks still have big mojo around here, it's all an underground network that officially doesn't exist. They're keeping as much of the traditional weaving patterns alive as they can, along with other things they don't talk about."

Lindsey nods. "What I picked up when I was living down here, their stories and weavings embody the sacred order of the world that the gods gave us. If they keep weaving and telling the stories, it keeps us *and* the gods alive."

"That's pretty much what I've gathered. I know they don't sell those special patterns, but those weavers produce the best work for export, too. I don't do much negotiating with them, just pay what they ask, unless they push it too far."

Lindsey smiles. "And that works for your business?"

He chuckles. "When I first starting coming down here, they were calling me *'el gringo loco'* because I wasn't haggling, just paid a fair price that was higher than anyone was getting before. So now I attract the best weavers and knitters. And all the exporters who deal with cooperatives are paying a little better, too. It comes out okay on the other end, so everybody's pretty happy."

"Good for you."

He shrugs that off. "Today I'm just checking in with the group, paying respects. It's like family, the people I work with. Got to have face to face contact."

"If I'd realized this was such a special family, I would have worn something fancier." She touches her plain cotton blouse.

He smiles. "You look perfect. They'll like you."

She smooths her calf-length skirt over her knees, hoping he's right. She's always dressed conservatively in traditional regions, to show respect for the native culture. That, and her Spanish that's picking up steam again after so many years away, has inspired an enthusiastic welcome among the women weavers of the cooperatives they've visited in the past couple of days. Yesterday, as Newman negotiated a shipment with the manager of a sweater-knitting group, a few of the women—mostly widows, she'd learned—let her know they regarded this export opportunity as a godsend to maintain their households. They'd urged her across the dirt road into a one-room, dirt-floored casita for refreshments and a "gal's-only" giggle fest conducted mostly in sign language, as this group of Mayan women spoke only a few words of Spanish. They'd all managed to communicate clearly enough their mutual admiration: The women stroked Lindsey's sunstreaked long hair, praised her green eyes "like the sacred jade," and feigned alarm at her height, while she soaked in the beauty of their gleaming dark eyes, smooth brown skin, and the colorful handwoven and embroidered blouses and skirts distinctive to each village. Mostly she envied their natural grace and femininity.

"*Hola, Señor Zender!*" A man in the local candy-striped trousers and loose tunic is waving energetically from the pier as the boat slows to nose in toward one of the assorted pylons of rough logs. "*Bienvenidos!*"

The young boy at the bow leaps out to run a line around the pylon, then scampers barefoot over the splintery boards to secure the stern. Newman makes a point of gallantly steadying Lindsey's arm as he assists her past cloth bundles and a tethered pig, over the gunwale onto the dock.

The local man sweeps off his straw hat and bows to her. After some elaborate introductions and welcomes in a mix of Spanish and Mayan dialect, Lindsey and Newman are ushered down the dock, up a steep dirt lane flanked by banana and mango trees, a simple whitewashed church, and the few shops of this roadless village. They turn down a dirt side-trail embraced by a fragrant tangle of greenery, blooms, and overhanging branches of the hardwood *jocote*, toward a compound of huts behind a fence of upright cut branches. As they enter the gateway to the central outdoor cooking area, it becomes apparent that yet another feast is being prepared. Any excuse for a fiesta in Latin America.

As they enter, stirring a hubbub of chickens and curious children, a cry goes up, and an old couple rise from chairs under a broad wooden trellis covered with shady vines. They are dressed in their best rainbow of colors, the woman's gray braid topped by an elaborately intertwined crown of a thickly-woven tubular scarf that crosses above the forehead and knots to leave fringes of blue, red, green, and yellow. Her profile beneath this headdress, with the proud jutting nose, could have been carved from an ancient Mayan pictograph. She spreads her arms, beckoning Lindsey and Newman toward the shade.

They pass a circle of women seated on the ground in their dark blue tubular skirts and their blouses woven in rich patterns of purple, red, gold, and green. They're rayed out around the trunk of an old mango tree, their hip-strap loom lines tied at one end around its trunk and the other end around their waists. They raise their heads to nod politely as Newman and Lindsey pass, quick fingers never pausing as they slide the spacer sticks and colored yarns through the warp lines of the emerging patterns.

Past the weavers, their progress is impeded by clusters of shrieking kids grabbing onto Newman's legs and being dragged along as he laughs and tosses phrases at them in awkward-sounding Mayan, provoking more laughter.

The silver-haired man waiting under the low trellis chops a hand toward the children and says something stern, which detaches the limpets from Newman's legs and lets him duck beneath the vines. The ceiling is a few inches too low for his height, which dwarfs the natives who make even Lindsey feel tall.

Stooping, Newman turns to gesture Lindsey in beside him. She's moving slowly herself, a little girl having become attached to her skirt, gripping it in a chubby brown hand. The other children have crept forward again after the rebuke from the patriarch. They're giggling, watching Newman with an air of intense anticipation.

Lindsey catches his eye, shrugs a question.

He winks at her, then takes a step toward her, straightening and pretending to whack his head on a beam of the trellis.

"Ow!" He rocks back in exaggerated dismay, smacking a hand to his head.

"*El Gringo! El Gigante!*" The kids erupt into peals of laughter, jumping and clapping their hands in delight. One little boy, bolder than the rest, runs toward Newman, pretends to ram headlong into a trellis post, and staggers back holding his head and groaning. The kids laugh louder, dancing around, which incites the chickens into flurries of squawking and flying feathers.

Another stern word from the old man, and the children subside, still giggling. Newman, stooping forward with a broad display of caution, winks at the children, provoking another wave of choked-off laughter. He takes Lindsey's arm with a gallant flourish and ushers her into the shade.

In the face of the dignified elders, Lindsey bows her head. As she straightens, the woman meets her gaze, and Lindsey is awed by the power in her eyes.

The elder's deep brown gaze, set in weathered wrinkles over the strong bones, shifts from Lindsey to Newman and back. A smile breaks over her face. "*Bienvenidos.*" *Welcome.*

twenty

COUGHING THROUGH CLOUDS OF copal incense, Lindsey
threads her way among the chaos of vendors seated on the
sweeping stone stairway of the Chichicastenango cathedral
for market day. She slips between two women with bundles
of lilies and exotic blooms, babies peering from the striped
shawls tied over their shoulders. While women and girls of
all ages tend their wares spread on blankets, creating with
their different village blouse patterns a wildly colorful
carpet, here in town the men loiter about in Europeanized
dress of cowboy hats and shirts, taking care of the
important male schmoozing, smoking, and drinking of
coffee or *aguardiente* spirits.

Lindsey can't resist a final purchase of some plump
avocados. She hurries down the last steps and across the
plaza to find Newman with the jeep ready in front of their
hospedaje. He's bending down to talk with a graying woman
in traditional garb, standing beside assorted bundles and
two young children.

He straightens as Lindsey approaches.

"*Hola*. Did you connect with Melani?"

"Finally." He beams and gives a thumb's-up, then turns
back to the Mayan woman, gesturing. "*Señora Vargas,
Señora Friedland*." In English, he explains that the woman
is headed with two of her grandchildren to a village along
their route today.

Lindsey smiles and tells the woman they have plenty of
room, gesturing to cover the gaps in the Mayan's Spanish
vocabulary.

She gives Lindsey a grateful, gap-toothed smile and
quickly shoos the boy and girl into the narrow back seat, as

Newman crams her cloth-wrapped bundles on top of their bags in the back cargo space. She starts to climb in beside the children on the cramped seat, but Lindsey touches her arm, gestures her toward the passenger front seat.

"*No, no, Señora!*" The woman looks appalled, starts again to get into the back.

"*Por favor, Señora!*" Lindsey insists, and Newman hands the grandmother into the front seat, where she adjusts her skirt and straightens her back, smiling. Lindsey squeezes in beside the kids, and Newman hands over the last of the baggage onto her lap, a wooden crate with two chickens oozing feathers between the slats.

As he climbs into the driver's seat and eases into the congested cobblestone lane, one of the chickens squawks and darts her head out to cock an eye at Lindsey and peck her hand. The kids laugh, as the grandmother claps her hand over her mouth in dismay.

Newman turns his head and meets Lindsey's gaze. "You okay back there?"

She laughs. "This is nothing compared to some of the bus rides I've been on. You know, the ones where you're standing for eight hours with maybe one foot contacting the floorboards between the livestock and produce and fifty people in the aisle? And there's a couple dozen votives and assorted saints hanging in the windshield?"

He glances aside at Señora Vargas, who is now looking rather smug, waving to everyone on the street. He looks back at Lindsey, and a slow smile spreads over his face.

"Oooph. Where are we headed?" Lindsey yawns and stretches against the Jeep seat, blinking drowsily at the dense green canopy closing over the dirt road, serrated leaves filtering the morning sunlight. Newman woke her up before dawn to drive east of Guatemala City, out of the highlands and into the fringes of the jungle sprawling toward the Caribbean coast.

"A surprise. You'll need your walking shoes."

"Well, how about a hint?" Lindsey's cranky with a stiff neck from dozing in the Jeep. "Is it a mile, or an all-day trek?"

He laughs, reaching over to tousle her hair. "Wake up, sleepy head! I guarantee you're going to love this. Trust me."

Lindsey, irritated, pulls away. "Don't—" Then she shakes her head.

"Hey. What?" He shoots her a look, eyebrows raised, then turns back to dodge a pothole in the rutted road as they jounce along.

Lindsey shakes it off. "Just a Nick flashback." She reaches to touch Newman's arm. "He'd get so high-handed, always wanting to run the show."

"Look, I just wanted to surprise you. This is a really special place we're going to, but if—"

She leans over to put her hand over his mouth. "I was letting my old buttons get pushed. Guess I still have some stuff to work through."

He nods. "Don't I know it! Look at me jumping into defensive mode, like I'm ready to dodge some bomb Kimberly's lobbing my way." He mock-cringes.

She chuckles.

Sobering, he asks, "Was it the same for you, Lindsey? It crept up on you? It must be different for women, that physical fear with the abuse. Did he hit you?"

Lindsey closes her eyes, heaviness of the old darkness pressing in on her, and she doesn't want to go there. She takes a deep breath. Newman wouldn't ask if he didn't want to know, so she tells him about some of it—the way Nick worked it, kept her always off balance between fear, hopelessness, and glimpses of light. How year by year the cloud she was living under kept getting denser until she felt the life nearly squeezed out of her.

She tells him about that final realization—Nick storming around the house in one of his rages, punching the wall while she was cowering in the locked bathroom. And how she'd suddenly straightened to take a good, long look in the mirror.

"That's when I knew I had to change. I couldn't change Nick—I'd tried it all, and he wouldn't even meet me a quarter of the way. When I looked in the mirror and saw myself becoming my mother, that's when I knew I had to get out, find myself again."

Newman reaches over to squeeze her hand. "You really got the double whammy, didn't you? Growing up with your dad, and then believing Nick was different? And now you have to watch your mother staying stuck in that same old dance."

She squeezes his hand back. "She was so *alive* when she was young, Newman. Always singing. I try to remember that, but it hurts to look at her now. How she's given herself away for the security—whatever the hell that means." She clears her throat. "But I want to spend more time with her. She's so frail, I don't know how much longer I'll *have* a mother."

She bites her lip then, turning to him. "I'm sorry, Newman, I wasn't thinking. Your mother...." *died of breast cancer.* Again, Lindsey's grateful to be alive, a survivor.

Newman squeezes her hand. "It's okay. Maybe what you're going through with your mom is harder in a way." He pulls his hand back to the wheel to negotiate a particularly rutted patch of road. "But I do miss her. Miss her for Melani's sake, too. She never got to meet her grandmother."

"Tell me about her?"

He hesitates, opens his mouth, closes it again, then blows out a breath.

"It's okay. You don't have to."

He shrugs. "Somehow being here in Guatemala, it's got me thinking about her. She was so beautiful, strong but quiet with it, like these Mayan women."

"They are amazing."

He clears his throat. "Hey, we're here. I'll...tell you about her later." Clearly he wasn't ready to talk more, so Lindsey sat back, settling into the light and shadow flickering over them as they turn off into an even narrower, rutted dirt road. Then they break out of the dense foliage into a dirt clearing with a wooden hut, a straggle of sheds, and some vegetable patches.

Barking erupts from behind the flowering-vine-festooned hut, and a shirtless man rounds the corner, calling back two scruffy brown mutts bounding toward the parked Jeep. He tilts back his straw cowboy hat and peers toward them, then a white smile flashes. "*Señor Zender! Bienvenidos!*"

After introductions to a shy wife and children who emerge from the hut, Newman arranges to leave the Jeep here while they take their knapsacks with picnic provisions down the trail behind the house. Newman's being mysterious again, refusing to reveal their destination.

They pass a tilled field of orange dirt, morning sun starting to bake it, then the dense tropical forest closes over them again in sliding tones of green, sparked by an occasional flash of red or yellow parrot feathers and the hanging clusters of white, purple, and orange blooms. Leading the way, Newman suddenly holds up a hand and makes a hushing gesture.

He steps back, and Lindsey peers around him to see a tapir ambling down the path toward them. The shy creature, like a cross between a giant pig and an elephant with its floppy long snout, pauses to fix a look of gentle curiosity on them. After a moment, it turns into the underbrush, disappearing in a surprisingly silent movement, given its size.

"Almost there." Newman gestures her ahead of him.

She rounds a curve of the trail, then stops short. The riotous foliage opens before her into a clearing where someone has been at work hacking back the engulfing vines and brush. An upright *stela* slab of dark stone nearly blocks the path, its carved Mayan face beneath an elaborate plumed headdress staring Lindsey down.

She takes a startled step back. "Wow."

Newman comes up behind her and lays a hand on her shoulder, squeezes lightly. "Hernando came across it a couple years ago."

"Incredible." Lindsey steps forward again and touches the cool stone, pushes aside a trailing vine to trace the lines of the ancient carving.

"There's a German group that started excavating, but so far they haven't done much. They don't want tourists finding out about it yet." He tugs her forward into the clearing, gestures across at a stone structure barely emerging from the lush greenery. Stepped stone climbs up the near side to a wall that disappears into the forest, a sprawling strangler fig having displaced a tumble of building blocks along its length.

Lindsey hurries across the rough clearing toward the structure.

She climbs up the tall steps, twice the height of an ordinary stairstep, and sits on the rough, lichened stone atop the wall. Slanted light beams ray down through the tree canopy, epiphytes and vines festooning the branches that spread like graceful candelabra toward the morning sun.

Newman climbs up to sit beside her. His voice hushed, he says, "This is a good spot to meditate. How about we sit with some silent mantras? If we keep our eyes open, we'll see what we invite in."

Lindsey stiffens, again remembering Nick, the way he'd try to dictate the "right" way to see. But then she lets out a breath and resets. Newman's offering her the gift of this special place, and he's obviously got something more up his sleeve. So far, with him, the exhilaration of discovery has outweighed the comfort of linearity.

She takes some deep, quieting breaths, silently reciting one of the mantras he's taught her as they've practiced morning meditation on the trip. Lindsey's been caught in the paradox of struggling to find the place of no struggle, striving to quiet her "brain whirl" while surrendering striving—more of those Zen-der twists? Now, with Newman beside her, welcoming his core calmness flowing through her as she learns to expand into new levels of perception, she finds herself in that place of peaceful ocean waves even as her eyes stay open, vision blurring to absorb the abundance of green life.

Time warps and bends into an infinite loop. And she somehow steps through it, or that doorway moves over her stillness, and she's in the presence of...the ineffable. All-encompassing, and she *is* that larger being. The shimmering contours of an eternal, maternal divinity enclose Lindsey, infuse her, and she's throbbing with the power of that compassionate connection to everything, everyone. She—Lindsey—all her former definitions melt into that union, and for a moment her ego voice panics into chittering protest.

"Hush," a deep, calming voice inside her soothes, father/mother love cradling her from without and within.

Suddenly a streak of blood-red flashes through the rich, nourishing green. Lindsey blinks and gasps. Newman's hand reaches to touch hers where it rests on the warm grainy stone, grounding her back in this place.

Lindsey blinks again, draws in a deep breath as another flash of bright yellow, punctuated with a crimson dot, sweeps through her visual field. She gives herself a shake, focuses, and sees a toucan perched on a branch at eye level across from their own wall perch.

The bird, with its sharp black, red, and yellow clown markings, tilts its head to check them out. Apparently finding nothing alarming, it reaches its oversized beak that looks like a ripe banana, and plucks a round red fruit or nut from the clusters hanging off the branch. It flies past again, the crimson orb vised in its beak.

As if at a signal, the air is alive with a flock of toucans, all swooping back and forth to pluck the red fruits, their sweeps of bold color intoxicating against the green backdrop. Lindsey hardly dares to breathe, for fear of breaking the spell.

A new player enters the clearing. The dark, lithe figure drops from an upper branch, hurtles downwards, then throws out a long, wiry arm to grip a branch and swing, landing on another branch. It leans forward to pluck some leaves and stuff them into its mouth, tilts over the edge of balance and drops, catching itself to swing by a long ropelike tail.

More spider monkeys follow the first, the troop of babies and adults sweeping through the branches they treat with a casual flair as their original jungle gym. The long-limbed acrobats scamper up trunks, leap from branch to branch, swing off by their tails and fly across to another tree, all of them passing and crossing each other in a complex aerial ballet. And all the while they're grabbing fistfuls of leaves and munching.

The bright toucans are still flying past these black monkeyshines, weaving a tapestry of living color. Newman's hand grips hers, joy reverberating, fountaining up to spill over them with the warmth of sunlight breaking through the leaves.

twenty-one

Dear Diary,

Now my "astral travel" journal? Newman talks so casually about connecting long-distance, or across time, with his departed Teacher or his own students abroad. Says that in India, no one would be surprised to hear about such spirit connections. Well, if I could pull it off, I know where I'd go— back to that magical jungle clearing with the flying toucans and monkeys, sitting on the Mayan ruins beside Newman. Haven't seen or heard from him since we got back a week ago. But I guess that's the point: If I get to the place of no-place in meditation, then I can be any place and all places.

So this morning I faithfully stacked blanket and pillow and plunked down in the closest approximation to lotus position my poor old knees will manage. Recited the mantra of surrender to divine will. Visualized a clear river washing away distracting thoughts....

Forty-five minutes and two hot flashes later, I was a sweaty mess from trying so hard not to try. My psychic drainpipe clogged with every trivial annoyance and stored-up resentment from the past five years, all tangled into a huge gunky hairball like those nauseating messes you finally get around to pulling out of the shower drain. The monkey mind really good at deciding that spiritual enlightenment rates a poor second after all those important things like, "Oh, damn, forgot to throw those dishtowels in the wash" or "Better schedule that screening colonoscopy my doctor's office keeps bugging me about."

Definitely not in the Om state! But at least now I know

it's there—that presence of timeless compassion. And Newman did remind me it's a practice. As in, lots of? Like those endless piano scales I repeated as a kid? It's worth it when all the Stuff falls away and I realize I'm Here. Now. Being.

And if all else fails on the road to bliss, there's always chocolate.

But enough transcendence for one day! Got a million things to catch up on, not to mention two needy cats with their whiskers all in a bristle over five whole days in the Feline Bed-and-Breakfast.

Damon wasn't thrilled with my putting off some of the articles and essays, so it's back to work. This being my own boss is going to take discipline. Not to mention a vigilant eye on the piggy bank. So maybe it's good Newman's off in his work-whirl again.

And what about that other moment at SeaTac, waiting to collect our luggage after the trip? I was asking him more about the women's weaving cooperativa, and what he'd said about positive female power. Did he think those women might be a good model for a matriarchy the world needs now? And I told him how at the Mayan ruins I'd felt the presence of an elemental nurturing Mother. Felt a part of Her.

Then he laid one of his damn Zender aphorisms on me, to the tune of, "That can be an ego trap. Feeling godlike."

I tried to tell him it wasn't like that.

But somehow the static was back. He pulled out his goddamn cell phone—"Have to check in"—and started answering his business messages. Damn. WTF??

"So, where are we?"

It's Damon on the phone, sounding a bit peevish. They're circling around Lindsey's short-notice trip with Newman, not talking about it while they're really talking about it while discussing getting back on schedule with the proposed *Whiplash* articles. "Can you at least get me that short piece on the pulp mill mercury cleanup by Thursday morning? I'll email all the facts and figures, should be a no-brainer."

"Thanks," she says drily. Probably a good thing to work

on, since her brain does seem to have dissolved into mush.

"Come on." He thaws with a chuckle. "Don't go all prima donna on me now, Lindsey. You know I like your flair. With words," he adds, "among other things. So if we can get a rhythm going..." a pause, "on these short pieces, it'd be sweet. I don't have time to sweat out the finished articles, and the other writers are stretched thin. I'll feed you the data, and you won't need to spend time on research. You've got the style, and a good eye for getting to the core."

"Thank you." She means it this time. "That sounds good, Damon."

"And maybe you can help me liven up this little cele-bration piece I've started about the hospital road access."

"What?"

"You haven't heard? They dropped the right-of-way application! We saved the park! Guess they didn't need any more negative publicity, what with the malpractice case and all."

"Damon, that's fantastic!" She must have missed the news while traveling. "That definitely makes my day!"

"Yeah, sometimes the people speak loud enough."

"They did. We all did.... Okay, once I finish these short pieces, we should get together to talk about the Kwamish project. I promise, no more distractions."

"That sounds pretty boring. You and Mr. Maybe burning out already?"

"Damon, that is *so* not your—"

Pounding on the front door interrupts them. She didn't hear a car pull in, wonders if it's Newman surprising her with a drive-by. Hopes so. She still hasn't seen or heard hide nor hair of him since they got back from Guatemala.

"Just a sec, Damon, there's someone at the door." She opens it to her sister Fran, face all blotchy, eyeliner smeared, fist poised to pound again.

"Fran! What's wrong?"

"Linny, thank goodness you're home! Joanie just called. Mom's in the E.R. We need to get up there."

Lindsey's mind spins.

"Lindsey?" A faint voice from the phone.

"Oh. Fran." Lindsey gestures her in, grips the phone and tells Damon, "It's my sister. My mom's in the emergency room, I've got to go."

"Oh. Sorry. Good luck."

"Thanks. I'll call you later." She turns to Fran. "Let me grab my purse. What happened?" The gears are spinning, throwing up every dire possibility she's been bracing for over the past few years.

"She fell and broke her hip."

"Oh." Conditional relief washes through her. "But she's okay?"

"Well, they're going to take her into surgery. But what Joanie said...." She takes a deep breath. "Dad wigged out in one of his rages, grabbed her and shook her, and that's how she fell. Or got thrown down. That's what Mom told her, I guess. I'm not exactly sure."

"Shit." She stares at Fran.

"Yeah. That shit-head! I could kill him." Her face is flushed, hands clenched.

Lindsey fights off her own wave of fury at their rageaholic father, thrusts through the drowning darkness of too many bad memories cresting like a tidal wave they've all been somehow holding at bay. The looming questions are suddenly right in their faces.

She takes another deep breath, reaches to give her sister a hug. Fran resists for a moment, rigid, the oldest sister who's always in control. Then she suddenly goes limp, leans into Lindsey's shoulder, shorter even with the stacked heels she wears. "Oh, God, Lin. What are we going to do with them?"

She pats her back. "Let's go. One step at a time."

Up at the hospital, Joanie's in the E.R. waiting area, rocking a crying Kendra against her shoulder. "Here, I'll take her," Fran says, seizing on the chance to step back into mothering mode. She sits and bounces Kendra on her knees, gets her playing patty-cake.

"Thank God you got here." Joanie scrapes her straggling hair back behind her ears. "Don's getting off work early, he'll come pick up the baby."

"Where's Mom? How's she doing?" Lindsey sits on the other side of Joanie on the slippery black settee.

Joanie blows out a breath. "They've got another doc in there, a surgeon, working her up for pre-op. Then they've got to admit her. Looks like they'll do a hip replacement tomorrow morning."

"What happened?"

"I don't...." She scrubs her face. "I'm not thinking right, this place is crazy." She shakes her head. "I don't really know. Lucky it's my day off, I was home with Kendra. Mom calls, she's crying, in pain, and Dad's ranting in the background, and I'm trying to get out of her what's going on. You know, how she always calls with all these false alarms. Like she just lives for those trips to see her doctors, wants us to run her around. But this time it's sounding bad. So I throw Kendra in the car and head over there."

Fran, holding a quieter Kendra now against her shoulder, asks, "So what is going on? Where's Dad now? Did he hit her, or what?"

Joanie glances around at the crowded waiting room. "All I know is I get there and she's lying on the couch crying. She says Dad pushed her down and she hurt her hip. Dad's yelling at her, denying he did anything. So I tell him to get the hell out of there, and he takes off in his goddamn truck, and I try to get some sense out of her. She says he shook her and she fell on those stupid tiles, landed on her hip, and now it's really painful. When I try to touch it, she screams. There's something really wrong. So I call the ambulance. Then she tells me Dad got mad at her over who knows what this time, and grabbed her, started shaking her and telling her he was going to kill her, cut her up in pieces and throw her in the pond. Then he shoved her and that's when she fell down and felt something snap and she screamed. He grabbed her off the floor and threw her on the couch and told her to stop being a baby."

"That bastard!" Fran grips Kendra tighter, and the baby starts crying again. "We need to file a report, get a restraining order—"

"Hey, there! Where's my girl?" It's Don, hurrying toward them and leaning over to scoop Kendra, shrieking again, out of Fran's grip. "Hey, now, pretty girl." He jigs her in his arms, and the exhausted baby finally goes limp. Rocking her, Don leans over to kiss the top of Joanie's head. "How you doing?"

She stands and leans into him, arm around his waist, tears breaking out. "I don't know!"

Fran's on her feet now, too, standing as tall as she can. "We need to get Mom to make a statement, get her away from that monster. Hasn't he messed up all our lives long enough?" She's itching for a fight.

Don raises his eyebrows, then turns to Fran. "Look, from what Joanie's told me, I don't think anyone really knows what happened. Let's just slow down."

"We need to take care of Mom first," Lindsey says, and turns to Joanie again. "Can we see her? Who's in charge?"

"Lord knows. It's so confusing in here." Joanie scrubs at her eyes. "I was in there with her, then they said to wait out here while the surgeon examined her and looked at the scans. Then they'll get her transferred into a hospital room, but that might take a while. I've been here," she glances at her watch, "a couple hours now."

"So where in Hell *is* Dad, anyway?" Fran's like a bulldog.

Joanie sighs. "I left a note at the house, and he finally showed up here. Mom started screaming when she saw him. Then he started getting loud and obnoxious about how they were poisoning her with those IV pain meds. She *was* rambling, pretty out of it. Another great scene...." She gives a shudder. "I think they figured she was delirious, told Dad to come back later. I don't know where he went."

"Didn't you tell them he shook her? Threw her down on the floor?" Fran's glaring.

Joanie shakes her head. "I don't *know* what happened, damn it! Before the ambulance came, I asked Mom if she wanted to file a complaint against him, and she flat refused. Said he didn't mean it. And *he* said he didn't do anything, so...." She sighs and spreads her hands.

"Why don't you come home with me, honey?" Don's looking concerned. "Rest up a little, then you can come back."

"That's a good idea. We'll take a shift," Lindsey says.

Finally they persuade Joanie to go home with Don and Kendra, so Lindsey and Fran take up the wait. Lindsey, stiff from the uncomfortable settee, paces past the various clumps of human misery packed in the unwelcoming room—some bleeding, some complaining, some just glazed over like Fran by now. She asks the harried-looking reception clerk one more time if she can go back to talk with her mother, and the clerk sighs and calls back to the nursing staff.

"Okay. Someone will come out for you."

Lindsey waves Fran over, and a green-clad, tired-looking young man escorts them past doorways and into a big open space echoing with footsteps, beeping monitors, equipment being rolled into spaces partitioned with curtains hung on ceiling tracks. They step aside for an aide pushing a gurney with a groaning bald man lying under a blanket.

"Friedland?" Their escort checks his clipboard and gestures them toward a curtained space, then hurries on.

Lindsey pulls the curtain aside and peers in. "Mom?"

Opal looks pale, sparse hair flattened over her head, so thin she's barely making a hump in the blankets, except where they've got pillows bracing her hip. Eyes closed, she groans, then blinks and gropes for her glasses beside her on a tray.

"Here, Mom." Fran hurries over and hands her the glasses.

"Fran? Linnie?" She peers. "Oh, thank goodness! This place is so awful, can't you take me home? I was so cold, and nobody would come. Where's Arlen?" She pushes against the covers as if to rise, then gasps and lies back again.

"Just relax, Mom." Lindsey strokes her hair back, squeezes her shoulder. "You broke your hip, so you need to lie still. They've got you on pain meds, that's why you feel a little confused. Dad will come back later."

Fran hisses, "Don't tell her that!"

Lindsey turns to give her a quick frown, but it's too late, Opal's caught it. She grips Lindsey's wrist with surprising strength. "I'm not going into a nursing home! I know that's what you want, trying to take me away from Arlen."

"Mom, we just want to get you healed. You don't need to think about this now," Lindsey tries to soothe her.

Opal shakes her head again. "He didn't mean anything. You know how he likes to yell, but he's a good provider. I don't want to be alone. We've got the animals, the garden. I just want to go home."

"Hush, now." Lindsey strokes her hair again. "Nobody's making you do anything, Mom. Try to get some sleep now." She turns to Fran, who's glaring at her. "Maybe we should see if they can give her a sedative or something."

"Lindsey, you're just encouraging her, covering it all over again," Fran whispers in a hot, angry gust.

Lindsey narrows her eyes, shakes her head. "Not now," she hisses. "Go get a nurse."

"Linny, please," Opal repeats, still clutching her wrist, "don't make me go in a nursing home. That's where people die."

Fran takes a deep breath, eases past the monitor lines on the other side of the bed, leans down to kiss Opal's forehead. "Don't worry, Mom. We'll take care of you." She gives Lindsey a significant look, then hurries out through the curtain gap, heels tapping staccato over the tiles.

"Ms. Friedland? Lindsey Friedland?"

"Yes." Lindsey, working at home, drops her pen onto the papers on her desk. "This is Lindsey." She doesn't recognize the voice on the phone, but there's a familiar quality to it. "Is this the hospital?" Opal's surgery went well the day before, but you never know.

"No, it's Sharon, Dr. Osborne's nurse."

"Oh." Lindsey gets a strange feeling in her gut, like she's just stepped into a plummeting elevator.

"It's about your mammogram. It's just a precaution, but...."

Lindsey doesn't hear the rest past a sudden rushing roar in her ears. It was just a precaution, they'd said at her checkup, calling her back in for those extra views after she'd gone through the drill and was waiting in the cubicle in their cotton gown to be told everything was fine, you can get dressed and go home now and celebrate your five-year mark. You beat the cancer!

Just a little shadow on the one angle. The radiologist looked at it again, and decided it was only scar tissue. And Lindsey so sick of thinking about her health, she was eager to forget about it.

"Ms. Friedland? Lindsey?" The phone's squawking at her.

"Oh. Sorry. I didn't catch that last part." She takes a deep breath, hands suddenly sweaty on the receiver.

"Doctor reviewed the mammogram; he thinks we should do a biopsy. Just to make sure. With your history...."

"I know." She steadies her voice. They have to cover

their butts, she knows that. It's nothing. Just jumping through hoops.

"Can you come in tomorrow? We have a cancellation at ten, might as well get it over with," Sharon continues in a perky voice.

"Sure. Yeah. That's great."

Damon's kissing her, and she thinks she shouldn't be doing this, what about Newman even if he has gone AWOL again? But damn, Damon's lips are delicious. *Carpe Diem.* Who knows how long she'll be here, and whole? And *he*'s definitely here, hot and spicy pressing over her, blue-black hair like gleaming wings hanging to curtain her face as he smiles and lowers his face again, tongue exploring.

"Mmm," is all Lindsey can manage, deplorably enjoying it.

Caw! Caw! Damon, with his mischievous grin, shapeshifts into a raven, long hair becoming blue-black, gleaming wings as he spreads them, lifts up and away into the air. *Caw! Caw!*

No, it's her phone's ringtone shrilling. "Damn! What time is it?" she croaks like the raven, groping over her bedside stand. She finds it as it stops ringing, blinks at the missed-call display. Joanie. A text message pops up: *Mom's having a rough day, can you check in with her at the hospital? I'll call you later.*

Lindsey has overslept, was juggling a lot yesterday between the hospital and her writing deadlines, then sleepless half the night with worrying about Opal, her own biopsy, Kevin in a coma, her precarious bank account, the empty static from Newman after the lovely connection on the trip....

"Jeez, then who do I dream about? Damon."

She groans. But somehow the dream has reclaimed her enjoyment of ravens, those delightful tricksters, after the nightmare of evil Nick and the bird. These days, she takes each gift when it comes.

She rides her bike to the hospital with a little garden bouquet for Opal, spends some time with her, trying to reassure her about the upcoming transfer to rehab for physical therapy, which Opal is convinced means a death sentence. When Fran shows up, Lindsey heads back home to work on those articles for the *Whiplash*. But she can't stop the brain whirl.

She feels weak, unable to get past the anxiety gnawing at her since the biopsy.

She hasn't heard the results yet. She's been trying to stuff it, telling herself it's no big deal, she's not going to buy into the medical paranoia trip again. And she'd decided earlier, going through it all, that if the cancer came back, she wouldn't take chemotherapy, wouldn't bow to the pressure. There's got to be a better way to heal than poisoning a person's immune system. But will she hold the line? Will she be strong enough?

She has to admit it now—she's afraid of more disfigurement. Of dying. Despite what she told Megan just a month ago. But then realizes it *was* true. When she went through it before, she was so dulled by despair, struggling through the Nick nightmare, she didn't care that much whether she lived or died. And now she does want to live. She wants to explore her writing, wants to find out where she can go with it. And she wants to love again. Feels so much waiting to flower, if she can only get clear of all these confusions with Newman.

She picks up the phone, then hesitates. She left him a message after Opal's hospitalization, just wanting to hear his calming voice, but she hasn't heard back from him. She knows he's busy with his daughter—and of course Melani does need to come first—and getting some shipments out from his warehouse in Seattle. And sometimes the cell phone messages seem to get lost in electronic limbo. But why can't he just do the thoughtful thing, and touch in with her? Like taking a minute to call and show he cares will mean he's somehow trapped in "expectations"? Is it supposed to be enough that they meet in "astral" time, as he claims when he "sends her blue light"? She fights an impulse to drive over to his place, since she doesn't want to show up uninvited if Newman's daughter is there. He hasn't introduced her to Lindsey.

She blows out a breath, shakes her head, and taps in his number one more time. Listens to it ring as she takes her phone out to the porch to watch morning light finger through the trees along her lane.

"Hello? Lindsey?"

"Newman, I caught you." She takes a deep breath.

"Barely. I've got Melani today, I'm on the run and I can't talk long." Voice sounding rushed, the static back.

Lindsey closes her eyes, heat surging through her—hurt and anger and confusion. "And how are *you*?" She wishes now she'd listened to her pride, hadn't called him, but plunges on, "Newman—"

"Wait. Hold on a sec." There's someone talking in the background, then Newman muffled, saying, "I'll go load your saddle and stuff in the van. Better hustle it, we should...." Some rustling and a door shutting, footsteps. "Lindsey? Melani's getting ready for her horse show. It's a big deal, first one since her accident. We've got to get the trailer and pick up her horse at the stable, so I don't have much time."

"Oh." She takes another breath. "Did you get my message?"

"I saw you called. I was going to call you back tonight, after I dropped Melani at her mom's. Are you okay? You sound upset."

"Well. I am. My mom fell and broke her hip, so it's been—"

"What? I'm sorry! Is she all right?"

"Well, physically okay. The surgery went well. But it's Dad, Mom and Dad, the whole mess. I mean, we're not sure, but it looks like he pushed her down while they were arguing. Now we have to figure out what to do." Now she's glad she didn't blurt out her anxiety over the biopsy in her message.

"Oh." A breath. "That's hard. Lindsey, I want to talk with you, it's just that I can't really focus right now. Can I call you back later today? I'd invite you out here, but I have to take off to Seattle right after I drop Melani off. I could call you from the road, and you can tell me about your mom."

"I guess." Is that the best he can do? "I'm wondering if you could teach me another mantra. I just can't get anywhere with the meditation practice. I could really use it right now."

Silence for a moment. Then, "Lindsey, I think you need to look inside yourself for this one. I don't think I should be your guru."

"What?" She blinks.

"I think you're starting to depend on me too much."

"Depend?" She holds the phone out and stares at it, then repeats, "Depend? How can I be depending on you when I hardly ever see you? When you won't even return a phone call?" *When I won't share my fears with you because I know you won't be there?*

"Lindsey, we just spent five days together on the trip. That's all I can give you for a while."

"Give me? What about give *you*? Wasn't that trip your idea?"

"Of course. I really enjoyed sharing that time with you, Lindsey. But now I've got to focus on—"

"'Really enjoyed'? Like really enjoying a good meal?" Lindsey shakes her head, blurts out, "What am I, some item on your To Do list you've checked off, now go away and don't bother you until the next time you get the urge?"

"Lindsey." His voice has cooled. "I tried to warn you from the start, I can't be there for you all the time the way you want. Maybe it wasn't so smart, inviting you on that trip. You wanted it to be a *luna de miel*, didn't you?"

"Damn it, that's not fair! Are you saying you didn't feel— *don't* feel all that's good between us? Every time we make a connection, you freak out and put your wall up. That static." She takes a breath. "I'm not asking for a long-term commitment. Just asking you to open up, let me in. Show some caring."

A pause. "Lindsey, I don't think you're being honest with yourself. You're building those scenarios we talked about, trying to put me—put us—in a box. Can't we just let things between us be what they are?"

"So what does that mean? Maybe you're not being honest with yourself, either. It's your excuse for every-thing—not falling into expectations, staying free of 'roles.' Maybe Megan's right, you only want me for booty call."

"Booty.... Megan said that?" Then he sighs, and his voice gentles. "Lindsey, this is what I was talking about. What I didn't want us to fall into. Slinging accusations. I'm sorry if I've hurt you, but I think I made a mistake. We're neither of us ready for this."

Lindsey's shaking her head, as Newman goes on, "Look, I wanted to tell you this in person, but I think maybe it's better that we don't get close enough right now to get physical—it just seems to take us over. I'm taking Melani on a trip to India. We're going to visit the ashram, it'll be good for both of us. She needs me to be really *there* with her. And I think you and I could use some space."

"What?" Lindsey scrubs at her eyes, wipes her dripping nose on her sleeve. She's a mess.

"We'll be gone until school starts. I think it's better if I don't call you. Let this cool off." He sighs. "You know, I tried to tell you maybe I'm just not relationship material. All this getting tangled up in longing, it takes us out of appreciating where we *are*. I don't want to get tied up that way now. Maybe never. And it's not fair to you to let you believe different."

She sits there staring over the lawn at the wild rose hedge. What *does* she want from him? A guru? Or a lover?

"Lindsey? Did I lose you?"

"Yep. Not even maybe, Mr. Maybe." She hits Disconnect.

So. Newman's off to India to transcend human emotions, and Lindsey's marinating in hers, despite best efforts to practice meditation. She supposes she might find it easier to enter the calm ocean blue if it weren't all wrapped around Newman's presence in her mind. But she doesn't want to chuck the effort just because she's untranscendentally pissed off at her "guru." And it *isn't* a guru she wants—she wants a lover who'll be open to learning from her, too.

"Why does everything have to be so damned complicated?" she mutters, then glances hastily around her, remembering she's not in her own home office where the cats don't care how crazy she acts. None of the *Weekly Whiplash* staff seems to have noticed, to her relief. The two reporters are glued to their computer monitors, fingers tapping, and the green-haired young man who handles the phone and miscellaneous is plugged into his iPod, nodding to an inaudible beat as he sorts mail.

Lindsey shifts uncomfortably in the chair, her breast still sore from the biopsy. And she's still waiting for the results, trying not to go down that rabbit hole....

She gnaws her pencil, scribbles another question for Damon about the traditional Kwamish shellfish rights, and blows out a breath, glancing up at the clock on the wall. He's late for their meeting. Making a point? She shuffles around the clipped reference articles, trying not to wonder why she'd dreamed about kissing him, then pulls out the photos he'd given her and studies them again.

Nana, 4th of July is scribbled on the back of one of them. Lindsey's already added it to the list of Damon's prints she wants, after attending his gallery opening.

She can't help smiling whenever she sees the silver-braided woman's smile. It's wide, full of humor and warmth as she looks up at her grandson over a partially-finished grass basket she's weaving with arthritic-looking fingers. There's a feeling of movement into and out of that moment, an air of teasing and affectionate admonishment, like she's ready to shake her head over whatever Damon's up to now. This is his gift as a photographer—he seems to capture whole stories in his images.

"Phew!" The office door is swinging open, propelled by Damon gusting in, long hair hanging loose today. "Lindsey, hey, sorry, I lost track of the time." He stops short, flashes his teeth, and shrugs.

"Well, I came up with some more—"

"Damon, that is such a hot idea! I'm, like, totally into Googling for you." Cutting Lindsey off, a bubbly young red-head in dangly earrings, extremely low-rise jeans, and equally missing-the-midriff tank top bounces through the door, bumping into Damon. "Oh, jeez, I'm such a klutz!" She grips a notebook and steps back just far enough to allow minimal air flow between them. "So, awesome, this is, like, so incredible. What do you want me to do first?" She tilts her head and straightens, thrusting her breasts out—all that smooth young skin and firm, healthy breasts. Lindsey swears they're brushing Damon's arm as the gal smiles up at him.

He clears his throat, glances from the young woman to Lindsey at the conference table, then at the two reporters who've stopped work to check out the action.

"Uh, everybody, this is Julianne. She'll be doing an internship with us for fall quarter." He gestures toward the green-haired reception guy. "This is Zeal." Then the writers.

"Nora, and Abe." Then, "And Lindsey."

Julianne waves at the others, then steps forward to offer Lindsey a handshake. "Nice to meet you, Ma'am. You just tell me if I screw up on anything, okay?" She gives Lindsey an earnest smile, then bounces back over to Damon's side like a wriggling puppy.

"Ah...." Lindsey blows out a breath. Now is one of those moments when she wishes she'd mastered that sardonic Mr. Spock raised eyebrow.

Damon's biting his lip as he meets Lindsey's eye.

"So, when do I start? I'm, like, ready for what*ever.*" Julianne is gazing up at Damon like she's ready, all right, for a double helping with whipped cream and a cherry on top.

Damon, holding Lindsey's gaze, raises his palms—*what can I do?*—and gives her a sweet smile.

twenty-two

AUGUST 23

Dear Diary,
   MEN !!!

Lindsey's sworn off them—inhumans of the male persuasion. Sick of succumbing.

She's ready to blast off to one of those sci-fi feminist utopias where they maintain a peaceful population through parthenogenesis or cloning. Y bother with nasty Y chromosomes? Ix-nay to the non-X! No more miraculous births via violation by divinely horny swans, bulls, or other Godly manifestations. So stuff it with your goddamned visitations....

Lindsey slams on the brakes, once again halting partway down the long grassy drive to the Friedland Folly. Prime male target ahead: Arlen. He's grumpily agreed to a talk about Opal before she's released from transitional care.

Lindsey closes her eyes, takes a deep breath, tries a calming mantra. Getting out of her Subaru, she walks into the hay field, the lush long grass of early summer shorn now to a rough dry stubble that catches at her sandals. She doesn't hold great hopes of breaking through with Arlen, but her own stubborn code of integrity insists she at least fill him in on the meeting with Opal's counselor.

Fran had arranged for the three sisters to meet with Vera, the counselor, after Opal refused yet again to file a report about Arlen's physical abuse. Vera, a motherly sort in flowing layers of lavender, seemed to be grappling with the failure of Opal's daughters to present a "united front" in this latest crisis. Instead, she faced a row of contentious chairs: Fran, still growling with her teeth sunk into the opportunity to punish Arlen; Joanie, chronically glazed-over with the exhaustion of baby Kendra and the guardianship issues; and Lindsey arguing the fairness of at least informing Arlen of the legal consequences if he ever attacked Opal again and they reported him.

"Great! So then he'll just get sneakier about it? And threaten Opal even more, if she rats on him? We need to get her away from him, *now*. Once she gets used to an assisted living unit, she'll be way better off," Fran had asserted with her usual surety.

Lindsey, irritated: "Aside from the question of whether they can afford that, how do you know what's better for her? Look what happened when she had her mental breakdown and we tried to get them to change. They made it pretty clear they didn't want any part of it."

Joanie, rousing briefly: "But they sure want us to come running when they call with one of their emergencies. They don't get it that we're tapped out. And they better not expect us to take them in when they finally crash and burn."

That's the one thing they all agreed on: No one is masochistic enough to take these crazymaking parents into their homes. To hell with guilt trips.

Well, almost. Lindsey feels enough daughterly duty to brave the wrath of pit-bull Fran and fill Arlen in on the situation. Who knows, maybe he'll step up and graduate from the emotional maturity level of a three-year-old to four, or even five.

And, as Lindsey steps through the prickling stubble toward the green, watered front yard, she remembers the gentle touch of her mother's fingers on her shoulders.

Yesterday, on her daily visit to the transitional care unit, she'd found Opal propped upright in bed, issuing Head-Nurse instructions to the aide about the proper way to fold hospital-corner sheets. When Lindsey rolled her eyes at the young man, he just winked and said, "She's feeling better today."

"Now sit here beside me and tell me about your trip with this new boyfriend." Opal was on a roll, enjoying the attention at the facility, almost sounding like her old self as she patted the bed beside her.

Lindsey's determination to stay perky collapsed around her. She broke into tears.

"Hush, now," Opal said. "Let me give you a shoulder rub. My patients always liked that."

So there they were, Opal the one in post-op rehab, insisting on giving her daughter a massage.

"Thanks, Mom," Lindsey whispered, turning to hug her.

Opal patted her back. "I'm glad *somebody* still needs me. Maybe I'm not so useless, after all."

Lindsey brushes at her eyes now as she steps from dry shorn hayfield onto the expanse of manicured lawn Arlen still insists on maintaining, driving himself to exhaustion to keep up the display. She takes a deep breath and squares her shoulders. Maybe he's had time to think while he's been on his own.

But by the time Lindsey corrals her cranky dad from his shop to sit down for a lemonade, then wades through piled-up fishing gear, muddy boots, and a week's worth of dirty dishes to get to the fridge—the cleaning gal having refused to set foot in the house alone with Arlen—it's not looking good. She suggests they take their glasses out to the deck, where he plunks down in a webbed chair and glowers.

"Goddamn, you'd think some of you yahoos might come out and give me a hand here! I can't keep up with all the yard work *and* the house." This, after he took off on yet another fishing trip the day after Opal's surgery.

"Well," Lindsey notes in a reasonable tone, "all of us are about maxed out right now, especially adding in trips to see Mom in the hospital and that care unit. You might try calling Marianne and apologizing for yelling at her last time. Maybe she'd come back and do some cleaning before Mom gets home again."

"Son of a bitch! Apologize to that cow? She's the one who—"

"Wait." Lindsey practices the traffic-stop gesture. "You can do what you want about the house. What I came out here to talk about is what Mom's counselor told us."

He narrows his eyes, gives her a suspicious look, and takes a gulp of his lemonade.

Lindsey sips her own, then takes the plunge. "Dad, you

need to know that it's not okay to push Mom around. She's too frail. You can't grab her and shake her, push her down. You ought to know that, but I'm going to spell it out—"

"Goddamn it!" Arlen thrusts up from his folding chair and onto his feet, slamming his glass onto the deck table and sloshing lemonade. "I told Joanie that was bullshit! I didn't do anything to her. She just wants everybody to feel sorry for her sorry ass!"

Lindsey grits her teeth. "Look, Dad, I don't know what happened. But Mom said you shook her and said you were going to cut her up in pieces, and if she decided to report that, then you'd be in big trouble."

"That useless old bitch!" Arlen's face is red now, vessels swelling in his neck.

"Don't you ever call her 'useless' again!" Lindsey snaps.

"Don't you tell me what to do, goddammit! Think you're so smart with your prissy college degree!" He steps closer, looming over her.

She tries not to grip the aluminum chair arm. "Sit down, Dad."

"No! You get the hell out of here!" He grabs the glass from her hand and throws it across the deck to shatter against a tree trunk.

Lindsey stands up to face him, takes a deep breath. "I came out here to do you a favor, but maybe I shouldn't bother."

"Favor! You call this a fucking favor?" His hands are fisted, face looking like it's going to explode, and he takes another step closer, bearing down on her.

His face looks like Nick's, right before he'd go on one of his rampages. Lindsey catches a quick breath, heart pounding, and a panicky voice is telling her to cut and run. But something else holds her there, facing Arlen down. She stands her ground, staring into his eyes, and finally he shakes his head, takes a step back, turns and looks out over the field.

She blows out the breath. "I told them it's only fair to let you know what would happen if you got reported for domestic violence. They'd take away your right to go into Canada on your fishing trips, for one thing."

"Like hell they would!" Arlen swings back around to face her.

Lindsey holds out her "Stop" palm again. "That's what Mom's counselor told us. And you'd have to attend weekly group counseling sessions on anger management. Which wouldn't be a bad idea, anyway. Dad, I don't think you have any idea how much damage you did to all of us. The way you're still hurting Mom."

His hands are fisted again, shaking, and Lindsey tenses, ready to dodge a blow. He raises his fists, then opens them, glares at his hands, flings them out in frustration. "You don't have to live with her! All she does is whine and fuss and act so goddamn pitiful I can't stand it."

There's a confused little boy in him—the one who got beaten by *his* father with a two-by-four—ready to cry or strike out at the world.

"Dad, I know. Mom drives us all crazy sometimes." She adds, "The thing is, you might *feel* like shaking her, but you can't do it. You've got to start thinking about what you're doing. Count to ten. Whatever."

He's turned away again, staring out at the field. Lindsey waits, but it looks like that's all she's going to get from him. She takes another deep breath, realizes she's shaking with adrenaline release.

"We're looking for someone to come out and help Mom around the house once she gets home, drive her to her appointments. That'll take some of the pressure off you. So you think about this."

Still no response. He seems to have sagged somehow inside his coveralls, and she sees a tremor in his hands.

Lindsey's eyes are burning. Maybe this is as close as they can get. "Okay, Dad. You take care of yourself." She turns and heads down the drive, and no word from Arlen follows her.

Lindsey's hands are shaking on the drive home, and she grips the wheel to try to still them. She eases into the clogged traffic on the outskirts of town, looks around her, realizes it's Friday afternoon rush hour. And she still hasn't heard the biopsy results.

Great. Another cheery weekend to look forward to.

She pulls over to the shoulder to call the clinic, but just

gets a recording telling her to "leave a message."

Something snaps. "Damn it! I'm not leaving another fucking message!" She pulls back into traffic, darts between honking cars to take the turn for the medical center instead of her neighborhood. She pulls into the clinic lot that's practically empty, jumps out, and pushes through the glass door ten minutes before closing time.

"I'm sorry, we can't take any walk-ins—"

"I'm a patient of Dr. Osborne's."

"Well, I'm sorry," the receptionist repeats. "Doctor's gone home for the day, and we're closing up."

"I just want to know my biopsy results. Look up my chart. Lindsey Friedland." She takes a deep breath. "The nurse said she'd leave a message. I don't want to wait another weekend."

"Well, I'm sorry, but the charts are on the nurse's desk, and she's done for the day. You'll just have to—"

Lindsey leans forward, slapping her palms on the counter. "Go get my chart and let me look at it. I have a right to see my medical records. I'll sign a waiver."

The receptionist opens her mouth, looks at Lindsey's face, and hurries into the back. There's a muffled sound of conversation, someone protesting. Some more muffled talking.

A new woman comes out of the back, wearing a white jacket, holding a manila folder. She steps around into the reception area, gives Lindsey a wary look.

"Lindsey Friedland?" She glances at the opened chart.

Lindsey nods.

"Birth date? Social security number?"

Lindsey provides them. "I just want to know the biopsy results."

The woman thumbs through papers. "Okay. Here we go. August twentieth. Benign calcification. No indication of malignancy."

Lindsey sags, lets out a long breath. "Thank you." She doesn't bother to ask why they had the report all week and couldn't be bothered to call her.

The woman looks up, into her eyes. She smiles. "You're welcome."

Summer's winding to a close, those lovely long evenings and all the sensual promise of hot sun and cool waters shriveling away into approaching fall. Tonight Lindsey feels old and worn out. After the confrontation with Arlen, the delayed news of the biopsy report has left her deflated, exhausted with all the emotional dramas. Not bothering with dinner, she crawls under the bedspread and closes her eyes.

She finally gives up on trying to sleep, sits up and opens the Rumi poetry book. She doesn't believe the poems are about only spiritual love. Those pesky rampaging emotions again:

>*You wreck my house and now my heart....*

"Oh, God!" Lindsey mutters. "I give up. Just lock me up in a padded cell. I'll go quietly."

Preserving these centuries-old traditional designs is more than a job for these women. They're weaving together the warp and weft of yesterday and tomorrow, creating the evolving Now of the village. Renewing its life. These beautiful women know their place—in the best sense of that phrase— and you can see the strength of that knowledge in their eyes.

"Arrgh." Lindsey rakes her fingers through her hair and scowls at the computer monitor. She can't seem to come up with the words to capture that knowing in the eyes of the mothers and grandmothers she'd visited in Guatemala. On impulse, she'd fired off an article proposal to the online *Feminist Fair Trade* journal, and now they want the piece right away.

She blows out a breath and glances at her notes again. HighJinks, ignored all morning, stalks into the office and jumps onto her desk, scattering papers and heading for the keyboard.

"Bad boy!" Lindsey scoops him up.

He starts purring, mission accomplished.

There's a knock on the front door.

Cradling HighJinks over her shoulder, Lindsey leans down to hit Save, then heads for the door. Pulling it open, she freezes.

Nick's standing on the porch, holding a bouquet of dahlias.

Lindsey's gut goes into that up-down lurching plummet as her stare fixes on the vivid coppery, crimson, yellow, and purple spiky blooms. The same kind of flowers they'd picked by the dozens for their outdoor autumn wedding. She catches a sharp breath, grip tightening reflexively on HighJinks still clinging to her shoulder. He yowls in protest and digs in his claws.

"Ouch! Damn!" Lindsey flinches, pain searing through her just as a hot flash triggers on a rolling wave of fire from the base of her spine upwards. Face flushed, she turns to disentangle the cat from her T-shirt and set him gently on the entry rug.

Nick squats, holding out a hand toward the Siamese. "Hey, big guy," he says softly.

HighJinks has gone still, sniffing the air of Nick's gone-strangeness. Then he steps over to him, rubbing against his hand, his legs. Nick looks up at Lindsey and slowly smiles.

He's undeniably handsome, face tanned and graying dark hair grown out a little longer now, feathering down the back of his neck, and he's looking healthy and fit in his worn jeans and t-shirt. Lindsey fights off a pang of remembrance, the old intimacies. She summons her caution, along with a golden orb of protection from her meditations.

Nick pets HighJinks and rises, offering the flowers to Lindsey. "Hi," he says.

"Thank you." She gingerly accepts the flowers.

"Can I come in?" He gestures toward the open doorway.

She hesitates. "Let's walk in the garden."

His sideways smile twitches. "All right." Then, tilting his head toward the dahlias, "You should put those in water."

She closes her eyes for a second, takes a deep breath. "Okay, just give me a minute. I'll be right out." She quietly closes the door on him, goes into the kitchen for a vase, and plunks the flowers into it. Then, not sure she wants anything from him in the house, she carries them out to the back porch and sets them there. Slips on her flipflops and heads around the house to the front yard. She visualizes that golden, glimmering light all around her, deflecting any threat. She's strong now. She's okay.

Nick's crouched beside the thorny wild-rose and Oregon

grape hedge, pulling a crab-apple twig through the grass for HighJinks to pounce on. He tousles the cat's head and stands as Lindsey comes over.

"I think he remembers me." He nods toward HighJinks, rubbing on his legs again.

"Of course."

Nick looks at the twig he's broken off the tree, shrugs, and tosses it under the branches. "It could use pruning, anyway."

"No doubt." Lindsey glances around at all the overgrown plantings, everything going wild and threatening to take over the stone walkway. "One of these days I'll have to hack a path to the front door."

He steps over to the wild fuchsia bush they'd started from seeds they'd gathered on a trip to southern Chile. "It's doing really well. I wasn't sure it was going to make it through that winter when we got all those hard freezes."

Lindsey touches a cascade of dangling purple-and-red blossoms. "The hummingbirds and bees are really going for it." She hesitates, then asks, "Do you want some apples? I can't keep up with them."

"That'd be great."

She leads the way down the drive to the back yard, grabs a sack from the porch. Nick's already moved deeper into the yard, standing by the raised vegetable beds he'd built and then never tended. He leans over to look at the dried stems of some mountain penstemons he'd started from seed, planning a rock garden. Another project that never got off the ground.

"Damn, you let the penstemons die!" He touches one of the branches like a miniature tree's, and it breaks off. "Don't you remember what a pain they were to get started?"

"I remember."

"You should have called me, I would have taken them where I could keep an eye on them."

Lindsey bristles. "I've had a few things on my mind, other than taking care of your specimens. You should have taken them when you left."

He spreads placating hands. "Yeah. I guess I forgot."

Lindsey leads the way past the garage to the old orchard, where the apples are starting to drop and litter the overgrown grass. "Pick whatever you want. I keep trying to give them away."

Nick takes the sack from her and picks a few apples from the lichened old MacIntosh, as Lindsey plucks one and bites into it, savoring the tart crispness. He starts to move on toward the younger red delicious tree, then stops short at the peeled yellow-cedar trunk with its two reaching arms that they'd salvaged from a river log jam and rooted in cement here. It was the start of another hopeful project to mount the "vulvular" cast-leaf birdbaths they'd made together, install a trickling fountain to fill them.

Nick reaches a hand and runs his palm over the cedar, then moves on to pick more apples.

Lindsey's caught in the play of filtered sunlight over the smooth yellow wood, the strangely runic patterns down the trunk that were probably the tracks of some burrowing creature but now look like the intertwining trails of raindrops, or tears. Maybe there's some message in the markings. Maybe it was always there, but Lindsey was too blind to see it. Blind and deaf to the warnings from her heart, from the way the world had gone muffled and silenced around her in those years with Nick.

She turns away, steps over to where Sombra is dozing in the dappled shade of the blueberry bushes. She sits crosslegged beside the cat and strokes her warm fur, picks some berries and pops them into her mouth.

Nick joins them and sets his bag down. Sombra startles, hisses at him, and runs toward the house. Lindsey shrugs.

Nick clears his throat. "It's good to see you, Lin. You look great."

"You look like you're doing well." She picks a few more berries.

"Things are smoothing out at work. You were right, I needed to work on my anger. I'm doing better with that."

She gives him a surprised look. He meets her gaze, gives her his crooked smile, this time flavored with irony. "You were right about a lot of things. I didn't realize what I was throwing away."

She goes still, watching him, wary. What has he come here for?

"You're so beautiful, you've probably got guys beating down the door."

She snorts. "Hardly."

"You don't have a boyfriend?" He sounds surprised. "I always figured you'd be marrying again pretty soon."

She frowns. "I had a lot of...." She starts to finish with "healing to do," but realizes it's none of his business. "I'm not ready for that."

"Yeah. I guess I wasn't, either." He picks some berries.

"What about your girlfriend?"

He looks down at the berries in his palm, jiggles them in his grip. "Didn't work out." He pops the berries into his mouth, chews, and swallows. Then shrugs. "Amy's too young. Immature. And she had that early-thirties thing going on, the biological clock ticking. She was pushing for having a baby, even though I'd told her from the start I wasn't into that."

"It's not a rational thing. So that's why you split up?"

"Not really. I mean, I cared—care—about her. So I finally agreed to try having a baby, and then *she* got cold feet. Dumped me." He shakes his head, pokes a finger into the grass beside him. "It's really for the best. It wouldn't have worked. She's a sweet person, but she doesn't have that... complexity you have, Lin. I miss that. And all the history we have."

Lindsey's gazing into the shifting leaves as a breeze stirs light and shadow. She can't hear them whispering, feels strangely out of her body, the world gone muffled.

"Lin." Nick reaches out to take her hand, tug gently at it. "I've thought a lot about what went wrong with us. I'm willing to work on it, if you'd give me another chance. I still love you."

From that strange, insulated distance, Lindsey turns her face to look into his eyes. He means it. He's opened something inside himself, and he's offering that.

For a horrifying moment, she's tempted. Tugged by his touch, by all the shared intimacies, like the cedar tree a foundation already laid. Longing for an end to loneliness. And the habit of loving, the innate attraction, is still alive in them. But that doesn't mean she can trust it. Trust him. Or herself, to hold firm.

"Nick." She reclaims her hand from his. "Do you remember when *we* talked about whether or not we wanted kids?"

He raises his eyebrows. "I guess. I didn't think you wanted them, either."

"That's not quite it." She braids her fingers, gazes down at them. "We talked about it for a while, when we were still in Oregon. It was getting to the point when it was time, if we were going to do it. You don't remember that?"

"Oh. Right."

"Finally I decided against it. Why do you think I made that decision?" She raises her face to meet his perplexed gaze.

"Well, partly our lifestyle," he says. "I mean, we wanted to be free to keep traveling, go backpacking, jump on our bikes when we felt like it. Frankly, I can't really see you giving all that up. Are you saying now you regret it?"

She shakes her head. "No. I realized it would be a mistake to have children with you, Nick. You were so angry, so often. And I know exactly when I made the decision. It was the first time you kicked Sombra. I realized our children wouldn't be safe."

He stares at her, his face flushing, darkening. He bursts out, "I never kicked Sombra! I don't believe this shit!"

"I know," Lindsey says wearily.

He jumps to his feet, pacing away from her toward the apple trees. He stands with his back to her. Presses his fists against his head. Gives himself a shake and takes a deep breath, visibly fighting for control.

Lindsey climbs hastily to her feet, groping for that shredded golden shield of light, ready to run.

He turns and paces back to her, stands stiffly. "Okay, I get it. This is still about punishing me for that affair, isn't it? Make up all this shit about throwing the cats, try to smear my name, even with my family. Christ, how did I let myself forget all that?" His face has gone red, and it's *déjà vu* all over again, back with Arlen looming over her.

Lindsey takes a deep breath, says quietly, "Nick, I hope you can hear yourself. You need to go now."

"What? Don't you pull this shit on me!" He reaches to grasp at her arms.

She takes a step back from him, plants herself and puts up the Stop hand. "That's enough, Nick. You need to go. Now." She hopes he can't see her shaking.

He clenches his fists, opens his mouth, snaps it shut. Turning away, he kicks at the bag of apples and stalks off down the drive. Familiar sound of a motor revving too fast, then he's burning rubber down the road.

"Whoa! Slow down!" A startled cry from the driveway, then a call, "Was that Nick? Lindsey, you okay?"

Lindsey hurries toward the voice, sees it's Crystal coming down the drive with a little gift bag, looking alarmed. The acrid smell of tire rubber hangs in the air.

"Crystal! Just in the...nick of time!" She takes a deep breath, still shaking, then steps closer to give Crystal a hug.

"Easy, now." Crystal pats her back. "Did he hurt you?"

"No." She takes another breath, eases back. "He just showed up out of the blue, I guess he wanted to make up. Then started acting like a jerk again. I told him to go."

"Good for you, beautiful Goddess!" Crystal beams, then pulls a small spray bottle from the gift bag. "Perfect timing with that horrible burned smell." She hands it to Lindsey.

"What is it?" She sniffs at the fresh citrus scent.

"Cleansing natural lemon and orange oils in spring water. I use it for a lift or purifying my space."

"Perfect!" Lindsey beams. "Let's spray the yard!"

"Yes!" Crystal claps her hands. "Then we'll circle the house."

Lindsey starts with the bouquet of dahlias Nick brought. She's tempted to throw them in the trash, then she smiles and takes the vase to the orchard, sets it atop the cedar stump. She intones a mantra and sprays the lemon mist over the flowers. Then, laughing, she kicks off her flipflops and runs barefoot over the grass toward the house, spraying purification as she goes, Crystal dancing along. Encircling her home with the scent of golden sunlight.

"Good-bye, Nick," Crystal sings.

"Hello, life," Lindsey adds.

twenty-three

TO: LINDSEY FRIEDLAND
FROM: HotDawg Horner

Hey, Lindsey, how's it hanging? Thanks again for the dating advice! Never thought after twenty years of marriage I'd be divorced and acting like a dorky highschooler again.

But, yeah, I got your drift about your mom sticking with your dad just because he was a "good provider." Guess I was figuring gals wanted to hear upfront what I could offer. Who'd a thunk ol' Horner had the true gold inside? Well, that's what Cheryl just told me. We were watching that new Neil Young DVD on my hi-def widescreen (ooops! ☺) and she turned to me and told me she likes MY "heart of gold." Well, hot damn....

You remember Cheryl VanHouten from high school? Ran into her at the Grizzly, she's a widow, and we're hitting it off. Plus, she likes cooking shows, too! We're trying out some spicy new recipes (heh-heh).

Great being pals with you, Lin. Talk about Heart of Gold, you got it, gal.

Luv, Ted

BOOM! Thunder overhead. And Lindsey had a gaggle of newbie tourists in her raft.

The dark cloud out of nowhere snagged on the treetops fringing the rocky canyon, burst open in drenching rain, and the river was swelling, racing faster through the rapids and black boulders. *Damn, where'd this come from?* But

Lindsey had handled worse before.

"Forward, forward. Okay, left back. All forward!" she called out to the tourist paddlers as they burst through another rapid, spray flying, rain stinging. They'd listened to her coaching, they were doing fine.

Then a blast of boombox punk rock behind them, drunken hooting, and a raft of idiots burst around the bend, out of control racing toward them.

"Left, left!" Lindsey shouted. "All forward!" They needed to get out of the way.

Too late. The idiots rammed them, went spinning and whirling on still laughing, as Lindsey's raft hit a boulder and tipped, spilling two. "High side!" she ordered the rest as she lunged partly over the stern, head and shoulders submerged in the swirling maelstrom, managed to snag the woman's life jacket. Lindsey dragged her in as burning pain ripped through her shoulder.

She ignored it, got her paddlers back on track, caught up to the bobbing young boy in his helmet, stabilized the raft as the boy's father dragged him back in sobbing.

"Okay, okay, everyone okay?" Lindsey was fighting red pulses of pain in her vision, fire running down her arm now. "Jimmy, you're a real trooper!"

The boy was okay, giving her a grin through tears. They all hunched in the downpour, whitewater crashing over them, racing down the canyon. Lindsey gritted her teeth against the pain as she steered. *No choice, gotta keep going—*

"Damn!" Lindsey wakes up in a damp tangle of sheets, sitting bolt upright and blinking in the dawn glow through the curtain. She rubs her aching shoulder along the surgery scar, souvenir of that rafting snafu. She groans. "What next?"

Thrusting the sheets from her, she staggers upright and out the back door to stand on the damp grass taking in deep breaths. A rare thunderstorm last night, bringing a cloudburst of rain, has cleared the air of its end-of-summer haze. The fresh morning breeze clears her head, too.

After a quick run through the awakening neighborhood,

Lindsey stands under the cold, bracing spray of the shower. It's Labor Day. She has her standing invitation to Megan's parents' beach cabin for their annual "Good-bye to summer" barbecue. Megan let her know yesterday that Newman's back from India, and he's coming, hoping to see Lindsey there.

He's tried to call Lindsey a couple times in the past week but she didn't pick up, and Newman didn't leave a message. She's had it with all the overwrought emotions. She just wants closure, wants to move on. She calls Megan to beg off on the barbecue.

"Giving Newman some of his own medicine, Lin?" Megan asks.

"No. No games. I'm just tired of the whole thing."

"Well, okay then. We'll miss you, sweetie."

"Say hi to your mom and dad for me. Ask if I can visit later."

"They'd love that. How's it going with your folks?"

"The best we can expect, I guess, for now anyway. All of Mom's care providers are clued in on our concerns, and everyone's ready to act if Dad crosses the line and someone witnesses it. And this new gal Patsy we hired to come in daily for a few hours to help out, drive Mom to appointments if we can't make it, cook something to heat up for dinner— she's a pistol. A real county gal, Dolly Parton hair and all, drives a big pickup, and she may just be a match for Arlen. Pitches crap right back at him if he starts up."

Megan laughs. "Oh, my god! I'd love to see that!"

"Let's go out for a visit, and you can see for yourself."

"It's a plan." A pause. "And Kevin? Any news?"

Lindsey sighs. "Not good. Every time I go up to read to him, it seems like he's shrunken a bit more. Rob thinks it's time, and the doc agrees, maybe best to take him off life support, let nature take its course. But Marci won't let him go. I get it, he's her boy, but it's all so awful...." A sobbing breath catches in her throat.

"Oh, Lin! Damn, I hope they make that doc pay!"

Lindsey takes a deep breath, pulls herself together. "Rob's going ahead with the lawsuit, and I really like his lawyer, he's dedicated. They want to stop this happening again, at least with Dr. Bennerton. And hopefully the hospital will actually make the audits meaningful. But it'll be months and months before anything happens, the whole legal tangle...."

"Will you testify?"

"Oh, yeah, if it helps."

"You go, Amazon woman! I'm proud of you, gal friend."

After she hangs up, Lindsey takes another quick shower, all the emotions triggering a sweaty hot flash. But they're not so bad now, thank goodness. She settles back down to her article about the Mayan weavers, finally making some progress. She's about to take a break when the phone rings. It's Newman.

Great. All the times I wanted him to call, and now....

She takes a deep breath, answers. "Hi."

"Lindsey? It's good to hear your voice." His voice tugs at her, that calm deep ocean vibe.

"Yes...." She takes another breath. "How was India?"

"It was great. Good for me, good for Melani. Getting back to the ashram, that peace. We did a lot of meditating together, and she loves the people, wants to spend more time there once she graduates. And it helped me get clear again. I realized that you were right—I *have* been afraid to open up." A gusting breath. "Lindsey, I'd like to see you again. I'm going to be home for a few weeks now. Would you like to come out for a sauna? We can talk?"

A pause. She shakes her head, realizes he can't see it. "Newman, I don't think that's a good idea."

"Oh." He sounds taken aback. "No, I get it, and I want to apologize. I wasn't being...caring before I left. I got sort of freaked out about the Guatemala trip, how it seemed like everything was moving too fast. Like I enjoyed it too much. We were getting too attached, too soon. Then I hurt your feelings."

"Yes, you did. But, actually, you were right—we did need some space. And when I thought about it, I realized that you'd been treating me disrespectfully all along, like I was on call for your convenience. And I'd been going along with it, which I never should have done."

"Wow, that's...." A stretched-out pause. "I didn't realize. Can I try to make it up to you? Get a fresh start?"

"Newman...." She sighs. "I'm not sure that's possible. Can you visualize your lifestyle changing? Not flying around so much? Actually able to make plans that stick?"

"Hmm." Another pause. "It is my business, Lindsey. And my spiritual work sometimes calls."

"And that's part of it for me. I know that's your life, Newman. I get it, I admire your work, and I care about you." Suddenly she's sure, and the words are there. "I've had time to think about what I want. And it's not a part-time lover, someone who's flying off in so many directions. I want companionship in a lover. So I'd like to be friends, but let's give it more time. I don't want the physical part to take over again. Maybe we could go for a hike or something this fall."

"Maybe...?" He sounds oddly off-balance. Then silence.

"Newman, you there?"

"Oh. Yeah. You just...sound different. Not that it's bad." Then he chuckles. "Listen to me, I'm babbling like a blessed idiot."

She laughs, too, relieved. "I think we've both been like Rumi's blessed fools. I've learned a lot from you, Newman, and I'm grateful."

"That sounds—"

"No, I mean it. I think I'm seeing myself more clearly now, too."

"Good." His voice has softened. "Hey, can I send you an astral hug?"

"I'd like that."

And she can feel that calm blue from her dreams, from their meditations together, flowing around her, touching her heart. She smiles, sends back her own warmth. *Peace.* It may not make sense, but that's okay. She's learning acceptance.

September 7

Dear Diary,

Take Twelve? Take some deep breaths....

So I did it, walked my talk, I am Woman and all that jazz. Lindsey who's taken on wild rivers and hospital corruption! Strong and sufficient unto myself. Learning to love who I am.

Maybe someday I'll be walking along a trail, happy in the sunshine, singing my own song, and there up ahead will be someone to keep me company. Someone to love. But today

I'm fine just as I am:
Lindsey Friedland. Lindsey freed!

twenty-four

LINDSEY'S DRIVING HOME FROM a quick visit to check in on her parents. Now that Opal has a home-care therapist and the take-charge Patsy for daily help, they can all take a breath of relief.

"Don't you worry your sweet head, Linny." Patsy has adopted Opal's pet name for her. "Opal and me, we're getting on like a house afire. And that Arlen, he's on notice he better watch his Ps and Qs. We all played cards yesterday, and we had some good laughs. Gets'em talking about the old days, happy memories. It helps."

"Bless you, Patsy!"

Lindsey decides to take a detour through the county farmland to enjoy the end of summer lull. The river meanders, muddy brown and serene, through the valley patchwork of golden shorn fields, vine maples along its banks already edging into fall crimson. Dark blue mountains in the distance etch sharp lines against the lighter blue sky flushed by rain of its August haze. Higher peaks still retain melting snowcaps dazzling white in the sunlight.

The openness of landscape broadens her thinking as she mulls over the Kwamish tribal project she and Damon have been focused on for the past month. The first goal is to "take the temperature of the tribe" about the contentious fishing and whaling rights issues and more. Can they visualize a convergence between preserving traditional ways and new environmental concerns? They've been gathering data, creating vision pieces, consulting with Lindsey's friend Ayako and setting a fast-upcoming date for a "circularity" meeting with the tribe to get people talking.

Lindsey's old high school pal, who squeaks in at 4 feet 11 if she stands tall, has always been a dynamo. And she's found her niche, facilitating open forums for communication, working a lot with the tribes.

"Hey," she's told Lindsey, "I kind of sneak in under their radar. They start out ready to resist some honky giving them advice, and here I come in all petite and Japanese, kind of look like them or at least on their side of the non-Anglo fence. So then I just have to open it up and let them see we can all listen to each other."

As Lindsey's been working with Ayako, Damon's been busy collecting state and federal grant-proposal possibilities. She's glad for the business focus, moving on from Newman. And Damon's been a bit more reserved, not pushing any overtures or touches. Maybe he's succumbed to the bubbly charms of the new intern? Or maybe he's just giving Lindsey the space she asked for.

But today they're taking a break from the project to fill a gap in *The Weekly Whiplash* production with a quick piece on Lindsey's native-plant restoration project in her creek ravine. He's coming by to take photos.

She pulls into her drive and sees his car already there. "Damon?"

No answer, so she heads for the back yard. She finds him sitting crosslegged in the grass at the edge of the creek ravine, beneath the soaring green umbrella of the venerable big-leaf maple tree. Sombra is nestled in his lap, eyes closed as he pets her.

Damon looks up then and sees Lindsey. A slow smile warms his face as he continues stroking the black cat.

"Wow, that's amazing." Lindsey steps quietly closer, and the normally skittish cat doesn't stir. "She's been terrified of men ever since Nick. I can't believe she didn't run and hide."

"I told her she's a beautiful warrior princess, and she liked it." His smile widens into a grin. "What's her name?"

"Sombra."

"Shadow girl. Okay, Sombra, we have work to do." He gently shifts her aside and rises.

Sombra stretches and wanders off.

"Sorry to keep you waiting. I was visiting my folks."

"How's Opal doing?" He's been keeping updated, asking about her family.

"Better, with more help around the house. We hired salt of the earth Patsy, who's just the ticket. Now we cross our fingers that Arlen will behave."

"Families.... Here's something from Nana." He steps over to retrieve something from the yellow-cedar stump and hand it to Lindsey. "It's for Opal."

She's speechless, staring at the beautiful woven-grass basket, like the one Nana was weaving in Damon's photo. Inside the basket are several flat cards with images of flowers and birds, well-wishes written on the backs in different handwriting.

"It's a hope basket. One of the things Nana and her friends do."

"Wow, I'm...." Lindsey feels tears welling. "It's beautiful. I can't believe.... Opal will love it. So generous.... Nana doesn't even know us!" She flings her arms impulsively around Damon. "Thank you. Thank her."

He hugs her back, and his strong solidity feels good. Then he eases back, takes the basket and sets it again on the trunk. "Let's not squish it!" He shrugs. "It's what Nana does. Takes care of people."

Lindsey's fishing a tissue out of her jeans pocket to wipe her eyes.

He gives her space, wandering over to look up at the sheltering maple boughs. "This place is incredible, Lindsey! It just drew me to sit under here and look up at the light glowing through the leaves."

"It's my favorite place to sit when I need peace. It's the Meredith tree."

"Who's Meredith?"

"She was my great-aunt. She left me enough money for the down payment on this place. That's why I could keep it in the divorce settlement."

"Well, thank you, Great-Aunt Meredith! So let's get some photos of you under the tree. Then we'll go down by the creek and see what you've been doing."

They tour the native trees, bushes, and ground covers she planted years earlier with the help of local Stream Steward volunteers who provide plants to restore salmon-spawning streams with cooling shade. The dense green foliage has created a quiet oasis in the middle of town, a refuge not only for the salmon, but for Lindsey in the hard years with Nick and the divorce.

"Shhh." Lindsey beckons Damon to follow her across her improvised log bridge over the mucky bog and onto the creek bank. Peering through the overhanging shrubs that have flourished in the past few years, they can see the red-tinged backs of spawning salmon. Undulating slowly, the salmon hang in the low current over the gravel spawning beds.

"Wow," Damon whispers. "I thought this creek was too polluted from the mall parking lot runoff."

"Work in progress. Still polluted, but the salmon give me hope."

Damon smiles into her eyes, then they watch quietly for a while, the only sound the subdued lapping of the creek and a winter wren warbling its melodious song. Damon snaps some shots of the salmon, then they edge back from the creek. He wanders over the replanted area, snapping a few more shots.

"Look, a bunchberry hiding under here. That's one of my favorites." He leans over to lift aside the fronds of a big sword fern to peer at the shy little plant with its shiny red berries. He straightens just as Lindsey's stepping around the fern, and they collide. "Oops." He takes her arm to steady her.

She doesn't move away.

He gives her an inquiring look. "Ah...Mr. Maybe?"

"History."

"Good!" He beams in clear delight and leans in to brush his lips over hers.

Surprising herself, she kisses him back. He's just as delicious as ever, slow warmth revving into more. A low rumble of pleasure makes its way up her throat.

"Phew!" Flushed, she steps back.

"And how." He grins. "But you still need a little time?"

"You are a mind reader."

"Hey, remember the shaman on the mountain." He strikes a pose, then sobers. "Let me know when—if—you're ready. But...don't take too long."

twenty-five

"DELICIOUS! THANK YOU." LINDSEY licks her fingers after accepting a sample of pit-smoked salmon from the man in the woven-cedar "basket" hat.

He smiles. "You're welcome, sister." He hands another sample to Ayako.

She smacks her lips. "Mmmm."

He laughs and turns back to tending the slabs of filleted salmon on grills angled over a long open fire pit. "We'll be feasting soon. You go dance now."

Inside the Kwamish tribe's new long-house community hall, drums are revving up, calling them back inside after the "circularity" meeting that Ayako facilitated with Lindsey's help.

"Hey, we rocked, gal!" Ayako gives Lindsey a high-five. "All of us!"

She sweeps an arm to include the tribal adults now being joined by kids of all ages, heading toward the hall. They're trailing in from the gravel parking area or the clapboard church across from it, dressed in dancing regalia: dark shirts with rows of miniature wood paddles dangling, dresses with fringe or feathers, some with small blankets over their shoulders decorated with applique images of Northwest-style creatures in geometric patterns of red and black.

The meeting earlier has surpassed their expectations, most of the adults speaking up about what they value, what they want for their children, how the salmon and trees and whales are part of their larger family and must be honored and protected. And now it's time to dance! And feast!

Lindsey takes a moment to breathe deeply, gazing out

at the magnificent view over the open Pacific Ocean here on the edge of the continent. It's a perfect early fall day, air crisp and clear, breeze ruffling whitecaps over the deep blue sea, distant sound of surf crashing against the rocks far below the cliff. An eagle soars overhead with its shrill cry.

Turning back toward the long-house, she tips her head in a silent thank-you to the carved wingspread eagle topping the tall totem pole in front of it. She nods to the bear with salmon, frog, and raven also carved into the pole, then stoops under the "blessing" cedar frond tacked to the oval doorway, letting it brush her head. Nana's coached her a bit on etiquette, like showing respect and humility when entering a gathering, bowing to let the cedar fronds cleanse her. She hasn't seen Damon since she arrived two days ago to meet Nana, who's been hosting her. He wanted to stay in the background of the project, but she supposes that eventually he'll show up again.

She blinks as she enters the hall, eyes adjusting from the brightness outside. There's a fire in the rock-lined pit at one end of the soaring space supported by thick, stripped tree trunks and topped by more cedar trunks as roof beams. Light streams in through opened skylights that let out the smoke. At the far end of the long hall is a gleaming wall of cedar planks with a mural of tribal-design eagles facing each other above killer whales.

Several men in basket hats or feathered headbands are seated around a huge drum, beating out a pounding rhythm. A few women in fringed dresses, along with children in everything from decorated shirts, feathered headgear, or appliqued blankets are moving in free-form dances around the wooden floor. Older women are seated around the perimeter, beating smaller hand drums or shaking rattles and chanting. A scent of woodsmoke and cedar-sage smudging fills the air.

Lindsey grew up attending local tribal celebrations, and loves the energy summoned by the drums, the joyful dancing. She's nodding to the beat as a line of kids dances past her, stomping and spinning, circling the hall, uttering bird cries and animal growls. She startles as a man in a wooden Bear mask touches her arm and beckons her into the dance. He lumbers convincingly around her like the animal, swathed in a bulky blanket, then herds her into the dance. She throws out her arms in surrender and joins the line, stomping, turning, swaying along.

Finally she spins out of the dance, joining some of the women along the side. One of them hands her a rattle, and she sits to join the rhythm.

A hoarse "Caw, caw!" breaks through the drumbeats, and a general cry goes up as the dancers part to welcome a new arrival.

The man is wearing a painted black raven mask with a long beak, and a black shirt with fringy ribbons and feathers. He crouches, tilts his head to give sideways looks at the other dancers, then raises his head as he pulls a hidden string to make the lower beak open and clack shut in quick snaps. "Caw! Caw!" he croaks, and chases the children in the distinctive bobbing, crouching style of Raven. The children shriek in glee and run as Raven pursues them, hopping and crouching. He dances then to the drumbeat, eerily embodying the bird. Lindsey's mesmerized, smoky dimness swirling around her, as reality seems to shift and sway, and it *is* a giant raven dancing before them, feathers shimmering with magic.

Then, bobbing his head, the dancer approaches the sitting women and singles out a graying elder. He pokes her with his beak and tips his head, spreading his "wings" and preening before her. She laughs and pushes him away, saying something in the native language.

Raven hunches, manages to look offended, then spreads his wings and dances off. "Caw! Caw!" He merges into the shadows, vanishes.

"That Chadis'kwis! Always the trickster." The women laugh, shaking their heads.

The drumming and the smoke are making Lindsey's head spin, so she slips outside for a breath of fresh air. Heading toward the view over the ocean, she notices the Raven dancer walking in normal human fashion now toward the parking area. He stops at a Subaru wagon and pulls off the mask. It's Damon.

"Wow." She starts to raise her hand, call out to him, then stops. She pulls back into the shade as he glances around, then hops into the car and heads off. She smiles.

"See you soon, Lindsey!" Ayako leans out the open window of her pickup, glossy short hair gleaming in the late afternoon sun. She laughs and gives Lindsey a thumb's-up as she turns and heads off down Nana's dirt drive.

Lindsey waves and pats the heads of the two yellow labs who amble over to butt her hands. "Hey, Mac. Ginger." She raises her face to the lowering sun, smiling, still resonating with the drums, with the stories she's heard that day, about grandmothers and great-grandfathers and how their ways are still alive here, still honored.

"Hey, Linny!" Nana, in her rocker on the porch, raises her face from her knitting and peers over reading glasses as Lindsey rounds the side of the mobile home, flanked by the dogs. "Take a load off." She picks some yarn balls off the folding chair beside her. "What a day, eh? My old bones just wanting to soak up this last bit of sunshine." Her silver braids swing forward as she adjusts herself in the rocker, gets a rhythm going to the clicks of her knitting needles.

Lindsey sits beside her as Mac and Ginger settle at their feet, gazing out over the scatter of cars parked on the lawn. For five dollars, Nana and her dogs provide secure parking for hikers on the nearby beach trail. Beyond the Subarus, pickups, and a rusty Buick sedan, the road winds along the curve of the shoreline flanked by wild rose and spiky grasses. The open stretch of the Pacific rolls in from a hazy blue horizon, spray shooting up around the jagged black rock stacks offshore, serrated wavelines sweeping in to break over the sandy beach. Nana's got a million-dollar view, and they sit drinking it in along with the sunshine.

"You hungry, girl? Got plenty in the fridge, and some lemonade."

Lindsey gets up, goes into the crowded living space, and pours them each a glass, bringing them back to the porch.

"Ah. Thank you." Nana takes a sip, sets the glass on a TV tray on her other side. "How about a smoke?" She fumbles for her corncob pipe and fills it with what Lindsey has figured to be a mixture of tobacco and various dried herbs Nana gathers.

"All right."

Nana smiles and fills her extra pipe for Lindsey, passes it over. Hands shaking with a slight tremor that the knitting seems to anchor, she strikes a match for Lindsey and holds it to the pipe while Lindsey puffs to get it going. She tries not to choke as she pulls in the spicy smoke, lets the taste fill her mouth, and blows it out.

Nana chuckles as she puffs her own pipe, rocking. "That's good medicine."

Lindsey's not sure if that's a joke, but getting to know Nana's sly humor these last couple of days, she just nods and takes another puff. It does have a strangely soothing effect.

"Hmm. Looks like we got us another hiker, getting a late start." Nana tilts her head toward another Subaru turning off the road, heading up the drive to park on the other side of the mobile home. A door opens and shuts, and the hounds jump up, barking, to run around the house. Footsteps approach the wooden pay box mounted on the porch.

"Now there's a picture!"

Lindsey, startled, turns in her chair, starts to pull the pipe from her mouth.

It's Damon, camera to his eye and snapping a shot.

Nana slowly lowers her pipe, blows out smoke, and smiles. "Baby boy, you still taking your girly pictures?"

"This time I got two beautiful gals for the price of one." Grinning, he bounds up the steps and leans over to give Nana a kiss on the cheek. He turns and gives Lindsey one, too.

Nana waves her pipe. "Bring another chair out. Linny's just going to tell us all about that big meeting." Nana had declined to attend, making an obscure reference to getting the "real news" later at her sewing circle.

"So, Nana's sharing her stash, eh?" He winks at Lindsey. "Better watch it, that stuff'll give you some wild dreams."

"Now, you don't start that nonsense. Linny's too smart for your tricks. You go get yourself some lemonade, come on back out and listen for a change."

"Yes, Nana," Damon says meekly, his eyes glinting mischief. "Whatever you say."

Nana snorts.

Lindsey tells them about the gathering, the stories she heard from the tribal members. "And then at the drumming and dancing, we had a visit from Raven. What was his name again?"

"Chadis'kwis! Up to your old tricks." Nana seems to have heard about it already. "That's his tribal name," she tells Lindsey.

Damon gives an abashed shrug. "Didn't want to miss out entirely."

The sun's a red ball now, flattening in the coppery haze over the ocean and laying a glittering trail of fire over the waves, subsiding into an evening hush. Nana suddenly looks her age, and tired.

Damon stands and, with a tenderness that belies all his teasing, strokes her head and eases her to her feet. "You take a little nap, and I'll cook us up this salmon I brought."

"No, no," she protests. "I'll cook you some dinner."

"No way." Arm around her, he guides her into the home.

Lindsey strolls over the yard with Mac and Ginger, toward the road to take in the last glimmer of sunset, breathe in the fresh salty breeze.

"Hey." Damon's come up quietly behind her. He leans over to pet the hounds, then glances up at Lindsey. "You done good here, gal."

"It was Ayako."

"You started it rolling." He straightens, face serious for a change, puts his arms around her and gives her a hug.

His strong body against hers feels good, and she inhales his spicy scent. He gives a little "Mmm," and presses closer to murmur against her ear, "Hello, Lin." He kisses her neck.

Tingles run up and down her spine, and she curves into his swaying embrace. They kiss, temperature rising, and time seems to get lost.

She eases back, catching her breath.

"So," he does his raising-one-eyebrow thing, "I do believe it now—you're done with Mr. Maybe."

"Oh, yeah."

"Then take me on your camping trip down the coast?"

She smiles and shakes her head. "Damon, this one I need to do solo. Check in on who I am. Just that wide open ocean and me for now."

Damon turns to the hounds, who are sitting on their haunches watching expectantly. He makes a comic face, lifts his palms, and tells them, "So, the beautiful maiden said take a hike. But not with me. And the devoted brave hunter threw himself off the ocean cliffs. That's him out there, getting pummeled by the waves forever." He jabs his thumb toward the distant rock stacks in the sea.

Mac gives him a big, slobbery yawn, then lifts a hind leg, bending double to lick his own balls.

Lindsey laughs.

Damon rolls his eyes. "See? I don't get *no* respect around here."

It's an easy hike among the big cedars, and it feels good to be out with her backpack again. Lindsey threads between the massive trunks and steps along logs laid across bogs, enjoying the lush mosses, ferns, salal, and salmonberry of the rain forest. She's been blessed by the weather gods, sunny days holding with a high-pressure front.

She raises her face to the burning crimson leaves of a vine maple backlit by the sun, tilting her head to play with the flickers of filtered light. Then she ducks around the bush to stand on the edge of the bluff, watching the ocean waves crash against dark rocks below. She finds the steep switchbacks, heads down, and strikes off along packed sand moistened by the retreating tide. Offshore, more jagged dark rock formations stand against the crashing sea, and ahead in the distance, the beach curves toward another steep headland she'll have to round at low tide the next day.

She sets up her tent beside a tannin-brown creek and stashes her food in a bear-proof container, just in time to save it from a bold party of racoon burglars who invade the camp and start poking around the tent. She shoos them off, then wanders out over the jumble of drift logs. An endless sweep of sandy beach runs from one rocky headland to another down the coast, seagulls threshing the air with their cries. She shucks her boots and wades out into the froth of rushing and retreating waves, savors the cold, tingling touch of the sea. Spreads her arms to the open horizon and all that boundless energy.

She smiles as she hears Nana's words again, from that morning:

"You stick to your guns, Linny. My boy Damon, he's not used to gals saying no. Not even maybe...." She chuckled, then sobered. "I know him, and this time he's serious. I do believe he's hoping to make something real with you. But you got to be ready. He knows that."

Lindsey, surprised, thanked her.

Nana nodded. "You're okay, then. You just stay in *your* story, don't worry about no happy ever afters."

Lindsey smiles now and closes her eyes, spreads her arms and turns in the swirling calf-deep water. The ebb sucks back to sea, pulling the sand out from under her bare feet. She laughs and spins faster, then runs to follow the flowing waterline. With the next surge of breaking waves, the flooding waters chase her toward shore again. She laughs once more and spins, running and dancing the edge of land and sea, leaping the questing fingers of tide, pirouetting along the foamy boundary as she leaves a trail of footprints gleaming in the sun.

Finally, wet and tired, Lindsey turns back toward shore, flushing up more gulls as she gathers polished pebbles along the drift line. Sensing a movement behind her, she turns.

A river otter, brown fur sleek and wet, runs with an awkward humping gait along the mouth of the creek toward the waves. Then another one, smaller, darts along behind. Lindsey catches a breath and holds it as the two eye her, tilt their heads, then relax and roll like puppies in the sand, wriggling on their backs. They jump to their feet, shake vigorously, and trot into the waves, where they dive and surface and dive in curves of sleek grace.

Lindsey's rooted, watching as the mother otter and her pup emerge from the waves to meander past her and nose along the creek again. She can feel herself beaming, realizes suddenly that she's happy.

She's being. Here. Now.

epilogue

Equinox

Dear Diary,

Shall we pause to take stock?

Female, liberated! Closing on 53, redefining "ma'am" and "power flashes."

Possessions: Self. 2 Best Cats in the World; 1 degree in creative writing and journalism (put to good use); zero job security, unlimited work potential. 1 charming 1920s bunga-low with 30-year mortgage and still in need of new windows, trim, and roof. Garden being reclaimed from weeds.

Green eyes (wide open); long sunstreaked hair (silver wisdom strands at the temples); "terrific ass" (holding in there); face framed with laugh lines and gravity; 1 and 3/4 breasts, Amazon Woman.

A new man? Stay tuned.

1 recently-renewed passport. 1 pair new wings.

Attention Book Clubs!

Discussion questions for PAUSE
can be found at
https://www.sarastamey.com/press-kit/

about the author

Sara Stamey's journeys include treasure hunting and teaching scuba in the Caribbean; backpacking Greece and New Zealand; operating a nuclear reactor; and owning a farm in Southern Chile. She also worked as a hospital medical transcriber. Now returned to her native Pacific Northwest, Sara taught creative writing at Western Washington University. A lifelong outdoors enthusiast, she shares her creekside land with wild creatures and her cat, dog, and paleontologist husband Thor Hansen.

Sara's SF novels with Berkley/Ace made the *Locus* Best New Novelists list, and *Publishers Weekly* wrote, "Stamey puts feeling into this tale of the prodigal daughter." *The Statesman Journal* calls her award-winning *Islands* "a superior mystery and suspense novel...a stomping, vivid ride." Her near-future Greek islands thriller *The Ariadne Connection* has received the Cygnus Award for speculative fiction and the Chanticleer Global Thriller Grand Prize: "*The Ariadne Connection* is a rocket-paced thrill ride that delivers complex, engaging characters in a laser-sharp plot."

Her novel *Pause* was awarded the Chanticleer Somerset Award for Contemporary Fiction and was also a Finalist for the Chanticleer Chatelaine Award for Women's Fiction.

Follow the author's weekly travel and writing blog, The Rambling Writer, at www.sarastamey.com, where you can also sign up for her newsletter.

Also by Sara Stamey

Wild Card Run

Win, Lose, Draw

Double Blind

Islands

The Ariadne Connection

ABOUT BOOK VIEW CAFÉ

Book View Café is a professional authors' publishing cooperative with authors from genres including mystery, romance, fantasy, and science fiction.

Readers can enjoy high-quality DRM-free ebooks from their favorite authors at a reasonable price, with select print editions available.

Authors can enjoy earning 90% of the proceeds of each book sold.

Book View Café authors include New York Times and USA Today bestsellers, Nebula, Hugo, Lambda, Chanticleer, National Reader's Choice, and Philip K. Dick Award winners, World Fantasy, Kirkus, and Rita Award nominees, and winners and nominees of many other publishing awards.

https://www.bookviewcafe.com